GRIM REHEARSAL

Press agent Pierce Kirby is thrilled when his Uncle Doc
visits, and takes him that night to a Manhattan play.
They all know Pierce at the theater, so he takes his
uncle backstage to introduce him around. While Pierce
is arguing with Ginette, the leading lady, his uncle
wanders off. When Pierce can't find him, he figures that
his uncle got tired of waiting and walked back to his
hotel. The next morning Pierce is informed that Uncle
Doc has been found murdered, and probably right there
in the theater. That's when he meets acting-Captain
Gridley Nelson. But Pierce isn't satisfied with the pace
of Gridley's investigation, and so sets out to discover
who killed his uncle himself. But who in the theater
could have wanted the harmless old man dead? And
why?

DEAD YESTERDAY

Thea had been a beautiful model until she met Count
Dino Mazzani. But after they married, his true
womanizing colors came out. And after his death, she
just let herself go. Now, overweight and barely
recognizable, she sits in her apartment and drinks.
Until her old love, Grant Barstow, shows up. Seeing the
shock in his face, the countess has her maid clean up
the apartment. Then Coley Spenser, her late husband's
former valet, makes an appearance, looking for cash
and whatever else he can find… soon followed by Thea's
niece, whom Thea has never met before, but who bears
a striking resemblance to her younger self. What
Spenser finds and how Thea reacts to seeing her niece
for the first time leads to a room full of death for
Gridley Nelson.

RUTH FENISONG BIBLIOGRAPHY (1904-1978)

Gridley Nelson Mysteries:
Murder Needs a Name (1942; UK edition, 1950)
Murder Needs a Face (1942)
The Butler Died in Brooklyn (1943; UK edition, 1946)
Murder Runs a Fever (1943)
Grim Rehearsal (1950; UK edition, 1951)
Dead Yesterday (1951)
Deadlock (1952)
The Wench Is Dead (1953)
Miscast for Murder (1954; reprinted in PB, 1956, as *Too Lovely to Live*)
Bite the Hand (1956; UK edition, 1958, as *The Blackmailer*)
Death of the Party (1958)
But Not Forgotten (1960; UK edition, 1960, as *Sinister Assignment*)
Dead Weight (1962; UK edition, 1964)

Unrelated Mysteries:
Jenny Kissed Me (1944; reprinted in PB as *Death is a Lovely Lady*, 1944)
The Lost Caesar (1945; reprinted in PB, 1950, and UK edition, 1946, both as *Death is a Gold Coin*)
Desperate Cure (1946)
Snare for Sinners (1949; UK edition, 1951)
Ill Wind (1950; UK edition, 1952)
Boy Wanted (1953; juvenile)
Widows' Plight (1955; UK edition, 1957, as *Widows Blackmail*)
The Schemers (1957; UK edition, 1958, as *The Case of the Gloating Landlord*)
Villainous Company (1967; UK edition, 1968)
The Drop of a Hat (1970; UK edition, 1971)

Plays
The Boiled Eggs: A Federal Theatre Project Play for Young People (1937)
Katcha and the Devil (1938)
The Speckled Band
The Mighty Mikko
A Valiant Little Tailor
The Totem
Babar the Elephant
The Children of Salem

GRIM REHEARSAL

DEAD YESTERDAY

RUTH FENISONG

Introduction by
Curtis Evans

STARK HOUSE

Stark House Press • Eureka California

GRIM REHEARSAL / DEAD YESTERDAY

Published by Stark House Press
1315 H Street
Eureka, CA 95501, USA
griffinskye3@sbcglobal.net
www.starkhousepress.com

ISBN: 979-8-88601-080-0

Book design by Mark Shepard, shepgraphics.com
Cover art by Shootelkora
Proofreading by Bill Kelly

First Stark House Press Edition: April 2024

A Genteel American Cop:
Gridley Nelson Returns to Action

By Curtis Evans

Seven years elapsed between the appearance of *Murder Runs a Fever* (1943), the fourth Gridley Nelson detective novel, and that of the next installment in the "Grid" Nelson series, *Grim Rehearsal* (1950), a theater mystery like such crime fiction classics as Patrick Quentin's *Puzzle for Players* (1938) and Ngaio Marsh's *Opening Night* (1951). In the intervening period, the author published five non-series mysteries. With *Grim Rehearsal*, however, "Grid" was back to stay for the next dozen years, during the Fifties making substantive appearances in a total of seven detective novels before taking his final bow in an eighth one in 1962. (He also pops up, briefly and inconsequentially, in Fenisong's 1960 juvenile delinquency novel *But Not Forgotten*.) For fans of mid-century "classic" detective fiction, the Gridley Nelson mystery series is a significant contribution to the genre and one thankfully now in the process of being recovered by Stark House. This latest "twofer" volume, the third in Stark House's Ruth Fenisong reprint series, contains both *Grim Rehearsal* and the Fenisong novel which followed it the next year, *Dead Yesterday* (1951), both of which are estimable additions to the Gridley Nelson canon.

Grim Rehearsal opens with New York press agent Pierce Kirby taking his kindly visiting honorary "uncle," Dr. Chadwick Miles, affectionately nicknamed by Pierce "Uncle Doc," to see a popular, critically bulletproof Broadway show called *Sea Change*. After the curtain comes down, he takes Uncle Doc backstage, where in her dressing room they visit star Ginette Arthur, with whom Pierce is currently having a romantic tiff. Said tiff, barely dormant, re-erupts between the two in Ginette's dressing room, leaving Uncle Doc tactfully to excuse himself to wander around backstage. While exploring the bowels of the theater, he overhears words that sound to him deeply nefarious, although we are not told what it is that he actually hears. The doctor goes forth to investigate at the end of Chapter One—and promptly disappears!

At the end of Chapter Two police inform Pierce that tragically the old man has been discovered dead in an alley—murdered. In Chapter Three the press agent calls upon Grid Nelson, temporary captain of the homicide division while his superior, Waldo Furniss, familiar from previous novels in the series, recovers in Florida from a bullet wound suffered in the line of duty. Soon Grid is scenting out crime in a complex case, with Pierce frequently tagging along.

Complication is added to the criminal conundrum when Toni George, a lovely *Sea Change* chorus girl whom Pierce encountered in Chapter Two, vanishes, just like Uncle Doc. Will she be found dead too? Before her disappearance Toni had been lamenting to Pierce that her love life with her proper and somewhat pompous attorney boyfriend, LeRoy Seagar, was being gravely undermined by importunate playboy and Broadway sugar daddy Bobby Drake, who just has not learned, apparently, ever to take "no" for an answer from attractive women. Pierce already has a down on Bobby, for Ginette on the night Uncle Doc disappeared informed him that she had actually become engaged to the wealthy and amorous man-about-town. With Pierce and now LeRoy querulously on his back, Grid needs the patience of a saint to carry on coherently with his investigation. Fortunately, the kindly cop has just that saintly patience, as followers of the series will already know from his previous cases.

Taking Pierce under his wing, Grid tells the press agent something about himself, in the process also reacquainting readers of the series with his back story as an American lawman who shares considerable affinity with the handsome and sensitive gentleman sleuths of British detective fiction:

> "You don't look as though you were born chewing a night stick."
>
> Nelson chuckled. "I wasn't." He began to talk about himself, easily, conversationally. He had gone to Princeton. There had been no special hurry for him to choose a career. He had tried all manner of jobs, separated from his fellow workers only by the fact that his mother had left him a small income and that he would continue to eat, whether or not he worked. Among other things, he had been garage mechanic, general factotum in a Little Theater movement, and apprentice in the laboratory of a criminologist. The last had held him longest, but he had an appetite for close contact with people, and after a while work on group theories became tasteless fare. "So I joined the force…. Some of my cases…yielded extremely valuable by-products. In one of them I acquired a maid…. Sammy's the best cook extant—with an intelligence that frequently puts the trained mind to shame…. And by way of another case I

acquired my wife. She's in Europe now and I miss her. That's the only part of marriage I object to—the missing."

Between sessions of listening to Mahler on the gramophone and devouring Sammy's delectable gumbo (accompanied by spoon bread and a chicory salad), Grid puzzles out a fiendish murder plot and routs the fiends who plotted it. The author even manages to provide some first-rate fair play clues for readers to decipher, if they can. What more could a vintage mystery fan demand from a mid-century baffler? As one myself, I emphatically agree with the *Berkshire Eagle* reviewer, who praised *Grim Rehearsal* for its "Broadway atmosphere done to a turn," "intelligent detection with no tricks" and "good writing about believable people."

In *Grim Rehearsal*'s immediate successor, *Dead Yesterday*, we initially encounter Countess Thea Mazzini—a once beautiful, former model who has gone to seed as a slatternly lush since the death of her wealthy, aristocratic Italian husband Dino—and the countess' none too devoted maid. In Chapter Two we meet lovely, seventeen-year-old Gale Upjohn, who has recently relocated to New York City from Connecticut with the rest of her family, which consists of her egotistical, intellectual parents and her equally annoying, slightly younger brother Rance (nicknamed "Rancid" in their new school). Fatefully Gale decides to make an impromptu evening visit to her aunt, who is none other than the countess, the family not having seen or heard from in years. Once she enters the countess' apartment, however, she descends into a maelstrom of murder, madness and Machiavellian plotting from which only Grid Nelson, it seems, can retrieve her—perhaps with a little help, one hopes, from brother Rance, who fancies himself something of a detective. There are some twists and turns to the tale, but it is more of a tale of suspense, peopled with some memorably drawn characters, portraits of good and evil.

Sammy is again on the scene, as is wife Kyrie, who talks over the case with Grid and has an important announcement of her own to make. During his down time at home, Grid listens to Debussy and sits down to another one of Sammy's dinners, consisting of "a thick broiled steak, a froth of mashed potatoes in a garlic-rubbed bowl, broccoli, watercress with a special dressing, crisp hot bread," and, for dessert, "a steamed rum pudding for which there was no room but nonetheless went down with miraculous ease." Meanwhile there is a brutal murder and other assorted nasty mysteries for this good, cultured man to solve, in this fine American crime story which artfully blends elements of Agatha Christie, Margery Allingham, Rex Stout and Ed McBain. The reviewer at the Book Corner of the *Wilmington Morning News* pronounced of *Dead Yesterday* that the novel, which s/he deemed "among the best [mysteries] of recent years," … "has convinced us that a really good mystery yarn is still about the most satisfying book that one can read." Surely no mystery fan will argue with that.

—January 2024
Memphis, TN

• •

Curtis Evans received a PhD in American history in 1998. He is the author of *Masters of the "Humdrum" Mystery: Cecil John Charles Street, Freeman Wills Crofts, Alfred Walter Stewart and British Detective Fiction, 1920-1961* (2012), *Clues and Corpses: The Detective Fiction and Mystery Criticism of Todd Downing* (2013), *The Spectrum of English Murder: The Detective Fiction of Henry Lancelot Aubrey-Fletcher and G. D. H. and Margaret Cole* (2015) and editor of the Edgar nominated *Murder in the Closet: Essays on Queer Clues in Crime Fiction Before Stonewall* (2017). He writes about vintage crime fiction at his blog The Passing Tramp and at Crimereads.

GRIM REHEARSAL

RUTH FENISONG

CHAPTER ONE

By now people had forgotten the critics' cold reception of *Sea Change*. On the strength of that freakish intangible known as audience reaction, the musical comedy had settled down for an indefinite stay at the Corridor Theater. And so studiously had Pierce Kirby, press agent, nursed it, that, although its unexpected rallying was no longer news, hardly a day passed without mention of it in one or another of the Broadway columns.

From the line outside the box office, it appeared that in all New York only Pierce Kirby was heartily sick of the production. His wide mouth drooped as he steered Uncle Doc through the crowded lobby. He thought glumly of the evening he had planned for himself, and then, glancing at his companion, was ashamed. Uncle Doc's face, wrinkled and weathered as it was, stood out among the faded town faces like a joyous old banner that had somehow managed through years of wind and storm to retain its original gallantry.

He was an uncle only by his own courtesy, and numberless were the plans he had waived in order to lead Pierce safely through the confused terrain of childhood. Pierce emerged from gloom long enough to resolve that Dr. Chad Miles, general practitioner of a vanishing school, making his first visit to New York in a decade, was going to have the time of his life.

Full cooperation made the task easy. From overture to first-act curtain, the old man applauded tirelessly, and almost any gag drew laughter up from his thin belly. In the intermission he could not be induced to leave his seat for fear of missing some fractional part of the second act. He ordered Pierce to run along and stretch his legs or whatever, and Pierce, after trying to convince him that the intermission was the best part of the show, ran along.

He had a good length of leg to stretch. He was a skinny dark individual, taut as a wound spring. His hunger for everything was prodigious, but Uncle Doc had remarked long ago that all the food he ate went straight to his brain. He was not as smart as Uncle Doc believed him to be, of course, but he was smart enough. At twenty-six he could hold his own against men of twice his age. Women were something else. Especially Ginette. Ginette was perhaps the chief reason that *Sea Change* stuck in his throat. He hated her role in it as much as he had ever hated anything, and since from birth he was a passionate character, his emotions rarely stopped at the halfway mark.

In the lobby he lit a cigarette and out of habit searched for familiar faces. The net result was not rewarding. A producer with irons in the fire plowed toward him and invited him to drop around for a business chat. An actress at leisure saluted him on both cheeks and announced that if he had been engaged to do publicity her last egg would have hatched too. He thanked her, expressed admiration for the scent she used, and hoped silently that her lipstick had not left a bloody trail along his cheeks. Over the massed well-groomed heads Bobby Drake waved to him. His right arm always seemed slightly crooked, as though he had fitted it around too many waists. Pierce waved back, idly wondering why the dapper little fellow had no woman in tow tonight and, for that matter, why he was among those present, since he seldom cared to be seen at anything but first nights. He finished his cigarette and went back to his seat. Until the final curtain he managed to blot out the frenetic doings on the stage, taking his pleasure in Uncle Doc's enjoyment.

When the audience, milked dry of encores, started to leave, Uncle Doc was still a claque of one. Pierce nudged him gently. "Those people next to you want out."

Uncle Doc stood up. "That was rich," he said. "Thank you kindly, Pierce. I don't know as I've ever seen anything to come up to that."

"You don't get out enough," Pierce said, his tone affectionate.

They joined the stream that flowed to the street. The winter air was good to drink after the sweetish heat of the theater. Pierce stood drinking it as though it might be some stimulant prescribed to lift his general tone.

Uncle Doc watched him. "Button your coat. You always were a boy to court disaster." He himself was tightly swaddled, exposing hardly more than the tip of inquiring nose.

"I'll get us indoors as soon as I can raise a cab. Any special choice of indoors? It's your night."

Uncle Doc hesitated. "Do you suppose—no—guess not."

"You guess wrong. Name it." For a moment he thought hopefully that the old man was ready for bed. In that case something might be salvaged of his own plans, which were as modest as the fairy-tale heroine's desire for one red rose, and apparently as difficult to achieve. For all he wanted was a few peaceful hours in the little apartment that should have been home and that had never been more than a place where he bathed and changed his clothes. He wanted to sit alone and read or play the unused gramophone, and somewhere between these entertainments to conduct an exhaustive search of self too long postponed.

But Uncle Doc had shoved back the brim of his hat to scratch his high naked brow, and the blue expectancy of his eyes showed clear.

"You dog," Pierce said. "Don't tell me you're hankering for a burlesque or a—"

"No. I had my fill of that stuff before you could word your natural wants. Besides, only thing to distinguish this show from burlesque is the suspense angle. Folks don't have to yell, 'Take it off,' because it is off." He coughed apologetically. "Pierce, I shouldn't be surprised if my wits are duller than they used to be—but I still don't know what you've got to do with all this." He turned toward the marquee of the theater. "You're not in it so to speak—not on the stage or managing it, I mean. Oh yes—you've told me you write newspaper pieces about it—but your name isn't on them—and back in Kincaid when Bick Standish wants news for the *Scythe* he sends a reporter to get it." He waited humbly for clarification.

Pierce had given up trying to explain the work of a press agent to the uninitiate. "I just see that the public isn't allowed to forget the shows that employ me." He tasted the statement and found it a triumph of simplification, because anyone who believed the eternal wooing of the press an easy task should try it. Sourly he reviewed the time spent on leg work and at his typewriter; the money allotted to lunches, cocktails, dinners; the meaningless contacts he was required to make that he might squeeze them for a yield of one small drop to be added to the releases he sent out, releases containing selected items calculated to pander to any and every style of keyhole journalism, his own tidbit sandwiched in and so cleverly devoid of special emphasis that more often than not even the toughest columnist was seduced into giving it space. He thought of the human-interest stories, most of them sheer invention, that he had woven about the separate members of the cast, even using the doorman's past to bridge a dearth of incident. He muttered, "A hell of a job. A combination Balzac and Barnum, that's me."

Uncle Doc was staring at him. Uncle Doc said, "Hmm. I still haven't got it quite straight in my mind. But if you like what you're doing, that's the main thing. You know—once I thought you'd be a real writer—showed all the signs of it when you were a kid. Funny—"

"Very." Pierce made his lips smile. "Now let's get down to pleasure. What's yours?"

"Well—I was wondering if you pulled enough weight to take me backstage. I've never been backstage."

"Follow me," Pierce said. His plans had included a total abstinence from Ginette, but how could you fast with the full meal thrust at you? He led Uncle Doc through an alley.

Uncle Doc commented upon the absence of stage door Johnnies. "In my time," he said, "with a cast like that, they'd have been swarming."

"These days the Johns are mostly autograph hunters," Pierce answered, "and *Sea Change* has been running long enough to glut even that market." He repressed an impulse to belch.

Steve, the doorman, sat guarding the entryway. Over him a bulb shone with cruel honesty on the unnaturally blond heads of two line boys. They greeted Pierce and glanced at Uncle Doc, and one of them made a snickering sound that hung in the cold dank air. They seemed disposed to linger, but Pierce brushed them off with forced good humor. "Go out and make some news that I can print, boys." Laughing merrily, they went.

"This your dad, Mr. Kirby?" the doorman asked.

"My uncle—Dr. Miles. He's visiting New York for the first time in years and he wants to see everything. All right with you?"

"Any uncle of yours," Steve said. He looked at the old man expectantly. "You a medico, sir?" He coughed. "I been feeling under the weather—"

"Nix," Pierce said. "He's a medico, all right, but strictly off duty."

Steve grinned. "I thought maybe he'd come to examine the girls."

"Steve was once chief comic at Minsky's," Pierce said. "He remembers all the jokes."

"Who helped me to remember? That story you dug out of me almost made my wife sore—except that on the strength of it she got promoted to queen bee of the neighborhood. Anyways—I know you didn't come to peep at the girls, Mr. Kirby—on account of you're star-minded." He shifted his chair to give them passage.

"Friendly cuss," Uncle Doc said. "An actor, was he? Must be about my age."

Pierce did not trouble to point out that the simian-featured little doorman was at least ten years younger than Uncle Doc. Steve had been born old.

"That cough sounded like a mixture of beer and tobacco, but I suppose if I were in his place I'd— Say—this is just the way I thought it would be."

He followed Pierce, who with practiced ease dodged stagehands and other impedimenta. Once or twice Pierce stopped for a word with players dressed to look like ordinary folk. Uncle Doc studied them frankly and, when a group of them had passed, sniffed the atmosphere. "Bet there's no other smell like this in the whole world."

"No—it's peculiar to theaters."

"Not what you might call a natural habitat. Your friends are a mighty peaked lot up close—and no wonder."

"Peaked, my eye. It's the light and the fact that they're clean of makeup to give their skins a rest. These kids are healthy to the bone. There isn't a girl in Kincaid who gives as much attention to diet and exercise as they do. Here—we can cross the stage to get to her—to the dressing rooms."

It was an old theater, the stage flanked by iron staircases. "Where do they lead?" Uncle Doc asked.

"To other dressing rooms. In this racket the higher up you go the less you rate. The chorus has two steep flights to climb."

He showed no impatience when Uncle Doc halted on-stage to crane at the ominous overhang of ropes and pulleys, and again to give detailed inspection to a flat of a village main street. Pierce considered himself a fatalist. If Ginette had left by the time they reached her dressing room it would be in the cards. It would confirm his resolution not to see her until the taste of their quarrel had been washed from his mouth.

"Could be Kincaid," Uncle Doc said, still studying the flat, "except that the signs on the stores are different. Well—I'll have something to talk about when I get home." He added wistfully, "Only there's hardly anyone left to talk to—"

"I'm sorry, Uncle Doc, I didn't hear—"

The old man's voice firmed. "I was just saying I'd kind of like to meet the leading lady face to face—I— Hey—wait—I'm not in that much of a hurry."

But Pierce, with goal in sight, could not control his sprint. Outside Ginette's dressing room he babbled foolishly until his knock was answered. "No flirting, Uncle Doc. None of the old line. She's practically engaged to be married." He kept his fingers crossed.

Uncle Doc said mildly, "I hope so—and I hope it's to the fellow she was making so free with on the stage."

Ginette's voice called, "Who is it?"

"Pierce Kirby and companion," Pierce said.

"Come in."

Ginette wore street clothes, a black softly tailored suit, and a small cap over the cap of her blond hair. Her face, too, was clean of makeup. But she did not look ordinary or peaked.

Pierce gave her a strained smile. "You're going to be a big disappointment to my uncle," he said. "You should be seated at your dressing table in a flimsy negligee, surrounded by flowers and cosseted by an adoring maid."

Ginette did not look at him. "The maid fits," she said, "except that her union says, 'Thou shalt neither cosset nor adore, and thou shalt leave early.' In fact, I was about to leave, myself."

Because Pierce said nothing, Uncle Doc said, "We won't keep you. Just dropped in to see if those footlights weren't stretching the truth a mite. They weren't."

She warmed and lighted suddenly. She held out her hand. "You must be the favorite uncle Pierce broke a precedent to talk about. He never does talk about important matters."

Uncle Doc chuckled. "I shouldn't wonder you'd drive most everything out of a man's head—including his manners." He shook her hand. "I'm Dr. Miles—and that's the only part of the introduction that's necessary, Miss Arthur. I saw you a few years ago when you toured the country with that repertory setup. Should have said the roles you played then were more your speed than tonight's caper, but I guess a real actress can turn her hand to everything. You got a mighty fine voice too. I mean singing voice. The other goes without saying. Most of the girls and boys nowadays seem afraid of their own strength when it comes to singing. They kind of keep half of it back and let the other half out through their noses, timid-like. In some ways we're backward in Kincaid, but—" His candid eyes finished the sentence. But we know the real thing when we meet it, his eyes said.

Ginette smiled. "If you're an average citizen of Kincaid there's nothing backward about it. I'm glad you like my voice. I was trained to be a singer before I became an actress."

"That so? Well—you've got that natural something that goes much further than training—"

Pierce was again seized with the urge to babble nonsense. "Watch yourself, Ginette. He's got enough soft soap to lather the city." And while he spoke he would have given much to know what Uncle Doc was seeing and how it corresponded to what he himself saw: a finely made woman of average height who could at will look small and helpless or statuesque and infinitely strong; whose face had regular features except for the eyes, which were proportionately too large; whose face in repose was not arrestingly beautiful, yet so mobile it could be shaped to fit a hundred molds. Even off-stage he had witnessed its changes to tragedy, to love, to rage, to joy, to icy arrogance, personifying rather than merely expressing these qualities. He shook himself. For what Uncle Doc saw, of course, in spite of his pretty speeches, most probably bordered on the clinical side. He would note the clear eyes and the clear skin and—

Uncle Doc said, "I was telling Pierce a while back that I thought stage people were bound to be a puny lot. But now I'm eating crow. Fact is, I don't know when I've seen a healthier specimen."

She was amused. "And I don't know when I've had a compliment I liked less. My favorite storybook heroines were always interestingly pale and fragile."

"Sure—and they suffered migraine and were tortured in childbirth." His eyes descended to her breasts, her loins. "You'll never have any trouble—"

"Break it up," Pierce said. "You're not in your dispensary." He went on babbling: "I warned you, Ginette, to watch out for Uncle Doc. He never stops practicing his profession for a minute, with or without the little black bag. Even when I was a kid I used to suspect that his equipment was only window dressing—especially the microscope in his office. I was sure that he was gifted with special sight and that his naked eye could detect germs at twenty paces." He wondered if

Uncle Doc's naked eye could spot the germs whirling about the dressing room, the germs left over from last night's dust-up. "He has a special gift for dealing with women too—otherwise he'd never have succeeded in remaining a bachelor. He—"

Uncle Doc said calmly, "Don't work so hard, Pierce. Miss Arthur hasn't taken offense. She knows an old fool when she sees one. Besides, glossing over a few of the lines she spouted on the stage tonight, she's practically a married woman. You told me so yourself."

"Oh God," Pierce said. And for the first time in memory he did not love Uncle Doc.

Ginette said clearly, "That's true. I am engaged."

Uncle Doc's time-stitched lips parted to form the first syllable of the word "congratulations," but he did not get the word out because Pierce had stepped between him and Ginette. Pierce had anchored his hands upon Ginette's shoulders.

Uncle Doc looked very pleased. "I thought it might be something like that," he murmured. He made his way out into the passage and closed the door behind him.

But it was not something like that. The brief silence in the dressing room could be translated to satisfy the most romantic leanings. It satisfied Uncle Doc. He stood savoring it until it was dispelled.

Ginette spoke first. Then Pierce said, "I couldn't have heard right." Then both spoke together, creating a landslide of words which tumbled about them without order or decency. "You heard—"

"You can't mean it!"

"Why can't I? At least he wants a wife—not a mother—"

"Stop—"

"And he doesn't need an intercessor—and he doesn't despise his lot—"

"What's wrong with being a press agent?"

"I never said anything was—it's your superior attitude toward it that makes it wrong. You'll keep on grumbling about it for the rest of your days—but you'll never make a move to change it—"

"It's money you want. Never expect me to believe you love—"

"I've given up expecting you to believe anything. You're unbearable—possessive—"

"Because I think you're destroying your stature as an artist in this—"

"I can't destroy my stature as an artist—I'm sure of myself. That's the difference between us. You're a floundering little boy. I'd rather marry a happy street cleaner than a malcontent who grumbles about trifles because of his own insecurity—"

"Trifles! Do you have to appear naked to keep your place on the American stage? Do you have to let yourself be mauled?"

Uncle Doc had been participant, and even detached observer, often enough to realize that the language of love has many strange variations. But this was something quite outside his experience. He did not like it at all. Uncomfortably he moved away from the door so that he should hear no more. He walked down the passage. A pity, he thought, that Pierce always seemed to place his bundle on the wrong horse. Pierce, although no blood relation, had been as close to him as a son could be. Once he had hoped that his own work might be carried on by the boy. When that hope petered out he had settled for a writing career. And in a sense, of course, Pierce had become a writer. At least he appeared to be making a better living at it than a great many writers. But somehow Uncle Doc could not accept his present occupation as real work. And by real work he meant a contribution that would improve or mitigate the conditions of the world in which he lived. Seeing Pierce after a long interval, he had at once noted signs of restiveness. Good signs, he thought, that could presage a will to change his lot. But from what he understood of the quarrel, the signs were not good after all. He had to agree with Ginette Arthur that the main thing about a man's occupation was the state of mind he brought to it. Perhaps he had let Pierce lean too hard upon him back in those days when the poor kid— He shook his head. No. Pierce was an ace. Once he realized his potentialities, there would be no stopping him.

Uncle Doc had recognized with delight the symptoms shown by Pierce in Ginette's presence. Ginette looked like a nice girl in spite of the somewhat bawdy stage doings to which she had lent herself. Maybe she was not really engaged to someone else. Maybe she was just riled with Pierce for something he had said or done. He could be mighty contrary. But marriage to a nice girl might be the very thing he needed to force him down to business. Marriage had much to recommend it, thought Uncle Doc. A loneliness settled upon him, making him wish that he himself had married. But in a town where until recently he had been the only doctor, it would have been unfair to expect a woman to— He straightened his shoulders. What nonsense to be dwelling on at his age. Not that he considered himself old. An inch or so to the right of seventy was not really old. He could look forward to quite a few more years, preferably filled with new interests such as Pierce's children. Only, from the look of things, it did not seem as though Pierce would get started soon enough for— He sighed. This visit to New York had been tonic until—

His steps had taken him back to the stage. He decided to climb one of the iron staircases. Might as well make thorough exploration of this strange life from life while he had the opportunity. He started the ascent. Just before he reached the second landing he came to a quick halt. What stopped him was not fatigue but another battle of the sexes.

These new combatants, whoever they were, did not at first sound quite so violent as Pierce and Ginette. At least they were permitting each other to speak without interruption. But there was something less wholesome than anger in the voice of the male. The female voice confined itself to uttering tepid protests.

Must be something in the air, Uncle Doc thought wretchedly. He felt trapped between two armies, each engaged in waging separate wars. He wanted no part of either of them. I'll get out of here, he thought. Go back to the hotel. Pierce won't feel like doing much, anyway, after that set-to. He'll want to be by himself and not saddled with— Well, I'll be—

A moment later he slapped his brow. My mind's wandering. I couldn't have heard right—or else they're rehearsing a new play. Yes, that's it. He clung to the theory even while it collapsed under the weight of reason. Because this was no acting. Nor were the lines just registered by his reluctant ears the lines of any play. Even in old-fashioned melodrama they would have been laughed off the boards.

As though he were about to brave a freezing blast, Uncle Doc tightened the scarf around his lean neck and hoisted his coat collar. He had to see who they were, assure himself that they were not monsters whose lips plotted such a monstrous undertaking. He had to size them up, weigh them, and decide how much of what he had heard to credit and how much to discard as the loose talk that people sometimes weave out of wishes and never really mean to implement. And, if necessary, they could be made to listen to him. He had never been one to dodge danger. More often than not he had successfully quelled it. He coughed a heralding cough. He took the remaining steps of the flight. There was a sudden silence as he appeared on the landing.

CHAPTER TWO

It could not go on forever. Having done all possible damage, the ugly landslide stopped as suddenly as it had begun. Ginette stalked out of her dressing room, and Pierce dropped into a chair as though felled. He sat inert for a few moments that seemed like an age. Then he roused himself and went out to look for Uncle Doc. But the passage was empty. He was seeking him in the regions near the stage when Ginette passed on her way back to the dressing room. "I forgot my pocketbook," she said, her voice aloof. "Is anything wrong?" She meant, "Is anything else wrong?"

"No. I was looking for my uncle. I guess he went home. I'll wait until you get your pocketbook."

"Don't bother."

But he waited, and the two of them walked out of the theater. She really did forget her pocketbook, he thought dully. She didn't come back for any other reason. As they left the stage door he said, "Steve's gone too. I thought he didn't leave until his relief came."

"He's probably around somewhere," Ginette said. She was a stranger addressing a stranger. Then she said, "I'm sorry about one thing."

His heart lurched.

"I'm sorry your uncle didn't wait."

"My intercessor, you mean. The one I brought with me because I couldn't stand on my own feet."

She had no intention of starting it again. "I like Dr. Miles—quite apart from you. This was to be his night, wasn't it?"

Pierce said, "Don't worry. I'll make it up to him." I'll make it up to him tomorrow, he thought, if I can manage to live until tomorrow.

"Is he staying with you?"

"No—at the Manhattan." Uncle Doc had refused to share the apartment, even though Pierce had assured him it would cause no inconvenience. The Manhattan Hotel had been his headquarters on his first visit to New York as a young man, and he insisted that to stay elsewhere would rob him of a very special tang preserved down through the years. Pierce was grateful now for his insistence. Feeling the way he felt, a talkfest such as Uncle Doc had every right to expect would have been impossible. He said to Ginette, "Would you like me to take you home?"

"No, thank you. Just get me a cab if you don't mind."

He was equal to no further protest. He hailed a cab for her. In the light of its lamps they both looked spent. Both of them said the formal "Good night" which meant "Goodbye." Then Pierce turned and started walking. It took heavy effort to move his tall slight body. And that was odd because he had the sensation that it was hollow, that all his insides had melted and drained away. He had no particular destination in mind. It was no longer necessary to go home and take stock. What was there left to take stock of? He was bankrupt, and at the same time he was his own chief creditor, and he did not give a damn if nothing was ever salvaged from the ruin he had become.

His coat flapped in the wind. "You always were a boy to court disaster," Uncle Doc had said. Painstakingly he buttoned his coat. The operation, inconsistent with his thoughts of a moment ago, restored him a little, protected him from the external cold. He decided that a drink might similarly react upon the chill within. A drink and lights and a frame of people he did not know, talking about problems that were not his. He might even get drunk. All desperate characters get drunk when they're thwarted, he told himself sardonically. It's in the best tradition.

He entered Shane's Bar and Grill on Sixth Avenue. It was frequented by members of the *Sea Change* cast, but at this hour he did not expect to encounter a familiar face. He was wrong. As he slipped into a place at the bar he saw three of the chorus girls occupying a booth. He pretended not to see them.

It did not work. He heard his name called and was forced to turn his head. One of the girls beckoned. "Come on, sit with us. We're that bored we'll buy you a drink."

He joined them. They were nice kids. No point in taking it out on them. "Hi, Toni, Jill, Stasia." It was part of his racket to remember names and faces. "What—no dates?" He sat next to Jill Batiste.

Jill said, "Stasia and I thought we were set, but we got stood up. Toni just happened to join us, but not for the same reason. She's going steady—only her boyfriend's the serious type and this is his night to woo the lawbooks or something. So we're having a wonderful time by ourselves." She had the smile of a street urchin, full of guile and charm.

"A wonderful time," Stasia repeated gloomily. "What makes me mad, we turned down a perfectly good invitation to a party on account of those two wise guys." She had naturally red hair. Her hands were forever at it.

Pierce said, "What'll it be, kids? My round."

Jill patted his arm. "There, now—conditions are beginning to improve. A Gibson for me. I'm fortified with a sandwich and coffee, so one little drink isn't going to give me a delicate morning." A Gibson was a martini without vermouth, and a pickled onion instead of an olive.

Pierce ordered three, and a scotch for himself. He tasted the scotch and found that he did not want it. He set the glass down.

Jill said, "Was that nice old man I saw you with when I was leaving the theater your papa?"

Stasia laughed. "It sounds like a switch on that chestnut that begins, 'Who was that lady I seen you with?'"

"It's not a chestnut. It's true. I did see him with—"

"My uncle," Pierce said. He toyed with the idea of calling the Manhattan to find out if Uncle Doc had got home safely. He decided against it. Uncle Doc might be asleep. He yawned, not because he himself was sleepy but in expression of deep discomfort.

Jill said, "Are you going to die on me too? Be amusing."

"Some guys don't know their luck," Stasia said. "Who else do you see with a redhead, a blonde, and a brunette on tap?"

It was true. They were all three luscious melt-in-the-mouth tidbits. But he had developed the captious appetite of an invalid. He was not tempted.

"So what's missing?" Stasia said. "No—don't tell me—let me guess.

I know—another blonde. But if you wanted her, you shouldn't have come in here. This joint is strictly for small fry."

He downed the scotch.

"Shut up, you dope," Jill said to Stasia. "Ginette Arthur's no snob. Hey, Kirby, shall I tell you the story of my life? I don't mean that malarky I fed you the first time but the real honest-to—"

"You're the dope," Stasia said. "Do you want to be jailed?"

Toni George was the only one who had not spoken. Nor had she touched her drink. The pickled onion in its depths might have been a crystal ball for the way she studied it. Pierce felt a wan glow of kinship for her merely because she seemed depressed. She was the brunette of the group, with poreless dead-white skin and deep-set eyes that were nearly black. She was not just young and fresh and highly colored as were her companions, but of a striking beauty. He had marked this during the early days of the show. But he had been strangely objective about it even before Ginette had taken an option on his senses. An option that she never meant to exercise. His sight dimmed. The table faded out. He was back in the dressing room. *I am engaged*, she said, *but not to you*. Again he trembled with shock as she said the man's name. *It's a joke—you don't need that brand of publicity—* And she, *I know what I need—which is more than you do—*

Jill raised her voice. "You got chronic malaria?"

He came back. He smiled meaninglessly.

"Because if you haven't you'd better see a man about something. You're shaking like you need a fix. What say we break this up? It's not a success. I can't imagine why. Here's you and here's us—and we're everything the ads guarantee after a ten-day trial. So why the lonely look? He has got a lonely look, hasn't he, Stasia? That's the reason I called him over. The moment I saw him my fingers itched to soothe his—"

"As long as the itch stays in your fingers," Stasia said, "it's okay."

"Why, Stasia Phillips—how you do go on!"

"And if you'll pardon the correction, you called him over because it never hurts to be nice to a press agent."

"There are times when the truth should be kept secret." Jill wriggled into the coat on the back of her chair. Pierce made vague motions of assistance. Stasia, too, prepared to leave. But Toni George sat still. The pickled onion continued to exert its fascination for her.

"Coming, Toni?" Jill asked.

"No."

"That's putting it in a nutshell. Well, suit yourself. And if you don't mind my saying so, you're easily suited." Jill smiled at Pierce to show that there was no hard feeling. "Thanks for the drink, anyway. If you should decide to give us another plug please don't mention that two blackhearted scoundrels welshed on us tonight. It would only start our public gunning for them."

Pierce stood up as she and Stasia eased their way out of the booth. From sheer inertia he sat down again. After a silence he asked the girl opposite him if she would like another drink.

"No, thanks."

Something to eat then?"

"No—I've eaten."

He ordered a second scotch. It tasted no better than the first, but he drank it. His stomach was a hard knot, and he did not believe a sea of scotch would untie it. He fiddled with the glass. He listened to a sticky interchange between a man and woman in the booth behind him. He actually heard himself saying, "Ha!"

Toni George stirred. She lifted her eyes. Behind the heavy screen of lashes they had a flat, almost opaque look. She said, "If you're waiting because you don't want to leave me here alone, you needn't. I'm expecting a friend of mine."

He assumed a synthetic jocularity. "The boyfriend—the serious student of the law?"

"He's not a student—he's a successful lawyer."

"Oh? Then I guess I'd better leave. He might find me out of order." She said, "Not you. He won't mind you."

She said it without inflection. Yet it carried an edge sharp enough to slice through his preoccupation. Pierce found himself examining the words with more care than they seemed to warrant. "Why won't he mind me? I've been considered worthy competition in my time." He looked at her. "You're feeling kind of low, aren't you?" He did not mean it to sound patronizing, but it came out that way. Because what did anyone else know about feeling low?

"Yes," she said. She seemed to be measuring him. "I'm glad you didn't leave. I've got to talk to someone before Roy gets here. I can't talk to him. And Jill and Stasia are swell, but—" She hesitated.

The same speech delivered by anyone else might have sounded like a desperate plea. But the voice of Toni George was rather thin and colorless, giving whatever she said a bread-and-butter flavor. Perhaps that was why he had never been attracted to her. He was highly susceptive to voices. Ginette's voice …

"You know Bobby Drake—don't you?"

He could feel his whole body stiffen. He had seen Bobby Drake in the lobby that night, and he had heard his name spoken by Ginette. He was sick to death of Bobby Drake. He managed to keep the sickness out of his voice. "Yes, I know him. Who doesn't?"

"I wish I didn't. I wish I'd never met him."

He squirmed. He said, "Oh no!"

"I beg your pardon?" She looked puzzled.

So she had to talk to someone—had she? A press agent for choice. What an act. He wondered if her apparent unhappiness was part of it, put on to make an impression the moment she had spotted him. A pretty competent performance at that, considering the flimsiness of the material. Those kids would go to any lengths to court the limelight. This time the patronage in his voice was deliberate. "What's the matter? Don't tell me he wants to make you wife number nine— or have I lost count? Well—it might be good for an item. But the columnists have become fed up with Bobby Drake. Unless he gets a new pitch I'm afraid he's on the way out." But Bobby Drake did have a new pitch. He was hitching his wagon to a star this trip. A real star, not some little pretender who didn't even know the present score.

Toni said in her thin, colorless voice, "He has got a new pitch. He's out of his head—and I'm terribly frightened."

Once more he was caught by the lack of inflection, the absence of any attempt at dramatization. Doggedly he clung to the role of skeptic. "Come now, Toni. Drake is harmless." Harmless to everyone but me, he thought.

She was staring at him. She said, "Oh—I get it. You think I'm cooking this up—trying to make the headlines."

"Well ..." He drawled it.

"Never mind—skip it. May I have a cigarette, please?" Her lips that usually seemed full and soft had shut tightly, as though closed upon any further confidence. She parted them to receive the cigarette, but the set line remained.

Pierce lit the cigarette and one for himself. He dragged on it. It tasted as the scotch had tasted. He wondered if frustration could spread to a man's palate, alter his entire chemistry. What the hell? He said to Toni, "Look, kid, if I've got it wrong I apologize. Go ahead— tell me why Bobby Drake has you scared."

"Don't humor me."

"All right, let's put our cards on the table. If you're stuck with the story that Drake has been pestering you because he wants you to join the parade of wives we *will* skip it. I happen to know otherwise— I happen to know that—" He could not get it out, that incredible fact that Ginette, his girl, had accepted the offer to be next on Bobby Drake's list.

She said quietly, "But he is pestering me to marry him."

"Then he *is* mad—"

"Yes—that's what I'm trying to tell you. At first I treated it as a joke. I thanked him just the same and told him that I was engaged to someone else. But he won't accept it. He keeps at me and at me. He comes to the theater and—and he sends things—flowers and candy—until yesterday. Yesterday he sent me a bracelet. Roy, my fiancé, was there when it arrived. He got furious, naturally, and he won't believe I haven't been encouraging Drake. Between the two of them I'm going mad myself. What makes it worse is that Drake is one of Roy's clients. That's where I met him—and now Roy doesn't want to handle his affairs any longer. Roy is just starting out on his own. Before his father died he was no more than a figurehead in the firm—but now he's in full charge because Mr. Cunningham's dead too. Seager and Cunningham have been handling the affairs of the Drake family for years. Roy was born in Chilton, the same as Drake, and he grew up with him. If he has to drop him now, for my sake, that makes a bad start for our marriage." She opened her pocketbook and extracted a jeweler's box. She pressed its lid and set it on the table between them. Its contents glittered wickedly. "When I tried to return it," she said, "Drake threatened to kill me. I know of course he wouldn't go that far, but just same—"

Pierce down at the bracelet. "He sent you that yesterday?" His head was starting to ache. "I think I need another drink, or maybe I've had two too many." Then the confusion in his brain cleared. Obviously the bracelet did not come from Woolworth's, so Toni George was telling the truth, or at least part of the truth. That much settled, the rest was easy. Toni had been the second string to Drake's bow— to be used if—if the first one failed. The futile egomaniac had not made the columns since his last divorce and he was probably desperate. And he was the man Ginette— Pierce said coldly, "I wouldn't worry about it anymore if I were you. You'd better put that bauble away if you're expecting your fiancé. It might stir him up again."

Absently she dropped the box into her bag. "It's easy to say stop worrying, but—"

"You might even—if you want to make a thing of it—sue the silly bastard for breach of promise. He'll pay through the nose now that—" He shrugged. Frustration could not only change a man's chemistry. It could change him into a rat.

"I don't know what you're talking about."

His voice was tired. "That makes us even."

She said, "I—I've confided in you for a reason—not just to get it off my chest. I—"

He nodded encouragingly. Now comes the gimmick, he thought. He was on familiar ground once more, having a good old reunion with his cynicism. It was like a shot in the arm.

"Could you—I realize that I've a nerve to ask it of you—but since you know Bobby Drake and since he knows you have an in with the press and he doesn't want unfavorable publicity—would you talk to him? You wouldn't even have to mention my name. You could just say you heard rumors he was annoying a certain girl and ask him to stop—"

"Full stop," Pierce said.

She turned her head. A man was approaching the booth, a short, stocky, no-nonsense man looking very prosperous and forthright in his neat business suit.

"Oh—Roy." Something that might have been anxiety flickered in her deep-set eyes. But she introduced the two men with considerable poise. "Mr. Pierce Kirby—Mr. LeRoy Seager." Before the handshake was completed she said, "Mr. Kirby's the show's press agent, Roy. He's been kind enough to sit with me until you came."

It was a definite dismissal. But Pierce, for no conscious reason except perhaps a will to control his own comings and goings, would not accept it. He heard himself saying, "Kind isn't the word. I always enjoy a tête-à-tête with a beautiful girl," and waited to see if the prosperous Mr. Seager would show jealousy, and realized with something like amazement that the trivial aspect of his nature still endured amid the surrounding rubble.

The prosperous Mr. Seager smiled, showing strong white teeth. "Toni is beautiful," he said, "and more than that. I'm a fortunate man."

Toni was right. He did not seem to mind Pierce. He sat down at Toni's side and gave her shoulder a quick squeeze. He glanced inquiringly at Pierce, ordered a drink with brisk competence, and said he was sorry to be so late but that he had been struggling with an important brief. He was, Pierce judged, almost twice the age of Toni, who could not have been much over twenty. He did not appear to be a man who would break out in a rash of fury because a crackpot millionaire client was sending his fiancée gifts. He appeared to be a man who would weigh the matter calmly and then proceed with extreme tact and caution.

Pierce drew breath sharply, remembering the part that same crackpot millionaire was playing in his own life. He wondered what sort of man he himself looked like. The haywire type, probably. But at the moment it did not seem to matter what he looked like, because his table companions were blind to him. They seemed to have worked up a communications system with dots and dashes understandable only to each other. He saw Seager nod slightly, and he saw Toni's eyelids drop as though a message had been received and acknowledged. "Nothing like love's young dream," he said bitterly, hardly knowing he said it.

Seager's close-shaven cheeks flushed surprisingly. "We've been separated for a whole day. You must excuse us."

Pierce arose, suddenly tired of them. "You must excuse me."

Neither of them even pretended sorrow at his leave-taking. Perversely he drew it out. "Toni, I'll see what I can do about that commission of yours."

"No," she said. "Don't do anything, please. I've changed my mind."

"I think that's wise. Better to ignore stuff like that." To Seager he said brightly, "We're talking shop. Some argument that Toni got into with another girl in the cast. Well—congratulations, both of you, and good luck. Do you want me to give the engagement a play?"

"Don't—there's a good fellow." Seager gripped his hand again in the best Dale Carnegie manner. "We haven't announced it formally as yet. I don't know if you've heard of my firm, but it's a conservative one—Seager and Cunningham. Both my father and Mr. Cunningham have departed, but I carry on as they would, and Toni agrees with me that it's best to tone down the theater angle. You understand."

Pierce said he understood. He turned and left the bar and grill.

He forgot them the moment he hit the cold. His head had begun to ache in earnest and he concentrated upon this feverishly, because a localized pain was better than the numbness that gripped him. He was seldom troubled by ills of the flesh, and he almost took a grim pride in this psychosomatic manifestation of deep mental distress. It proved something or other.

He ignored a cruising taxi. He started walking across town to his apartment. He thought that if he filled his lungs with the good night air he might be able to sleep and that tomorrow he could go on as usual. He took long strides, his head pounding with every one of them, but yet not sufficiently to dominate his thoughts. He could be detached enough to experience honest disgust at the way he was taking the blow delivered by Ginette. He told himself that people did not love that way anymore, that it had either gone out of fashion with *Godey's Lady's Book* or had never existed. He tried to analyze his suffering and came up with one part wounded vanity. But that left at least three other parts, and he was incapable of isolating them. He thought of Uncle Doc. His earlier mood had changed and now he regretted that Uncle Doc was not staying at the apartment. It would, after all, have been healing to talk to the old man. Uncle Doc could prescribe for him, psychosomatic headache and all; help as he had always helped to make him see things straight. He decided to go to the Manhattan Hotel first thing next day. He felt a little more normal even thinking about it.

He reached Third Avenue, walked uptown a few blocks, and turned East on the side street where he lived. He went into the small building and took the self-service elevator to the third floor. As he let himself into his apartment the phone was ringing. He thought that it would stop by the time he reached the living room. But it kept on ringing. He lifted the receiver to his ear, knowing that it was not going to be the one call he wanted, and desperately hoping that it would be. He said, "Hello," and an impatient male voice said, "Is this

Mr. Pierce Kirby?"

"Yes."

"We've been trying to reach you for an hour."

"I go out sometimes," Pierce muttered.

"Lathrop speaking. Homicide Squad."

"Look," said Pierce, "I never liked practical jokes. Say who you are and get it over with."

"This isn't a practical joke, Mr. Kirby." Some of the impatience drained out of the voice. "We wish it was. An old man has been brought in. We found a typed letter in his inner pocket—no envelope— but your return address on the stationery. We want you to come down to identify—"

"Wait a minute," Pierce said. "Wait a minute—"

"Kirby?"

"The man—doesn't he—isn't he able to—"

"He's dead. That letter's the only paper on him. Late sixties—blue eyes …" The voice went on, machine-like, and with an accuracy that left no room for doubt.

CHAPTER THREE

Pierce had gone two blocks when a policeman intercepted him. "What's your hurry?"

"The m-morgue," Pierce stuttered.

"You can't run all the way to the morgue, mister, unless you're planning to increase its population." He sorted out the incoherencies that poured forth. Then he propelled the wild young man with the flapping overcoat to the nearest call box and got in touch with Homicide. He was an alert policeman, and no one was going to put anything over on him. When he was satisfied he shoved Pierce into a cab and gave the driver the address on East Twenty-ninth Street.

Pierce did no conscious thinking in the cab, but he was visited by a memory. He was a small boy again. He could have been no more than three. He had been playing with his toys, and then suddenly he had given way to an irresistible compulsion to bellow, without understanding that he was protesting a universe recently stripped of its warm and comforting bosom. His bosomless aunt had rushed into the room. He was unable to explain his panic, and finally she had slapped him hard, shouting, "There—now you've really got something to cry about."

Later, inside the morgue, with the sheet replaced over Uncle Doc's fragile old bones, he thought, Now I really have something to cry about, and he pressed his fists against his hot dry eyes, and all that he had cried about before was without meaning.

There had been a sequel to that particular memory of childhood. His aunt never meant to be unkind. She was merely harassed and tightly limited. When his hysteria persisted and he refused to eat or sleep she had summoned Dr. Miles. And soon after that the child stopped longing for the mother and father who had left him to go off on an archaeological expedition. Nor did he mourn them three years later when an epidemic swept through their camp in some remote part of the world which meant as little to him as did their deaths.

Uncle Doc had fathered and mothered him. And now it did not matter that the years had brought articulateness, even glibness, with which to express his grief and fear. Once again he wanted to throw back his head and bellow at the top of his lungs. Only this time the bellow would send no one running for advice. There was nowhere to run. Perhaps it was this realization that helped him to contain himself, forced him a step toward latent, fully realized maturity.

The morgue attendant stared at Pierce, his eyes dropping to the clenched fists. He said, "It always gets you that way the first time. You better catch some air. When you're not used to this formaldehyde it's liable to—"

"His neck—why is his neck—"

A plainclothesman had been leaning against one of the human filing cabinets. "Broken—from a fall, we think. You're sure about the identification?"

Pierce nodded.

"That helps. I'm to take you to Homicide. You might have some answers that will put us on the right track."

Pierce said, "Must he be left here? He—he liked fresh air. He'd have wanted to be buried in Kincaid—"

"Kincaid? Well—you can make your arrangements at Homicide if you prove authority."

Pierce tore his eyes away from the sheeted body. He followed the plainclothesman out of the morgue. He got into the waiting police car and was driven to West Twentieth Street. The building that housed the Homicide Squad was peopled by a dispirited night shift. The plainclothesman left him in an anteroom and returned presently to usher him into the adjoining office.

At the side of a large littered desk sat a man with a blunt, legible face which at the moment stated only that he was sleepy. He held a pencil poised over a stenographer's notebook. Behind the desk was another sort of man, and he was wide awake. He dawned slowly upon the consciousness of Pierce. At first he was no more than an unexpectedly pleasant voice.

"Sit down, Mr. Kirby. My name is Nelson." His head was covered with white wiry curls. He nodded it at the plainclothesman. "Thanks,

Lathrop." He waited until the door had closed, and longer than that, as though it was up to Pierce to speak first. His brown eyes were calm, yet busy while he waited.

Pierce spoke with difficulty. "Are you the head of—of the Homicide Bureau?"

"Yes—acting captain—temporarily. My chief is in Florida."

Pierce found makeshift dumping ground for his piled-up resentment. "They're always in Florida—always taking vacations." His rising voice included every public servant who had ever made the news. "Loafing while a man—while men of ten times their worth are murdered on the streets—"

Nelson said quite gently, "Furniss, my chief, never took a vacation in his life. He's away now to recover from an injury received in the line of duty." There was nothing prosaic in the way he delivered the worn phrase. "I've worked closely with him for years. I'll do whatever can be done." He paused. "I understand how you must feel, Mr. Kirby."

Pierce stared at the pointed olive-skinned face, young beneath its astonishing thatch of white hair, and almost believed that the man did understand. He muttered something apologetic for the outburst. But it had served him well, had cleared the area around his constricted chest. He breathed more normally.

"You're next of kin?"

"Yes." Then, confused, he said, "Well—no—not legally. He hasn't any living relatives. He—he practically raised me."

"Lathrop said that you mentioned a place called Kincaid."

"In Ohio. My father was born there and I lived there with my aunt. Uncle Doc—he—he was a general practitioner—the only doctor in town. He—" Pierce shrugged helplessly. Words were a surging mob upon his tongue. He could not bring them to order.

Nelson said, "What was his full name?"

"Dr. Chadwick Miles."

"Dr. Chadwick Miles," Nelson repeated, "Kincaid, Ohio." He glanced at the stenographer. "How long had he been in New York?"

"Since this morning—I mean yesterday morning."

"Did the trip concern his profession?"

"No. He came to see me."

"He was staying with you?"

"He wouldn't. He'd always stayed at the Manhattan. I met the train and took him there in a cab." Pierce moved restlessly on the hard straight chair.

As though reading his thoughts, Nelson said, "This isn't a waste of time, Mr. Kirby. I want you to tell me just what you and Dr. Miles did from the moment you accompanied him to the hotel until you saw him last."

"We had lunch," Pierce said. "Then I left him because I had to go to my office. We met for dinner, and I took him to the theater. We saw the show. Then Uncle Doc wanted to go backstage—so we went. We—he waited while I talked to someone—and I guess he must have been tired. When I went to look for him he was gone—"

Nelson had let him get that far without interruption. Now he interrupted and Pierce was grateful. He had all he could do not to collapse under the guilt that rode him. In fruitless attempt to keep what he had never possessed he had lost the one real friend he had ever known.

Nelson said, "You aren't giving me facts. I want the name of the show—"

"*Sea Change*," Pierce said, "at the Corridor. I don't see—"

"And your connection with it? I assume you are connected with it since you seem at home backstage."

"*Sea Change* is one of my accounts. I'm a press agent."

"In that case you don't exactly deal with facts." For only a moment his eyes were less grave. "Are you in business for yourself?"

"I have an associate. I do most of the outside work."

"Was Dr. Miles familiar with the cast of *Sea Change?*"

"Familiar? How could he be? I told you he hasn't been in New York for years."

"No—you didn't tell me that, but it's the sort of thing I want to know. Very well—you went backstage—"

"I introduced him to a few people—that's about all. He looked at a piece of scenery. Then he wanted to meet the star, so we went to her dressing room."

"Ginette Arthur?"

"Yes." The name, impersonally uttered, was any name.

"Go on."

"He—they talked for a few minutes. Then he wandered out into the passage and—he didn't wait for me."

"How long did your own conversation with Miss Arthur last?"

Pierce said tonelessly, "I don't know."

"Ten minutes—fifteen—a half-hour?"

"I don't know—I didn't time it—under a half-hour, I guess."

"Were there many people in the theater when you left?"

"No. It seemed empty. Even the doorman was gone."

"That's unusual, isn't it?"

"I suppose so, but he might have quit his post for a— Wait—it was about twelve—time for his relief—although I didn't see the other man either. There are three of them. They work in shifts—8 A.M. to four—four to twelve—and twelve to eight—"

"I see." Nelson pressed a buzzer on his desk. Absurdly the notion crossed Pierce's mind that the acting captain of Homicide, merely on the basis of seemingly irrelevant questions, had unearthed the murderer of Uncle Doc and was now about to give orders for his arrest. But to the policeman who answered the summons Nelson said, "It's chilly in here. Could you manage to get us some hot coffee?"

"Sure—right away."

"Thanks." To Pierce he said, "Aren't there some questions you want to ask?"

Pierce said dully, "I know enough."

"You do seem to know that it was murder and not death by accident. Did Lathrop tell you that?"

"No—I—"

"Then he must have told you where the body was found."

Pierce shook his head. He said, "What difference does it make? I suppose Uncle—Dr. Miles decided to walk back to the Manhattan." His wide mouth went crooked. "He trusted everybody. In Kincaid he was accustomed to being out at all hours of the night. He wouldn't have stopped to figure that New York was different. He'd have gone down a dark street without giving it a thought. That's how it happened, I guess. Somebody held him up. He'd have tried to resist— to reason—but his sort of language wouldn't make a dent. So he was killed." He quivered, thinking of that wryly bent head, so upright in life.

Nelson said, "It would seem that way—except for several factors. The ordinary hoodlum robs his victim and if he offers resistance attacks with fists or a knife or a gun or a garrote or whatever happens to be his choice of weapon—but the ordinary hoodlum doesn't stick around for long enough to strip a man of all identification. Dr. Miles's wallet was gone—and that fits. But the labels were torn off his clothes. And if the murderer hadn't missed that letter of yours folded up in an inside pocket, the chances against identification for at least some time were small." He opened a manila folder and took out the one sheet of paper it contained. "This was written six months ago. It must have held special significance for your uncle because he kept it. Luckily it was the one where you told him of your change of address."

Pierce winced. He remembered that letter, full of cheerful nonsense intended for Uncle Doc alone. He had boasted of his rising fortunes, of the new apartment … He said lamely, "I was going to have breakfast with him at the hotel this morning. If he hadn't been there I'd have known something was wrong. I'd have reported it to the police—I—" With every word the loss came home to him. "It doesn't make sense —it doesn't—"

"Did you have any reason to expect something wrong? I mean you spoke of going to the police in that event. Most people don't—not right away."

"Of course I had no reason to expect anything. Why should I?"

The policeman returned with three cartons of coffee. Nelson doled them out. The stenographer looked alert for the first time. Nelson sipped and grinned. "My chief wouldn't approve—he's an epicure. But at least it's hot. Drink it, Mr. Kirby."

Obediently Pierce drank the cardboard-flavored liquid.

Nelson went on conversationally, "Was Dr. Miles carrying a large sum of money?"

"I don't know. I didn't ask him." Every time Uncle Doc had taken out his wallet Pierce had made him pocket it again, insisting that the visit was to be his treat. His treat! He set the container of coffee down carefully.

"I won't keep you much longer," Nelson said. "You're right about it not making sense. Yet someone went to a great deal of trouble, convinced that it would. Do you live in a hotel?"

"An apartment house. Why?"

"A foolish question. Mine, I mean. Your letter mentioned the apartment. Does the building have a central switchboard?"

"No—it's a small house—self-service elevator—"

"Anybody to take phone messages when you're out?" He answered it himself. "No—Lathrop was trying to get you for an hour before you arrived home. We'll get back to that later."

"Look Mr.—Captain—"

"Lieutenant's my real title—a recent promotion from detective sergeant." He added, "By your expression you don't think the promotion's merited. What I'm trying to get at is that the murderer might not know your situation. He might have planned to phone and leave a message that he was Dr. Miles and that he had been called back to Kincaid. You'd have accepted that, wouldn't you? And a considerable interlude might have passed before you discovered the truth."

Pierce said, "Maybe. But what I can't accept is your idea that this— this murder was planned. How can I explain about Uncle Doc? Nobody had a thing against him. He—"

"How long since you'd seen him?"

"What difference does that make? Two years. I went home for my aunt's funeral two years ago, but nothing had changed. He was still the most popular—the best-loved man in Kincaid. Another doctor had moved in, but Uncle Doc was everyone's first choice." Because the attentive pointed face seemed to be expecting something further, Pierce went on, "You'll be getting it into your head next that the new doctor followed him to New York and killed him to do away with the competition."

Nelson said mildly, "It never hurts to consider even the most remote possibility."

"Well—you can throw that one out. Uncle Doc was delighted with his colleague—and vice versa."

Nelson seemed willing to throw it out. He said, "So you've had two major bereavements in two years."

"My aunt's death didn't hit me very hard." Pierce managed to keep his voice steady. "How do I get him out of the morgue?"

"Do you plan to accompany the body back to Kincaid?"

"Yes—yes, of course."

"The arrangements for release will be made as soon as possible." Nelson stood up. He did a funny little jig step to flex his legs. He was a slim, triangular figure just under six feet. He took a coat from the rack and slung it about his wide shoulders. He said to the stenographer, "All right, Sugs. You needn't type that now." His eyes hoisted Pierce out of the hard chair. "I'll drive you home, Mr. Kirby. We're almost neighbors. I live on Lexington. You don't have a car, do you?"

"No. Aren't you going to do anything?"

"There isn't much I can do at this hour. I'll send a man to the theater to look around. And the doorman will be questioned—the one on the eight-to-twelve shift. What's his name?"

"Steve Gillian—but that won't help—"

"Do you know his address?"

"I have it written down somewhere." Pierce searched his pockets. He littered the desk with memoranda and finally tossed a slip of paper at the stenographer. "There. But Steve won't be able to tell you anything. I've told you what happened. Uncle Doc—"

"Barring possible witnesses, only the murderer can give an exact accounting of what happened. It's just possible that the doorman might have seen or overheard something that will provide a clue. Come along."

On the dark street a wet snow fell. The clock on the dashboard of Nelson's car said "Two-thirty." Pierce stared at it blindly as the car slid forward. To the man at his side he said, "If it isn't the way I thought—if you intend to start investigating at the theater—why send a man? Why not go yourself? Or doesn't it seem important enough?"

"It was important enough to get me out of bed. But with the chief away I'm more or less chained to the office." A note of regret had entered Nelson's voice. As though he were analyzing it, he added, "I preferred my old job. I'm not a desk man at heart. But don't worry. All of the men on the Homicide Squad know their business. You'll get your taxes' worth."

Pierce did not answer. His words had been prompted by the confidence the acting captain had somehow managed to instill him. To explain this would have sounded fatuous. A short while later he broke the silence. "You've driven past my street."

"I know."

"Where—" He tried to peer out of the streaked window. "It looks like Fifty-ninth—the entrance to Central Park."

"You recognize it?"

"Why wouldn't I?" He turned from the window to stare at the impassive face beside him. A thought knocked at his brain for entry. He sent it away. The man's credentials were authentic beyond doubt. But if he had not seen him behind his desk at Homicide …

The car stopped. Nelson got out. He beckoned Pierce. It was no idle gesture. It was a command. Pierce obeyed it. His arm was clasped in strong fingers. He was led to the side of the road. The wet snow fell on his hatless head. He watched Nelson take out a flashlight and aim it downward. Behind a row of bushes the crusty winter earth showed signs of disturbance. And one of the bushes was out of alignment.

"Those footprints—if you can call them prints—were made when the body was moved," Nelson said. "There were none when it was discovered."

Pierce found his voice. "But the Manhattan Hotel is on Thirty-sixth Street. What would Uncle Doc have been doing up this far?"

"He didn't come of his own accord—nor under his own power. He was brought here in a car and tossed into the bushes, his body crushing that one as it landed. A patrolman making his rounds noticed a gray car stopping. He thought it might have stalled and ran to see if he could be of help—but by the time he got here it was gone. That broken bush drew his attention to the body." Nelson raised the flashlight suddenly and shone it full on Pierce's face. Pierce blinked but made no further protest. Nelson went on, "He didn't get the license number nor the make of car, and so many vehicles pass along this road that it's impossible to distinguish one tire print from another."

Pierce said, "Why didn't you tell me this before?"

"I thought it would be more graphic if you were on the actual scene."

Pierce said without resentment, "That's not the answer." He was glad that Nelson had suspected him. Let him suspect everybody until he touched goal. "Did he suffer?" He gritted his teeth. "I mean had he been beaten? I didn't see any bruises —but his neck—"

"The medical examiner believes his death was caused by a fall—not from the car—wrong angle. The autopsy hasn't been performed yet—but—here." He took a package of cigarettes from his pocket and thrust it at Pierce. He lit a match, shielding it deftly from the falling wet.

Pierce inhaled. "Must there be an autopsy?"

"It's the usual procedure in a murder case."

Pierce started walking back to the car. He said over his shoulder, "Next time you'll have real cause to suspect me—because if I find the bastard I'll kill him."

"I don't think you will, Kirby. My instinct didn't suspect you this time—but a policeman mustn't let his instinct rule." He did not say that logic had backed instinct; that a man with something to hide, a man as tightly strung as this one, did not empty his pockets willynilly on a policeman's desk. "I'm sorry I had to bring you here—or I will be sorry if events prove my instinct."

This time he drove Pierce to his door, and Pierce surprised himself by saying, "If you'd like a drink—" But it was not really so surprising. Nelson, within the past hour, had become the only link with Uncle Doc. Pierce felt reluctant to part with him.

Nelson seemed to find nothing complicated or unusual behind the invitation. He accepted it. The two men went up in the self-service elevator. While Pierce was fishing for his key Nelson swooped to remove a card that had been placed beneath the door. "Notice of a telegram," he said.

Pierce took the card and pocketed it absently. He unlocked the door and switched on the foyer light. He led Nelson to the living room. It was well furnished with functional chairs and lamps and tables, but plainly no one lived there. Pierce eyed it with distaste and wondered drearily if anyone ever would. He was glad he had company.

Nelson lowered himself to a chair that cared for everything but his legs. He watched Pierce busy himself at a portable bar. "Before we drink, hadn't you better call Western Union? It might be important."

The skinny taut young man recognized the importance of only one matter. This was implicit in his grunt. But he went to the telephone, consulted the card, and dialed. He gave his name and address and chewed on a pencil while he waited. Then he tore the pencil from his mouth and said, "Repeat that.... Yes.... Yes, I've got it.... Yes—I want you to send it over. What's the time on it?" He nodded, as though he were face to face with the operator. He put the receiver back in its cradle. He turned to Nelson, his expression a compound of bewilderment and respect. "The telegram was signed Chadwick Miles. It said he had been called back to Kincaid. It was sent out an hour and a half ago."

"And when we check we'll discover that it had been printed on a grubby piece of untraceable paper and brought in by an anonymous character who was stopped in the street by another anonymous character and paid to do the errand." Nelson left the chair and was across the wide room in three strides. He seized the telephone and spoke into it for about five minutes. He hung up and said, "Well, we're checking, anyway."

Pierce said, "I still don't see how the telegram would accomplish anything. You try to identify people brought into the morgue, don't you? A story in the newspapers—a description—"

"Yes, we try all the usual channels. There'd be a story—a brief one tucked away on the third or fourth page—and even if you happened on it, the chances are you'd make no connection. And even if you or anyone else came forward, enough hours would have passed to wash away the trail. Perhaps a small delay is all the murderer needs to suit his book." He noted that his young host looked old, that he was shaking his head like a very old man who had seen too much and yet despaired of living long enough to accept or evaluate the sum total. "I'll have that drink now," Nelson said.

He seemed in no hurry to leave. He sat opposite Pierce, glass in hand. And presently Pierce talked. He unloaded sentence after sentence and fitted them together to make a series of pictures. In every one Uncle Doc was the central figure, a man carrying a full program who had yet found time to devote to a lonely child. It was he who had presented Pierce with his first books, his voice that had translated their heroic content. It was he who had bought Pierce the first fishing tackle and been the best of companions while it was put to thrilling test. And Pierce had him to thank for the first fountain pen, the first watch, for everything an unimaginative aunt did not think to supply, and for intangibles beyond her power to supply. Encouragement. Balm for failures, for wounds garnered in first physical encounters when youthful dignity had been upheld with fists. Suitable gravity to speed him on his first important date. Guidance ...

"I've got to know why he was killed," Pierce said. "In a way it's my fault." Then, quite naturally, he went on to talk of his quarrel with Ginette. He did not give the cause of the quarrel or its climax. He simply said that it had taken place and that Uncle Doc had obviously not wished to remain as a third wheel. "So you see," he ended, "he came to New York to visit me—and I was so busy with my own affairs that I let him down. If—"

Nelson had been no more than an eminently satisfactory listener for a good half-hour. Now he shook his head. "No, I wouldn't dwell on that if I were you. It's exceeding the bounds of normal egotism to blame yourself for something you couldn't possibly have foreseen." He arose. "Is there anyone in the theater who doesn't like you—who might want to hurt you?"

"I don't think so. I don't think I'm taken that seriously."

"Well—I'll keep in touch with you. Get some sleep." He did not state his own plan to go to the theater at once and see what might be seen. "By the way—who in *Sea Change* uses brown grease paint?"

Pierce considered the question. "Everybody. Yes, men and women alike—in the Tropical Tease number—except Miss Arthur. She's supposed to have been a prisoner and she's pale in contrast to the others."

"Then your uncle couldn't have picked up grease paint in her dressing room?"

"Picked it up? No—"

"When you were walking about the stage did he brush against anything? There was a smear of it on his jacket."

"On his jacket? But he had his overcoat on. Oh no—I can't believe it—that he was killed in the theater—that someone there—"

After he had gone Pierce could not bring himself to take the preparatory steps toward bed. He sat on in the living room, his mind taking stab after ineffectual stab at the puzzle, growing blunter and blunter, until at last sleep came to his chair to call a temporary truce.

CHAPTER FOUR

Pierce brought the body of Uncle Doc to Kincaid. In the bereaved town he was met with sorrow, reproach, and even open hostility. The sheriff said he guessed the New York police force was not all it was cracked up to be, not by a damn sight, and he had a good mind to take a hand himself, except that he believed folks should stay where they belonged and look what happened when they plunged into unfamiliar waters. Not that Chad Miles had plunged without invitation. He eyed Pierce angrily.

At first Pierce, armored by his thoughts, did not feel the harsh consensus that he was at least the indirect cause of the tragedy. Nor was he aware after the funeral and during the reading of the will that there were a few who struck the word "indirect" from the record of their convictions. Uncle Doc had come of wealthy stock. Pierce inherited the bulk of his worldly goods, and men had killed for less than the antiques that furnished the sturdy Miles house, or the bank balance accrued long before the family's last descendant had turned to his unlucrative profession.

When finally the thickening miasma of suspicion did penetrate, making it difficult for Pierce to draw free breath, he wanted, in spite of it, to stay on in Kincaid for a while. He wanted to sit in Uncle Doc's office and imagine the old man there with him. He wanted to revisit the places they had visited together. But he denied himself, partly because scoffing at any manifestation of sentimentality was a habit, and partly because stronger forces urged his return to the scene of the crime that he might find the criminal.

The rumormongers would never have believed that even the

significance of the will had fallen below his level of consciousness. Only hours later for one bitter moment did he catch himself wondering if his new status would have influenced Ginette. In ugly self-disdain he hoped never to know. That episode was finished. He was determined to put it behind him. He would get to the bottom of Uncle Doc's unwarranted death, and then he would come to grips with life. If he remained a press agent he would be the best press agent ever. If he decided upon another field he would top its record too. The material legacy made no difference. It was that other legacy of Uncle Doc's, coupled with his own best effort, that would decide his fate.

He took a plane to New York. En route he read the newspapers. These, along with the few he had managed to pick up in Kincaid, added little to the sum of his knowledge. Since Uncle Doc had been a figure of importance in his own hometown, his death had spread beyond the usual column. No paper had splurged to the extent of sending a reporter to Kincaid, but one sob sister had chalked a long-distance call to her expense sheet and out of it and out of thin air had woven a maudlin story. It was the sort of thing that Pierce himself had often written, tongue in cheek. Sickened, he almost decided then and there to seek another outlet for his talents.

The news released by Homicide was more succinct but just as unenlightening. As soon as the plane landed Pierce called Nelson to ask if any facts had been withheld.

But Nelson offered nothing. "Sorry—we're working every angle. We haven't closed the case by any means."

Pierce hung up. There's only one way this case will be closed, he vowed. It was understandable that he felt disheartened. Not quite so understandable was his disappointment in issues other than the central one. During his ordeal in Kincaid he had thought frequently of the white-haired detective. The pointed olive-skinned face had become a symbol for him, an assurance that justice would be done. Contemptuously now he blamed himself for his excessive faith, incepted within the space of one hour when a stranger had taken on the seeming of a friend. Will I ever, he thought, learn not to go overboard backward or forward for everyone who crosses my path? And immediately his mind did a backward flip, dismissing Nelson and the entire force behind him. So much for that. I'll get there alone, someway, somehow.

He went up to his apartment to deposit his suitcase. The mailbox was stuffed with an accumulation of five days. In the living room he opened and scanned the letters without interest. Then he came to the one from Ginette. He had a fine dramatic impulse to tear it to shreds but found himself incapable of the gesture. He did manage to invoke enough discipline to wait until his betraying pulse had subsided before he slit the envelope.

DEAR PIERCE
I was sorry to hear about your uncle. The few things you said from time to time made me realize how much he meant to you. I told the Homicide man all that I could, but of course it did not help. If you want to call me, please do.

                                                             GINETTE

He stared down at the dark unwavering script. He told himself that it was not the fact that she had troubled to write that was important. At the news of a death the most unlikely people tendered condolence almost by reflex. To prove it there was a note signed by the entire company of *Sea Change*, prompted, he supposed, by the sob sister's account of a grief-stricken young Broadway press agent who had taken time out from his hectic activities to give an old friend safe conduct to his final resting place. No, it did not matter that Ginette had written, nor would he take advantage of the slight opening she had provided. What mattered was the proof that Nelson and his squad had not been soldiering. If they had questioned Ginette, then it followed that they had talked with other members of the cast in an effort to discover the wherefore of Uncle Doc's death. Pierce was both warmed and chilled by this realization. He felt that he had misjudged Nelson. Yet he felt that failure of a whole squad to whom precedence had donated a full bag of tricks held little promise for his own amateur essay.

Pierce sat down. He did not know where to begin, but because Nelson had hit upon *Sea Change* as the starting point he decided to follow in his footsteps. There had been so much red tape to unwind before Uncle Doc's body was given up by the morgue, and so many arrangements to be made before the train trip could be undertaken, that it had been impossible to go to the theater. He looked at his watch. It was a quarter to three. Steve did not come on until four. Steve was a forlorn hope, but he was a hope. He must surely have been there when Uncle Doc left. Perhaps Uncle Doc had said something to him on the way out, something that he had not thought worthwhile to repeat to the police. No. He was floundering right at the start. According to Nelson's theory, Uncle Doc had picked up a smear of grease paint on his jacket. That meant his clothes had been removed before he left the theater, or at least that his overcoat had been removed. Yet he had shown no sign of being uncomfortably warm. The coat had been buttoned even during his conversation with Ginette. So—

Pierce tried to visualize each separate member of the cast: the leading man who was a foil for Ginette, the sparkling ingenue, her partner, the dancer who performed two show-stopping solos, the colored vocalist, the members of the chorus. Quite successfully, using the ever-silent gramophone as a focal point, he conjured up face after face. But he could not succeed in vesting any one of them with evil. He tugged at his hair. He rubbed the dark stubble on his cheeks and, unaware of motivating suggestion, walked like an automaton to the bathroom and shaved and showered. The grooming did not erase the shadows under his eyes or improve his color, but it improved his spirits. When he had dressed again and called his office it was time to go to the theater.

Steve was at his post, reading a torn copy of *Variety*, feet propped against the wall, chair balanced on its hind legs. When Pierce said his name the chair came down on all fours. "Hey—you scared me. Oh, it's you, Mr. Kirby." He blinked. "Say, you'd scare anybody— regular dress circles under your eyes." Then he composed his simian features. "Excuse it. I know how you didn't get them. Tough about your old uncle. Seemed like a nice fellow."

"Steve, you were here when they—when he left—"

"Funny thing about that." Steve dropped the copy of *Variety*. "Got a cigarette?"

"Here."

"Thanks." He lit the cigarette. Piano chords heavily struck swelled out to the stage door. "Listen to that," Steve said. "Those poor kids have—"

Impatiently Pierce dismissed the music. "Well—were you or weren't you here?"

"That's what's funny. You know I'm not a guy to imagine things, but after you and he went in I was sitting here—and I was damn glad I didn't have much longer to go because I'd had some extra beers with my supper and I felt dopey. Not drunk, you understand, just dopey. So after a little while—me fighting to keep the lids up—I heard someone calling me. Sounded like it came from outside. I thought it kind of screwy because practically everybody had checked out, and anybody who had sense enough to use the stage door would have savvy enough to pick a better visiting hour. Anyway, I waited a minute or two to see if it would come again—and sure enough, it did—plain as day. So I stepped outside, but no one was there. I went almost to the end of the alley, and still no one. And when I tried to get in again the damn door had snapped shut—a spring lock—they'll do it every time in a wind—only how the latch got on I'll never know—it was off all evening—and me with my keys hanging on the hook inside. There was nothing I could do but climb the fire escape on the side where I'd left windows open for ventilation. After I made it—being as how I was up there anyway, I did my rounds so's I could tell the relief man everything was under control. It was five to by my watch—about the time I take my last look-see. Come to think of it, you and Miss Arthur must have checked out while I was upstairs too—because there were no signs of life when I came down and passed her dressing room. Couldn't blame me for guessing your uncle had been with you—"

"Did you recognize the voice that called you?"

"Nah. The police asked me that."

"They did?" Pierce was deflated.

"Sure. Maybe ten-twelve repeats on it, like they didn't believe me the first time."

"Was it a man's voice or—"

"A man," Steve said without hesitation.

"Did it sound as though he might be calling for help?"

"I don't think it was like that. Anyway, I'm telling you there was no one there. If someone had conked your uncle in the alley he sure was whisked away on the double—but he couldn't have been in the alley in the first place or I would have seen him pass."

Pierce said, "You're sure you really heard a voice—and that it came from the alley?"

"I heard it twice, so it must have been the McCoy. All I'd taken was beer. I could use some now. Between you and the police I can't even work up a good spit. Not that I don't want to help, Mr. Kirby." He thought a moment. "That voice either came from the alley or some comic stuck his head out of an upstairs window and yelled for the hell of it. Jokes yet."

"But you said there was no one upstairs."

"Yeah—that's right."

Pierce stood there frowning, struggling with his thoughts. Someone had leaned out of a window and shouted Steve's name, someone who knew that the key ring hung on its hook and who counted upon Steve's doing exactly what he had done. Then perhaps that someone, not leaving it to the wind, had rushed down the stairs, fixed the latch, slammed the door, and rushed back to get his victim. He had carried the fragile old body out before Steve could return to his post. Had Uncle Doc been dead then or only unconscious? Had death come later?

"You don't look like yourself, Mr. Kirby. You don't want to let a thing like this get you down. We all got to go sometime—"

Pierce nodded like a deaf man who pretends to hear. He wondered if Nelson had come to the same conclusion. Not that it led anywhere. All it did was strengthen the theory that Uncle Doc had met his death in the theater. He shook his head. He did not find it difficult to believe that in the end he would find the criminal. But he did find it difficult to believe that anyone in the cast was responsible for the crime. There had to be a motive for taking a life, or there had to be some form of insanity that would create a motive. Nobody had a motive for killing Uncle Doc. And nobody could weather the arduous demands of show business and be that kind of insane.

"Like I was saying—there's no use knocking yourself out. Leave it to the police. The way they've been going at it, your uncle might have been Rita Hayworth."

Pierce said, "Were there any special visitors that night—anybody who stood out?"

"Nah. Regulars, most of them—the mama who always comes to call for that chick with the walk-on—and Audrey's husband, the one with the two heads—and about seven or eight fellows, property of the other kids in the chorus—and Mr. Drake. That's the lot."

"Mr. Drake came backstage that night?"

"Right. Wouldn't make me mad if he came every night. A real gent. He tipped me a wink and a fin."

"What time did he come?"

"Just before last curtain. He don't waste a minute when he's going someplace."

"Who— Did he ask for anyone?"

"Nah. He ain't all that particular—and I didn't ask him, on account of there's no tomato living would get sore if he busted in. I been doorman long enough to figure who has to be announced and who don't."

Pierce held his breath. Then he said carefully, "Of course you saw him leave."

"Natch. Came out with a crowd before you and your uncle went in—had a load of curves on each arm, and more tagging behind. He must've took a notion to give one of his parties."

Pierce said flatly, "You're sure?" The eyes he turned on Steve were skeptical. Drake was engaged to Ginette. Then why should he come backstage without visiting her, and why should he give a party to which she was not invited, unless—unless they were both going on as before at her insistence, until such time as she saw fit to publicize the engagement?

"What gives?" Steve looked injured. "Maybe I hear voices, but I don't see things yet. When Mr. Drake came out was when he tipped me the fin."

"And he couldn't have come back—forgotten something—or wanted to see—to see someone else?" Pierce had allowed his mind to slip its track for a moment. Surely Drake must have taken time for a visit with Ginette that night to get her answer, because on the night before she had not mentioned the engagement.

Steve said defensively, "I guess he could've. I got to leave my post once in a while. My kidneys ain't—" He squinted up at Pierce. "Say, you wouldn't be trying to pin this on a gent like Mr. Drake?" He laughed. "Honest—for a minute you had me worried. Mr. Drake's one of the sweetest little guys in this burg—not to mention him being rich from money. No disrespect intended, but your uncle wouldn't have been carrying enough in his wallet to buy the mayonnaise at a Drake shindig."

"The police don't think my uncle was killed because someone wanted his wallet," Pierce said unwillingly.

"Why don't they? He was rolled, wasn't he?" Steve looked disgusted. "Can you beat those cops? Always trying to make themselves seem smart by dragging in complications."

Pierce turned away. "Well—thanks, Steve. Have a couple on me." Instead of making for the door, he walked toward the inner passage.

Steve's hand closed over the bill. "*Thank* you. Hey—going to sit in on that hassle of your own free will?"

For the first time the background music to their talk registered. "Hassle? What goes on? This isn't matinee day."

"Course it isn't. Last night Sarkoff caught the show and blew his top because he said the chorus was taking indecent liberties with his routines. So he called for a rehearsal. He's been at it since eleven this morning. The company manager came up a while ago and told me about it. He says his desk in the basement is vibrating so much he can't work—and he wants to know why did they have to pick the day he goes over the books. The kids'll be dead on their feet for tonight's show."

Pierce was out of earshot. He had intended to go to Ginette's dressing room. It would be locked, but if he stood outside as Uncle Doc had done, he had some vague notion that he might be able to reconstruct the events that had led to the crime. He had counted upon the theater's being empty. Now, of course, it would be impossible to cross the stage without making himself conspicuous, and that he wanted to avoid. He shrugged. It had been a silly idea, anyway. If the police, going over the ground while it was fresh, had found no clues, what could he expect to find? A far better idea would be to observe the individual members of the cast, see if he could detect any changes that might be expressions of guilt. And the chorus was a good starting place.

On the way to the stage he sketched a mental timetable. The final curtain of *Sea Change* was at ten fifty-five. Say it took five minutes to get out of the theater. That made it eleven. And another five minutes of standing on the pavement until Uncle Doc asked to go backstage. Pierce groaned. If only he had denied the request. No, that line of thought was unproductive. All right. They had gone backstage at eleven-five and looked around for about fifteen minutes, outside estimate. That meant it was eleven-twenty when they entered Ginette's dressing room. Uncle Doc had spent no more than five minutes there. Then, thought Pierce grimly, the fun had begun. Uncle Doc had tactfully retreated, and twenty minutes later, according to Steve, he had made his last exit. What had happened in those twenty minutes? He knew the old man better than to suppose he had stood outside listening to the quarrel. More likely he had walked a good safe distance away. Safe!

Pierce halted. He stepped back a little so that he could see without being seen.

Sarkoff, the show's choreographer, was in the pit trying to communicate with the pianist, who idly beat his instrument. Sarkoff's muscles, the set muscles of a retired dancer, jumped dangerously beneath his leotard. The floor of the stage looked like a battlefield. It was strewn with recumbent bodies.

Sarkoff shouted, "All right—so we take it once again," and the bodies, clothed in practice outfits, rose at the signal and took it once again.

Pierce watched, and sighed because he could tell nothing from the fixed theatrical smiles turned toward the imaginary audience. They looked the same to him as they had always looked, and so, for that matter, did the routine. He could not see why it should invoke either Sarkoff's pleasure or displeasure.

Sarkoff, however, was stretching his Tartar lips to full width. "Good," he shouted at intervals. "Good." When the routine was over he jumped up on the stage and beckoned until the dancers were a tight group around him. "So—we have it at last," he said, "and we must not lose it again. Also, it is for you to remember that stale liftings of the body stink as bad as stale fish—and you tell this wicked girl who stays away from Sarkoff's rehearsal that she pays a fine. What's further, she should be careful how she is behaving or Sarkoff can arrange like that"—he snapped his fingers—"not to need her at all."

One of the boys giggled. Sarkoff nodded dismissal. He disappeared into the wings opposite to where Pierce stood.

A buzz of talk zoomed up. "Get a load of him …" "Talk about stale …" "Someone should call Toni.... Maybe she's sick...." "Just let him arrange to do without her. Equity might have something to say...." "My feet …" "Me too … I've worn a hole through these slippers...." "He's the one should be fined...." "Holy smoke—it's half-past five.... Hardly worthwhile going home...."

The sexes separated. The girls rushed for the iron stairs on Pierce's side of the stage. Several of them said hello to him in passing. Most of them seemed too tired to make the effort. One of them halted.

"Why, Mr. Pierce Kirby! When did you get back?"

"Hello, Jill. Today."

"Welcome. Sorry about your—"

"Thanks." He added, "It was nice of the company to send me a note."

The girls jostled her. She stepped out of their way. She stood massaging her legs. "I'm so beat I couldn't hurry to a bargain sale."

"You do look tired."

"Well, so do you—like you been going through a couple of dozen routines yourself. Some life. Toni George doesn't come near to guessing what a good day she picked to stay away."

"You shouldn't be standing here. You'll catch cold. Go up and put some clothes on."

"Now that's an unmanly invitation." She brushed the sweat-darkened yellow hair back from her child's brow. She grinned up at him.

"What's that you said about Toni George?"

"Didn't you hear Sarkoff sounding off? She skipped rehearsal. I'm kind of worried at that. She's always spelled her career with a capital *C*."

"She's marrying a successful lawyer, isn't she? So now maybe she can afford to be less conscientious."

"Yes—I guess that's it. You haven't got a sandwich in your pocket? I need some energy to take these stairs."

She looked rather grubby and pathetic, standing there. Besides, at the mention of food his own stomach felt hollow. He had not had a good meal in days. Getting sick at this point would be a mug's game, he told himself. Also, it was just possible that he might learn something from Jill. He said, "You find the energy to dress and I'll feed you—unless you have a date."

"I have no date." She took the stairs two at a time, calling over her shoulder, "Fifteen minutes. Where'll I meet you?"

"I'll be out back—with Steve."

But he waited in the alley to spare himself any comment that Steve might make at the new coupling. And presently Jill, bearing no resemblance to the tired girl in practice shorts, thrust her arm through his. "Come on—before you have the whole crew on your hands. Is this a steak or cafeteria date?"

"Steak. Wherever you say."

"McClune's. Their windows have been making me drool for weeks. Anyway, none of the kids eat there."

"Are you ashamed to be seen with a lowly press agent?"

"Nuts—I'm afraid the word will get back to Miss Arthur. I need both my eyes."

"Don't worry about that," he said, trying to keep it light. She glanced at him curiously but bit down on anything further she might have wanted to say.

Because it was early the dinner crowd had not begun to line up at McClune's. They chose a table and Pierce ordered. He ate as much as he could and watched Jill eat more than any woman should:

oysters, a man-sized steak, mushrooms, baked potato, and a dessert snowed under by whipped cream. When she had finished she gazed at him anxiously. "I don't usually do this before a show—but everything ought to be under control by curtain time."

"Sure—relax."

"I hope you didn't think I was hinting when I asked if you had a sandwich on you. I hate people to see through me."

In spite of his preoccupation he was able to smile.

"Well—anyway, thanks. Right now I could lick my weight in Sarkoffs."

"Jill—you know Bobby Drake, don't you?"

"Not as well as I'd like to. Why?"

"Does he seem particularly fond of Toni George?"

"What little bird told you that?"

"I've got my sources."

"So you have. I'm not making hay, am I? That yummy food made me forget your trade. How about an exclusive on little Jill—her indomitable courage in the face of adversity—her steady progress toward certain stardom—"

"Later. I'm a one-story-at-a-time man." He was still striving for the light touch. "What about Toni and Drake?"

"Oh, all right. He is giving her a play. Last night it was a corsage pinned with a little diamond heart. But believe it or not, she doesn't want it publicized. That's on the level—though why she clings to that stuffed shirt of a lawyer when she could be the next Mrs. Drake is by me. Say—you're a louse."

"I don't get you." He was frowning. He did not get anything, least of all why Bobby Drake should continue to court Toni when he was engaged to Ginette.

"I think it's a pretty low-down trick."

"What is?"

"Bringing me here to pump me about Toni. What are you—a Turk? First Miss Arthur, and now a girl who's on her last lap to the altar. Let me tell you something, Pierce Kirby. Carrying that torch will only light you as far as the icebox. Toni's the faithful type—misguided, maybe—but—"

"Be quiet. I'm not carrying the torch for anyone."

"Cross your heart?" She beamed angelically. "Then there's a chance for me. I could go for a lean, lonely press agent. No kidding."

"No kidding goes. So quit it."

"Well, I just thought that maybe a couple of orphans from Ohio might—"

"Are you from Ohio?"

"A long way." She dropped the subject. "Will you wait until I call Toni? I want to find out why she didn't show up today."

"I'll wait."

When she returned to the table she said, "Sorry to be so long." She looked worried.

"Is she sick?"

"I don't know. I didn't get her. The girl she shares with says she didn't come home last night."

"Well—"

"Don't say 'Well' like that. Toni's no tramp."

"She doesn't have to be a tramp to spend a night away from home."

"But she has no girlfriends except Stasia and me. And you could even count Stasia out in a pinch."

"If you're really worried why don't you call what's-his-name—Seager?"

"She might not want me to—just in case she—"

"You're a funny kid, Jill."

"I'm a boffola."

"Never mind. She'll probably be at the theater."

"Are you going back there?"

"Not right now." He added belatedly, "I'll take you back though."

"Gracious offer declined. I'm staying out awhile to catch some air. Toni wouldn't be there yet anyway."

"I don't know how you can walk after the strenuous day you've put in."

"That's Jill all over—untapped hidden resources. Good thing, too. I've got to take this meal down a peg."

They parted at the door of the restaurant. On the phone, Marc, his partner, had mentioned a new account. Pierce thought it only fair that he put in some night work on it to make up for his absence.

Marc had left a scribble on his desk telling him to take it easy. He did not take it easy, but he accomplished very little because his mind was elsewhere. The new account was from the producer he had met in the lobby on the night of Uncle Doc's death. All roads seemed to lead back to that night. He glanced through the notes that Marc had taken. A serious play by an up-and-coming young American, scheduled to go into rehearsal in March. The publicity to start at once. Trying to work up an interest, he looked through the names of the tentative cast. His eyes remained fixed on Ginette Arthur's name, which headed the list. So she was leaving *Sea Change*? And not because he had wanted her to, since he no longer counted. And apparently she would not permit marriage to interfere with her career. Well, he hoped that the new play would be worthy of her talent. He shoved the sheaf of papers away. He was not going to do publicity for it. Either they turned down the account or Marc would have to handle it alone. He would give up *Sea Change*, too, as soon as he had accomplished his ends there. His shoulders drooped. He supposed that in the natural course of events Ginette would cross his path again, but to place himself in a position where he must deliberately seek her out was, he felt, asking too much of him.

Discouraged, he quit the office. For he was in that position now and could not help it. He was going back to the Corridor to carry on where he had left off that afternoon, and he would have to see her. Might as well get it over with.

When he entered the stage door Steve was not alone. He was invaded by a one-man army, and his customary aplomb had deserted him. The man was both familiar and unfamiliar. He was LeRoy Seager, completely shorn of the smug, successful air that had characterized him for Pierce.

Steve said, "Sure—maybe I have seen you before—I see a lot of guys. What's that got to do with it? There's still no sense letting you up. Go out front if you don't believe me. Being as how you're so important, they'll give you standing room. The curtain's up—that door's closed, but if you listen good you can hear for yourself. If she was where she should be she'd be onstage right now. But she isn't. I ought to know. Didn't they have to call Sarkoff back again to rearrange the whole damn lineup? See can't you get it into his head, Mr. Kirby."

Seager turned toward Pierce. He did not greet him, but recognition flickered in his eyes. "He won't let me pass. I'm—I'm frantic. I couldn't meet Toni after the show last night, but she had a luncheon engagement with me today and she didn't keep it—and when I called her apartment she hadn't been there—not even to sleep. Now this man insists—"

"Who's insisting?" Steve said belligerently. "I'm telling—that's all—just telling. She doesn't turn up for the rehearsal and she doesn't turn up for the performance—and what's more, she doesn't even telephone."

Seager had removed his hat and was destroying the smooth set of his light brown hair. Pierce said to him, "You've tried every place she might be?"

"Yes—yes. I don't know what to make of it. It isn't like her—"

Pierce said abruptly, "Did you try Bobby Drake?"

Seager's face reddened. After a moment he answered the question in a strained voice. "I could only get his man. He said that Mr. Drake was out."

Plainly Pierce heard another voice, the voice of the white-haired detective. *You spoke of going to the police. Most people don't—not right away.* He said, "Then I think you'd better call the police." He interpreted the queer distortion of Seager's neat features and added, "This isn't the time to think of your conservative law firm, Mr. Seager. When a trouper like Toni George misses a show and doesn't notify the company, there must be something very wrong."

CHAPTER FIVE

But in the end it was Pierce who called the police, because LeRoy Seager, that self-assured Dale Carnegie model of success, seemed unequal to the blow that had so suddenly befallen him. He clung like a frightened maiden to the younger man. "There must be some logical explanation for this. Toni's so sensible—always in full command of a situation—I know she—"

Pierce cut his dithering short. "We'll see. You wait here."

Steve called after him, "Hey—you can use my phone." But he was halfway down the alley, striking out for the nearest drugstore.

He shut himself in a booth, dialed Homicide, and asked for the acting captain. It did not occur to him to speak with anyone but Nelson. He waited, drumming impatiently on the black metal box. But Nelson was not in his office, and whoever took the call did not know or would not say where he could be reached.

Outside the booth, Pierce hunted through a tattered Manhattan directory. There were more than five columns of Nelsons, and he had neither a given name nor an initial to go by. He recalled then that the detective had said something about living on Lexington Avenue. That narrowed it down. He bought some cigarettes, took his change in nickels, and went to work. After seven tries he hit goal. A rich contralto said, "Yes, sir, my Mr. Grid-dely Nelson work for the police." But when he asked to speak with her Mr. Gridley Nelson she said sternly, "He ain't working now. He ain't through his coffee." She stood firm until a quiet voice that Pierce recognized said, "Sammy, I'll take that," and took it.

Pierce identified himself and immediately gave the reason for his call. He made a long story of it, starting at Shane's Bar and Grill on Sixth Avenue. When he had finished he said, "I'm sorry to disturb you—"

Nelson was friendly. "That doesn't matter. Only I'm afraid this isn't my department—at least I hope it isn't. I'll turn it over to Missing Persons for you."

"Oh." Pierce felt like a fool.

"Will you give me the girl's name again—a description—and her home address? I've got it in the files—we interviewed all the chorus girls—but the files aren't handy."

Pierce supplied the name and the description. "I can't remember her exact address. Steve, the doorman, will have it."

"Do you know what she was wearing when last seen?"

"No—but some of the girls will know. The chorus shares a dressing room, and she wouldn't have changed after she left the theater last night because she didn't go home."

"Missing Persons will send someone over to the theater and to her address. I suppose getting a picture of her won't be difficult."

"There are groups in the lobby, but I'll bet Seager has a studio portrait in a silver frame. He's waiting at the stage door for me."

"Keep him there."

"All right." After a pause Pierce said, "There's nothing else about Dr. Miles? You didn't trace that grease paint to any—"

"No—there were smears of it in every dressing room except Miss Arthur's—and unfortunately the whole cast uses the same brand, so we couldn't narrow it down."

"Steve said he told you he heard a man's voice—"

"Yes, we know about that. It seems obvious, doesn't it, that someone wanted him away from the door."

Pierce said irritably, "It seems obvious all right. What doesn't seem obvious is the name of that someone."

Nelson's next words sounded irrelevant at first. "Do you intend to carry on your work as a press agent, Mr. Kirby?"

"Of course—or at least until—" He broke off. "Why do you ask?"

"I just wondered. I understand you've come in for a large inheritance."

In the background Pierce heard the deep rich voice of the maid calling something about cold coffee. Nelson said, "I'll get onto Missing Persons right away and put the wheels in motion."

Pierce hung up. He walked back to the theater. Anger made his face a shade whiter. Inheritance, he thought. That was a crack. The damn fool still suspects me. He's frittering away precious time suspecting me. That's why the murderer's still at large!

He did not want to go where he was going. He wanted to storm Nelson's apartment and beat some sense into him. And for good measure he wanted to take a poke at the contralto voice which had intimated that hot coffee took precedence over bounden duty. At least I'd furnish him with grounds for making an arrest, he thought. At the rate he's going he'll never find better.

He stalked through the stage door. Seager looked at him and around him, as though he expected to see Toni George tagging at his heels.

"I put the call in," Pierce said.

Steve said, "They didn't take it serious, did they?"

"As seriously as they take anything."

"Say—what's going on here, anyway? Do you think the show's jinxed? First your uncle—"

Seager groaned.

Steve said grudgingly, "I'll let you up during the intermission if it will make you feel better."

"No," Seager said. "I didn't mean to doubt your word." He seemed beaten.

Pierce said, "Was Toni with anyone when she left the theater last night?"

Steve shook his head. "She was alone—one of the first to check out."

"Had Drake been here?"

"No. Look—I'd pay a sawbuck if I had it to know why you're so interested in Mr. Drake—"

Seager muttered, "No sense waiting here. I'll—"

"We're to wait until the man from Missing Persons comes," Pierce said.

Unheeding, Seager started for the door.

"You'd better wait," Pierce said dryly. "Orders."

Steve said, "The gentleman needs a drink, Mr. Kirby. You take him out and get him one. I'll hold the fort. With the training I've had lately I can answer questions like a quiz kid."

Seager said, "I don't want a drink—I'm going somewhere." He circled Pierce and stepped out into the alley, closing the door behind him.

Steve shrugged. "He sure is upset—the poor cluck. I would have let him use—"

"I'd better go after him," Pierce said, and went. He caught up with Seager at the mouth of the alley. "It would be more sensible to wait and cooperate with the police," he said, not meaning it.

"I'm going up to Bobby Drake's place. Maybe he was at home when I phoned and didn't want to talk to me. I intend to have it out with him once and for all. I should have done it sooner. He wanted to get Toni away from me. Perhaps he—"

"All right, I'll go with you." Pierce had mixed motives. For one thing, Seager looked as though he needed support. For another, it seemed necessary to reappraise Drake in the light of Ginette's announcement. But even more consciously, he hoped for provocation to use some of the violence inspired by Acting Captain Nelson, and he could have asked for no better outlet than Drake. He thrust his hands into his pockets, ashamed because he had not outgrown the age when fists seemed the only possible means of exorcising a mood.

They reached Sixth Avenue. A woman standing beside them on the curb had just signaled a cab. When it drew up Seager stepped into it. He called to Pierce, "If you're coming, hurry."

Pierce apologized to the angry woman and got in beside him. Seager gave Bobby Drake's address.

Annoyed, Pierce said, "Is that a habit with you—stealing women's cabs?"

"I beg your pardon?"

"You should have begged hers."

Seager's voice was piteous. "Do you think that Toni finally— Drake is a millionaire—I'll never be that wealthy, although I'm far from poor. Naturally I wouldn't have asked her to be my wife if I couldn't give her every comfort—"

"Naturally you're talking rot. Succumbing to Drake wouldn't explain her absence. She could still have notified the theater." Pierce dropped the matter of the pirated cab. Seager was in no state to be called to task for his rudeness. He did not even remember to pay the fare when they arrived at the towering building on Beekman Place. He stormed the aristocratic doors and darted into an elevator. He was shot upward before Pierce, delayed by his transaction with the driver, reached the lobby.

Talk about one-track minds, Pierce thought. He addressed an operator lounging in the doorway of his car. "Mr. Drake's penthouse, please." The penthouse had been widely publicized.

"If you walk over to the desk the clerk will announce you."

"I'm with Mr. Drake's lawyer. He just went up."

The operator nodded. "All right. Sorry, but we have to be careful. So many people just think they've got business with Mr. Drake. You'll have to wait for the other car to come down. Mine doesn't go up to the penthouse."

Pierce waited. He, too, just thought he had business with Mr. Drake. Yet it was a thought that persisted although there was very little to back it.

He made the swift, well-oiled ascent, climbed the few remaining steps to the penthouse, and clattered the knocker on a portal that would have done credit to an English manor. Ordinarily, so would the man who answered his summons. He was correct in every detail, except for the expression of bafflement on his close-shaven face.

"Sir?"

"Mr. Drake, please."

"Mr. Drake is not at home."

"But Mr. Seager is here, isn't he?"

"Yes, sir. He's here." The baffled expression deepened. He studied Pierce for a moment and, seeming somewhat comforted by what he saw, stepped aside to let him pass.

Pierce walked through an opulence of rich tapestry and mellow wood. The grandeur made him wince. He tried to see it through a woman's eyes, a specific woman. From the material standpoint he had no blame for her. He entered a square, softly lighted room that had everything but a tenant. He turned inquiringly to the correct English servant who had dogged his steps.

"I thought Mr. Seager was in here, sir. But he seemed to doubt my word when I told him that Mr. Drake was out—so perhaps he's—"

Seager came into the room. He took up a stance near the Adam mantel. "Well," he said, "he's not here." He had obviously been on a tour to prove the statement. He had not flushed out Bobby Drake, but to some extent he had collected himself.

"We'll go back to the theater," Pierce said.

"Just a moment." He straightened his shoulders, and the manner now assumed was patently the one he used in court. He fixed a steady eye upon the gentleman's gentleman. "When did Mr. Drake go out, Barrows?"

"I don't know, sir. I've been on holiday. I just returned this morning."

Seager said skeptically, "A funny time to take a holiday."

"There were three weeks coming to me, sir, and I'd had a cough, so Mr. Drake kindly suggested it."

"All right—all right. You returned this morning. Do you mean to say that Mr. Drake wasn't here then and that you haven't seen him all day?"

"That's true, sir. He left no instructions for me either. Perhaps he's gone to his place in Chilton."

Seager pounced. "What makes you think that?" It was plain that no witness had a hope of concealing evidence that he, Seager, wanted disclosed.

Barrows's smooth face reddened. Pierce wondered what his boiling point was. It struck him that Seager's nose would do as well as any for a well-aimed punch. He made what allowance he could for emotional stress.

Barrows said stiffly, "It seems logical, sir. A suitcase and some clothes are missing."

"How about the cook and the maid? Weren't they informed of Mr. Drake's plans?"

"They said not, sir. And they wouldn't be in a position to make the inference that he'd left town since they're not concerned with his wardrobe. However, if you wish to question them they have quarters in another part of the building. They always leave after dinner, as soon as they've washed up, unless Mr. Drake requests them to stay. Tonight I gave them permission to leave a bit earlier since there was little for them to do."

Seager's courtroom manner dissolved. "If Drake skipped town without telling me, his lawyer, it's because he didn't dare tell me."

Barrows said, "But, sir, Chilton's no more than fifty miles away. You wouldn't really call that leaving town."

"I wasn't talking to you."

"You're running away with yourself," Pierce said. He meant it in more ways than one. "He wouldn't need to let you know if he only planned to be gone for a day or two—and with one suitcase, that seems a likely bet."

"Not necessarily. He told me once that he keeps a complete wardrobe at the Chilton place."

"Well, if Toni's with him she'd certainly have made some preparation—and the girl she shares her apartment with would have seen the signs and said something when you phoned. Certainly she'd have said something to Jill Batiste when—"

Seager said hopelessly, "I don't know—I don't know—with his money, she could afford to replace everything she owned."

Barrows kept glancing from one to the other, the baffled expression plowed under by very human curiosity. He cleared his throat. "I beg pardon, but if it's a matter of importance why don't you call the Chilton place?"

Seager looked at Pierce. "I can't—I don't want to find out—"

"Of course you want to find out." Pierce was liking Seager less with every passing moment, but he could not help feeling sorry for him. "Anyway, I want to find out—and so do the police now that I've rung them in."

Barrows said, "Shall I get the number for you?" He, too, wanted to find out. At Pierce's nod he hurried across the room, opened a wall cupboard, and extracted a telephone set.

"You—you speak to him," Seager said to Pierce.

"Why me? What shall I say?"

"Anything. Ask him if she's there—that's all."

Pierce shrugged and went to stand at Barrows's side. Barrows had given the number to the operator. He was holding the receiver away from his ear, and Pierce could hear a series of rings. After a few moments Barrows said, "No one seems to be in the house. Shall I try the caretaker's cottage? The caretaker and his wife do for Mr. Drake when he's there without a staff. They'd know."

"Go ahead—try them," Pierce said.

Barrows broke the connection and called the operator again. This time there was a response to the ringing. Barrows said, "Hello—Foster? Barrows at this end.... Yes, very much indeed.... I returned this morning.... Quite fit, thank you...."

From the other side of the room Seager shouted, "For God's sake, is he or isn't he—"

"Sorry, Foster, I haven't time for a chat. Did Mr. Drake—Oh, he did.... Late last night? ... You haven't? ... I see.... Was he— I see.... Hold on a moment, won't you?" He covered the mouthpiece with his hand. He said, "Mr. Drake got there late last night. He was—er—a young lady was with him."

Seager clapped his hands to his head.

Pierce said, "It doesn't necessarily mean Toni—it could be—" He did not want to imagine further.

Seager strode over to the telephone. "Tell him to put Drake on—I'll talk to him. I'll—" He grabbed the receiver from Barrows. "This is

Mr. Seager. Call your—call Drake. I want to speak to him.... What? ... All right, all right, I hear you.... The young lady—was she— Damn it, do you know anything?" He slammed the receiver back into its cradle.

Barrows's lips were a line of shocked disapproval. Pierce said, "Well?"

Seager glared at him. "He says Drake came after midnight. He didn't speak to him. He heard the car drive up and he saw Drake and—and a tall young lady get out and go into the house. Then he says he telephoned over to see if he could be of service but got no answer. Evidently they did not wish to be disturbed."

"You still don't know it was Toni." Pierce thought with disgust that, even if it had been Toni, no man who professed to be a lover should be so ready to accept defection. He added, "Almost any woman would look tall next to Drake." He did not continue with that line of defense because Seager, although strongly built, was actually just as short as his erratic client. "Where's Drake now? Did the caretaker say?"

Seager's "No" was bitter. "It appears that Chilton was only a stopover in this—this romantic elopement. When the caretaker went to the house this morning there was no sign of either of them. Come on."

Barrows escorted them to the door. Pierce thanked him, and Barrows accepted the thanks with dignity. He carefully avoided looking at Seager. As an afterthought Pierce asked him to telephone the Corridor if he received any word from Drake within the next hour.

When they reached the street Seager said angrily, "I wish you hadn't been in such a hurry to call the police. It's bad enough without my being a laughingstock. I'm not going back to the theater to face—"

"Yes, you are." Pierce tried to look menacing. "I called because you were in too much of a froth to do it yourself. I don't intend to hold the bag for it." He could not help his next statement. "If Toni has gone off with Drake it's my opinion she's well out of it."

Seager made a sound of anguish. "Don't say that. If you could put yourself in my place! I'm sure you meant well and I've no wish to put it all on your shoulders. I'll go back with you and explain that she's been found."

"I must say you're a man of little faith. How can you be so sure she's the girl the caretaker saw? Drake has a million women—" Then he thought of Ginette, who was, after all, only one of those women. He wondered if she had any idea of what her husband-to-be was up to and just how much she was prepared to countenance. And why? Ginette had never given the appearance of being mercenary or grasping. In fact, she always leaned the other way. She gave generously. She kept open purse for anyone who approached her for a loan. She could not resist the appeal of a beggar on the street and was often down to rock bottom before payday came. But lack of money did not seem to worry her. Nor had she ever expressed any fears concerning the insecurity of her profession. The remaining explanation for her engagement to Bobby Drake he could not accept. She did not, could not, love such a man. But that's your ego talking, he told himself. No matter who it was, you'd refuse to believe that she preferred him to you. He stopped trying to look menacing. He looked humble and lost.

They had walked to the corner of First Avenue. Seager came to a halt before the entrance to a hotel bar. "I'm going to have a scotch." He announced it as though he expected to be denied.

"Why not?" Pierce followed him into the bar and was immediately reminded of the last occasion when a drink seemed like a good idea. Then he had been thinking only of Ginette. Now Ginette and Uncle Doc and Toni George became an inextricable tangle in his head. But whatever linked them together was invisible, or at least it eluded the fumbling of his mind.

Seager had collected himself sufficiently to order a special brand of scotch and to ask to see the bottle. He did not attempt to drown his sorrows. He had specified one drink and he meant one drink. After he had drained it he squared his shoulders, counted his change, and looked at the remaining liquor in Pierce's glass. "As soon as you're ready," he said.

Pierce was bored with him. "Don't wait if you're in that much of a hurry. I'll catch up with you."

But he waited, although Pierce took his time, divided between irritation and amusement at the pompous show of impatience. He had reached the point where he was quite ready to believe that Toni was the tall young lady seen with Drake. He did not blame her. He wished her luck.

They took a cab back to the theater. This time Pierce, who was often more than generous, left Seager to pay the fare. He walked around to the alley, entered the little cubicle, and found that Steve had company.

Steve seemed relieved to see him. "I said I'd hold the fort, Mr. Kirby, but I didn't mean until the war was over." He gestured toward the man who came forward.

"Missing Persons," the man said, "name of Tarr." He looked Pierce over. "You're Kirby—the fellow who put in the call?"

"Yes, I called. I guess maybe it was a mistake—"

Tarr put his hands in his pockets. He was a young man. He might have been a put-upon clerk addressing a half-witted customer. "Well, maybe you have too much time on your hands. Where I work we don't. I've been standing here almost an hour waiting for the show to finish so I could question somebody."

Steve said loyally, "It wasn't Mr. Kirby's fault. The way that shyster acted was enough to send anyone hotfooting it to—"

The door opened. Seager entered as though on cue.

Tarr said, "Well, is she found or not?"

Seager opened his mouth. He closed it, took out a handkerchief, and blew his nose loudly. Steve's telephone offered unexpected competition.

Steve said, "Ain't this my busy night." He reached for the receiver. "Corridor Theater.... I don't get you—maybe you want the box office.... Who? ... Why didn't you say so?" He turned to Pierce. "Some fellow with marbles in his mouth asking to speak to you. Here—but don't make a habit of it. I got troubles enough."

Pierce took the phone. He said, "Hello—Kirby speaking." Then he listened. Out of the corner of his eye he saw Steve yawn and look at his watch. Listening, he looked at his own watch and noted that the final curtain would come down in five minutes. Everything seemed perfectly ordinary and normal except the words that came to him from the other end of the wire. When he was able to cut in he said, "Wait a minute, Barrows. Hang on."

Seager, hearing the name, came forward. "What is it? Why has he called? Does he want to speak to me?"

Pierce ignored him. He said to the man from Missing Persons, "I didn't make a mistake after all." His voice was as bleached as his face. "It was Nelson who made the mistake by dumping it in your lap. It's bounced right back. His coffee's going to get a lot colder—"

"Nelson? You mean Grid Nelson? What are you talking about?"

"You've heard of Bobby Drake?"

"Yeah."

Pierce said rapidly, "Well, we paid him a visit while you were waiting here. He wasn't home. I gave his man this number in case he received word from him. We'd tried to reach Drake at his house in Chilton and the caretaker said he wasn't there but he'd arrived late last night with a young lady and left early this morning. Now the caretaker's called Drake's man again. He says he went over to the main house to see if it needed tidying up. He says there's been some kind of a struggle in the living room. He found a woman's shoe under the couch, a heart-shaped diamond pin in the fireplace, and blood— blood all over—"

"Give me that phone."

"Take it," Pierce said. He watched Tarr's large hands close about the instrument. He heard him ask a series of competent questions. He slumped against the wall and clumsily lit a cigarette.

CHAPTER SIX

By the time Tarr had finished questioning Barrows, Steve was working to close his unhinged jaw. But Tarr was not interested in Steve's reaction. He had stepped away from the phone and seemed to be making an unbiased survey of Pierce and Seager. He drawled, "So you had something after all."

Seager's jaw hung too. Pierce would have liked to fix it for him. He no longer sympathized with the man, perhaps because Seager, so ready to expect the worst, had found the worst beyond his small imagining.

"In the first place," Tarr said, "what made you rush over to this fellow Drake's apartment?"

Pierce answered shakily, "That's a long story."

"Condense it. We'll get the trimmings later."

"I think you're out of your depth. You should call Homicide. They'll be out of their depth, too, but—"

"Never mind what you think. What do you know?"

"I only know that Toni George was engaged to him." Pierce jerked his head toward Seager. "But Drake began to send her presents—to make a general nuisance of himself. She was frightened of him. She told me so and I laughed it off." He gave an imitation of that laugh. It sounded like a very bad imitation. He would have liked to go on practicing it, laughing his guts out mirthlessly at the brush he had given Toni George when she appealed to him for help. He controlled himself with everything he had.

"How come she told you?" Tarr said.

"She had no one better to tell, poor girl." Once more his head jerked toward Seager. "That tower of strength professed to be in love with her, but he didn't profess to trust her." It was good to shift some of the blame he had taken to himself. "Besides, Mr. Seager was in a delicate position. Drake is his client—"

Seager said hoarsely, "That's unfair. I wanted him to get another lawyer. Toni wouldn't hear of it. Toni—" He repeated the name incredulously. He closed his eyes.

"Keep going, Kirby," Tarr said.

"I explained it all to the acting captain of Homicide, but I guess he didn't think it worthwhile to brief your department. Toni walked out of the theater after the performance last night, and that was the last any of the company saw of her. A rehearsal was called today and she didn't turn up for it. She had a lunch date with Seager. She didn't turn up for that. He came to the theater to see what it was all about and he discovered that she hadn't turned up for tonight's show either.

He was in a dither, and I thought he had reason to be, so—"

"Where were you last night?"

"Out of town. I got back this morning." Pierce added flatly, "Obviously you haven't heard—but something else happened recently to make me extra cautious. So when this thing about Toni came up I took the liberty of disturbing the police again. After that I felt sorry enough for Seager to want to lend him moral support when he went to Drake's. You know the rest. I suppose Seager's excitement on the phone made the caretaker curious. Anyway, he decided to go over to the main house to see if he could tell whether Drake was coming back, he said, and to tidy up. Well, there was more tidying to do than he'd bargained for. I don't consider myself a pessimist, but as far as I'm concerned that heart-shaped diamond pin in the fireplace clinches it."

Seager had opened his eyes. They glinted strangely. "No, she isn't dead. She can't be. He—if he's hurt her I'll—I'll—" He was a lawyer to the bone. He did not complete the threat.

"Why do you say the heart-shaped pin clinches it?" Tarr asked.

"Because Jill Batiste, a girl in the chorus, told me that Drake had sent Toni a corsage last night fastened with a heart-shaped diamond pin."

"I'll talk to this Jill," Tarr said.

Steve gave tongue. "Holy, holy! It won't get into my noggin. Mr. Bobby Drake never hurt a flea, let alone bumped one. He's the sweetest little—"

Tarr said, "You can testify as a character witness when we catch him."

"You won't catch him this way," Pierce said. His voice was so hot it scorched his throat.

Tarr went to the telephone. He spoke in what sounded like gibberish or code. But the gist of it was plain. He sent out an alarm for Bobby Drake, alone or accompanied by one Toni George, showgirl, thought to be injured.

"Optimism," Pierce muttered.

Tarr hung up and called the Chilton police and went through it again, not once but several times. The recipient on the other end must have been just as unbelieving as Steve, who kept up a running conversation with himself.

The calls completed, Tarr said, "Is the show over?"

"Just," Steve said, "but so help me—"

"Then I'm going up. Want to point out that Jill, Kirby?"

"No—call Homicide."

"Homicide's funny—they don't like to play unless there's a body."

"Didn't Drake's man tell you about the blood!"

"People are apt to exaggerate. So until there's a body or enough evidence to point to one it's a job for Missing Persons."

"How much evidence do you need? Can't you add?"

"You add for me."

"All right, I will. Toni received the pin from Drake. She met him to return it. She got into his car, and he either persuaded or forced her to go for a drive with him. He drove to Chilton. He'd threatened her with violence before, and this time he carried out the threat. Look—if the blood doesn't convince you, there's her shoe. She had no other clothes with her but the clothes she was wearing. A girl doesn't walk out of a house with one shoe on. But she's not in the house—so she was carried out—by Drake."

"We don't know it's her shoe. We don't even know that pin was the one he gave her. We'll check. Our boys will be en route to Chilton right now, and the Chilton police will stand guard to see that nothing's disturbed until they get there."

"I'm sure those things are not Toni's," Seager said loudly. "She would never have gone with him." He seemed intent upon making a complete reversal. "Someone else went with him—not my—"

Pierce said to Tarr, "You don't even have a recognizable description of her."

"I came here with a partner. He got one of the group pictures from the company manager and had her face picked out for him. He took it back to headquarters, where it will be blown up and broadcast from here to hell and gone. But if you're adding right, it's not her picture we want. It's Drake's. And that's not hard to get from what I see in the papers. Coming backstage with me?"

"No." His voice held less hostility. "Anyone can point out Jill Batiste for you. Take the first stairs you come to and climb two flights." He intended to go backstage to talk to Ginette. But he did not want Tarr at his heels when he went.

"Suit yourself." He spoke to Seager. "What about you?"

"I don't know—I don't know what to do."

"What's your address?"

"The Morrow Arms—on East Fifty-seventh Street."

"Right—why not head for it? You don't look as though you'll be of much use right now." Tarr opened the door behind him, stepped through, and closed it firmly before the noise within had time to penetrate the cubicle. Simultaneously Seager took the door to the alley.

"That shyster could have forced himself to say good night," Steve said. "You treated him pretty good for a while—playing nursemaid and all. Some people—honest—" He brightened. "Say, the wife's always grumbling about why don't I tell her something exciting. Wait till she hears—"

A buxom, furred woman and two spruce young men came in from

the alley. One of the men said heartily, "Hello, Pop."

Pierce muttered, "Don't let anyone up until the detective comes down."

Steve nodded. He gave the men an evil stare. He did not like to be called "Pop."

Pierce disappeared through the inner door. He walked slowly. He passed the first iron staircase and crossed the stage. When he came to Ginette's dressing room he turned the knob and entered.

Ginette's maid was hanging costumes in the wardrobe. Ginette sat at the dressing table removing her makeup. He saw her startled expression in the mirror. "You should have knocked," she said. Then she said, "Pierce." Her voice throbbed with it, and his heart echoed the throb.

The maid settled the last costume in its place. She turned and said cordially, "Well, look at the stranger. You been away, Mr. Kirby?"

"Yes, Dora, I've been away." He had the sudden illusion that he had been very far away and that he had just returned to his own country. He found it impossible to take his eyes from Ginette.

She seemed to be working against time with cream and cleansing tissues. The maid went to her and hung a robe about her lovely bare shoulders. "You ain't hardly decent, Miss Arthur."

Ginette struggled into the robe and stood up. She went to Pierce and put her arms around him.

He was not proof against the soft, fragrant contact. He held her close. He kissed her mouth, and for as long as the embrace lasted he was possessed of only the sense of taste and of touch and of smell.

The maid said, "I guess there's nothing else you'll want tonight, Miss Arthur," and Pierce thrust Ginette from him.

Ginette murmured uncertainly, "You got my note?"

"Yes—thank you."

She walked back to the dressing table. The maid put on her hat and coat and left quietly. Ginette, standing with her back to Pierce, said, "Why did you push me away?"

He answered roughly, "I'm protecting Bobby Drake's interests—in his absence."

"Pierce, do you have to be so damn melodramatic?"

"Is that melodramatic? You're going to marry him—aren't you?"

"No, you idiot. Of course not."

"You mean the grapevine works that fast?"

She turned toward him. "Has he been up to something? Pierce, you couldn't have thought I meant it. You made me angry and I said the first name that popped into my head. I said I was engaged to Bobby Drake only because he'd been sitting in the third row that night and I happened to single him out while I was singing the 'Daddy's Little Helper' song. I ought to be insulted because you believed me. I didn't think you were all that gullible."

"Gullible?" Cold air seemed to be creeping down his spine because he could not now be gullible. She was a good actress, perhaps a great actress. She could have made the most trumped-up nonsense sound genuine. And what frightened him was the source of his doubt. He was as bad as Seager, he told himself.

She was coming toward him. "No," he said, and while he said it he took a step to meet her and reined himself back before the distance between them had lessened to danger point. He could not afford to be mindless again.

"Pierce! We quarreled and I'm sorry. I tried to say it in my note. I guess it didn't come through. I'm leaving *Sea Change*. That's part of what you wanted, isn't it? As for the things I said, I wish I could take back most of them—not all—because you were getting awfully possessive, and I hate being possessed"—she smiled—"in that sense, anyway. It seemed to me that if you could be so critical of me, then it should work both ways—and you have no idea how disgruntled you'd been lately about your own work—as though it were beneath your talents. Well, maybe it is—that has to be proved—and only you can prove it. But I just don't want you to develop into a chronic grumbler, and you should be glad I care enough to—to care. The other things— the ones I didn't mean—about you not being a grown man, of having a father fixation on Dr. Miles and bringing him to intercede for you— I know that wasn't true. Oh, Pierce, I wish I hadn't—"

"It doesn't matter. Everybody who can spell psychoanalysis feels free to toss its vocabulary around." He had been listening to her dispassionately. The things they had quarreled about seemed young and trivial to him. He wondered why he had taken them so to heart. This is Ginette being reasonable and tender, he thought. If I didn't know I never would suspect the countless other facets to her personality. How beautiful she is in this role. How gracefully she brushes the soft fair hair back from her forehead. How touching the childlike sincerity of her regard—the way her mouth curves. How soft and vulnerable she seems. He said, "What matters is finding out who killed my uncle—and that's all that matters to me now."

"All?"

"Yes. I'm not an actor. I can't make those swift transitions. That night you gave me one idea, and I've spent the time between getting used to it. I'm used to it now. I can even bear it. Why start the rat race again? About that night—not the quarrel—about Uncle Doc. You remember you left this room first. Then you came back. I wanted to ask you if you saw anyone—"

"If I had I'd have told the police officer who questioned me." Bewilderment caught at her smooth brow. Then her face cleared. "It was a terrible shock for you. You look dreadfully tired. Would you like to come to my house and talk?" Absently she had removed her robe and was putting on a dress. "Would you mind shutting the door? Dora left it open."

His mind not on it, he went to the door and almost closed it in the face of the detective, Tarr.

Tarr did not even have the grace to look embarrassed. "I was just about to knock."

"How long were you just about to knock?" Pierce said. He saw that a frost had settled upon Ginette, covering the soft vulnerability of a few moments back.

She said crisply, "No, don't come in, whoever you are. You'll have to wait outside until I'm dressed."

"Yes, ma'am." Tarr removed his foot from the threshold. "I guess that means you too, Kirby." He drew Pierce out of the room and closed the door. "I see you came backstage anyway. I got a description of what Toni George was wearing, including shoes. She had on open-toed black pumps, medium heel, size seven A."

Pierce said, "Then why are you waiting—"

"I wouldn't call it waiting. Whenever I hear voices I always stop to listen. It's part of my training. You never know—do you?"

Pierce turned and met the deep-set brown eyes of Gridley Nelson. His stomach turned over. If he had held any hope that Toni George was alive, Nelson's appearance robbed him of it. If Nelson was here it was no longer a job for Missing Persons. To hide the sickness in him he said angrily, "I see you finished your coffee in good time to eavesdrop."

Tarr shook his head. "No, he missed the best part of it. He don't know, for instance, that your friend in there was engaged to Drake."

"If you heard that," Pierce said evenly, "you heard her deny it."

"Sure, but I could tell you weren't sold, so why should I be?"

Nelson said, "You'll send out that description of the clothing right away, won't you, Tarr?"

"You bet." Tarr grinned. "It's a beaut, isn't it? That Jill who watched her dress didn't miss a trick from drawers on out. A case like this is a nice change from— Well, I'm on my way." He walked briskly down the corridor.

Nelson said, "Does Miss Arthur know of Toni George's disappearance?"

"I guess so. She must have heard some talk of it when she came in—but she doesn't know that Drake has any connection with it." Pierce spoke with too much vehemence. "Miss Arthur has nothing to do with Drake. She told me she was engaged to him in order to end a quarrel we were having. It's the sort of thing any woman might do."

Nelson said, "Or any man—under sufficient provocation." Then he said, "I'm driving to Chilton. Want to come? You might be useful."

"Some use I've been." It was a cry of frustration.

"Tarr told me that Toni George had appealed to you for help."

"That's what I mean."

"That's what I thought you meant."

"I'll go with you," Pierce said. "I don't see what good it will do, but anything's better than— Look—two fatalities—do you think—is it screwy to think there's a connection?"

Nelson said slowly, "The only link we have is *Sea Change*—and that could be no more than coincidence."

"Big Disclosure Department," Pierce said.

"What sort of girl is Toni?"

"Beautiful—quiet— What makes you speak of her in the present tense? You know she's dead. You wouldn't be here if she wasn't. You managed to make that definite when I telephoned you. Or are you here because Drake figures in an unexpected way? He's news, isn't he—a big name? If he doesn't appear soon with a nicely packaged explanation I guess even the commissioner will leave his coffee to take a hand."

Nelson had a wide, very expressive mouth. Now he seemed to have difficulty controlling it. He said mildly, "Would it surprise you to learn that policemen sometimes have days off? This is mine, and I'm here because I want to be here. And the drive to Chilton has no official significance. If it had I wouldn't take a passenger."

"Especially a suspect passenger," Pierce muttered.

The door of Ginette's dressing room opened. She said, "I'll be out in a minute, Pierce. Is that barger-inner still there?"

"Captain Nelson's here," Pierce said.

Nelson corrected him: "Lieutenant."

Ginette called, "Who?" Then she came out, struggling with her coat.

Automatically Pierce helped her with it. She was looking at Nelson. She said, "Oh—Lieutenant Nelson."

"You've met?" Pierce asked.

"Yes—the lieutenant questioned me about Dr. Miles."

Nelson's lips twitched again. "I'm not always drinking coffee," he said, "and you may not believe it, but it wasn't because Miss Arthur's famous that I decided to go back to leg work."

"I'm groveling," Pierce said.

Ginette glanced from one to the other. "Lieutenant, have you found out anything about Dr. Miles?"

"Not yet, Miss Arthur."

She said regretfully, "I'd so hoped for Pierce's sake that—"

Pierce said abruptly, "I'll have to talk to you another time, Ginette. I'll put you in a cab."

For a few seconds the silence was as thick as a fog. Her voice labored through it. "Very well, Pierce. Just as you like."

Nelson said, "A cab won't be necessary. We'll drive you home—unless you want to come to Chilton with us."

"To Chilton? Is something happening in Chilton?"

"Something did happen," Pierce muttered.

She turned to him. "I'm trying to be awfully patient and understanding, Pierce, but I do hate to be talked at."

Nelson said quickly, "Sorry—we've both been assuming that you knew of Toni George's disappearance."

"Disappearance? I heard when I came in that one of the girls missed the show. I didn't realize it was a matter for the police."

Pierce said, "She was last seen with Bobby Drake at his home in Chilton. Now there's nothing to be seen there but bloodstains and a few other souvenirs."

She seemed shaken. She said blankly, "You're joking, Pierce—"

"No, just repeating someone else's joke."

"Bobby Drake, that harmless little man, gone violent—abducting a chorus girl? I'll never believe it."

"Do you know Bobby Drake well, Miss Arthur?" Nelson asked.

"Not really well. I've met him here and there. He's rather a sweet, defenseless—" She looked at Pierce. She bit her lip.

"That rumor of your engagement to him isn't true, then?"

"Oh lord, Pierce, you didn't—"

"He didn't, Miss Arthur. The detective from Missing Persons overheard your conversation a little while ago and passed it on to me."

"Is that who that man was?" Pierce waited for her anger. It did not come. She shook her head slowly. Her voice was rueful. "I told Pierce I'd give almost anything to unsay the stupid things I said to him that night. Now I'd double the offer. I'm not and never was engaged to Bobby Drake. Does that satisfy you, Lieutenant? It doesn't satisfy Pierce because he can't be objective about it. In fact, I doubt if he'll ever believe another word I say."

A charmer, Pierce thought, fully conscious of her appeal and of its effect on the very male, very distinguished-looking detective. He heard himself saying, "Belief is another of those things that should work both ways." He had to touch her even if it was only to inflict a hurt. "You don't believe me either—about Bobby Drake being responsible for—for God knows what."

"Good night, Pierce." The throb in her voice was a dangerous weapon to all mankind. "I hope you feel better about everything soon. Good night, Lieutenant, and thank you. But I won't go to Chilton. We've made you uncomfortable enough as it is."

Nelson did not urge her. If there had been any purpose behind his invitation he seemed entirely willing to relinquish it.

When they reached the cubicle Steve was checking out a group of performers. The habitual grin was missing from his face, the wisecrack from his tongue. The players also seemed subdued. Speculative glances were flung at Pierce, Ginette, and Nelson, but no one spoke. In response to a gesture from Steve the trio hung back until the cubicle had cleared.

"That detective gave me a note for you, Lieutenant." Steve handed him an envelope. He looked expectant while Nelson slit it and read the contents. But Nelson only said an absent "Thank you" as he put the note in his pocket. The cubicle began to fill up again. Nelson herded Ginette and Pierce before him to the door.

Steve bellowed after them, "Giving me a sealed envelope and warning me not to open it! Some crust—police or no police—using my phone and talking so's I couldn't understand a word. I ain't going to be responsible for all those extra calls when the bill comes in—"

Nelson closed the door behind him. "Sorry to thwart the poor man," he said, "but I didn't see any point in making a general announcement."

In the darkness of the alley Pierce made a small sound of foreboding.

"Yes," Nelson said, "it begins to look very bad. Tarr called the Chilton house again. The shoe conforms to description. And Drake's abandoned car has been found on the outskirts of Chilton. The upholstery's badly stained."

CHAPTER SEVEN

Pierce saw Toni. For one brief moment the dark alley was the booth where she had sat opposite him at table. Her face was classically beautiful. Then the beauty was shattered by her prim flat voice sifting all drama from the words she spoke.

She vanished as Ginette drew gasping breath. He was suddenly and confusedly grateful to have Ginette standing there beside him. He thought he could feel the warmth of her body through his heavy winter coat. Seager came into his mind, a bereft Seager. Why question? Why doubt? He muttered, "It isn't so easy." And as though Ginette knew what he meant, she moved away from him and walked on ahead into the lights of the street.

"My car's around the corner," Nelson said, "but I'm afraid I'll have to rescind that invitation, Kirby."

"They still haven't found a body?"

"No."

"Then, according to Tarr, you're still not on official business. I'm going to Chilton. Alone if not with you."

Ginette made one more attempt to reason with him. "What can you do there? The lieutenant's accustomed to dealing with—"

"I don't know what I can do, but I'm going."

"But it isn't as though you really knew the girl—"

"I did—I knew her."

"Oh?"

"We won't stand here arguing about it," Nelson said. He strode down the street, darting into a drugstore before they caught up with him. They waited on the pavement. Pierce supposed aloud that he was making a telephone call and Ginette agreed with him. Beyond that there was no exchange. He reappeared, flashed them a quizzical look, and led the way to his car. He said, as though resigned, "All right—get in. Miss Arthur?"

"Thank you, but it's no trouble at all for me to take a cab. I'll be hoping it isn't what you think."

They watched her as she turned and walked away, moving, as she always moved, with grace and pride.

Nelson said noncommittally, "I would have been glad to drive her home. It's on our way."

"You know where she lives, then?"

"Yes." He was behind the wheel of the car.

Pierce did not pursue the subject. He climbed in.

They rode for a few miles, each apparently behind his own wall of thought, Nelson seemingly relaxed, driving with no waste motion or effort, Pierce so tense and withdrawn that he jumped at hearing the other's voice.

Nelson said, "I have all their addresses." He sounded amused. "Everyone connected with *Sea Change*, actors, stagehands—the lot. That much is routine." Then he said irrelevantly, "Miss Arthur was right. You shouldn't be here. I don't think you're temperamentally suited to this sort of thing."

"Is there a special temperament needed? You don't look as though you were born chewing a night stick."

Nelson chuckled. "I wasn't." He began to talk about himself, easily, conversationally. He had gone to Princeton. There had been no special hurry for him to choose a career. He had tried all manner of jobs, separated from his fellow workers only by the fact that his mother had left him a small income and that he would continue to eat, whether or not he worked. Among other things, he had been garage mechanic, general factotum in a Little Theater movement, and apprentice in the laboratory of a criminologist. The last had held him longest, but he had an appetite for close contact with people, and after a while work on group theories became tasteless fare. "So I joined the force," he said, "and I was lucky. It was from raw rookie to detective sergeant to ..."

Pierce was interested until he got the idea that this disarming, likable man was treating him as a nurse might treat a fractious, unpredictable child, spinning a yarn to calm him. He stirred restively.

"Some of my cases," Nelson was saying, "yielded extremely valuable by-products. In one of them I acquired a maid—the woman who put your back up. She wouldn't if you'd met her. Sammy's the best cook extant—with an intelligence that frequently puts the trained mind to shame." He swerved without comment to avoid an oncoming car that was in the wrong lane. "And by way of another case I acquired my wife. She's in Europe now and I miss her. That's the only part of marriage I object to—the missing. And yet I'd convinced myself that bachelorhood was the only tenable state before Kyrie—"

Pierce said rudely, "To get back to police work—what else do you do but take people's names and addresses?"

"That depends."

"On what?"

"To quote a recent newspaper article, about eighteen thousand people a year bow out under circumstances that require investigation. We try to give as much attention to each as seems warranted. A proven suicide, of course, is usually clear-cut, but murder—" He cut the sentence short as Pierce yawned. "You didn't ask for a lecture, did you? You want me to be specific. Well, your uncle's death appeared simple enough on the surface. If the murderer who stripped him of identification had taken even more pains, had thought, for example, to dress him in the clothes of a derelict and had been able to get him to drink heavily, the autopsy would have revealed high alcoholic content in the blood and we'd have assumed that it was just another Bowery-style killing for immediate gain. But since your uncle's clothes were good and since the percentage of alcohol indicated no more than one cocktail with his dinner—"

Pierce said weakly, "Stop it," remembering that dinner and Uncle Doc's air of experimentation as he sipped his daiquiri.

"I'm sorry. You give the impression of being such a hardboiled young man that you almost had me fooled."

Almost, Pierce thought. Almost. His voice was something less hard when he spoke again. "I still don't see the point of that name-and-address routine."

"A starting point—from which we backtrack as far as we can into the past."

Pierce said, "You do that all the time—for everyone?"

"It's fairly simple research. In this case it was unrewarding. With one exception, no one even came from your uncle's part of the country."

"Jill Batiste did. Was she your exception?"

"Yes." He added, "She seems to be Toni George's best friend."

Pierce said heavily, "She's a nice kid."

Nelson, offering him a cigarette, said, "Temperament or no, considering that you haven't the facilities of the police department at your command, you've done rather well."

"Oh, sure—walking over ground already covered." He held a match to Nelson's cigarette. "I guess I owe you an apology, Lieutenant."

"Owe it to me, then."

"I'll buy you a drink if you want to take time out."

"At the risk of having you at my throat again, I'll settle for a cup of coffee. Mine *was* cold."

Pierce smiled. "Tell me more about Sammy—and your wife."

Nelson said obligingly, "You'll have to meet Sammy. My wife too— when she comes home." His voice warmed. "She's blonder than Miss Arthur and she doesn't depend upon mood or facial expression. Her beauty's there to start with—" His slight pause seemed to hold embarrassment. "I didn't start out to make comparisons—disparaging or otherwise. Miss Arthur has a rare luminous quality—"

"Let's get back to your wife."

"I wish she'd get back to me. In addition to everything else, her brain's king size." He laughed. "And she'd have her doubts about the size of mine if she could hear me now." He began to talk about general matters.

They were deep in a discussion of the cold war when they stopped for coffee at a lunch wagon outside of Chilton. Both seemed to have forgotten the nature of their errand. But as they entered the town proper Nelson said, "Do you know where Drake's house is located?"

Pierce felt his hackles rise again. "No." His tone said, "Take it or leave it."

Nelson half turned in the driver's seat. He seemed surprised. "We'll get directions at that all-night drugstore."

About ten minutes later they rolled through the gates of a broad driveway. Just within stood a small cottage, but no one came out of it to challenge them.

The main house was a red brick Georgian structure, simple and dignified. Pierce thought that it was not the type of house a Broadway playboy might be expected to inhabit, and Nelson apparently was of the same opinion because he muttered something about its being inherited. Nelson pulled up behind another car and stepped to the landscaped soil. Feeling superfluous, Pierce joined him. Salt air entered his lungs. He thought he could hear a distant sea.

Every bulb in the house seemed to be burning. A party might have been in progress except that fragments of talk drifting out from an open window contained no festive note.

Nelson laid his hand to the brass knocker on the sturdy door. His summons was quickly answered by a uniformed policeman who looked like an adolescent impersonating the law. He said, "Yes?" and eyed the newcomers doubtfully.

Nelson said, "Homicide—Manhattan." He and Pierce were led through a spacious high-ceilinged hall into a room that at first glance seemed to be chiefly windows and marble fireplace. The furniture was unostentatious enough to have grown naturally out of the thick rug. For occupants the room had two other policemen, a plump, pink, distinctly unhappy little man in blue serge, and a giant specimen in tweeds who stepped forward to greet Nelson.

"Grid—always glad to see you under any circumstances."

Nelson shook hands with him and introduced him to Pierce as Chief Maddox of the Chilton police. Maddox seemed to assume that Pierce, too, was a member of the Homicide Squad, and Nelson said nothing to disabuse him. Nelson's eyes were roaming the room, resting briefly on the fireplace, on an overturned chair, on an ugly stain on the couch.

"Your lab men have been and gone," Maddox said. "I told them to disturb as little as possible. Of course I don't know how much damage Foster did before we arrived."

Foster, the plump little man, came away from the wall that had been supporting him. He cleared his throat nervously. "I disturbed nothing." He had a guileless, button-featured face.

"But you called New York instead of calling us," Maddox said.

"I told you why. It looked bad to me. I was taken by surprise—and I'd just spoken to Barrows. It seemed the natural thing to call him."

"You stick to it that you weren't working a delaying action—giving somebody time to get away?" Maddox glanced at Nelson.

Foster said, "I'm sure I don't know why you keep saying that. I've told you—"

Maddox shrugged his giant shoulders. He had an almost insulting aura of health. "Foster's been with Drake for years," he said. "He won't for a minute admit that his master could be a criminal. And the thing is, Grid, I'm kind of stunned, myself. The Drakes were always highly respected in this community." He waved back possible arguments, although Nelson had given no indication of speaking. "Sure—old families grow a weed now and then. Still—"

Foster said, "Mr. Drake may be a bit wild and restless, but there's no real harm in him. He's been kidnaped—that's what it is, pure and simple. There'll be a ransom note any min—" He gulped. He looked startled and rather pleased at his own temerity.

Maddox said, "No self-respecting kidnaper would choose a time when his victim was entertaining. He wouldn't want to complicate his job that way. And you yourself admit to seeing the girl. Suppose you go over it again for the benefit of Lieutenant Nelson and his assistant. You might remember something you left out. Sit down and take your time—we're not against you." He sat down himself in a large club chair, but Foster edged back to his supporting wall. The others, too, remained standing.

Foster said, "There's nothing but what you took down in the statement, sir."

"Maybe not. But Lieutenant Nelson hasn't read the statement. He'd rather hear it at first hand."

Nelson nodded.

Foster looked at no one in particular. "Well, it was late last night." He spoke in the tone of a pupil reciting a lesson. "About this time. My wife and I had gone to bed. She was asleep, but I heard the car drive in. I hadn't expected Mr. Drake. He usually lets me know when he's coming, but once in a while he doesn't—not that I mind—I always try to keep the house ready, so that part of it was all right. I hurried into my bathrobe and slippers and went to the window facing the house and I saw him help a young lady out of the car and go into the house with her. I wondered should I get dressed in case anything was wanted. Then I thought I'd phone and ask because I was tired and I didn't want to put my clothes on for nothing. I phoned, but there was no answer and I thought, That's all right—he doesn't want me there. I can go back to bed. And I went to the window again to pull the shade down. I'd pulled it up to look out, and my wife doesn't like the sun to shine in her eyes in the morning. I saw that the lights were on in the house and that the car wasn't in the front driveway anymore, so I guessed that Mr. Drake had come out and driven it around to the garage while I was at the phone and maybe that was why he didn't answer. I didn't know whether to try again or go back to sleep and wait till morning. He's pretty considerate. It wouldn't be like him to want me at that time of night, barring he had a crowd with him or it was some special occasion—but still I thought I'd better sit up awhile and see. For one thing, his bed— Well, then my wife woke up and asked me what was the matter, and when I told her she said to forget it and come to sleep. So I did. That's all there is to it. Except that my wife was angry because I'd waked her and she couldn't manage to doze off again. She got hungry, being waked like that, and I had to go to the kitchen to get her something. I had a bite, too, while I was about it—and what with one thing and another, we both overslept, so that by the time we were up and doing Mr. Drake and his—his lady friend had gone."

"You'd started to say something about his bed."

"I was rambling, sir. It had nothing to do with what you want to know. My wife always says I ramble—"

"Do you always keep the beds made up?"

Foster said miserably, "No. Mr. Drake likes fresh linen, well aired, and when I expect him I always leave the beds to the last minute. So you can see why I was in a quandary—because as far as I knew he'd never made a bed in his life, and unless the young lady he'd brought with him was handy—" He seemed to hear his own words with horror. His face became a deeper pink. "Well, that's all, except that my wife says she didn't sleep as well as I did—and that toward morning she heard a woman scream. She says it went through her like a knife—and then it stopped suddenly before she could make up her mind to do anything about it."

Nelson started to say something, bit down on it, and glanced at Maddox. Maddox opened his eyes and yawned loudly. "Sorry, I had a hard day—made a speech at the opening ceremonies of our new hospital, and tomorrow there's another ceremony I'm expected to take part in. Got the picture, Grid?"

"Not quite."

"Well, take over. It's all yours—or at least half yours. The showgirl belongs to you, anyway, and I guess we split Drake since he has residence both here and in the big city—except that if he's a murderer I'll gladly relinquish my half."

Cute, Pierce thought sourly. His skin had prickled when Foster told of the scream. He did not see how anyone could air a sense of humor in the face of tragedy.

Nelson said to Foster, "Did you hear them talking when they arrived?"

"No, sir, I didn't—they were very quiet."

"And later, before you went back to sleep, did you hear anything?"

"Well, no, but I wouldn't. The walls here are very thick—and unless the windows are open—"

"Didn't Mr. Drake open the windows? That's almost the first thing anyone does—entering a closed house."

"It wasn't a closed house, really. I mean I'm in and out all the time."

"I see—then you're responsible for the windows being open now?"

Foster looked uncomfortable. "I opened them when I came over tonight. I guess I did it without thinking. There was such a frowst of cigarettes and—"

"And?"

"Liquor, if you must know," Foster said defiantly.

"Drake hasn't the reputation for being a hard drinker."

"I—not in the ordinary way of things, sir. But—but someone had spilled a drink." He pointed toward the slightly blemished surface of a squat Queen Anne table. "It had evaporated, but it gave out a nasty smell, so I—"

Maddox said in a suffering voice, "The man doesn't disturb a thing. He only opens all the windows and wipes off a table."

"It's solid mahogany, sir. I'm very particular about the furniture—and a liquor stain can do a lot of damage—"

"He hands us a theory of kidnaping with one hand," Maddox said, "and wipes away possible fingerprints with the other."

Nelson said, "Do I understand that you waited until Barrows' phone call to enter this house? You say you're in and out all the time and yet you didn't come over all day today?"

"Not since this morning, sir." Foster seemed relieved to have the subject changed. "You see, the garage door wasn't operating properly and I'd been meaning to repair it before Mr. Drake came again. It was the first thing I thought of when I heard the car. Mr. Drake hates things not to work—and I thought he'd be sure to notice it and complain and I'd better be able to say it was attended to when he brought it up."

Nelson said, not too subtly, Pierce thought, "I suppose, being a rich man and rather spoiled, Mr. Drake could fly into quite a rage when things didn't go his way."

Foster seemed to miss the implication. "Well, no." He added, "That is, not very often—which makes it worse somehow—if you know what I mean."

Nelson signified gravely that he knew. "So you went over to fix the garage door?"

"Yes—as soon as I was dressed." He added apologetically, "That would have been about half-past nine. Usually I'm at my work much earlier, but as I said, we'd overslept and—"

"Weren't you afraid the noise of repairing would disturb Mr. Drake? Or is he an early riser too?"

"No, he has no call to be, but it wasn't a noisy job—just a matter of oiling and an adjustment of the weights. As it turned out, I could be as noisy as I wanted because Mr. Drake's car—the one he uses in town—the one they found—was gone."

"And neither you nor your wife had heard it drive away?"

"No, sir." He lowered his rather high voice. "My wife always says she wakes at the drop of a pin—but between you and me that's only a notion of hers. And I never have any trouble that way myself once I get to sleep. It could have been a truck and it wouldn't have disturbed me."

"Yet your wife was awakened by the scream."

"Yes—but—well—that's another sort of noise, sir, and she's sensitive—"

"What did you do after you'd fixed the garage door?"

"I was just going into the house to put it to rights when my wife called. She'd an upset stomach and a headache—it never fails when she eats late at night—and nothing would do but that I drive to town to have her prescription renewed. When I got back it turned out that she was feeling much better and didn't need the prescription after all. My niece was with her. She's a smart girl. She'd been working in Europe since the war, and this was the first time we'd seen her in years. She had a lot to talk about—very interesting, it was. Well, the day was gone before I knew it, and what with one thing and another, I didn't get much done. When Mr. Barrows called from New York, Mr. Drake's lawyer, Mr. Seager, sounded so excited on the phone that I thought I'd better come over and get busy because it seemed likely that if Mr. Seager expected to reach Mr. Drake here he'd be returning. You could have knocked me over with a feather when I saw the state of this room—"

"Mr. Drake has entertained here before. The room doesn't look much more disorderly than it might after a party. Except for that overturned chair—"

Foster said with naïve satisfaction, "After I'd recovered my wits, so to speak, I didn't touch that—I left it just as it was—and I didn't try to wash out the blood on the couch—or on that rug where the gentleman's standing." He nodded toward Pierce.

Pierce looked down and hurriedly stepped away from the bladder-shaped stain at his feet.

"You knew it was blood at once?"

"It was stiff—and when I smelled it—" He squirmed and looked distressed. "I did think at first it might be wine, except that Mr. Drake seldom drinks red wine. He prefers champagne."

Nelson said, "Just a few more things I'd like to get clear. Then you can go back to your wife."

"Yes, sir. She'll be on pins and needles—"

"Did Mr. Drake have breakfast before he left?"

Pierce read a whole history into the fact that Nelson had not said did *they* have breakfast before they left.

Foster answered, "No, sir. I always keep a supply of food on hand—things that won't spoil—but nothing was touched. The kitchen's as clean as a whistle."

"Was that fire laid—or did Mr. Drake attend to it himself?" Nelson was looking at the logs and kindling in the fireplace.

"It was laid. It kind of surprised me that he hadn't lit it because it gets pretty chilly here at night—especially when the oil burner's been turned low for a while. I keep it set low when the house is empty—just high enough to prevent freezing. I think he must have started to light the fire, though, and then changed his mind and—and gone to bed." Foster had relaxed somewhat, but now he blushed again.

"Why?" Nelson was not inquiring about the blush.

"Because the logs were disturbed. That's how I happened to find the diamond pin. From force of habit, you might say, I went over to straighten them, and the pin was under that big log which had slipped off the andirons."

"I see," Nelson said. Pierce wondered what he saw. "You say you were up late last night? How late?"

"It must have been after two when we finally dropped off."

"While you were fixing something for your wife you had the lights on, of course. And you didn't hear the car leave during that time or until the time it took you to get to sleep?"

"If it had left then I'd have heard it—my wife too."

"How much illumination was there when you saw the two people get out of the car?"

"Very little—no moon—but I saw Mr. Drake and the girl for a minute in the splash of the headlights. Mr. Drake was wearing his favorite overcoat—the kind he gets in England—and his Borsalino hat."

"Did you get any idea of what the girl was wearing?"

"No—I could just see that she was tall. I'm not much good at women's clothes. She had no hat on—or if she did it was one of those little caps they wear. Her coat looked like fur, though. If my wife had seen her, she'd have been able to tell you—"

"One more thing. *Had* Mr. Drake's bed been slept in?"

"No, sir—at least—I don't know—I should have gone upstairs to look, but I—I'd better go now and—" He started toward the door, an eager servant on familiar ground once more. Nelson checked him. "Don't bother. You can attend to it in the morning. Thank you—and good night."

"I—I'm excused?"

"Yes, if it's all right with Chief Maddox."

"It's all right with me," Maddox said.

Foster almost raced toward the door. Then he turned, moistened his lips. "Will I come back to lock up after you've left?"

Maddox said, "Give me your keys. I'll do the locking up."

"Well—" Foster took a large key ring from his pocket. He surrendered it to Maddox as though he were betraying a trust. "You won't know which is—"

"I'll use the trial-and-error method. Good night, Foster."

"I beg pardon, sir, but you won't want to question my wife any more tonight? She'll be needing her sleep after—"

"That's up to Lieutenant Nelson."

Nelson said, "I'll take a look at her statement and if I find I want more information I'll see her tomorrow."

"Thank you, sir."

Nelson walked to one of the windows and watched the little man's progress along the driveway to the cottage. Maddox said, "It doesn't add up to sickem, eh, Grid?"

Nelson turned back to the room. "Doesn't his wife do any of the work?"

"She's supposed to, but she's a spoiled would-be beauty who thinks she's married beneath her. Shouldn't be surprised if Bobby Drake was the lure that made her swallow such a menial position. She squawked like a mid-Victorian spinster with migraine when we took her statement. She's strong as a horse, too, but it's Foster she's got blinkered."

"May I see her statement?"

"It's still in shorthand. Want to take it with you and have it typed in your office? Might be quicker."

"What system?"

One of the policemen came forward. "It's Gregg, Lieutenant. Anyone who knows Gregg can transcribe it—not like some of those other systems." He handed Nelson a notebook and seemed relieved when he slipped it into his pocket. "Both statements are in there."

"Never saw a cop yet who wasn't allergic to typing," Maddox said. "You'll find her account substantially the same as Foster's, Grid, except she insists Drake has a terrible temper—and except for the scream which, incidentally, she says didn't stop of its own accord. She swears it was choked off."

Nelson said, "And yet she didn't do anything about it."

"She was too petrified to move, she says, and anyway, it was none of her business."

"Was Drake attracted to her?"

"Who knows? There's no accounting for tastes. Say—how's this for a theory? She and Drake were carrying on and she got jealous of his new girlfriend and did away with her."

"I'll buy it if you can stretch it to account for Drake's abandoned car and the rumors that a woman could carve out a full-time career disposing of his girlfriends."

Maddox grinned. "I'll sell it cheap if you do the accounting."

Pierce wanted to shout, "What do you think you're playing at?" Unnoticed, he stood there glowering.

"Speaking of the abandoned car," Maddox said, "he must have been in a panic—worked like crazy to obliterate all fingerprints. Now why would he do that? Any half-baked rookie could trace the car back to him."

Pierce said, "Toni's fingerprints were what he wanted to obliterate."

Maddox wheeled in his chair to stare at him. "I shouldn't think so, mister, considering he didn't take the trouble to destroy her fingerprints in the house. The lab boys got them everywhere they turned—fine clear ones. Of course we're not sure yet they're hers, but we've made sure they're not Foster's or Mrs. Foster's. So you knew the missing girl? Thought you were one of Grid's young hopefuls."

"He's a friend of mine and of the missing girl," Nelson said.

"Okay by me. I've heard you generally know what you're doing—

witnessed it too. I'll never forget that Warner case that had all of Westchester County climbing trees until you—"

"Exactly where was the car found?"

"Just past the town limits—where the road forks. If he continued on foot along the right fork and went at a good clip he'd have come to the railroad station in about fifteen minutes."

"Carrying a dead or injured girl?"

"You can search me. He didn't dump her along the way or we'd have heard by this time. After the car was found I recruited all the citizens I could to search the surrounding territory."

"Good job." Then Nelson said, "I'll take a look upstairs."

"Help yourself." After a moment of deliberation Maddox hefted his bulk out of the chair. "He's got a picture on his dresser that tallies with the girl's description. You'd think he'd have been more concerned with getting rid of that than wiping his car clean." He led the way into the hall and up a polished staircase. The three policemen formed a rear guard behind Nelson and Pierce.

"Third door on the right," Maddox said, "is his bedroom."

The room was well proportioned, well furnished, and, except for the rumpled bed, in good order. A studio portrait in an ornate frame looked out of place among the dresser's masculine appointments. Nelson and Pierce halted before it. Pierce declined his head in brief confirmation and turned away.

Nelson gave no further attention to the picture. Starting from the top, he slid dresser drawers open and shut, glancing swiftly into each. The bottom drawer received a somewhat longer scrutiny. It was piled high with photographs of women, most of them framed.

"He keeps a morgue of his own," Maddox said. "The queen is dead—long live the queen."

Nelson walked over to the bed. He touched his fingertips to the linen.

Maddox, watching him, said ruminatively, "Funny aspects this case has. Downstairs she struggles for her virtue and bleeds enough to predicate a mortal wound. Then she trots up here meek as a lamb, makes her bed, and lies in it. Or did the struggle come later—and why?" He answered himself: "Later—or she'd have tracked blood. But why should she struggle when she'd given in so gracefully? That bed was made by an expert all right—and if what Foster says is true, Drake is anything but an expert. Hey—"

Efficiently Nelson was whipping sheets and pillowcases off the bed. He folded them neatly, with a minimum of handling. "Get me a laundry bag or a large container of some sort," he said to one of the policemen.

A prurient expression settled on Maddox's broad face. "What would you want with those, Grid?" His tone accused Nelson of excessive bad taste.

"An oversight of the lab squad. Tests will determine whether or not the bed's been used. It may have been rumpled to confuse the issue."

"For God's sake—what issue?"

"I'm not sure. Perhaps the time of departure from this house."

"According to Foster, Drake must have left between the hours of two in the morning and ninish."

"Yes—and the nearness to two or to nine would depend on whether or not he went to bed." Nelson shrugged. "I can't see why a few hours one way or another would make much difference, the way it turned out—unless he thought the police would come on the scene earlier. As you remarked, there are some funny aspects to this case."

"I move that we sleep on them," Maddox said.

CHAPTER EIGHT

To the obvious discomfort of the three uniforms, Nelson said, "Which one of your men is going to stand guard?"

It was plainly a new idea to Maddox. "I hadn't got around to picking one. It's unlikely, of course, that with all the damn-fool frills Drake used to cover his tracks he'll be returning here in a hurry. Still—" He fixed his eyes on the youthful policeman who had answered the door. "You're elected, Jack. You can brew a pot of coffee to keep you awake. I'll send a relief in the morning. Here, might as well take these keys. Coming, Grid?"

"In a little while."

"Suit yourself. Be seeing you." He lumbered out, followed by his retinue. One of the men carried a laundry bag containing the bed linen. Jack, the last in line, carried a burden of grief.

Nelson seemed in no hurry to leave. After the police car had pulled away he sat down on the edge of the stripped bed, a withdrawn expression on his face. Aimlessly Pierce wandered over to a large closet, opened it, and gazed at the orderly array of men's clothing.

Nelson glanced at him. "I'm sure that all the places large enough to conceal a body have been searched," he said, "if that's what's on your mind."

"Nothing's on my mind—except that it's hard to understand why Drake would have to pack a bag when the drawers are stuffed with shirts and underwear and there are suits enough here to outfit an army."

"What's this about a bag?"

"His man in New York mentioned that a suitcase and some clothes were missing—"

"I wish you'd brought that up sooner."

"I only just thought of it. Why?"

"I could have asked Maddox if he'd seen or heard about it."

"I don't—"

"Unless Drake owns some favorite articles that can't be duplicated, packing a bag means he was planning to go on to another destination. It gives the whole business a more calculated look." He got up from the bed and went to the closet.

Pierce moved away to take up a stance before the dresser. He found himself staring at Toni's photograph and wished fervently that the pictured mouth could open to pour out flat, unaccented words of guidance.

Presently his exclamation called Nelson back from the exploration he had been conducting in the closet. "Say something?" Nelson asked.

"No—I mean—look—Seager comes from Chilton too."

The information did not excite Nelson. "Who told you that?"

"Toni did—at the bar and grill—"

"Well?"

"Seager's her fiancé—or was—or maybe is. Wouldn't it be possible— couldn't she—"

Nelson said gravely, "Don't rush it."

"All right, I'm mixed up—it's only an idea—but, being engaged to him, she'd know where his house is here in Chilton. Say Drake didn't kill her and she managed to get away from him—but because she was hurt she couldn't make it back to New York and went to the one safe place she knew of that was near." He looked at Nelson eagerly.

"Does Seager keep the Chilton house open? I understand that he lives at the Morrow Arms on East Fifty-seventh Street."

The eagerness faded from Pierce's face. "I don't know. I guess it's a crazy notion. I forgot about her having only one shoe. Anyway, if she's there she'd have telephoned for—"

Nelson said briskly, "We'll have a go at it anyway." He went the telephone on the bedside table. He jiggled the hook, and when the nerves of Pierce began to battle the light, harmless sound, he said, "Hello—will you give me the number of LeRoy Seager's residence in Chilton? ... No, I haven't a directory.... Let's not bother Information. This is the police.... Thank you—will you try it for me, please?" He held the receiver away from his ear. For Pierce, the long series of buzzes had a hopeless, sterile ring. He wondered at Nelson's interminable patience and drew breath heavily as the receiver was replaced.

"At any rate, the telephone hasn't been disconnected," Nelson said. "We'll drive over, just to stay on the thorough side."

But from his subsequent actions it became apparent that he did not think Pierce's theory important enough to put to immediate test. He went back to the clothes closet and took one last comprehensive look. He went into the adjoining bath, leaving the door open, and Pierce could see him poking into a huge hamper and standing before a linen press as though he were taking inventory. Then he strode out into the hall.

Pierce trailed after him, up the stairs to an incredibly neat attic, and down again to the second floor, where every bedroom and bath was given a quick, competent search. In the main hall Pierce gritted his teeth and said, "If you put any stock in Toni being at Seager's house you wouldn't waste—"

But Nelson had ducked into a small square library, nor could he be nailed down until the kitchen was the one remaining room to be explored.

The young policeman sat at a scrubbed pine table obediently drinking coffee. He set his cup down and muttered, "They put the bag of sheets in the luggage compartment of your car."

"Thanks." Nelson stood in the doorway, his eyes at work the length and breadth of the room before he brought them to settle on the glum boyish face. "You're new to the Chilton force, aren't you?"

The "Yes, sir," was defiant. Jack grimaced strangely. He might have been trying to look old and experienced.

"I thought so. I've worked with Chief Maddox before. I'd have remembered your face. He must repose a lot of confidence in you to trust you with a job like this."

"Well, I only got my appointment last summer—but I'm older than I look." He was trying hard to quell the smile. "The other fellows have wives and kids. I guess that's why I was picked."

"Chief Maddox wouldn't allow considerations like that to interfere with his duty. You were around when the men from the laboratory came?"

"Yes, sir."

"Did you happen to notice whether they took a suitcase back to the lab with them—something that wasn't part of their regular equipment?"

"A suitcase? No, sir. I helped carry the stuff out after they were through. Nobody had a suitcase or I'd have seen it—nobody had anything but regular outfits for chemicals and camera supplies—"

"Did you hear any mention of a suitcase being left in Mr. Drake's abandoned car?"

"No—only talk about bloodstains on the upholstery and the way there wasn't a print even on the door or the steering wheel." He had brightened considerably. It was clear that Nelson's confidential approach had made him feel "in," one officer of the law discussing an important case with another. He added, "Of course it's wintertime and people like Mr. Drake and his friends almost always wear gloves—but still, when you light a cigarette or do something like that, you're bound to take gloves off, so that's why it's funny."

"True enough. Do you know where the Seager house is?"

"Not exactly. You see—until last year I lived in Creston— Wait a moment—I'll find out." He dashed out of the kitchen before Nelson could raise a hand to stop him.

"Impetuous lad," Nelson said ruefully.

"Where's he gone?"

"To wake the Fosters, I'm afraid." He was exploring the pantry when the youngster returned.

"Got it for you," he reported breathlessly. "It's about three quarters of a mile down the road toward Pine Harbor. When you see the sign 'Miggs Cove' you take the first turn to your left that runs along the beach. You keep going for about ten minutes and you'll see a rustic gate leading to the house. You can't miss it—but Foster says it's been closed since Mr. LeRoy, Sr., died—boarded up tight—"

"I see. Isn't there a shorter cut?"

"I guess not. Foster didn't say."

"Thank you—you've been a big help." He beckoned Pierce. They went out through the kitchen door.

The night air was sharp and clean and still. A scattering of fading stars did little to brighten the dark sky. Unconsciously Pierce pitched his voice low so that it blended with the surrounding quiet. "Do we still try it?"

"Might as well—it's not much out of our way." He added inconsequentially, "Someday I'll live in the country—near the sea for choice."

"I don't call this country. You should have seen the places Uncle Doc and I—" Pierce bit his lip. "What are we waiting for?"

"The question is, do I disturb Foster again and ask if he saw Drake carrying a suitcase?"

Pierce looked toward the black outline of the cottage. "Oh, let them sleep," he said, less out of consideration for the Fosters than out of a gnawing will to take action, any action. "I still can't see why the suitcase is important."

"Frankly, neither can I. Just the same, it bothers me. We're agreed that Drake's packing for a brief visit to his own house would be a 'coals to Newcastle' proposition. So I want to know what was in the suitcase. It might supply a clue to his real goal—although if he had one why he should deliberately stop off to foul his own nest is another thing to be figured."

Pierce said, "Barrows, the man in New York, would be the one to tell you what was in the suitcase."

"I guess you're right. Let's go."

They got into the car. Pierce said, "Toward Pine Harbor. Do you know where that is?"

"Don't worry. This is old territory for me."

In a short span of conversationless driving they came upon a sign nailed to a tree just beyond the road's shoulder. Nelson drew over and braked suddenly.

"Why are you stopping?" Pierce asked. "We didn't come to the turn."

Nelson took a flashlight from the glove compartment. He got out of the car and shone it upon the sign. Pierce read the painted legend aloud. "'Miggs Cove.' But he told you that Seager's house was on the road that went along the beach."

"I thought I might take a look at the beach first." Nelson's voice was noncommittal. "You wait in the car."

Pierce could hear the sound of waves. He said thinly, "You mean that the car might have been planted where it was to put us off the track? You mean that Drake might have drowned Toni?" He slid along the car seat to the open door. "I'll go with you."

He froze with one foot on the ground as Nelson said, "Hold it."

Two lights came bobbing unevenly over a small rise where the road widened. Nelson started walking toward them, his own light transferred to his left hand, his right thrust into a pocket. Pierce followed him. He looked down and saw the spread of the shale beach, punctuated with the scattered silhouettes of small boats. He saw the two figures plodding up the stony rise. As they reached the road Nelson trained his flashlight upon them.

They made instinctive motions of recoil. They stared openmouthed at their reception committee. They seemed sturdy, prosperous-looking men dressed for a camping expedition. They wore heavy woolen shirts, corduroy slack suits, and thick-soled shoes. One of them said uncertainly, "Yes, mister?" His companion was trying to sidle past Nelson.

Nelson moved aside to let them by. Then he took Pierce's arm and walked after them until they reached the bath of the car's headlights. "Wait a minute," he called.

They turned. The spokesman said, "Your car break down? Afraid we can't help. We walked here. But when we get home we could telephone and try to raise the garageman."

Nelson opened his coat and produced a wallet. He held it so that they could see his cellophaned credentials. They crowded close to read.

One of them chuckled and slapped the other's back. "You should have seen your face, George."

"Well, you didn't look so healthy either, Mervin. Police officers, eh?" He included Pierce in the designation. "Thought you might be anything but at this time of night. Matter of fact, we're sort of policemen ourselves—temporarily, that is. Other days I'm George Phillips, department store magnate, as they say in the papers. You must have passed my emporium if you came through Chilton. And this is Mervin Pomeroy, a competitor of mine, although I've got more and better hardware in one little corner of Phillips and Company than he has in his whole shop. That right, Mervin?"

Mervin responded good-naturedly and at length. Nelson broke in upon the wordy exchange: "Were you on police business just now?"

The department store magnate shuffled uncomfortably. "I guess I shouldn't have mentioned it—only that I didn't want you getting suspicious about what we were doing on the beach at this hour. You see, it's kind of a town matter, and maybe Chief Maddox wouldn't want us shooting our mouths off—"

"I've just left Chief Maddox," Nelson said. "I take it you're part of the group that volunteered to help in the Drake affair."

"That's right, Lieutenant." The magnate sounded relieved.

"I thought you were asked to comb the location where Drake's car was found."

"We were. Coming here was our own idea. Mervin and I got it at the same time. So we kind of sneaked away. Of course the car wasn't near water, but it struck us he might have left it there to keep people from thinking he'd drowned her."

The hardware merchant evidently considered that he had been silent long enough. He said with satisfaction, "We figured where would we go if we wanted to get rid of a body—and for first choice we picked Miggs Cove."

George said, "Far back as I can remember, nothing like this ever happened in Chilton—not even on the wrong side of the tracks. And when you think of a man like Drake, who should be setting everybody a good example, it makes your blood run cold. Of course she might be washed out to sea by this time, but they'll probably drag Miggs Cove anyway, just in case she's wedged in someplace. Believe me, I'll think twice before I let my kids go crabbing or clamming here this summer—let alone eat their haul. Might even have to build that swimming pool the wife's always wanted because she hates the Chilton summer crowd. It being so near New York City, we get some mighty undesirable—"

Pierce cried, "Why will they have to drag the cove? Did you find anything?"

"Well, now—no offense—but I guess we should make our report to Chief Maddox, seeing as how we got our orders from him in the first place. You go along with that, Mervin?"

Nelson said solemnly, "Chief Maddox has gone to bed after a long, tiring day. It wouldn't be fair to disturb him now. Of course if what you've discovered is unimportant enough to keep until morning—"

George bridled indignantly. He looked at Mervin. "Unimportant, my foot—"

"Then I think you'd better produce it. I'm afraid this is no longer a town matter."

"You mean Chief Maddox called you in on account of the New York chorus girl?"

"Something like that."

"Go on, show it to him, George," Mervin said. "We don't want to hold up the works."

George unbuttoned one of the huge flap pockets of his corduroy jacket. Gingerly, between thumb and forefinger, he drew out a wadded lump of colored silk. He flicked his hand and the material unfurled. It had been vivid once. Now its figured pattern was caked with a thick brown substance. "Blood—looks like," George said unnecessarily.

Nelson relieved him of it. He glanced at Pierce. Pierce shook his head in answer to the implied question. He said, "She probably had a hundred scarves—women do."

"Where did you find this?" Nelson said.

"It had caught on a piece of driftwood near one of the rowboats. See—it's got a small tear in it. We found something else too. At least Mervin did." He paused as though to give Mervin time to take a bow. "Don't know as it means anything, but I brought it along. If it had been in a place where there was other litter I wouldn't have, but we keep signs posted all over the beach asking people not to dump stuff on account of we don't want our clams and crabs feeding off sewage— and anyway, there haven't been any picnics there since fall." He was fishing in the other flap pocket. He came up with a button. "Could have ripped off a man's overcoat," he said. "Wasn't cast up because it isn't worn a bit."

"Anything else?"

"Anything else!" He sounded hurt. "We must've walked a mile along that beach back and forth before we found this much. And all we had was flashlights—"

Nelson said, "If ever I need deputies I'll know where to come." He stowed scarf and button away and got back into the car.

"Both Mervin and I are always ready to do our duty. We don't want anybody—no matter who he is—to get away with shenanigans in this town."

Shenanigans, Pierce thought bitterly. Two fine upstanding citizens, and neither of them with so much as a token expression of sympathy for the fate of the New York chorus girl. He became aware that Nelson was calling his name. He climbed into the car.

Mervin shouted hopefully, "Say—you wouldn't be driving back to Chilton? Our feet are wet—and beat up, besides. We walked here because we didn't want to make a noise starting up our cars and have the others needle us in case the hunch didn't pan out. One thing—they won't needle us now."

"Sorry, I've an errand down the road." The car was away before they had time to reply. "A dirty trick," Nelson said, "but I didn't want an audience."

Pierce said tiredly, "What *do* you want? Why go to Seager's now?"

"One scarf doesn't make a body." Nelson took a left turn. "Excuse it. I'm not trying to be facetious. Call it nerves if you like."

"Nerves?" Pierce glanced at him and saw with surprise the grave set look of his face. "This should be an old story to you."

"It should be, but it never is. I'd like to take a look at that beach myself—and examine the boats—but I guess it had better wait until daylight."

"Tell me—was a scarf included in the list that Jill Batiste gave Tarr?"

"Yes—a figured silk scarf. That must be the house."

He maneuvered the car so that its headlights were trained full upon the low white building set about twenty feet back from the road. Old elm trees, planted at precise intervals, margined the overgrown driveway, and what had been a lawn was a tangle of coarse high grass. Equipped with flashlight, he led the way to a sagging front porch.

Equipped with nothing, not faith, hope, or even healthy curiosity, Pierce followed. The impetus was missing. His lagging feet took him no farther than the porch. He sat down on a step, waiting tense and chilled and lonely while Nelson carried out the sleeveless errand. Of its futility Pierce had no doubt. He saw a wavering Toni at the bottom of the cove. He had never seen men dragging for a body, but he saw them now. They were men of George's and Mervin's stamp. They talked incessantly, some grumbling, some cheerful, all wearing smug faces, none thinking of the object of the quest but rather of their own satisfyingly important roles. None giving a thought to a girl living and beautiful a day or so ago. And when they found her, the icy warped flesh, the lank black hair, once gleaming, lovingly tended, would they still talk of projected swimming pools, of an unjust stricture put upon the pleasure of their young?

It seemed to him that he sat there for a very long time. He heard sounds with which his brain refused to cope. Ghost sounds. The blow struck by a swinging shutter. The scuffle of small animals. A sighing wind. What might have been the prizing of an outbuilding door. The darkness of the night began to lift while he sat there, and the gray sky labored to bring forth a day that for him was doomed at birth. He peered to the right and the left of him, and for as far as he could see there was no other human habitation. He was not in Westchester County. He was in some desolate wilderness into which he had stumbled through no fault of his own on the night of Uncle Doc's death. And the shock which had pursued him then was now fully upon him. He felt condemned to struggle with it forever. His teeth chattered. Yet inertia strong as chains prevented him from arising and seeking Nelson out.

When he heard Nelson's voice at last, it was like an echo from another world. "Was I long? The house is boarded up all right. I made unlawful entry by way of a loose shutter—and from the signs I wasn't the first to think of it. My predecessors were tramps, probably. There's a store of canned foods in the kitchen, and a couple of the cans had been opened quite recently and stowed in the garbage pail. Very tidy tramps. They left no other clues to their presence but—"

Pierce heard himself saying, "Detection for the sake of detection." His voice sounded remote. "Time means nothing to you, does it?"

"I'll admit that I didn't expect to find Toni George here when we started out. My mind had been working on much the same lines as those two merchants'. Water has always been the easiest way to dispose of a body. If that is Toni George's scarf she could have been here—or by the same reasoning she could have been on the way back from here, believing mistakenly that the danger had passed. So I gave the place and grounds a going-over—but a flashlight isn't the best aid to such an expedition. Good heavens, boy, is that noise your teeth? Get up—move about—"

Pierce got up. He stretched his cramped limbs.

"It wasn't too bright of you to sit all huddled up like that."

"I'm not too bright."

"You'll be surprised at the way your I.Q. will mount after a breakfast, a hot bath, and sleep." He urged him toward the car.

They passed no one on the road out of Chilton. The volunteer citizens had evidently suspended operations. Pierce closed his eyes and did not open them until they were far along the highway. Then he came awake sharply.

Nelson said, "Glad to have you with us again. Cigarette?"

Pierce lit one and inhaled. "That scarf caught on a piece of driftwood. It must have been pretty much in evidence if those men found it. Under the circumstances you'd think Drake would have made pretty sure he left no traces."

"It struck me that way too. Of course he might have let his hurry to be off override caution, not realizing that anyone would go near the beach until the warm weather set in. No, he comes from Chilton. He'd know the fishermen and professional clammers keep at it through the winter."

"I guess there's no answer except that he's completely insane."

"Well, I'll get the name of his tailors and see if the button means anything to them. And I'll show the scarf to Jill Batiste, and if those items add up—"

"Then all you'll have to do is to find him. And he's probably in

Mexico by this time—with a suitcase full of money." Pierce had not known how he would end the sentence. It ended itself.

Nelson said calmly, "Now that's a thought. We'll check his sources of supply, of course, to learn which one has been tapped lately—and for how much."

Suddenly Pierce found himself thinking with unusual warmth of his own job as press agent. Compared to the laborious step-by-step plodding required of a detective, it took on new desirability.

CHAPTER NINE

Nelson dropped Pierce at his door, put the car in the garage, and walked the few blocks to his own dwelling. He slept for three hours. Then he bathed and dressed. He did not wait for Sammy to arrive and start his day auspiciously with a good breakfast. He left a note for her, fared less well at a cafeteria, got his car, and drove to headquarters. He handed the statements of the Fosters to a typist, requesting that they be transcribed at once, deposited the scarf and the bundle of bed linen in the lab, succeeded in exacting a promise that the reports would reach his desk in record time, and went to his office for a session with the telephone. He got the name of Toni's doctor from the girl with whom she had shared an apartment. He got extraneous information along with it that had more to do with the girl's failure to sleep a wink all night than with the case. He was able to hang up by promising that he would go into the matter further and in person. He phoned the doctor, who used no more words than were necessary to state Toni's blood group. Barrows, Drake's man, was next on the list. He came through with a description of the clothes that were missing from Drake's wardrobe; in short, which Barrows was not, the outfit Foster had glimpsed from his bedroom window, plus a dark gray suit and brown shoes. Barrows seemed troubled because he could not estimate the number of shirts, pairs of socks, sets of underwear, or ties that were missing. "Mr. Drake has so many, you know." But he could say what watch and what cuff links Mr. Drake would be wearing, and did, going into such finicking detail that he might have been examining the articles under a microscope. Nelson congratulated him for his powers of observation and asked the name of Drake's jeweler. Barrows misunderstood the request and was at tactful pains to inform him that both the watch and the links were originals, made to Drake's own specifications, could not be duplicated, and would not, in any event, be suitable for a—well—for everyday use. He took a few more minutes to add that he was deeply shocked at the whole affair and that there must be some mistake.

Nelson said he hoped so, instructed him to carry on until further notice, and held out the doubtful treat of a face-to-face meeting as soon as it could be arranged.

The typist brought in the Foster statements, and Nelson pondered over them for some time. He was on his way out of the building when a horde of reporters descended upon him. It was his turn to answer questions. He answered, agreeably and with dispatch, his mind carefully blue-penciling the words before they passed his lips. Convincingly he regretted that he would have no further information until the laboratory reports came in, and with the exception of one ratty specimen from a tabloid the horde scattered. He had to thrust the ratty specimen out of his way, a luxury which he knew he would pay for as soon as the next edition of the tabloid hit the street.

He left his car outside of headquarters and walked over to Fifth Avenue. The jewelry store that received Drake's patronage had windows of invisible glass. They exhibited nothing but an emerald as large as a bird's egg and a few chunky lumps of gold. He was tempted to reach through deceptive glass and pre-empt the emerald for Kyrie. He grinned, thinking what a fine thought that was for an officer of the law to entertain, and his grin became a smile as he went on to speculate upon Kyrie's reaction to it. The smile faded as he remembered that he had left home before the mail was delivered, and he hoped there would be a letter from Kyrie when he got back that night, whatever time he did get back. He forced his thoughts away from Kyrie. It was difficult, but he did it. He strode into the shop, an officer of the law on duty, not noticing that the mirrors on either side of him imaged a tall, well-clothed man of distinction, or that the clerk who came forward on his best foot was accepting the image at face value.

"Yes, sir. May I serve you?"

"I'd like to see the manager."

"But I'm sure I can help you—if you'll tell me what you have in mind."

"I have police business in mind."

The clerk recoiled. "You don't want to make a purchase?"

"No—not this time. Perhaps I won't need the manager. Who waits on Mr. Bobby Drake?"

"Mr. Bobby Drake?" Excitement replaced frustration. It roughened the genteel voice. "Is it about that chorus girl? I heard it on the radio this morning. I can't believe it. I don't wait on Mr. Drake personally, but I'm a good judge of people. That chorus girl must have been blackmailing him. Mark my word, unless he had extreme provocation—"

"Does this come from here?" Nelson laid a small tissue-wrapped packet on the counter, opened it to expose a heart-shaped pin.

The clerk fingered it, turned it over. "Why, yes. It doesn't carry our signature because it's not an original. It's made for us by—"

"Thank you. Will you please call the manager—or the clerk who takes care of Mr. Drake?"

"Well—" He was reluctant to do the errand. He wore that "give-me-the-inside-story" expression. He used delaying tactics. "May I ask to see your credentials."

Nelson produced them. When the lingering scrutiny became too much for him he said, "You needn't bother to read the small print." He sat down and followed the little man's stiff-legged progress toward the rear of the shop. He watched him signal a younger clerk who was paying breathless homage to a mean-mouthed woman in mink. There were no other customers, either because it was early or because business was bad. The mink woman looked as though only the Koh-i-Noor would have lured her from bed before noon. She seemed annoyed as the two clerks conferred discreetly, lips to ears. Then Nelson's man placed himself at her disposal, freeing his colleague, who shed his breathless homage as he came forward. He had no handkerchief in his hand, but he gave the illusion of a man mopping his brow.

"Mr. Margrave said you wanted to see me or the manager. The manager won't be in until late afternoon."

"I won't take much of your time," Nelson said.

He was rewarded with a genuine smile. "Glad to be rescued. Take all the time you want."

Nelson returned the smile. "Did you sell this pin to Mr. Bobby Drake?"

The clerk looked down at it. "I think so," he said, "or one like it. It's a popular item."

"You can show me a record of the sale?"

"Certainly."

Nelson sat down again and waited. He thought that the clerk was taking much longer than necessary to produce the record. He did not blame him. The mink woman seemed to have set a goal for herself. Clearly she was determined to touch every piece of jewelry in the shop.

The clerk returned at last, tiptoeing past the danger area. He carried a leather-bound volume. "Sorry to be so long," he said without sorrow. "All of the sales slips are copied into these books along with notes which we refer to when we wish to analyze a client's—um—interests. See—Mr. Drake bought the pin and a bracelet on the same day."

Nelson read the date, the price, and a brief description of the articles. He frowned. He turned back the pages of the book. He saw Drake's name repeated several times. Within a month he had bought two gold cigarette cases, twelve compacts marked party favors, and a star sapphire. Nelson's frown was not for his extravagance. He was trying to remember something that he felt he should remember.

"Mr. Drake's butler or valet or whatever he calls himself telephoned that day," the clerk said, "and told me approximately how much Mr. Drake wished to spend. The selections were left to me. Mr. Drake has confidence in my taste."

"Barrows telephoned?"

"I don't know his name. Mr. Drake usually comes in to make his own selections, but once or twice he's telephoned when he's in a hurry. He has an account here, of course, and we're always glad to give him special service."

"I see. The pin and bracelet were delivered to him?"

"No—he didn't want them sent to the penthouse, his man said. A special messenger called for them. It was the recipient's birthday, and the messenger was to pick up flowers on the way so that they could be delivered at the same time as the jewelry."

"Isn't that a risky way to do business? Anybody could call pretending to be Drake's man and send a special messenger for the loot."

"I wasn't born yesterday. I called the penthouse back. I described the things I'd chosen and asked if they'd do. The same voice answered. It was all in order."

"Were you given the birthday girl's address?"

"Say!" He forgot the decorum of the establishment. He clutched Nelson's arm. "Sure—no wonder the name they were broadcasting sounded familiar to me. I was told to print it plainly on the package so that the messenger wouldn't slip up. It went to Toni George all right—that's the one, isn't it?"

Nelson nodded.

The clerk hesitated. "Could you—would you mind telling me what it's all about?"

"Sorry, I haven't time. Thanks for your help." He left the shop. With all the time in the world he could not have gratified the clerk's curiosity. He did not know what it was all about, nor exactly what he had hoped to uncover beyond verifying the fact that Drake had been sending gifts to Toni George. Perhaps, too, he had hoped to establish complicity on her part which would clarify her reason for going to Chilton with Drake. For example, she might have accompanied Drake to the jeweler's.... He thought of Pierce Kirby and of Kirby's belief that she was an innocent victim. He thought of the bed in the Chilton house and of Foster's contention that Drake was incapable of bedmaking. Indisputably, in the face of things, that meant that the task had fallen to Toni, and indisputably it was an odd task to be undertaken by a girl who fought for her virtue. It stuck in his craw. He liked Pierce Kirby very well. He liked his loyalty, but—

He started to cross Fifth Avenue against the lights. He stepped back before the bus could do more than fan his trousers, piously thankful for his reflexes. Pierce Kirby and Toni George. Bracelet and pin. The lights were with him. He crossed the avenue safely and continued due west. He was no longer absentminded. He was onto something. He was recalling Pierce's account of his conversation with Toni in the bar and grill. She had set the bracelet on the table. Yes, he was onto something. He did not know its worth, but it was something. No other bracelet had been listed among Drake's purchases. And if the bracelet and pin were delivered at the same time in the same package, why had one been received so long before the other? Jill Batiste said that the pin arrived on the night before Toni's disappearance. It had been attached to a corsage. Wait a minute. Don't lose it. Follow it. Back to the bar and grill. In her appeal to Pierce, Toni had said that her fiancé, LeRoy Seager, had been there when the bracelet came. He had been furious....

Nelson quickened his pace. He could check that. Seager figured in his plans for the day. He would drop in at the lab first to find out if the reports were ready. Then he would take his car, drop in on Seager, and after that proceed with the rest of his program.

The reports were not ready. They had run a precipitant on the blood and it checked with Toni's group, but the rest of the findings were still to be made. The wizard in charge swore unscientifically at Nelson, accusing him of expecting the impossible. And Nelson said that in his job he had to expect the impossible or give up. He stopped in his office for what he hoped would be a short while. But business was good that day, not spectacular but good, and he spent more than an hour mapping out the initial tactics to be used in ferreting out the murderer of an apparently respectable white-collar worker who had been beaten to death in a Greenwich Village rooming house. The commissioner cut off another slice of time by way of an extended telephone talk. He told Nelson that the Drake affair had already aroused national interest and indignation. He told him that he was to work closely with Missing Persons and that the entire force had been instructed to cooperate. He said that with Furniss in Florida it was up to Nelson to prove his mettle, as he had so often proved it in the past. And when Nelson was able to get a word in the word was "Amen."

He drove to the building that housed the firm of Seager and Cunningham. It was half-past one. He was hungry, but he did not stop for lunch and he hoped that Seager was not lunching. He rode up to the fourteenth floor of the building and entered a very conservative reception room. The woman at the desk looked conservative too. She had undoubtedly grown old and gray at her job, because few firms these days had sense enough to hire women of her stamp. She turned her sharp, knowledgeable face upward, asked his name and business, and without audible comment retailed the information to Seager's office. She said that Mr. Seager would receive him and offered to lead the way. Nelson thanked her and refused the offer. He took the door she indicated and walked to a rhythm of typewriters through a narrow lane bordered by offices. He found LeRoy Seager crouching behind a strictly utilitarian desk, attempting not to avoid the law but to close a jammed bottom drawer. Nelson, approaching the desk from the side, saw that the obstacle looked like a large square picture frame.

Seager sat up, exhibiting a distressed yellowish face, a nervous play of features. He muttered, "Old furniture—drawers always getting stuck. If it weren't for sentimental reasons I'd get rid of it. My father—" He coughed. "Sit down, Lieutenant. I was just about to go to lunch, but I can give you a few minutes." He said it as though even the mention of lunch soured his stomach, and he looked as though his visitor was not improving the situation. "You aren't the man I spoke to at the theater last night. I've forgotten his name, but—did they take him off the case?"

"I'm from Homicide," Nelson said. He lowered himself to a chair near the desk. "There are a few matters you might be able to throw light on—"

"I doubt it. I'm in complete darkness myself." Seager's voice shook. "All I ask is to be allowed to forget—"

"I realize you're under a strain—"

"Strain? I haven't slept a wink—or been able to swallow a—" Then he said, "Excuse me. I'll try to cooperate."

"Do you know if Drake ever consulted a psychiatrist?"

Seager said bitterly, "So that's the angle. Because he's important, the good old insanity plea—"

"We haven't progressed that far. Did he consult a psychiatrist?"

"Not to my knowledge."

"Then give me the name of his doctor. He probably has a good one who'll know something of how his mind works."

"I don't see—well—" He supplied the doctor's name.

"How long have you been engaged to Toni George?" At Seager's grimace he said, "Whatever I ask you won't be prompted by common garden curiosity, Mr. Seager."

"I know. I know. I asked her to marry me three months ago, and she accepted. Please understand that I'm not the sort of man who chases after chorus girls. I happened to meet Toni about six months ago when I went to the theater with an out-of-town client. He had a date with one of the girls in the show and she brought Toni along. I fell in love with her—much against my better judgment. I thought she was sweet and unspoiled and would make a fine wife and mother.

And she never gave me any reason to believe that I was mistaken until Drake began to— Oh, what's the use? I want to believe in her. I want to keep her memory unsullied because there's nothing else left me—but it's hard. I can't reconcile the girl who went to Chilton with the girl I knew. Why did she go? What could have prompted her? If she had told me outright that she preferred—that she no longer—I wouldn't have tried to hold her—I—"

Nelson checked him. "You were there the night Drake sent her the bracelet?"

"Yes—yes, I was. It made me sick. I wanted to terminate connections with Drake, but Toni wouldn't have it. She promised to return his gifts—"

"Gifts?"

"He'd been sending candy and flowers regularly."

"But no other jewelry?"

"Not that I was aware of. Do you mean she'd been concealing—"

Nelson shook his head. "I wondered if anything had come with the bracelet—some matching piece—a brooch, perhaps."

Seager looked puzzled. "I don't understand. Wasn't the bracelet enough? When she opened the box it shone like a beacon—flashy and in poor taste—but more valuable than anything I could run to." He added hastily with what might have been pride, "And I'm not a poor man by any means."

"You're from Chilton too, aren't you?"

"Yes, I'm from Chilton. I haven't lived there for several years, barring a few weeks at a time now and again when my father was alive. The house has been closed since he died."

"I know. I went there last night."

"To my house?"

"Yes. One of the men had a theory that Toni George might have headed for it to escape Drake's clutches."

"Toni in my house? No—no—ridiculous—unfounded. She didn't know where it was. She'd never been there." He pressed a hand to his head. "I kept planning to take her, but something always interfered." Again his voice shook. "That's my fate—to have my plans interfered with—"

He seemed so close to the rim of hysteria that Nelson introduced a practical device to draw him back. "By the way, when you closed the house you neglected to have your telephone service discontinued— or the telephone company neglected to carry out your order."

Seager said dully, "That last is what happened."

"What I'd started to say was that since you were brought up in Chilton you must have known Drake a long time. Is it your opinion that he's capable of murder?"

"No—but my opinion doesn't count. I've been wrong all along the line." He got up from behind the desk. He went to the water cooler. He stood drinking with his back to Nelson. Water slapped the floor.

Nelson leaned over and peered into the half-opened bottom drawer. Unconsciously he was actuated by the same impulse that had led Pierce to study Toni's picture on Drake's bureau, the seeking of some clue that only she could provide. For he was certain that the frame which Seager had removed from his desk contained her picture. People reacted to bereavement in strange and different ways, he thought. He could not imagine himself disposing of a loved one's picture under any circumstances.

He straightened as Seager turned from the water cooler. "I won't keep you any longer. If anything else occurs to me I'll come back."

Seager said, "There's been nothing accomplished so far—no trace of Drake—not even a lead?" He answered himself: "No—and I don't wonder—not if your men get brain waves about finding poor Toni in my house."

Nelson said reasonably, "We didn't know that it was closed or that she'd never been there."

"Of course, I realize that—I don't mean to criticize. I know you'll do all you can."

On that note Nelson left, pausing for a few words with the receptionist on his way out. Yes, she knew Mr. Drake. He had visited the office only a few days ago. No, she did not think he was capable of murder....

He made for the wheel of his car, thinking that for choice he would take Pierce Kirby's response to tragedy. Pierce at least wanted to do something about it even if it meant wearing himself out in the process, while Seager seemed capable only of sitting back and wearing himself out with self-pity. No one could say he was not making a thorough job of it. Nelson did not know what Seager was like normally, and so he had no basis for comparison. But right now he could not help wondering why a beautiful young girl had chosen him as the object of her affections. He grinned crookedly. He would have to make a more thorough study of the man. Snap judgments were unfair.

He parked the car on a side street and went in search of a restaurant. He made an unfortunate selection, and while he was eating he thought of Furniss and wished he could hear that epicure's fruity comments about the food. Amusement value aside, it would have been helpful to run through the case with Furniss, who was a friend as well as a superior officer and who could be counted upon for good horse sense and for his knack of arousing it in others. You're on your own now, Nelson told Nelson, so dry your pretty eyes and get going.

He arrived in Chilton at a few minutes past four. There were no signs of activity as he turned into the driveway of the Drake house, but as soon as he left the car a woman hurried out of the caretaker's cottage. She did not appear to notice him. She made a beeline for the garage. He followed slowly. He found her a short distance from the side of the two-story building. She was busily removing washing from a clothesline. Not a family wash, he observed. Just a few intimate flimsies. They had a homemade look.

"Mrs. Foster?"

"Yes?" She blasted it at him. She had the proportions of an Amazon, topped with a cheap assembly-line face. "Got to get this washing in. I think it's going to rain."

Automatically Nelson glanced at the sky. "I don't think so. My name is Nelson—Homicide." He almost added, "I'm a family man, so you needn't be embarrassed about that stuff you're trying to hide."

"Following me all over the place," she said. "What do you want? My husband and I gave our statements to Chief Maddox."

"I know. I'm working with him. I'd like to have you tell me what you told Chief Maddox, and anything else that might have occurred to you since."

"Nothing has occurred to me." She wore a large apron over her very large curves. She was stuffing the underwear into its pockets as she walked away from the garage. She did not look like a woman who enjoyed wearing an apron, nor did she look modest. Brash was the adjective he fitted to her. He would not have been surprised to find sequins under the apron. Her hair and her mouth and her fingernails were too red, and she exuded a rather strong odor that was not all cheap perfume. She said in her too loud voice, "I don't see why I have to go over it again." They had reached the door of the cottage. "I'm busy."

"Sometimes under the stress of circumstances important facts slip one's mind. Surely you must have been thinking a great deal about Mr. Drake since last night—"

"My husband and I work for him. That doesn't mean we have to think about him." Her eyes were on the cottage door. "Anyway, how do I know what your real business is?" She turned to appraise him, giving peculiar attention to detail.

He could not help grinning. It struck him that now he knew how a maiden felt when pawed by the gaze of a libertine. He did not produce his credentials. "If you phone Chief Maddox he'll vouch for me. I want to talk to him anyway." He was curious to see the inside of the cottage, to discover what sort of background she had created for little Foster.

"Never mind. I guess you're what you say you are. You can't blame me for being suspicious, though." She sounded slightly less aggressive. "You certainly don't look like any policeman I've ever seen—and what with all the reporters and other nuisances who've been here today—"

"Didn't Chief Maddox leave one of his men here to deal with them?"

"He left some unhatched kid and called him off early this morning. The Chilton Businessmen's Club is having its annual doings today—and Miggs Cove is being dragged, besides. I guess the chief needs all of his force on tap. Besides, it wasn't necessary to leave anyone here. We're around. No one gets past us."

Nelson said, "Of course. I should have had your husband come out to identify me. I met him last night."

"He's gone to town to do some shopping. Look—here's what I know—and I hope it's the last time I'm asked to repeat it." She told her story rapidly. Except for the scream she had heard, it was the same as Foster's story.

"You're sure the girl did scream—sure you weren't having a nightmare?"

"I'm sure all right. I don't see why it's so hard for everyone to swallow. She's gone, isn't she?"

Nelson was chilly. He turned up his coat collar. Mrs. Foster wore no coat, but she did not seem to feel the cold. And no wonder, he thought. Cold was her own atmosphere. She generated it. He said deliberately, "What's hard to swallow is that one woman could hear another scream and not go to her aid."

"Well—you know how it is." She was far from being abashed. "It happened suddenly and stopped suddenly—and what could *I* do about it?"

Fragile little old you, he thought.

"I did think of waking my husband, but he's not exactly lionhearted. Maybe if he had a build like yours—" Her light blue eyes were like two busy hands. "Well—first thing I'd fallen asleep again."

"How long have you worked for Mr. Drake?"

"Since I married Fostie. That'll be three years in April." She did not sound as though she thought it three years well spent. "Fostie's been with him at least ten."

"Then he probably knows him better than you do. Your statements seem to disagree on certain points."

"How do you mean?"

"Your husband gives the impression that Mr. Drake is usually a mild-tempered man."

"Mild-tempered my—" She smiled unpleasantly. "I've seen that high-toned jerk so mad he'd pick up the nearest thing and fling it at you. Believe me, mister, I'd be glad to make book on that scream I heard being the last of its kind. I didn't need even three weeks to see what Drake was like under his fake manners."

"What did you do before you were married, Mrs. Foster?"

"That's kind of nosy."

"I was wondering what had made you such an astute judge of character."

She studied his grave face. "Yeah? Well—I was a professional—on the stage. Sure, I've knocked around enough to know the score. I guess that's why this kind of life looked good to me for a while."

"Doesn't it look good to you now?"

"Sure—swell. Fostie's okay as husbands go—and I ought to know. He's strictly a small-change man—needs a shove once in a while— but—" She broke off. "Say—beat it, will you? I got work—"

"What did you do on the stage?"

"Anything I could get. Satisfied?"

He was not satisfied, but he had work to do too. He bade her a rather tentative goodbye.

CHAPTER TEN

The disappearance of Robert "Bobby" Kenmore Drake, socialite, suspected of foul play in connection with Toni George, showgirl, occupied major space in all of the New York newspapers. Even the country's outstanding conservative sheet gave it sedate play, and one sensational tabloid went so far as to take the President of the United States to task, hinting that such a thing could never have happened under a Republican regime. Leading radio commentators evidenced, according to their lights, shocked surprise at the little playboy's breaking of the rules, or contempt for a system which condoned such parasites. A Russian publication gave the incident a contemptuous nod in a paragraph headed "Capitalism Is Death." Television devoted a whole quiz program to the puzzle. But neither the newspapers nor the radio nor Russia nor television nor the police succeeded in bringing Bobby Drake to book or in discovering the remains of Toni George.

Pierce, increasingly frustrated as the days passed, performed the motions of his normal existence as well as he could. But he felt close to reality only when he haunted the Corridor Theater or when he was badgering Lieutenant Gridley Nelson.

For the most part, Nelson accepted the badgering calmly. Apparently the nature of his job had created in him a special immunity. This was fortunate, since he was being criticized on all sides. The press, which had never seemed overly appreciative of his absent chief, now so openly yearned for the old man's return that the commissioner felt called upon to issue a statement citing Nelson's past record. But the intention of the statement backfired, serving only to emphasize present failure. It was not surprising that Nelson accepted and even seemed to welcome the ubiquitous Pierce, recognizing the validity of his interest, his right to question. In fact, he sometimes wished that Pierce had official standing so that he might give him full confidence.

As it was, Pierce learned before the papers did that Jill Batiste had identified the scarf found near the water as Toni's and that its stains matched the blood group supplied by Toni's doctor. After that, all other information seemed extraneous. In the face of such indisputable testimony to crime how could it matter that the cove had yielded nothing, that the body had not been washed ashore, that the bed linen subjected to serology tests had shown evidence of human contact that checked with experiments on a piece of Toni's abandoned clothing?

This latter fact had been played down by most of the reporters. They had elevated Toni to saint's status and obviously did not want to eat their words. So they glossed over her seeming lapse with the theory that Drake had carried her to the bed after she was unconscious. They explained the absence of blood on the linen by stating that Drake had knocked her out first and wounded her later. The more they blackened Drake, the more they kept their heroine's virtue unassailed.

The articles missing from Drake's wardrobe had cast no light upon a possible destination. But it was made public that his bank had converted certain of his securities into a cash sum amounting to five hundred thousand dollars. The bank official said that Drake had been quite mysterious as to what he intended to do with that princely sum, and of course the official had not felt free to press him, had simply delivered it into his hands. Nor could Seager, his lawyer, give any information about the transaction. His former client, he said stiffly, had not seen fit to mention it to him.

But what did it all matter? thought Pierce. Toni George was dead, and Bobby Drake had fled to parts unknown. The important thing was to find Drake, to take the straightest possible road toward that end without stopping for piddling research into the whys and wherefores. Find Drake. Find Drake. Find Drake. He wanted to shout it from the rooftops. He wanted to tour the country on foot, sniffing at every inch of ground along the way until he came upon the quarry. As time passed, tormented by his inadequacy, by primitive instincts that could find no outlet, he lost more weight. He was a sick young man.

The affair of Toni George had revived the "lesser matter" of Uncle Doc. His picture, which some enterprising reporter had prized from the hometown, appeared one day with the picture of Toni George which some other enterprising reporter had managed to steal from Drake's bureau in Chilton.

Pierce all but wept at the incongruity of the juxtaposed faces, at a society whose balance was so askew that it demanded the sensational in order to accord even passing notice to such a man as Uncle Doc had been. It was not a recent picture. He had probably been photographed no more than once in his adult life. It showed a much younger man than the one who had come to visit Pierce in New York. The mouth and chin were firm. The eyes held clarity and wisdom and encouragement for all who cared to meet them. As Pierce stared, his own blurred eyes cleared and the incongruity faded. Uncle Doc and Toni, unknown to each other in life, and now placed side by side, seemed joined beyond the mechanical offices of the paper which featured them. Pierce nodded his head, as though agreeing with a thesis offered by his innermost self. He was certain that one murderer was responsible for both tragedies. Find Drake. Find Drake!

Notable among the by-products of the crime was the boom in *Sea Change*. It no longer needed a press agent, nor even competent performers. People thronged the theater not to see the show but to enjoy the pleasurable chill of speculation on its connection with sudden death. A fashionable game had been launched in which a member of the audience would tug at a companion and whisper, "I've got it—that man doing the monologue—notice the sinister expression? He's mixed up in it—I just know it." Or, "I'll lay odds on the dancer—with that mouth she's at least an accessory. She knows where Drake is hiding."

An acquaintance who had overheard a similar exchange gave Pierce an account of it and Pierce almost threw up. Yet it did not seem more farfetched than his own conviction that Drake had killed Uncle Doc. He thought of possible reasons that Drake might have for doing away with the old man. He could arrive at nothing better than that he had, Steve to the contrary, come back to the theater that night, discussed his plans for Toni with someone, caught Uncle Doc listening, and killed him to prevent interference. Pierce did not pass this bit of conjecture along to Nelson. What good would it do? Everybody in the cast had been questioned, and none had so much as hinted at such a conversation with Drake. Find him. Find him!

In the beginning, Ginette Arthur had refused a "run-of-the-play" contract, and the producers, glad to have her on any terms, had agreed to a "suitable-replacement" clause. She took advantage of the clause, and the producers, drunk with the new cards dealt by providence, allowed her more than the usual leeway. A week after Pierce's drive to Chilton she made an unobtrusive exit from the show, and her understudy stepped into the role. The audience did not comment upon the switch. It is doubtful if they noticed it. Nor did it receive much publicity. One columnist intimated that there was more to the move than met the eye, but none of his colleagues took up the ball. Ginette Arthur was popular with the press. They seemed willing to accept her withdrawal from *Sea Change* on the grounds that she had signed for a new and more serious play and wanted a rest before it went into rehearsal.

Pierce made no further attempt to seek her out. Aside from the doubts he so stubbornly cherished, he felt that he had nothing to offer her and would have nothing until in some way he was free of his constant preoccupation. And his frame of mind was such that he believed he would never be free of it. At least that was the way he rationalized his fear of reaching for undeserved happiness, of being totally disarmed by her propinquity. He had embarked upon an endless circular journey.

On a Sunday, a few days after Uncle Doc's picture had appeared with Toni's, Pierce, sitting in his apartment, heard the confident ring of the bell downstairs. He pressed the buzzer that released the mechanism and immediately wished that he had ignored the ring. He did not want callers. He was unshaven. He was in bathrobe and slippers, and although it was past noon he had not breakfasted. When he heard the elevator stop at his floor he decided to lie low. But his visitor was persistent, and finally he opened to him.

Nelson said, "If you're hiding out you shouldn't have answered in the first place."

"I answered before I thought. I had no idea it would be you." He felt a sudden spurt of hope. "Is there—"

"No—no news. I've missed your nuisance value these last few days, so I thought I'd look you up."

"Come in."

Nelson followed him to the living room, saw the accumulated stack of papers on the floor, the page bearing the odd mating uppermost. "I'm sorry about that," he said.

It struck Pierce that he had come merely because he was sorry about that. "Sit down. It doesn't matter—not more than anything else. Uncle Doc would probably have laughed like hell."

Nelson stood, taking him in. "It wouldn't do you any harm to laugh like hell. When did you eat last?"

"I was just about to—to think about coffee."

"Coffee? Breakfast coffee? My own mind was fixed on lunch. I know a good restaurant near here—"

Pierce shook his tousled head. "Not me—but thanks." Then he said, "I'm a rotten host. The maid who cleans for me keeps eggs and stuff in the refrigerator. If you can do with that I'll get a meal together for you."

"Don't bother. It will be ready by the time you've shaved."

"Well, you couldn't do a worse job than I do."

When he came out of the bathroom, groomed and dressed, breakfast was ready. The kitchen table had been set, the coffee was drinkable, the toast unburned, and the eggs of a decent consistency.

Pierce ate and drank. "You give me that cared-for feeling," he said dryly.

Nelson grinned. "It took me a long time to achieve this state of perfection. If my teacher hadn't been an expert you'd be toying with slops."

"You're a damn funny policeman."

"So they've been saying lately."

"I didn't mean it that way. I don't suppose anyone else could do more than you've done."

"Thanks."

Pierce looked at him and saw a reflection of his own depression in the deep-set brown eyes. He said awkwardly, "I hadn't thought much about your side of it."

Nelson placed a cigarette between his lips. He got up and began to pile the dishes in the sink. "Even as a rookie I never counted on it being all flags and glory. I've had times like this before and will again." He ran the tap water over the dishes.

"Don't do that. The maid will take care of it in the morning."

"I'm just rinsing them."

"Has the public griped as much as this in other cases?"

Nelson came back to the table. "My chief usually bears the brunt when he's around because he's a more colorful character. But I don't mind the gripes."

"You mind something."

"I mind murderers running around loose. I always have."

Pierce nodded in heartfelt understanding. They smoked in silence for a few moments. Pierce said, "I don't remember sitting in this kitchen before. It's not bad."

"I think that's the healthiest remark I've ever heard you make."

"I feel a little healthier for some reason."

"You should eat oftener."

"Maybe. Tell me—have you ever had another case—you personally, I mean—where you didn't find the murderer?"

Nelson sighed. "I thought we were going to forget it for a while. I thought we were going to have a really healthy conversation. Yes, I've had unsolved cases."

"You think that this one—"

"No." His tone held conviction. "This one will be solved."

"But why? Unless you've been holding out—"

"I'm hopeful because the unsolved murders were of the simpler variety. Their perpetrators weren't trying to be clever. It's the extra touches—the tendency not to let well enough alone—that give a murderer away. Things like—"

"You're not going to start on the printless car and the made-up bed routine again—"

"All right. I'm not."

"Those letters you spoke of—nothing there?"

More than the usual flow of crank mail had flooded the department. People had seen Drake as far away as California and as near as Brooklyn. They had run across him in every city on almost every street. They had caught glimpses of him in Canada. They had seen him wearing dungarees. They had seen him in tails. They had seen him afoot. They had seen him in cars. They had met him on boats and trains and planes. He had carried an ax. He had been burdened with a bag from which blood seeped. According to their letters, he had frequented hobo jungles and grand hotels at one and the same time.

Nelson said, "All of those that just barely cleared the lunatic fringe were followed up. Two of the more lucid ones came from Chilton, but they were dead ends too. One was from an old and sociable lady with time on her hands—the other from a little boy with a highly developed sense of drama. Speaking of Chilton, I discovered a back road that—"

"You seem to be hanging around there a lot. I don't see anything to be gained by—" He broke off. "Now who the hell can that be?"

The downstairs bell was ringing. Nelson unwound his legs from the legs of the kitchen chair. He looked at his watch and said as though remembering an engagement, "I'll be on my way."

"Stick around. I'm not expecting anyone, if you're trying to be tactful. I'm not even home."

"You're not," Nelson said, appraising him again, "but you should be. If you don't watch it, Kirby, you'll find yourself saddled with an obsession you'll never be able to shake. Go on, answer the bell. It might be important."

"What's important?"

"Anything's important that will give you a breathing spell." Nelson sounded impatient. And that was phenomenon enough to send Pierce out of the kitchen.

He pressed the buzzer. When he opened the door and saw the girl, his vision tricked him. But it was not Ginette.

After a moment he said, "Stasia."

She wore no hat. She was prodding the tendrils of her red hair into place. "You scared me. I thought you weren't going to come through with my name. You had 'the-face-is-familiar-but' expression."

"Is anything wrong?"

"Wrong? Not yet. I haven't got past the door yet—but I'm hoping."

"I'm sorry. Come in."

"Well, if you insist. I'm not intruding, am I?" She crossed the threshold, linked her arm in his, tugging him toward the living room.

"I didn't know you had my address," he said foolishly.

"I got it in the most unorthodox way—looked in the telephone book, and there it was just as plain—"

He laughed. "I'm honored, Stasia, but—"

"Are you? I'd never have guessed." She stood in the doorway of the living room, her arm still linked in his. "Nice place you have—so free of the woman's touch. Don't you want to take my coat?"

He took it. He seated her. She opened a cigarette box on the table near her chair. It was empty. He gave her a cigarette, lit it, and watched her drag on it. Then she threw back her head and bared her perfect teeth to a gust of laughter. "I can't help it," she said. "You should see your face. Okay—I'll tell you why I came—partly—and maybe I'll tell you the rest of it later. It's Sunday afternoon—see? And it suddenly begins to smell like spring outside—and I'm lonely— and naturally I thought of you."

"Naturally. Now what's the rest of it?"

"Not so fast. I want to be plied with liquor first. Jill told me you bought her a dinner once. I don't see why I'm not worth similar courtesies." Her face soured. "Not that I'm the type to cut in on a pal's time—especially when the pal can't—" She turned her head. "For Pete's sake, why didn't you say you had company?"

Nelson had entered the room from the foyer off the kitchen. "Hello— I'm not company—just kitchen help."

Her eyes, tinged with the russet color of her hair, widened. "I know exactly who you are."

"Miss Phillips—Lieutenant Nelson," Pierce said.

"I'm discriminated against everywhere I turn, Lieutenant," Stasia said. "How come when I was questioned about Toni I drew a lunkhead who really looked like a comic-strip policeman?" The flippancy fell flat. She started to rise. "I only dropped in for a moment—"

"Didn't I hear a drink mentioned?" Nelson asked.

"It depends on how long you were standing there. Have you come to arrest my host? Is that why he looks so puny?"

"A purely social visit," Nelson said. He walked over to the portable bar. He glanced at Pierce.

"I'll get some ice," Pierce said, and started for the kitchen. "Don't go, Stasia."

She was there when he came back with the ice cubes. She did not look too pleased about it, but she was there, making very small talk with Nelson. "When I came in," she was saying, "he made like a goosed hermit. He might never have seen anything but trousers in the whole of his natural life."

Pierce said, "I always react that way to the unexpected—even when it's delicious." He gave the ice tray to Nelson. "I'm slow on the uptake. It used to worry my teachers."

"I'll bet. Honest, boys, I was passing, so I thought I'd drop in—I'd only planned to say hello and—"

Nelson fitted a glass into her hand.

"Well …" She glanced at each of them in turn. She settled back in her chair. "Here's looking at you—and I must say it's a nice change after the mixed ladies of the ensemble. You're both fine men I wouldn't be ashamed to be seen with in public or private." She tasted her drink. "Mmm—good."

"Do you live near here, Miss Phillips?"

"Not what you could call living, Lieutenant."

"You're still sharing the apartment with Jill, aren't you?" Pierce said.

"Not what you could call sharing." She finished her drink. Nelson refilled her glass. She said, "Thanks, you've a deft hand with the rum, Lieutenant." She slanted her russet eyes up at him. "Is this really a social visit?"

"Of course. Do you think I'm wearing out my welcome?"

"No, but I'd counted on finding Master Kirby alone. Anyway, I hadn't counted on his being thick with the police."

Pierce said, "Could it be that you're the one not making a social visit?" His pulse quickened. "Is it something you found out about Toni?"

She shook her head with vigor and immediately went to work on the slight disorder created by the movement. Pierce wanted to tear her hands from the red curls. She said, "Not about Toni—post-Toni. Nothing criminal—only sick-making. I'm supposed to be the selfish one—but believe me! I'm up to here with it. I had to shoot my mouth off to someone or bust, and I chose you because you belong to the family." She gestured with her glass in Nelson's direction. "But *he* is as outside the family as anyone can get."

"If you have something you want to tell Pierce in confidence, I'll leave," Nelson said.

She looked at him crossly. "Don't get wrong ideas. It isn't up your alley."

"Well, then—if the law isn't involved—"

"The law? That's a laugh. Tack a syllable to law and you'll have something—at least Jill must think he's something. Nope, the beef's strictly personal—not your dish at all. Jill had a kind of a thing for Pierce. That's really why he rates a slice. Just for spite I want him to know what type has a thing for him."

Pierce said, "I don't get it."

"Honest, I don't either. I purely don't. Toni was her best friend—"

"Jill and Seager? Is that what you're saying?"

She focused on her empty glass. "Did I say it? Oh well—once a bitch, always a bitch, I guess. But at least I'm sincere. And she had the nerve to lay me out because once I wouldn't let Toni borrow a new evening wrap for some clambake he was taking her to—"

They had both forgotten Nelson. Pierce said, "But Jill doesn't like Seager. She thought Toni was a fool for wanting to marry him. She told me so herself. She called him a stuffed shirt."

"Sure. She told me the same—and what's more, I believed it too—so you aren't the only bunny on the block. But it turns out to have been a carload of sour grapes. Coming at her, it gets sweet all of a sudden. You'd never suspect she cried her face raw the night Toni bowed out. I hate hypocrites—I could spit."

"How long has she been seeing him?"

"How should I know? I found out Thursday—by accident. I had a date after the show, but he was full of paws and not to my taste, so I shook him and went home and made myself comfortable. And who walks in but Jill and Seager. Did they get red. They didn't even stop to take in my negligee. It was the quickest vanishing act in history."

"Maybe there's some explanation?"

"Yeah? I asked for it and all I got was a 'mind your business.' That's explanation enough for me. If she has nothing to hide why is she hiding it? I haven't spoken to her since. Anybody but Jill, and I wouldn't bat an eyelash. Even if she'd waited a decent length of time I'd say okay—because you've got to be realistic about those things— but with the body not even turning up to be nailed down—" She paused, as though to review the words she had just spoken. She looked surprised. "Mix another shakerful, Lieutenant. Damn it—I need a few."

She had said what she had come to say. The remainder of her visit was dedicated to variations of the theme. But no new chords were struck. An hour later Pierce took her home to Fifty-second Street, helped her up three stiff flights of stairs into a living room with lighting effects supplied by a neon sign across the way, and left as soon as he could without damaging her ego. But it was not soon enough. His feelings were mixed as he descended the stairs. He felt better and he felt worse.

He heard music as he unlocked his door and for a moment thought he was in the wrong apartment. He had not expected Nelson to wait until his return. But Nelson had revitalized the long-silent gramophone and was sitting back in a chair listening to a Mahler recording of *"La Cathédrale."*

Nelson's attitude of relaxation irritated Pierce. "Well?" he said rudely.

"Hold it, will you?"

Pierce held it. When the record was finished he turned the gramophone off.

"You have a good selection," Nelson said.

"Listen any time you like—but not now."

"Why not now? Music can be very helpful."

"Would you like me to go out and buy you a violin and a deerstalker? What did you make of Stasia?"

"I deduced you wouldn't be back so soon."

"I have no sense of humor," Pierce said. "Let's start again. What—"

"Was Jill at home?"

"No, she wasn't. Look—"

"I'll have to know a lot more about Jill before I make anything of Stasia." He added, "Seager did mention in passing that it wasn't his habit to chase after chorus girls—Toni George being the exception."

"Find out what it means, then."

"I'll try. Every little bit helps—the bed linen—the heart-shaped pin—the—"

Pierce twisted the knob of the gramophone savagely. "You might as well listen to music," he muttered.

CHAPTER ELEVEN

Pierce went to his office early the next day. He was determined that he would not call to see if Nelson had got to the bottom of the Jill-Seager combine until he had caught up with his work. He had been struggling along at a rate that was becoming increasingly unfair to his partner, and he felt that either he must take hold again or bow out entirely. Strangely enough, the idea of bowing out was more sour to him than it would have been a month ago. He worked feverishly for a while, enjoying it in spite of himself, managing to forget everything but the release he was writing. When he looked it over it was not bad. It had a completeness about it, a good rounded flavor. He spotted an error and went to Marc's desk to search for an eraser. He picked up an unfamiliar manuscript and opened it to the first page. His interest caught, he began to read. It was Ginette Arthur's new vehicle. It was good. It was something a man would not be ashamed to publicize. His mind began to teem with ideas.

He was still reading when Marc came in. "Hi, Pierce." He was a heavyset young man with a deceptively lethargic face. "Sorry to keep banker's hours. I had to see—"

"I know. You've been having to do everything around here. Say— this is the real thing." He put the manuscript down.

Marc whistled with relief. "You're going to tackle it?"

"You bet."

"That's the old fight. I've been trying—but what I turned out was damn dull. The play went into rehearsal Friday—"

"Don't worry. I'll have something cooked up by Wednesday at the latest."

"Boy, if I were as creative as you—"

"Me creative?"

"Are you kidding? Haven't you heard the rumors? You're getting the Lansing Prize for that doorman story—which means a reprint in *Zest* with your by-line and—"

"Marc, wait till Uncle Doc hears—" His smiling mouth twisted. "Oh hell—hell—"

Marc said understandingly, "No break on that yet?"

Pierce shook his head. Listlessly he tackled the work on his desk again. There was no joy in it.

At one o'clock Marc went to an appointment. Pierce sat on. After a while he called Nelson. He did not succeed in reaching him, nor could the answering voice be persuaded to hint at his whereabouts. Pierce was enjoined to leave a message, but he had no message to leave. Angrily he doubted that Nelson had done anything at all about Jill and Seager. He was probably wasting valuable time hanging around Chilton. Pierce played with the idea of going to Chilton and prying him loose from the incomprehensible magnetism that it seemed to exert for him. He tossed the idea aside. Nelson might be unwilling to be pried loose, or he might not be there at all. At three o'clock he decided that there was nothing to prevent him from drawing his own firsthand conclusions about Jill and Seager.

He looked up the numbers and called Jill's apartment. No one answered. He had better luck with Seager. At least he spoke to Seager, putting on a phony cordial accent.

"Hello—this is Pierce Kirby. I'm in your neighborhood and—" It was a lame start. He improvised rapidly, "I need some legal advice and I thought I'd consult you—"

"Pierce Kirby?" Obviously the name held no charm for Seager.

"Yes—press agent for *Sea Change*. I was with you when—"

Seager did not allow him to get any further. "I remember you—of course. I'll be glad to recommend another firm if you like. There's nothing personal in this, but I'd as soon not be reminded of the circumstances under which we met."

Pierce muttered nastily, "Rumor has it that you're being reminded constantly."

"I beg your pardon? About that legal matter, you might try Forbes, Henderson, Satterlee, and Hitzig. They're very sound. Now if you'll excuse me, I have a client waiting." He hung up.

Pierce banged his receiver back into place. That's what comes of using roundabout methods, he thought. I should just have dropped in on him and asked him if Jill was another exception to his rule of not chasing after chorus girls. Well, who's to stop me? He flung himself into his topcoat.

Spring had invaded the February day. It invaded him too. Unconsciously he straightened his shoulders. In the act of hailing a cab he changed his mind and walked to Seager's business address.

Just as he entered the lobby of the office building Seager stepped out of an elevator. He was conversing with a tall, thin, elderly man. All tall, thin, elderly men reminded Pierce of Uncle Doc. Perhaps that was why he did not interrupt the conversation, or perhaps it was because the change in Seager's appearance shocked him. All the cockiness and confidence seemed to have deserted the stocky lawyer. It was difficult to believe that he had taken a new lease on life by way of a romantic alliance with Jill.

Sheepishly Pierce ducked behind a pillar, stepping on the toe of a nondescript man who gave him an offended stare. Nelson was right, he thought. He did not have the temperament for detective work.

Within the next few minutes he was given a second chance to prove or disprove it. Having allowed sufficient time for Seager and his client to be well away, he went out into the springlike air. And as though she were a reward of virtue, Jill Batiste came walking down the street. He stretched his legs, meeting her halfway.

"Hello, Jill."

She did not turn pale because she was pale, but she exhibited no pleasure at the unexpected encounter. "Hello."

"Going my way?"

"No—I—"

He took her arm. "You might as well be. Let's have a drink."

"Thanks." Her eyes went past him to the office building. "Another time. I have to run now."

"You weren't so hard to get last time we met, Jill." Baiting her was no more fun than stalking a sick puppy. Murder was like radioactivity, he thought. The blight lingered and spread long after the explosion. Himself. Seager. Jill. He hardened, thinking of why he had wanted to see her. He said, "Seager's left. I saw him go out."

"What are you talking about?"

"You were on the way to his office, weren't you?"

"Suppose I was. Do you have to make everything your business? All right—give this one to one of your fine-feathered columnists. I'll even word it for you. 'What chick horned in on what vanishing sidekick to form a new twosome?'" Then she began to cry, the tears flowing freely right there in the open for all to see.

The detective in Pierce bolted. He panicked. "Use your handkerchief. Do something—stop it—" He glanced wildly to either side of him, seeking cover. He saw a luncheonette sign and steered her toward it. She went with him blindly, sniffling, wiping her eyes with the sleeve of her coat.

He thrust her through a door and sat her down at a marble-topped table. He extended his own handkerchief, relieved that they were the only customers in the bathroom-tiled interior, and annoyed because both the counterman and the lone waitress appeared to be cynical students of human nature.

Jill blew her nose. She searched in her pocketbook for the tools of restoration. She gave him a quivering little smile.

"Sorry, fellow. Everything's under control now. Nice place you've picked. Just tell the *maître* not to over-ice the champagne."

"You should have had your fit in front of the Waldorf. What's it all about, Jill?"

"That's what I'd like to know."

To the approaching waitress he called, "Coffee—hamburgers—anything."

"Just coffee for me," Jill said.

"No, you'd better eat. You can stand it."

"Listen to Mother. Have you looked in your own mirror lately?"

"I enjoy small talk, Jill, but this isn't the place for it."

"This isn't the place for anything. How did you manage to contrive our rendezvous? You *must* be hard up for news."

"I'm not on that business at the moment."

"A likely story. What business are you on—cops and robbers?"

"Jill, I didn't contrive this meeting, but I did want to see you."

"You're turning my head. Ah—coffee." She sipped it. "Well—anyway, it comes in a coffee cup."

He leaned across the table. He wanted to shake her. "When did you decide that Seager wasn't a stuffed shirt?"

"Who says I decided it?"

"Never mind."

"I won't if you don't." She bit into a hamburger. She chewed away, eying him defiantly.

"Jill!"

"A lady can't talk with her mouth full." She filled it again.

"I'll wait," Pierce said. He thought of Nelson and tried to emulate his patience. "Damn it—if you stuff yourself with every hamburger in the joint I'll still be waiting."

"Perish the thought." She set the half-eaten roll in the center of her plate. "I think I'm going to be sick."

"No, you don't—"

"Hold the thought. Make me believe it." She swallowed. She sat back with her eyes closed. Her long blond lashes gave her face a babyish, defenseless look.

"You ought to leave the chorus and get an act of your own."

Her eyes still closed, she said, "I'll settle for a glass of water."

The waitress had disappeared. A third customer had entered, a shopper who deposited herself and her bundles at a table near the door.

Pierce lowered his voice. "Sure—I go to the counter for water and you skip. You'll have to think of a newer gag."

"Don't use that word—please."

He stared at her. He went to the counter and came back with a glass of water. She drank some of it.

"Feeling better?" he said uncertainly.

"A little. I want to go home."

"You're not popular at home."

"Oh—so it was Stasia who spilled the beans," she said, "high-minded pal Stasia."

"What difference does it make who told me?"

"Get me out of here. I need air." She was not fooling. Her battle with the hamburger had displaced her lip rouge, revealing a blue-white tinge. She swayed as she stood up. Pierce left his chair to steady her. He put some money on the table. He supported her to the door.

Outside, she leaned against him. "I do feel rotten, Pierce."

"I'll get a cab. Will you wait here? I'll stand more chance if I go to the corner."

She nodded.

It took him several minutes to find an empty cab. He got in and returned to the luncheonette. Jill was not standing where he had left her. He told the driver to wait and dashed inside. The woman shopper was still there. The waitress was mopping up the table he and Jill had vacated. He went up to her. "That girl I was with—did you happen to see which way—"

The waitress gave him a malevolent stare. "So you had a change of heart—pussyfooting back—maybe to make more trouble for her." She gestured toward the counterman. "Nicky and I seen she was crying when she came in—and then he seen you leave her on the doorstep, so he called me and we stood watching because we didn't like how she looked. So sure enough, she starts to fall over and we haul her in before she draws a crowd."

Pierce said stupidly, "She's here?"

"Laying down in the back. I wanted to call an ambulance on account of she's out like a light—and don't tell me that don't mean what I think it means even if it isn't showing yet."

Pierce looked nervously toward the woman customer, who appeared to be minding her own business.

"But she come to right away and says she'll be okay if I let her rest a couple of minutes," the waitress said, "which suits me. If an ambulance pulls up some louse is sure to crack it's the food—"

Jill came out of the back room. "I'm all right—I—"

The waitress turned. "You bet you are, honey. Look who's here.

See—you don't have to worry anymore."

"I'm sorry, Pierce. I don't know what happened to me."

"Come on, kid," Pierce said. "I've a cab waiting." He put an arm around her. With his free hand he rooted in his pocket.

"That's the way it should be," the waitress said. "I don't want your money. Just you be nice to her. Well—all right."

Jill said a meek "Thank you very much." But when they reached the cab she began to giggle. "Oh, Pierce, you *will* make an honest woman of me? Promise?"

"Can't." He helped her into the cab. "Maybe I should have told you about my wives." He gave his own address to the driver, got in, and closed the door.

"Hey," Jill said, "I want to go home. Tell him—"

"Please don't be silly. You've three flights of stairs to climb. You'd never make it."

"How do you know there are three flights? You've never—"

"Relax. Here—have a cigarette. No—" He put the package back in his pocket. "It might be bad for you."

"Pierce—I'm not in an interesting condition—"

"It interests me."

"I'm only sick and tired of everything. I wish I'd never come to New York. Back home I had a boyfriend—he was something like you—but steadier—"

"He must've had everything."

She said seriously, "He pretty nearly did, but I couldn't see it that way. What a dope I am."

"You don't have to keep on being a dope. You can go back to him."

"Oh, sure. What time is it?"

"Not too late to correct your mistake."

"No—I mean it."

He glanced at his watch. "A quarter past five. Why?"

"I want to know how long I can rest before curtain time."

"Don't give it a thought. Start resting now."

"You're nice, Pierce. You must have had nice parents."

"Yeah."

"You're not nagging me anymore. I appreciate that."

"I'm saving it until you look healthier."

"Do I look so awful?"

"You couldn't look awful. A little white around the gills is all. Do you faint often?"

She said indignantly, "Of course not. I'm not the fainting type."

But she fainted again while he was unlocking the door of his apartment. He caught her just in time and carried her into his bedroom. He put her down on the bed, ran to the medicine chest, looked blankly at its meager display, ran back to rub her hands, thought of the bar, stormed it, poured brandy, spilled some, but managed to force a few drops between her lips. Presently she began to fight him off. She opened her eyes and tried to sit up.

"You're among friends, kid. Hold your fire."

She said wonderingly, "I did it again. I guess it's because—"

"Don't talk."

She lay back. He took off her shoes. He put a blanket over her. He tiptoed into the living room and picked up the phone to call a doctor. But he could think of none to call. There had been no occasion for him to get medical advice in New York. It struck him then that the only doctor he had ever consulted aside from army medicos was Uncle Doc. He sighed deeply. He dialed Ginette's number because it was the first that came to mind. He did not expect to find her at home, but he thought that her maid could give him the information he needed.

Ginette herself answered the phone, recognizing his voice immediately. "Pierce—it's good to hear you."

"Thanks." In passing he was pleased to note that her voice had no effect upon him. "Will you give me the name and number of your doctor?"

"What's wrong with you?" She sounded concerned. "You're not—"

"I'm fine. I haven't time to explain."

"Dr. Stern," she said. "If you can't get him, try Dr. Holloway. Wait a minute, I'll give you the numbers." She gave them and hung up.

Dr. Stern's secretary said that he had been called to an accident case. She could not say when he would return. Pierce tried Dr. Holloway. The line was busy. He dialed at brief impatient intervals until he made the connection. The girl who answered took his name. She said brightly, "Oh yes. Miss Arthur just phoned about you. Is it an emergency?"

"Yes—that is, I guess so."

"What seems to be the trouble?"

"Fainting spells—"

"I see. How long have you had them?"

"I—I'm not sure—" He halted on the verge of correcting the misconception. The doctor might be the sort who attended only celebrities or the dear friends of celebrities.

Evidently the girl thought he was too ill to explain. She said reassuringly, "The doctor's with a patient now. He'll come as soon as possible."

Pierce thanked her. He went to take another look at Jill. She seemed to be sleeping. She looked very innocent. She did not look like a girl who had allowed no time to pass before she snatched at a dead friend's property. Neither did she look like a girl who would have strength enough to dance in the chorus in a few hours. He decided to give her no choice.

Just as he had completed the call to the Corridor the bell rang. He smiled cynically as he released the catch on the downstairs door. He had not expected the doctor to arrive so soon. Nothing like having friends in power when it came to getting service. He wondered if Ginette, with a clearer view of the situation, would have been willing to take so much trouble.

When he heard the elevator stop he raced to the door, flung it wide, and said, "Good evening, Dr. Holloway." Then he groaned.

"Pierce, is it that bad? You shouldn't be up and about." Ginette came in, shut the door firmly, and led him back to the living room. "Lie down. The doctor will be here any moment. I hope you don't mind my being so officious—but you sounded strange—"

He was completely at a loss. Hearing her voice over the phone was one thing, seeing her in the round another. The fair hair drawn back from the smooth brow. The lovely clean planes of her face ... He stammered, "It's damn nice of you. I didn't mean to give the wrong impression. I was just in a hurry. I should have—"

"Don't apologize. If it embarrasses you to have me here I won't stay."

He had a feeling that his embarrassment was in its infancy. "I'm afraid there's been a misunderstanding. It's my fault, of course, but I don't need a doctor—I called him for Jill—"

"For Jill?"

"Jill Batiste—one of the girls in *Sea Change*."

She widened her eyes. Then she said, "Oh," as though she meant, "Oh, of course."

"Well—now that you've come, won't you have a—"

"But, Pierce, I gave him this address." She turned toward the telephone. "I hope I can catch him before he leaves. Why didn't you tell me? I—never mind—I'm glad it isn't you."

Pierce took her arm. The contact did not help matters. "Don't call. Jill's in the bedroom—she's sleeping—"

Ginette sat down on the couch. Her face was expressionless, a blond wood carving. "I haven't seen you lately," she said, "so you can't expect me to be informed about your—"

"No—no—it's not that way at all. Jill's— Look—you must know Jill—"

"Not so well as you do, obviously."

"Hell! Please kindly give me a chance to tell you—"

"You owe me no explanations."

"I don't at that." He wanted to hit her, to kiss her, make her smile or cry, make her do anything that would bring mobility back to that infuriating wood-carved face. "I owe Jill something, though. I can't have her reputation ruined."

That did make her smile. But it was not a smile of which he could approve. "What a gentleman it is," she said.

"Listen to me. I met Jill on the street—by accident. I had wanted to see her, but—"

"Will you ever know what you do want?"

He raised his arms, dropped them. He said deliberately, "Yes, but that has nothing to do with the current rate of exchange. As I was saying, I met Jill by accident and she fainted—"

"Swooned at the sight of you, no doubt."

"And I brought her here because she lives in a noisy trap with three flights of stairs to climb and I'd had enough of a hassle lugging Stasia up yester— Oh lord!"

"Stasia too? Well, perhaps there's safety in numbers." Her little smile broke into laughter. He could not determine whether or not it was genuine. She thrust her coat from her shoulders. "I'll wait until Dr. Holloway comes. Just mark it down as my contribution toward saving a reputation. Meanwhile, should I see if I can do anything for the girl?"

"It's very kind of you."

"Superhumanly kind." She went into the bedroom.

Pierce started to follow, sat down instead. He lit a cigarette. He drew a book from the bookcase. He tried to look like a man relaxing in the privacy of his living room.

From the doorway Ginette said, "The patient is sleeping soundly." She used the efficient tones of a nurse.

"I wish you weren't an actress, Ginette."

"No one will ever accuse you of being an actor. What are you pretending to read?"

He could not answer. He put the book down.

Ginette took a chair at the opposite end of the room. She kept a formal conversation afloat until the bell rang. It was she who let the doctor in, calmly explaining the situation to him. "I'm afraid I got my patients mixed, Doctor. Mr. Kirby is one of those men who panics easily. It's his young cousin who's ill. He was so excited when he telephoned me that I jumped to the wrong conclusion."

The doctor said that it was not uncommon for the layman to panic in the face of illness. He gave Pierce a fatherly pat on the shoulder. He gave Ginette a far from fatherly look.

Pierce resented him. He thought that doctors should be old and mellow. This one was a dapper specimen, hardly more than his own age. Grudgingly he showed him where he could wash his hands, pointed out the bedroom, and came back to pace the living room floor.

"For all the world like an expectant father," Ginette said at last. She had picked up the discarded book and appeared to be making headway with it.

"Don't you start that," he said, not meaning the book. When pressed he told her about the scene in the luncheonette, about the expressed conviction of the waitress. She seemed amused. He had forgotten what a warm, responsive audience she could be. He went on talking. Before he knew it he had told how he happened to meet Jill on that particular street, and what events had led to the meeting.

Ginette said, "I don't see why you think it has any special significance, Pierce. Just the fact that this man Seager and your Jill both loved the missing girl would be a natural enough basis for bringing them together. Do you know if there have been any real developments not revealed in the papers? I've been longing to ask, but—" She broke off. "What's the matter now?"

He was remembering tardily her own possible connection with the case, her connection with Drake which she had later denied. He closed his lips tight. He wished that he had sense enough to keep them closed more often.

She said, "You actually do suspect me—don't you? You're sitting there flaying yourself because you've just presented most secret and important information to one of your chief suspects. That's probably why you've been keeping away from me."

He said lamely, "You're talking rot."

"You're thinking rot." She stood up. Her voice rose too. "I had only to tell you in the heat of anger that I was engaged to another man and you lost faith in me forever. But I walked in here, found another woman—in the flesh, mind you—and very pretty flesh—occupying your bed, and I was able to dismiss at once or almost at once the notion that she was your mistress—"

The doctor spoke from the doorway. "Your cousin," he said, "has been trying to starve herself to death. Luckily she has a strong constitution."

They both turned. Pierce said, "What?"

"I don't mean she's been starving herself deliberately. But she can't recall one square meal eaten within the last few days. It's my opinion that she's deeply disturbed about something—but you probably know more about that than she was willing to tell me." He handed Pierce two prescriptions. "Vitamins and a sedative. Have them filled at once. But it's even more important that she rest in bed and take plenty of nourishment—not too much at once, but often—eggnogs, custards, fruit, small portions of beef and liver, green vegetables. Is that clear?"

Ginette glanced at Pierce. He looked dazed. She said, "Miss Batiste doesn't live here, Doctor. Can she be moved?"

"Yes, provided it doesn't upset her. May I drive you home, Miss Arthur?"

"No, I'm staying awhile. Thank you very much for coming."

"It's always a pleasure to do what I can for you. Good evening."

Robot-wise, Pierce escorted him to the door. When he returned he said helplessly, "I can't send her home. Stasia would never lend herself to a routine like that. I should have asked him to make arrangements at some hospital."

"I doubt if they'd take her in at a hospital. You have to have something really spectacular to get a room without advance notice these days." Ginette sounded completely detached. "Speaking of notice, hadn't you better call the Corridor?"

"I did. Look—what'll I do? I haven't any food in the house—milk and eggs, maybe—but nothing like meat or greens. Even if I had I wouldn't know how to cook—"

From the bedroom Jill called, "Pierce, where are you? Come here."

He shrugged defeatedly.

Jill was huddled into one of his robes. Her wrinkled dress hung over the back of a chair. She looked at him reproachfully. "That was a dirty trick, sicking that Mr. Park Avenue onto me. I needed him like I need pimples."

He shouted at her, "You need a good beating. Were you broke or what? Couldn't you have touched me—or coaxed your new beau to buy you a meal?"

A spot of color blotched her white face. She said primly, "Sorry to have been a nuisance." She sat up and reached for her dress.

"Where do you think you're going? Jill! Hey— Goon! Look, baby, I didn't mean to shout—"

"Okay." She smiled. "I'm not mad, but I've got to scram, anyway. What time is it? I must have slept. First thing I knew Lord Piddlecoop was feeling my pulse."

"You're not going on tonight. I phoned the theater."

She said in dismay, "You shouldn't have done that. I'm all right. That sleep I—"

"That sleep was only the beginning," Pierce said. He wished he knew what the end was.

Ginette entered the room. She carried a drinking glass full of light frothy liquid.

Jill looked from her to Pierce. "Miss Arthur! I thought I heard voices, but I didn't know—"

Ginette brushed Pierce aside. She sat down next to the bed. "Drink this. Doctor's orders."

Jill said doubtfully, "What is it?"

"Milk and egg."

"Do I have to?"

"Yes—take it slowly." Ginette's voice brooked no argument. "Pierce, go down and get a cab. Jill's coming home with me."

He said, "Oh no—you mustn't think of it," and was appalled at the false ring of his protest. "There's no reason why you—I'll manage—"

"You can't manage—and it won't be any trouble. Edna loves nursing people." Edna had been in charge of her domestic arrangements for several years.

Pierce went on making false protests, praying they would not be heeded, until Jill muttered, "Thanks for arguing over me, but I'm not a stray cat. I've a roof to call my own."

Ginette said finally, "You need attention that you can't get under your own roof, so just be a sensible girl—unless you'd rather be a very sick one. Pierce hasn't read the book that says show people always stick together. Finish your eggnog. Pierce, get that cab."

Jill finished the eggnog, and Pierce went before Ginette could change her mind. When he came back Jill was dressed and quite ready to accompany Ginette. In fact, the understanding that had sprung up between the two during his brief absence made him uncomfortable.

"I could get a nurse here and move to a hotel for a few nights," he said, meaning it.

Ginette answered "I promise I won't let her come to harm, Pierce. It would be a bit obvious, wouldn't it—in my own home? And even you must admit that I'm seldom obvious."

CHAPTER TWELVE

Ginette had leased from friends a small brownstone house in the Sixties off Fifth Avenue. There were two large high-ceilinged rooms on the ground floor and three bedrooms upstairs. Scattered throughout were comfortable no-nonsense chairs and couches, bookcases where shabby classics and bright current volumes rubbed bindings, a catholic array of pictures, including reproductions of old masters and modern originals, and fireplaces whose carved marble of another era just refrained from making war on stark new andirons. Because Ginette was vague about her possessions, Pierce could never figure out what had been in the house when she arrived and what she had added to it. Yet because he loved her and because the whole seemed oddly expressive of her personality, it had always seemed friendly and dear to him.

But now, as he helped Jill up to the bedroom that she was to occupy, it was as though his quarrel with Ginette had spread to include her surroundings.

He said uneasily, "Sure you want to stay, Jill?" They were alone in the bedroom. Ginette was downstairs conferring with Edna.

"Look at that bed," Jill answered. "Me in a four-poster under a tester and a down quilt. I'm just beginning to live."

A white-haired woman came into the room. She was large and solid. She had guileless eyes and a pug nose. She was the sort of woman Pierce had met on many a street in Kincaid. She made his qualms seem ridiculous. He smiled at her. "Hello, Edna."

"Hello, stranger."

"Jill, this is Mrs. Schoonmaker."

"So you're the little invalid," Edna said. "Never mind calling me Mrs. That was a long time ago. Now if this fellow will take a walk I'll have you in bed in two shakes."

"I don't have a nightgown or anything," Jill said. But she did not sound worried.

"We'll fix you up."

Pierce left them alone. He went downstairs. Ginette lay on a couch before the fireplace. She was staring at nothing.

Pierce said awkwardly, "In the excitement I forgot to ask you how the rehearsals for the new play were going."

"The way all good rehearsals go—reassuringly rotten. Would you like to stay to dinner?"

"No, thanks. Thanks for everything." He wanted to stretch out beside her, to be marooned on the little island of her scent, to turn, to open his arms, to— "Good night, Ginette. Don't get up. I'll find my way out."

She murmured something that sounded like "I hope so."

Standing in front of the lighted house, he felt lonely. It occurred to him that in the course of his rounds he had met quite a few people in New York and that there was none among them with whom he shared a real bond of friendship. They were people to eat with, to drink with, to laugh with, but never to cry with. Let a serious subject be unloaded, and you could cut the restlessness and boredom with a knife. How often he had seen it happen. And no bouquets for me, he thought desolately. I'm no better than the rest. Perhaps if I'd really listened to Toni that night … It's a hell of a life I've been living. It's got to change. I've got to change it.

He thought of how he had dreamed of marrying, of having kids and giving them the love and affection that had been denied him by his own parents. And he thought of Uncle Doc saying that Ginette was built for childbearing, and silently he addressed Uncle Doc.

"She's a career woman. She doesn't want kids."

Uncle Doc answered, "Sure she does. She just doesn't want a kid for a husband. You could work something out."

"But she said she was engaged to Drake."

"That was your fault. You were acting up. She had to say something."

"How can I *know?* That night I turned my back on you to quarrel with her, she left the dressing room first—"

"Nonsense. Why should she want to kill me?"

"Why should anybody?"

"You'll find out. You always were a boy for finding out. You always were a boy for tripping over stuff you left in your own way too. You trust Ginette. Proof is, you left Jill with her. Don't think for a minute you'd do that if you really doubted her."

"But I haven't given Jill a clean bill of health either. I got sidetracked is all—because she looked so miserable. Maybe I was willing to leave them together because—"

He had started walking. He bumped into a woman carrying bundles. That put an abrupt end to the silent conversation. He walked to Fifth Avenue, got on a bus, and went downtown. He walked east to his apartment because he could think of nowhere else to go. When he was upstairs he told himself gloomily that he should have stopped at a restaurant. He investigated the barren refrigerator but saw nothing there to tempt him.

He thought that the apartment looked more deserted than ever before because Ginette had been there and was there no longer. He thought that Uncle Doc alive might have used words similar to those he had imagined. He *did* trust Ginette and he was tripping over obstacles furnished by himself. Why? Because he wanted to punish himself. What right had he to happiness when his own cheap self-absorption had caused him to neglect a man he had cherished and a stranger who had sought his help?

He thought defiantly, That's the way it is. And as though under orders, he went to the telephone and called Nelson's apartment.

The maid with the rich voice answered. She admitted that Mr. Grid-dely had just come in and put him on without delay.

Nelson barely allowed Pierce time to furnish a sample of his voice. "Hello, Kirby. I was just about to sit down to dinner."

"Look—why haven't you done anything about Seager and—"

"I'll keep it hot for you. Hurry."

"Keep what?"

"Something extra special," Nelson said, and hung up.

Five blocks separated Pierce from Nelson. Pierce had covered three of them before it registered with him that he was hastening to dinner and not to some important revelation. He cursed and slowed his steps. He entered the vestibule of a modest walk-up, rang the bell without enthusiasm, and climbed three flights of stairs, cleaner than the stairs in Jill's house, but just as steep. Nelson stood within an open door to welcome him, tactfully ignoring the fact that he was panting.

He was ushered into a room that seemed almost arrogantly alive as compared to his own quarters. There was a long ash table set for two. There was a premature spray of fresh white lilac in a green vase. There were books and records in and out of cases and cabinets. There were vividly draped windows and sturdy armchairs. And there was a fragrance that suddenly made the prospect of dinner agonizingly bright.

Nevertheless, he said stubbornly, "Yesterday you seemed to think it important to get onto Seager and—"

"I'll take your coat," Nelson said. "Sammy's busy in the kitchen or she would do the honors. Sit down." He raised his pleasant voice. "Sammy, is there time for a cocktail before we eat?"

"Be there directly, Mr. Grid-dely." She came directly, bearing a tray on which there were a pitcher and two iced martini glasses. Her handsome head was six feet off the ground, and she had a fine thin mouth and nose, and heavy-lidded eyes set in flesh the color of dark honey.

She said, "Good evening, Mr. Kirby. We glad you here."

Pierce said, "Good evening," and accepted the drink she poured. He drank because she was waiting for him to drink. "It's very good."

She gave him a dignified nod and went back to the kitchen. He set the glass down on a coaster. He opened his mouth. "Give it a rest," Nelson said. "I'll hear your recriminations after dinner."

Presently Pierce discovered that he was enjoying the meal and that it was the first meal he had enjoyed in a long time. There was a great bowl of gumbo, large pieces of chicken, saffron-tinted and flavored with okra and tomatoes and onions and sassafras and something he could not name. Sammy had framed this art with mountains of rice and eked it out with hot spoon bread and chicory salad.

"It's the filé powder that makes it special," Nelson said. "Hard to get, but Sammy manages. She always says, though, that gumbo's better on the third day. This is only the second."

"There won't be any third." Pierce took a liberal second helping. "Where on earth did she learn to cook like this?"

"New Orleans."

"She's wonderful."

"Understatement, according to my chief. He's not a man to take stairs lightly, but he climbs these without a murmur whenever he's asked and often when he's not."

Pierce stopped eating for a few moments. He said delicately, "You chief sounds enterprising. Maybe he could give you some advice about—"

Nelson said without expression, "I've had three telegrams and one book-length letter from him in two days."

"Oh. Well—have you lived here long?"

"Too long. It was fine when—before I was married—but the ceremony took place in the densest part of the housing shortage, and the best we could manage was to get the apartment next door as soon as it fell vacant—so at least we're able to spread out a bit. Kyrie's coming home in a week."

Pierce envied him for the look in his eyes, for his Kyrie, for Sammy. Then he thought, That's all very well, but it could be making him soft. It might account for his— Yet even the one-track mind of Pierce found it difficult to run down a host at his own table.

It was Nelson who invited the onslaught when they had carried their coffee to the easy chairs. "All right—fire. But before you start, perhaps you'll want to know a few facts."

"All I want to know is why you didn't question Seager and Jill after Stasia—"

"That's exactly what I want to tell you. Questioning doesn't always provide answers. You've proved that today, haven't you?"

"I—well—they didn't have to talk to me—but you could have made them talk."

"By beating Seager until he blubbered the traditional 'Stop—I'll sing'? By terrorizing a girl who faints in the street?"

"How—"

"I'm not attempting to confound you. LeRoy Seager and Jill Batiste have been going about equipped with the most efficient of tails. Rudimentary, my dear Watson."

"Elementary," Pierce said without thinking.

"Not as applied to tails."

"Damn it—I didn't see anybody who looked like—"

Nelson said dryly, "Then I must send them both my heartiest congratulations. They saw you—in the lobby of Seager's office building and in the luncheonette—to mention two places."

"There was no one in the luncheonette—only a woman who came in after—"

"That's our girl."

"Would she be the one carrying bundles outside Ginette's?"

"Quite likely. Latest reports have it that Jill rests under Miss Arthur's roof while Seager dines alone in his service apartment at the Morrow Arms."

After a moment Pierce said, "You may not believe it, but I don't get any special kick out of acting the fool. You might have told me your plans."

"It hadn't occurred to me that you could know so little about ordinary police procedure."

"Rub it in."

"I don't feel smug enough to rub it in." He looked far from smug. "You were trying to go it alone. I've the combined facilities of the law behind me, my own squad, and the pick of Missing Persons—and I'm still waiting for—for things to break."

"Do you really think Jill and Seager might be in on it?"

"If Seager has reason to abet a man suspected of murdering his fiancée I haven't hit upon it."

"You're hedging. Couldn't money be a reason?"

"You mean Drake might have hired Seager for other than legal business? We've been unable to discover that Drake's been in touch with anyone since his disappearance, and it's pretty farfetched to imagine that he confided his plans to Seager beforehand and paid him to keep them secret."

"Yes, I guess so, but maybe Drake did Seager a favor by ridding him of Toni. Maybe he was sick of her. Look how quickly he turned to Jill."

Nelson said thoughtfully, "No—I don't think it's that way. Jill sticks to her story that the heart-shaped pin arrived on the night before Toni vanished—and she's backed by a few other girls who were in the dressing room when it came."

"Are we on that again?"

"Wait a minute. You're always clamoring for facts, aren't you?" Nelson gave an account of his visit to the jeweler. "So you see—the bracelet Toni showed you sometime earlier and the pin were on the same order and delivered to Toni in the same package. So how does the pin turn up later attached to a corsage?"

Pierce shrugged.

"Furthermore, Barrows, who was supposed to have telephoned the order, denies any knowledge of it. Yet the jeweler insists he checked back to the penthouse and received confirmation."

"Interesting," Pierce said, "but I can't see its importance. Couldn't Drake have phoned and pretended to be Barrows?"

"Why?"

"He's too far from sane to need a why." Pierce struggled with it. "How about this? Barrows is lying to protect Drake because he has some foolish idea it will help Drake's case if it can't be proved that he was serious enough about Toni to send her the diamonds. It won't, of course. There's too much against him. The blood—that button found on the beach that his tailors identified—"

"I don't think Barrows is lying." Nelson turned his head as Sammy came into the room. "Sorry we've kept you so late. Couldn't you leave the dishes until morning?"

"I in no hurry. 'Sides, everything's done but these." She put the coffee cups on a tray and carried them out to the kitchen.

The telephone rang. Nelson called, "I'll take it, Sammy," and went into the bedroom.

Pierce sat upright in his chair, staving off a pleasant food-induced languor. He could not hear Nelson's voice, but he did hear light domestic clatter from the kitchen. He could have slept to it. He felt vaguely discomforted by a well-being he had not earned. He was glad when Sammy halted before him on her way through the room.

"Mr. Kirby, I gone next door if Mr. Grid-dely want me."

"I'll tell him. Thanks for the best meal I've had in years."

Her heavy-lidded eyes appraised him. She said severely, "You eat good as that all the time and meat comes to your bones." Then she smiled at him and he smiled back. "I got a notion Mr. Grid-dely going to ask you here some more."

"I won't need coaxing."

He sat on alone. He thought that Nelson's phone call was taking a long time. He strained his ears. He thought he heard him hang up. Then he heard the phone ring again and settled back in his chair. He lit a cigarette, stubbed it out, and was lighting another when Nelson appeared with two coats over his arm.

Nelson said, "Here's yours. Did you have a hat?"

"No—where are we going?"

"In opposite directions. I've got two destinations. Maybe I'll call you later and have you go with me to the second one." Nelson's pointed face looked strained. "Sorry—hope I can be a better host next time."

"Official business?" Pierce put on his coat.

"Yes." Nelson lifted his voice. "Sammy, I'm leaving."

"She's not in the kitchen. She said she'd be next door if you wanted her."

"Well, I'd better let her know. Come on."

Sammy had left the door of the next apartment on the latch. Nelson opened it and strode in, Pierce following. Sammy was in a lighted bedroom to the right of the door. She was evidently tidying bureau drawers. Pierce watched her folding a minute pair of briefs and thought that Kyrie must be neatly made.

Nelson watched too. He said absently, "No need for you to bother with this place yet, Sammy. Miss Kyrie won't be back for a whole week."

"I got me a schedule," Sammy said. "They plenty to do in that week." She stared at him. "Something bad happen, Mr. Grid-dely?"

He shook his head. "I just wanted to tell you I'm leaving."

She nodded. "You get everything cleaned up good before Miss Kyrie come. Hear?"

Going down the stairs, Pierce said, "Does she sleep in?"

"What? Oh—no. There's a room for her when she wants to use it, but she likes her own home best."

"There is something wrong—isn't there?"

Nelson did not answer. He raced to the street. Pierce hurried to catch up with him. "You sound funny and you act funny. Should I be interested in that phone call?"

Nelson's car was parked before the house. He got into it. Pierce caught the door before it slammed, climbed in beside him. "I don't care where you drop me. I've nothing to do anyway."

"You're a damn nuisance." Nelson was not smiling. He started the car. "All right—we're headed for the Morrow Arms. It seems that Seager has a caller."

Pierce felt the sudden hammering of his heart. "Not Drake!"

Nelson said flatly, "No—not Drake. Ginette Arthur."

Pierce heard his own voice shouting belligerently, "Other people live at the Morrow Arms besides Seager. What business had the woman to follow Ginette? She was assigned to Jill. She—"

"Operatives are encouraged to use their judgment right or wrong. This one used hers."

"Is that what your damn-fool phone calls are about?"

"Partly."

"Then you're more than partly full of it," Pierce shouted, "and that goes for your operatives—"

"I've seen evidence of a corresponding fullness in you—and you know Miss Arthur better than we do." He stopped the car.

Pierce gaped at him, then at the empty driver's seat. He shook himself and got out in time to see Nelson disappear into a canopied entrance at the end of the street. When he reached the lobby of the Morrow Arms, Nelson stood near the door talking to a woman who looked vaguely familiar. Nelson broke off the conversation and walked to the rear of the lobby. Pierce started to follow. The woman's voice detained him.

"He's gone to telephone," she said.

"What for—the reserves?"

She grinned.

"If you ask me," he said, "this judgment you're encouraged to use needs simonizing."

She kept on grinning. "Is the lady another girlfriend of yours? Then why not look at it this way? That fellow upstairs is on the suspect list, so maybe I'm here to protect her from him."

"Miss Arthur's a famous actress. She knows a lot of people, and it just might happen that some of them live here."

"It might. But it's Seager she's honoring."

"I don't believe—" He did not finish because her attention was no longer his.

A nondescript man had taken up a stance a few feet away. He kept glancing at his watch as though he were waiting for a tardy date. The woman operative caught his eye and winked. He responded with a leer. Pierce felt like Alice in Wonderland until it dawned upon him that the man was Seager's tail. Forgetting the issues at stake, he hated the pair of them. He walked to the elevators and waited there for Nelson.

Nelson came toward him. With an aloof nod he stepped into an elevator and said, "Eleven." To Pierce he said nothing until they left the car. Then he muttered, "A body was washed ashore two miles from Chilton."

"No!"

Nelson treated the exclamation as something more than reflex. "Just a little while ago when Sammy—"

"Are you sure it's—"

"No more questions. I'm sure—and you've given me an idea." He knocked on a door.

"Yes?" Seager said. He opened the door cautiously. He recognized them and took a backward step. "Good evening. What is it you want?" His stocky body centered the frame of the door.

"A few minutes of your time," Nelson said, "preferably inside."

"I can't ask you in. I have a client with me."

"I know," Nelson said. He put his foot on the threshold. Seager had the choice of moving aside or of being thrust aside. He moved. Pierce crowded after Nelson. He tagged him across a small foyer into a hotel living room whose stereotyped character was relieved only by the presence of Ginette.

Behind them Seager complained bitterly. "I consider this behavior extremely highhanded. I shall ask for an explanation from the management for allowing anybody and everybody to come up unannounced."

Pierce drew a deep breath. "Ginette, why are you here?"

She looked at him. It was a look of cancellation, plain as a black line drawn through a name on a visiting list. Why his doubts, painstakingly nourished until now, should choose this moment to desert him, he did not know. He said, "I didn't mean— I'm sure you had a good reason for coming."

Nelson said, "Suppose I give my reason for being here first." He turned to Seager. "I was misguided enough to think you'd want to be informed about developments in our investigation of your fiancée's disappearance."

"I am—I do—but—"

"Very well, I'm asking you to come with me to Chilton to identify a body."

"A—a— What did you say?"

"A body—washed in from Long Island Sound—and thought to be Toni George."

Seager tottered. Nelson pushed a chair under him. He collapsed into it, gripping its arms. He did not say, "No," as Pierce had done. He said, "Oh," drawing it out like a practicing vocalist.

Ginette addressed him with odd impersonality. "I'll get you some whisky if you tell me where you keep it."

He did not look at her. "I—I'll—it's in that cabinet. Perhaps you'd all— It was a shock. Of course I expected it—I—nevertheless, it was a shock." He took the small glass from Ginette's hand and drank. He said, "In a way I'm almost relieved. Now that I know beyond the shadow of a doubt perhaps I can—"

"The doubt will remain until you've identified the body," Nelson said.

"I can't. I must ask you to excuse me—I've been far from well lately—surely you understand how I—"

"The girl has no living relatives. You, her intended husband, will have to stand as next of kin."

Pierce said in deep disgust, "Perhaps he'd rather send his new flame."

Ginette came in strongly: "I'm only an understudy tonight, but I think that's my cue."

CHAPTER THIRTEEN

She held her audience. "I'm here because an unhappy girl asked me to do her a favor. She should have gone to the police with her troubles, but because of something that happened to her once she held back. Not that I have any way of judging whether the story is police-worthy. I'll leave that to you, Lieutenant. Last week a picture of Dr. Miles appeared in the newspapers with a hitherto unpublished picture of Toni George. Jill saw it and worried about it. It wasn't a publicity shot. Jill had gone with Toni to have it taken, and the photographer was so expensive that Toni bought only one print, which she gave to her fiancé as a birthday present."

Seager made an attempt to heckle. "It's all a tempest in a teapot—"

Nelson silenced him. "Please go on, Miss Arthur."

"Jill checked with the photographer to see if Toni or anyone else had gone back to buy a second print. Nobody had, so it's understandable that she was puzzled when, according to the newspaper account, the picture given to Mr. Seager was the same one that had decorated Bobby Drake's bureau. So Jill took what was in my opinion the hard way of finding an answer to that riddle. She had never liked Seager. It must have made her crawl when she had to pretend to a romantic interest in him. Yet she felt that was the best means to discover why he had presented Toni's picture to Drake, for whom he was supposed to have entertained a violent jealousy. She had worked up some pretty dark ideas about Mr. Seager. It didn't seem at all illogical to her that he might somehow be involved in Toni's disappearance. She was so disturbed by these ideas that she found it difficult to eat or sleep." Ginette paused briefly. "Undoubtedly Mr. Seager is a lonely man and Jill is a lovely girl. But it couldn't have helped her physical or mental state much to be forced to endure his—well—attempts to forget his grief—as part of the role she had set herself to play."

"Now look here!" Seager shot out of his chair.

"We're looking," Nelson said.

Seager sat down again. After a moment he shrugged. "These women," he said, and his inflections were strictly man to man. "Out of a clear sky Jill Batiste practically deposited herself in my lap. After all—I'm human—and yes—lonely, too, in spite of Miss Arthur's intended sarcasm. And you may put it down to male ego if you like, but I can hardly believe that my—er—longing for affection was distasteful to the girl. She certainly encouraged me to think just the opposite—and if she was seeking me out simply to discover why Drake was in possession of that particular photograph she had only to ask—"

"I asked," Ginette said. "I was quite direct about it, but I didn't get an answer."

"I didn't consider it any of your business—if you'll excuse me for—"

Pierce offered hoarsely to sit on his face. Nelson gave him a warning look. Seager ignored the byplay. "Jill was poor Toni's friend. She had a right to her curiosity. There was no need for her to employ such a roundabout method—unless I was rather less repulsive to her than she seemed ready to admit."

Pierce said ominously, "I've been aching to sock you since the first time I laid eyes on that smug face of yours." At least half his rage was for the insolence directed at Ginette. "Most likely Jill didn't dare to let you know what she was up to because she was afraid you had killed Toni. I wouldn't put it past you—"

Ginette nodded and made a sound that might have been approval. It was her first acknowledgment of Pierce since he had entered the room. Pierce did not notice. He had moved very near to Seager. His fists were clenched.

Seager said, "Lieutenant, you brought this man with you. I'll hold you responsible for anything he may attempt to—"

"He won't attempt anything," Nelson said. "Before you get your coat, tell me in short sentences why you gave Toni's picture to a rival."

Pierce retreated of his own accord. He listened.

"I didn't give it to him. He stole it. It was on my desk in the office. Sometimes I had occasion to leave him alone there for a minute or two. Right after his last visit I noticed that it was missing."

"When was his last visit?"

"I can't recall the exact date."

"It seems to me that such a theft would mark a date for you."

"It did—I was very much upset—but so many things have happened since then—"

"Well, undoubtedly your efficient receptionist will be able to supply the information."

"Is it—why is it important?" Then he said, "Let me think—it was about three weeks ago—yes, just about that. Would you mind telling me what bearing—"

But Nelson, after a visible struggle with himself, said curtly, "We'll get started for Chilton."

Without a word Seager got up and went into the bedroom.

"Thanks, Miss Arthur," Nelson said, "for speaking your piece."

"I'm glad you turned up. It saved me a trip to your office—a fruitless trip, since the revelation doesn't seem to have any particular value. What shall I tell Jill?"

"Anything reassuring that comes to your mind. By the way, what sort of run-in did she have with the law?"

"You mean the thing that made her afraid to come to you? Well—it was a confidence, but I'll break it to keep you from unnecessary speculation. Jill came from a rather poor home. At the age of eight she was caught shoplifting. It seemed her brother was badly in need of a baseball glove, but the town policeman had a heavy hand and no imagination. She's hated the law ever since."

Nelson smiled. "You managed to extract a lot from her in a little while."

She gave Pierce a sidelong glance. "Perhaps I'm the latent mother type. Good night, Lieutenant." She started toward the foyer.

Pierce looked after her. He said to Nelson, "Do you want me to go to Chilton with you?"

Perversely Nelson said, "Yes."

The outer door closed upon Ginette as Seager came from the bedroom. Pierce rushed to the elevator, hoping for a word with her before the two men caught up with him. But she was gone.

In the lobby neither the woman operative nor the man with the leer was in sight. Nelson led the way to his car. Seager climbed into the back as though he were taking a taxi.

For a distance of several miles no one spoke. Then Seager leaned forward and tapped Nelson's shoulder.

"Yes?"

"The body they found—they're sure?"

"It's possible, of course, that Chief Maddox is allowing himself to be swayed by the fact that there have been no other reports of persons missing in that area."

"It seems to me that all possible tests should have been made before subjecting me to this terrible ordeal."

"If you're able to make positive identification, perhaps time and some of the taxpayers' money can be saved."

Seager said no more. He settled back. Pierce wanted to say a great deal. He glanced at Nelson's profile and forbore, but he thought that it was just as well he had come along. He would force himself to look, at whatever cost. He would surely recognize whatever remained of that striking beauty, the black hair, the deep-set near-black eyes, the poreless flesh … He swallowed. He did not trust Seager, would not take his word for anything.

Nelson supplied a cigarette as though on demand. Pierce accepted gratefully.

With the exception of the blazing drugstore, only dim night lights picked out the shops in the town of Chilton. Nelson drew up before a window displaying an elegant casket. "They don't have a morgue here," he said. "When necessary they commandeer the basement of the undertaker." He looked at Seager. "But I keep forgetting that you're a native of Chilton."

Seager was the last to leave the car. He averted his eyes from the window display as though even that upset his delicate sensibilities.

The muted, sorrowful character of the establishment was violated by a policeman who asked their business and directed them across thick carpeting to a flight of stairs concealed by black velvet drapes. In the basement, apparently used for storage of funeral accessories as well as for police work, three men sat waiting. Chief Maddox was the central figure. He heaved himself up when he saw Nelson.

"Hi, Grid. You've met our Doc Traub. This other Gloomy Gus is Emmett Foley, the proprietor of Chilton's least thriving business, thanks be."

Nelson shook hands. Both men were short and fat. The doctor was sallow and had hair. The undertaker was ruddy and bald.

"Grid," Maddox said, "according to Doc Traub—"

Nelson said, "I've brought Mr. Seager, the fiancé of the dead girl."

"Sure—I recognized him. When are you coming back to settle in a real town, Mr. Seager? Sorry—guess you don't feel much like light chatter. A tough errand for you—but at least—"

Nelson took his arm and steered him to the other end of the long, harsh-smelling basement. He spoke briefly, and Maddox answered at length, obviously taking special pains to lower his hearty voice.

Pierce looked about him. His eyes lit upon piles of lumber, upon a pair of sawhorses placed at a sinister distance apart, upon a stack of folding chairs, a carpenter's bench, a bolt of purple satin, upon a door opposite to the one he had entered. His eyes kept returning to that door, his thoughts to what might lie behind it. He heard Seager mutter, "For God's sake, why don't they get it over with?" and was for once in accord with him.

Nelson and Maddox rejoined them. "In through there," Maddox said.

Nelson motioned to Seager. Pierce started to follow. The door closed in his face,

Maddox came up to him. "No need for a crowd. Sit down. Make yourself comfortable. Believe me, you're not missing a thing."

The doctor yawned. "You might have given me my innings before they went in, Maddy. I haven't seen the inside of my house since six o'clock this morning."

"Grid Nelson didn't seem to want it that way," Maddox said.

The undertaker crammed a stick of chewing gum into his mouth and champed it so vigorously that his bald scalp moved. He addressed Pierce companionably, "You fellows must lead an exciting life. Now take me, for example—"

The terrible door opened and Nelson and Seager emerged. Seager was livid.

Nelson said, "Mr. Seager is unable to identify the body."

Pierce stiffened. He had expected that. He had worked himself up to believing that Seager was at least an accessory to murder. He had thought that the body would prove to be Toni's body and that Seager would deny it on the premise that it would be more difficult to establish his guilt without the evidence of a corpse.

He heard Maddox say, "I'm not surprised." He saw that the doctor and the undertaker had both left their chairs.

The doctor said, "I don't get this. I don't see why we need his—"

"I'll talk with you in a few moments, Doctor," Nelson said.

Pierce took a step toward the door. "Let me look—I'll know—"

Nelson gripped his arm. "Stay put."

Seager was stumbling, trying to reach one of the chairs. His voice came thinly. "Why did you bring me here? How could that—that poor thing be Toni?"

The doctor whipped a small bottle from his pocket. He uncorked it and held it to Seager's nose. As the strong ammonic fumes reached out Pierce felt his own nostrils twitch. Seager sputtered and coughed. He thrust the bottle away. His eyes were streaming.

The doctor said, "Thought you were going to faint. Don't have to be ashamed. Lots of men can't stand to see—"

Seager choked. "Take that—cork it—" He swabbed at his eyes. He blew his nose. Then he stared at the handkerchief balled in his hand. He said, "I'm sorry—glad, I mean—glad that it isn't Toni. I—" He got up and made for the stairs.

Nelson motioned for Pierce to follow. Pierce took one last look at the closed door and obeyed. He and Seager stood on the sidewalk until Nelson and Maddox appeared.

Maddox said, "My car's parked down the street. Did you drive out in yours, Grid, or Mr. Seager's?"

"I don't use a car in the city," Seager said. The fresh air had revived him. "I find taxis more convenient."

"Yes? Well—couldn't get along without one here. You had a beauty, I remember. Sell it?"

Seager nodded vaguely. It was obvious that he found the conversation irritating. He looked longingly at Nelson's tried-and-true Buick.

"Be seeing you," Maddox said, and strode away.

Seager again pre-empted the rear seat. As Nelson started the car he said, "Under the circumstances I won't apologize for making a fool of myself. I doubt if you could have found a more unpleasant way to waste my time."

Nelson did not answer.

"Watch where you're going," Seager said. "You're headed in the wrong direction—or is it too much to ask that I be driven home by the shortest possible route?"

"I have an errand to do first."

Seager leaned forward. "Errand! I never heard of such a thing. I won't stand for it. My time isn't completely valueless, you know. Drop me off at the railroad station. I've had enough—"

"It's five after ten," Nelson said. "The trains leave on the hour. You might as well come with me." That was his last lip service to the continued bluster in the rear seat. Seager was still at it when the car stopped about halfway between the Foster cottage and Bobby Drake's house.

Armed with a flashlight, Nelson left the car. He ignored the cottage. He by-passed the house and disappeared into the darkness beyond it.

Pierce thought there had been lights in the cottage when they drove up. Now they were out. Nelson reappeared, his tall triangular figure crossing the yellow pool of the car's headlights. He strode up to the Foster door and knocked.

"Do you happen to know the nature of this errand?" Seager addressed the back of Pierce's head.

"No." Pierce, too, got out of the car, only to put distance between himself and Seager. He did not know the nature of the errand. He could have gone on to elaborate upon all he did not know. The scene in the undertaker's basement had been for him devoid of meaning. Yet he thought that below the surface was something that his limited equipment could not fathom. Nelson, he could have sworn, had known in advance that the corpse was not Toni. Why, then, the futile ceremony of identification? Feeling tired and stupid, Pierce went to stand beside Nelson.

Seager called from the back of the car, "They must be asleep. People in the country retire early. Have you no consideration at all?" His voice sounded very loud. Pierce could hear him strike a match, could almost hear him inhale cigarette smoke. His ears attuned to the stillness, he heard other sounds within the cottage. A muttered stream of words, feet pounding a floor, a woman's voice demanding to know what was wanted.

For answer Nelson knocked again, two short authoritative knocks, and as though recognizing their official significance, the woman cried, "I don't care—it's late. We've gone to bed." Then she did open the door suddenly and closed it suddenly, herself shut out as well as the would-be intruders. She stood on the step confronting them, a huge silhouette of a woman.

"Mrs. Foster," Nelson said, "I want the key to the garage." It was a simple statement, without apology or a by-your-leave.

She began to shout. "Is that why you woke us up? Of all the nerve! What country do you think this is?" She was featureless, standing there in the dark. She was a bludgeoning voice hurting the quiet night.

"I'll have the key," Nelson said.

"You—" Her mouth was like an oven from which she pulled hot unsavory lumps of invective, and when the supply was exhausted she screamed, "Fostie—Fostie—come out here!"

There was no sound of hurrying footsteps from within the cottage, but the door opened and Foster was there. He pressed a wall switch and the light shone upon his small trembling figure. He was fully dressed. So, it could now be was his large screaming wife. "It's all right, dear. This is a police officer—not a burglar." To Nelson he said apologetically, "You must excuse her, sir. She's been very nervous lately—she must have thought—"

"Mrs. Foster and I have met before," Nelson said.

Pierce stared at the woman in wonder. She looked powerful enough, he thought, to take Nelson in one hand, him in the other, and bang their heads together. She was silent now, her face composed; masked would be more like it. And the night was still again except for a distant sound of some animal among rustling leaves.

"Would you—did you want to come in?" Foster said.

"No, I just want the garage key."

Foster slapped at his clothing. "I'll get it for you," he said. "We were preparing for bed. I'd just turned out my pockets." He stepped back into the cottage, drawing his wife with him. "You're sure you won't come in? I could give you some refreshment—"

"No, thank you."

"Well …" Foster left the door ajar. Pierce glimpsed a stodgy interior before he and Nelson turned their backs upon it to face the car.

Seager was a static bulk on the rear seat. Nelson called, "Why don't you get out and stretch your legs? I might be quite a while."

"Your concern for my welfare comes a little late," Seager said.

Pierce marveled at his control. He himself could not have sat quiet and aloof in surroundings so marked by ugly incident. Curiosity alone would have impelled him to be at least a close observer even though his wits refused to interpret what he saw and his lips had lost their knack for asking questions.

Perhaps five minutes passed before both Foster and his wife emerged. "I mislaid it," Foster said.

"No matter. Chief Maddox has given me authority to pick the lock if necessary."

"You didn't give me time to finish." Foster produced the large key ring. "I just meant that I had to hunt for them. I'm sorry to have kept you."

"There's no particular hurry," Nelson said.

The woman mimicked his mild tone. "No particular hurry. Then why couldn't it have waited until daylight? Why did you have to disturb us at this hour?" She caught her husband's arm. "Fostie, how do we know he really is a police officer? I haven't seen any credentials—even if he has some they could be phony—"

Foster said, "But, dear, Chief Maddox places a lot of confidence in him. Didn't I tell you about ..." He went on to tell her while Pierce and Nelson stood by.

Pierce expected that at any moment Seager would roar a protest from the car. But Seager had evidently thrown in the sponge. He remained static and mute. Pierce realized that the Fosters were engaged in something more than zany conversation. They were using delaying tactics, deliberately keeping Nelson from whatever it was he sought in the garage. He thought with small comfort that he was not the only one whose wits had dulled. What was the matter with Nelson that he could not penetrate so obvious a ruse? He nudged him in the moment that Nelson reached out and calmly extracted the key ring from Foster's hand.

Nelson walked toward the garage, not seeming to notice that he led a procession. He flashed his light on the lock and by guess or touch selected the matching key. He rolled back the sliding doors. Over his shoulder he said, "Turn on the light," and Foster stepped forward, fumbling a bit before he complied.

It was a spacious garage. It held a station wagon, a gray sedan, and behind these a convertible, painted black. Pierce, at Nelson's heels, observed that the convertible carried no license plates. Nelson had halted to give it cursory inspection, to flash his light on its interior before he continued his march toward the stairs at the rear of the garage. He climbed the stairs as though he knew where he was going, and why. He called down to Foster, "Where's the light switch here?"

"Inside the door. I hope it isn't shut. It has a spring lock, and I'm not sure the key is on that ring. Let me—"

He did not finish because Nelson had found and applied a key that fit. By the time the others reached him he had also found the wall switch.

The room had two beds covered with yellow chenille spreads, two chests of drawers, three straight chairs, a large old-fashioned wardrobe, and a crammed magazine rack. The walls, broken by two doors, were papered with black and yellow triangles, a pattern more or less echoed by the linoleum on the floor.

Nelson stood in the center of the room taking survey. One of the doors was half open upon a white-tiled bath. He went in but did not linger. He was at the other door as Mrs. Foster came over the threshold, pushing her husband and Pierce out of her path. She, too, seemed to be taking survey. She exhaled gustily.

Her voice halted Nelson. "Where do you think you're going? If you're looking for something in there you've got your work cut out for you. It's used for storage. Even we've lost track of half the junk it holds." She snorted as he closed the door behind him. She said to Pierce, "You're his stooge, aren't you? What's he after?"

Pierce saw no reason for replying. He saw her throw an unreadable glance at Foster. Then she announced that she had to go to the bathroom, and went.

She reappeared before Nelson did. Again she and her husband exchanged glances. They said nothing, but she tapped her foot steadily until Nelson came out of the storage room, closing the door behind him. He looked at the two beds, chose one, and sat down. Absently he rubbed his dusty hands on the chenille spread.

"Who occupies this room?" he said.

The Fosters answered like a trained chorus, "Nobody." Mrs. Foster continued solo. "Except when Mr. Drake's in residence. Then it's for the chauffeur or gardener or—"

"But this bed I'm sitting on is made up, and I don't imagine that window's been left open all winter."

Beds again, Pierce thought. The guy has a bed fetish.

Mrs. Foster said, "Sure it's made up. I come here when I feel like it to get away from it all." She followed Nelson's eyes to the magazine rack. "I keep a supply of stuff to read and I have myself some peace. I even go so far as to take a bath here and maybe a snack—like it's the good old days and I'm single again. But you had to go and spoil it for me. It won't be fun anymore with Fostie wise."

Foster did not look hurt. He looked admiring.

"You do light laundry here too," Nelson said. He drew a minute garment from his pocket. "This fell off the line in the bathroom. I rescued it. You're right to hang it indoors. I meant to tell you the other day that silk yellows in the sun." Almost tenderly he spread it on the bed so that its shape could be seen. "So small," he said. "It's hard to believe you can get into—"

Foster made a weak, sputtering sound. His wife said negligently, "Don't try to play the he-man, Fostie. Let the poor cop get his kicks where he finds them." She reached the bed in two steps. Whether her outflung arm was aimed at Nelson or the pants remained undetermined. She stiffened. "What's that?"

It sounded as though a parade was marching up the stairs. The voice of Chief Maddox shouted, "Grid—hey, Grid—are you there?" At Nelson's answering shout he lumbered into the room. "You had something. Yessir—you had something. Only it's a blonde." He moved aside to let the rest of the parade pass. It came on, single file. It comprised a uniformed policeman, a limping spectacled girl with cropped yellow hair, LeRoy Seager, and a second policeman bringing up the rear.

Foster moved over to his wife and reached for her arm. It was no idle gesture. He needed support. She shook him off. Her assembly-line features were all at once transparent, the shadowy thoughts scurrying behind them in great disorder. Pierce was staring at the girl. She wore dungarees and a white shirt. The delicate skin on her face was scratched. Her shirt was torn and showed the stains of earth and grass. With difficulty Pierce shifted his gaze to Seager. He cried harshly, "What's the matter? This time it's real!"

But he felt his mind to be suspect as he went to the girl. "Whatever he's done to you he'll pay for—everything's all right now."

Her eyes behind the disfiguring glasses were opaque. She said in her prim flat voice, "That's what you think." Someone pushed a chair under her, and she sat down.

CHAPTER FOURTEEN

Mrs. Foster went into her screaming act again. Rage made her incoherent. "The stupid bitch—don't even know enough—never saw her before—a frame—you can't prove—"

Chief Maddox gave her a light, impersonal tap to quiet her. Her fist came up against his jaw. His next blow was more vigorous and less impersonal. A weeping Foster rushed blindly to her aid. Nelson and the two policemen intervened. Pierce bent over the seated girl, his body protecting her from involvement. The girl had removed her glasses. She held them before her, seemingly entranced by their glitter. Pierce remembered a pickled onion in the depths of a cocktail and its hypnotic effect upon a pair of fixed dark eyes. Seager was paying no attention to her or to the confusion around her. He was half out the door when Nelson hauled him back.

"Don't leave," Nelson said. "They're going to need a lawyer." He nodded toward the Fosters, now sandwiched between the two policemen. The tears still rolled down Foster's plump cheeks. His wife's mouth was closed and set. Pierce did not know at what point she had stopped her noise, but he was suddenly aware of the room's suffocating quiet.

Seager's voice provided little ventilation. He said fastidiously, "I don't know what's going on here—but you can't seriously expect me to have any part of it."

"Hear that?" Maddox said at large. "Hear what the man says? No sinking ships for him."

Foster was the only one who responded. He ground the heel of his hand into each streaming eye. He exclaimed in deep reproach, "Mr. Seager!"

Seager was moved to the extent of amending his words. "Of course if these people are in trouble, I'll be glad to do what I can."

"Listen to me," Pierce said, "all of you. Don't you realize— This is Toni George. There can be only one reason why he's pretending not to recognize her."

He produced no startling effect. Nelson said, "What about it? Do you want to explain to Kirby why you're not dancing for joy at seeing your fiancée again?"

Seager said aloofly, "He's a press agent. He should be able to figure it out for himself. It's quite obvious to me. Her disappearance was a put-up job—a publicity stunt—and since she did not choose to take me into her confidence I don't see why I should be expected to feel happy at seeing her again."

"Is it your theory," Nelson said, "that Bobby Drake aided and abetted her in this scheme?"

"I shouldn't be at all surprised. Mr. Drake's humor is infantile. It would be his idea of a good practical joke."

Unexpectedly Mrs. Foster shot forward. Her lips were working. Before she managed to get them apart Seager added, "Probably Drake engineered the whole affair and threatened his employees with the loss of their livelihood if they refused to hide her. I intend to do my utmost to see that it doesn't go hard with them."

Maddox was smiling and shaking his head in wonder. Nelson was not smiling. Neither was Toni George. She had emerged from her trance. She raised a hand to her dry bleached crop and she winced.

Nelson said, "I understand, Mr. Seager. You intend—if necessary— to champion the underdog. You feel that the Fosters have become embroiled out of self-preservation and you'll go to their aid in court. But because of quite normal resentment you won't lift a finger to keep Toni George from her just punishment."

Toni George looked at her lover. "Won't you, Roy?"

Seager met her eyes. He turned away, clearing his throat. He said brokenly, "Yes—yes—I'll help her—for the sake of what she meant to me—"

"Meant, Roy?" said Toni.

"Give me time," he groaned, and then more urgently, "You *must* give me time."

"Virtually," Nelson said, "Toni has been a prisoner for several weeks. And she's going to be a prisoner in actual fact for a great deal longer than that while you take time to consider ways and means. It isn't good enough. Your theory isn't good enough either. Drake's sense of humor may have been infantile, but jokes aren't funny—especially to the infantile—unless they can witness the outcome."

"He probably got cold feet—"

"He got very cold feet—and Toni is realizing too late how wrong she's been—but not too late to refuse the role of scapegoat. No lawyer can help her now—least of all you. And you can't help the Fosters either. But they can help themselves to some extent." He stopped talking as Toni George stood up.

She said, "He's right. It isn't good enough."

Seager cried out. The Fosters exploded according to their natures. But she would not be silenced. Grimly she rode through interruption. It seemed that the words she delivered in her toneless, undramatic way had been accumulated during a long and painful solitude, and now she could not wait to be rid of them. Even Nelson's frequently interposed questions hardly served to halt her. She answered mechanically and hurried on. One of the policemen wrote busily, his notebook resting on a chest of drawers. But Pierce had no need of pencil or notebook. For days after he could repeat her words almost verbatim.

"Roy thought the whole thing up," she said. "I must have been crazy to go along with him. I knew it as soon as I had time to think—only that wasn't until it was over and done with—and I was stuck here. But when I was with Roy he made it seem so reasonable. We couldn't get married any other way, he said, because since his father's death the firm had been slipping. Most of the worthwhile clients had pulled out because he wasn't conservative enough for them. Drake was the only rich one left, and handling his affairs was peanuts compared to what could be had if I'd cooperate. When you're in love—even when you think you're in love—you get wacky. I did. All I could see was that an educated, professional man wanted to marry me. I'm not excusing myself. I'm not smart enough to make excuses—not like Roy—"

"Shut up," cried Seager. "It's not too late—"

"You're bad news, Roy. I knew it when you went for the old man—I just wouldn't let myself admit it." Her eyes shifted to Pierce for a moment. "I didn't know who he was then, but I guess it wouldn't have made any difference. He was in the way. That's all that seemed to matter."

A sickening lump had formed in Pierce's throat. He had moved as far away from her as the room allowed. He thrust his hands behind him, secured them there with ropes woven by his mind. Yet crowding hatred and aversion was pity for her.

"Roy had come up to the dressing room," she said, "and—"

"It was an accident!" Seager repeated wildly, "It was an accident," seeking belief in the withdrawn faces.

"Tell us what happened to Dr. Miles," Nelson said.

"There was a lot of confusion. Bobby Drake had looked in to round up some girls for a party, and the takers were busy getting themselves ready. My table was near the door. Roy knocked and I opened it and he whispered that he'd be back—he had to go to the washroom. By the time he did get back to the dressing room it had cleared. So he sat down to talk things over with me. I must have been hoping we wouldn't have to go through with the Drake business—that there'd be some other way we could get married and live the kind of life Roy wanted—"

Maddox boomed, "If he says one word, gag him—and if that doesn't work, knock him out."

Seager closed his mouth.

Toni went on dispassionately: "We were at it for quite a while—talking back and forth. The last girl out had left the door open—it was kind of smelly in the dressing room, so we didn't bother to close it. Nobody was on the floor, anyway. When we heard the cough right outside Roy almost had a fit. Both of us went to look, and we saw the old man standing there. He had a nice face—not mean or anything—and he started right in to talk to us. If he'd kept quiet and gone about his business it wouldn't have happened. But he let us know he'd heard too much. Roy got kind of purple and called him senile and said he'd been imagining things. The old man looked surprised. You could tell he wasn't fooled, although he muttered something about it being his mistake and turned to go. Roy followed him—and at the head of the stairs he reached out suddenly and gave him a hard push. That was how it happened. Roy ran down and saw that his neck was broken." Her mouth twisted. "Give the devil his due," she said tonelessly. "I don't think Roy meant to kill him. He'd just lost his head. He carried him back up to the dressing room, and we closed the door and tried to think of something. At first I wanted to call the police, but Roy said they'd ask why we were there so late and that they had ways of putting two and two together. He said we couldn't afford to be on the scene of any death—accidental or otherwise—not with what was to come. If a body was found in the theater there'd be an investigation, with everybody questioned—and he didn't want me touched by it—it might cause suspicion later. I said surely we wouldn't go ahead now, but he acted like I was stupid. We were both in too deep to turn back, he said, and we could make this a kind of rehearsal. If we had nerve enough to see it through it would prove that we could carry off that other. I got a headache listening to him. I didn't know what was right or wrong anymore. I told him to do anything he wanted—only hurry, because Steve might make the rounds or something. Well, he started to tear the labels off the old man's clothes. When he took his wallet and stuff, that seemed worse to me than anything—like common stealing—but he told me it wasn't that he wanted the money—it was to keep the police from finding the old man's name for a while. The more time it took them to check, the less chance there'd be of connecting the death with the theater. The name of Dr. Miles didn't mean a thing to me—but there was a snapshot of Pierce Kirby in the wallet—so we knew how he'd happened to come backstage." She licked her dry lips. "We thought first of carrying him down the fire escape, but Roy was afraid we'd miss our footing in the dark." She touched her slim throat. "I think I'm getting laryngitis—that wet grass—"

Nelson said, "So Seager leaned out of an alley window and called Steve—and Steve, thinking the voice came from the alley, went to investigate—and one of you ran down to slam the door so that Steve would have to use the fire escape to get back in."

She nodded. "Me—I was the one who locked the door. Then I ran back up and Roy said it was okay, Steve had started to climb. So he slung the old man over his shoulders and I went on ahead to be sure the coast was clear. Steve had disappeared from the fire escape by the time we reached the alley. When we got to the start of it Roy told me where his car was parked and gave me the keys and I brought it around. When Roy drove off it was just like he had a passenger in the front seat.... Could I have a glass of water?"

Nobody moved. Then, at a gesture from Nelson, one of the policemen went into the bathroom and got it for her. Nelson said, "So you got rid of your car quite recently, Mr. Seager? I think I can tell you when."

Seager did not answer. Foster coughed dryly. His wife said, "This is all strictly news to us—understand?"

Nelson said, "We'll get to you." His eyes commanded Toni to proceed.

"Roy didn't make me go with him. He told me to wait in Shane's Bar and Grill. I didn't know what he'd do with the body. I was glad I didn't have to be with him when he did it. I went to Shane's. Jill and

Stasia were there. When Pierce Kirby came in they called him over. I didn't want to look at him or talk to him, but Roy had said the rumor that Drake was chasing me would have to be started somewhere, and if the opportunity came up there'd be no better place to start it than with a press agent." Her shorn head drooped on her neck.

Nelson said, "Drake had never singled you out, had he? It was Seager who sent you the bracelet and the pin. But he made the mistake of ordering them at the same time. You turned over the original package to him and he had it sent back to you in two installments. Drake must have trusted his lawyer implicitly to supply him with a key to the penthouse. I suppose Seager just walked in and used the phone and answered it when the jeweler checked back."

"You're insane," Seager said defiantly. "I never had a key to the penthouse. I went there only by invitation, with the exception of the night I went with Kirby. I can prove that by the servants—"

"You're not telling me that Barrows was in on the plot? Barrows was vacationing at the time the jewelry was ordered."

"I'm telling you nothing."

Toni said, "Barrows wasn't in on it."

"I see. This is where the Fosters come in. Foster had a key to the penthouse—probably because he was sent there on occasional errands." He looked at the cowering little man. "You're not a good conspirator, Foster. To be on the safe side you should have removed that key from the ring you gave me."

"It isn't there—I got rid of it after—"

His wife hit him on the side of the head.

"That won't do you any good," Nelson said to her. He might have used the same tone to reason with a juvenile delinquent.

Foster was sobbing openly, talking through his sobs. "It's not my fault. I was satisfied—I was making good money—I begged her to leave me out of it. I knew I'd give everything away—I'm not cut out for—"

"You're not," Nelson said, with no intent to extend comfort. "But Seager needed help, and you and your wife were his obvious choice. It was he who sent you to the penthouse to order the jewelry. He knew Drake would be out that day and that Barrows was away. And he knew that the maids wouldn't question your right to be there or to use the telephone."

Maddox shook a fist under Foster's quivering chin. "It's true, isn't it? Answer yes or no—and it better be yes."

"Y-yes." Foster dared not look at his wife.

Nelson said to Toni, "Do you want to get on with the rest of it? You're not being coerced. So far you've made a statement of your own free will. You can continue or not as you choose."

"Why not?" she said hoarsely. Then she said, "Laryngitis on top of everything else."

"All right," Nelson said, "I'll talk for a bit. On the night scheduled for your disappearance Seager drove his car out here and parked it in the garage of his own place." He waited for her nod. "I don't know how you arranged the date with Drake. Probably you were told when he'd be in Seager's office so that you could just happen in."

She said painfully, "Yes—I flirted with him. He was surprised, because I was Roy's girl—but I told him I'd had a secret crush on him for a long time and he was pleased. Roy left us alone in the office, and we made the date to drive out here. I was to meet him right after the performance. It would have been better for him to come to the theater and let the girls see him, but he didn't want to. I guess he was nervous about it getting back to Roy." She clasped a hand around her aching throat. "I met him and we drove to Chilton. About half a mile from the house there's one of those road signs with the arrows pointing in all directions. It had been fixed that Roy would be hiding in the bushes there. I told Bobby Drake to slow up, I'd seen something moving on the road. He stopped the car, and Roy jumped in and banged him on the head with a rock. He didn't die right away, but he was out. He never knew what hit him. He bled all over—"

Seager was sneering. His sneer said, "Prove it."

Nelson said, "And Seager put him in back of the car and took the wheel, after pre-empting the Italian hat and the English overcoat in case anyone besides the Fosters should happen to be present when you arrived at the Drake house."

"Yes."

"And Drake's body was carried into the living room and his blood was dabbed about to make us believe what we did believe for a while. One of your shoes was left there to complete the picture. I suppose the tale we were expected to attach to the pin in the fireplace was that you had cast it there in righteous indignation to show that you couldn't be bought with jewels. It was all carefully thought out."

"Roy's a good thinker," she said without admiration.

"And it was you and Seager who went to bed in order to refresh yourselves before you disposed of the body."

Incredibly her pale face reddened. She could admit to murder, not to the loss of virtue.

"Did you know beforehand that you and Drake had the same blood type? Seager at least must have realized that the lab would run a precipitant."

"Roy knew."

"Shall I go on? All right. The original arrangement was for you to hide in Seager's house until he could get you out of the country, where he might or might not join you. But when Kirby, by way of a wrong premise, hit on the idea that you might be there, and the policeman ran to Foster for directions, Foster streaked along the back road, which I discovered later, to hustle you away. He probably had some telephone signal arranged to warn you in case of danger, but he didn't dare trust to it."

"Yes, Foster got me and sneaked me into their cottage. The next morning, after the policeman had been called off, they brought me to this room—kept me here ever since because they were afraid someone else might get the idea that I was at Roy's. Some fun. They didn't even dare to buy me stuff to wear for fear they'd be caught shopping. These things I have on were left by their niece." She gave Mrs. Foster a look of cold dislike. "She even had to cut down some of her underwear for me."

"I know," Nelson said. "She was kind enough to wash it out for you too."

"Kind?" said Toni. "I made her hang it in the sun before I'd put it on."

"You two-bit tooth dancer," Mrs. Foster yelled, "I'll—"

Nelson made himself heard. "And tonight when we arrived, the Fosters obligingly raised their voices in warning and you climbed out of that window—"

"Yes—I helped myself down by that tree outside. I fell on the way back to Roy's house. I hadn't got very far when the police jumped me."

Nelson turned to Seager. "Would it change your mind about talking if I told you we've found Drake's hat and overcoat?"

Seager said in attempted mimicry, "No, it wouldn't change my mind. Why should it? As for this demented girl trying to worm her way out of a stunt by attempting to cast suspicion on a man of my standing—"

"Are you aware that tests will prove you wore the coat and hat?"

Seager said quickly, "I tried them on when he bought them—he—"

"Would that have been on the same day he stole the picture from your desk? Never mind. I don't want you to answer. It would be a useless tax on your ingenuity to find all the answers you're going to need." Nelson looked very tired and not very happy.

"Shall I take them away, Grid?" Maddox asked. "I've a stack of blank warrants—"

"Give them hospitality for one night. I'll arrange for an immediate transfer."

"You and your pal there had better tag along to the jail in case anyone makes trouble. You're armed?"

"Yes," Nelson lied.

But nobody made trouble.

At 4 A.M. Nelson and Pierce were headed for New York. Pierce thought of another drive along the same road, of the way it had all started, of Uncle Doc, of a girl with cropped bleached hair who was no one he had ever known, of Ginette, who was blessedly free of the whole mess.

"Why the hair and glasses?" he asked suddenly, as though it were a major point.

"At a guess she was practicing the disguise that would get her out of the country when the heat died down a bit. Also, if any of the townspeople caught a glimpse of her they wouldn't connect her with the descriptions in the papers. The Fosters would probably claim she was their niece, who actually does wear glasses and has short blond hair."

"When did you get to know that?"

"Foster had mentioned the niece in his first statement. I wanted to verify his excuse for not entering the Drake house sooner. How do you feel?"

"Like a convalescent. As though recovering isn't what it's cracked up to be." He thought again of Ginette.

"I feel almost like that after every case—even without being personally involved."

"I was a big help." Ginette. He had practically accused her. She would—

"You put me on Seager's trail by suggesting that Toni might be hiding in his house. It started me thinking. There was so much to think about—his pantry that was almost as well stocked as Drake's— the suitcase—Mrs. Foster—"

"That horrible creature—"

"Foster didn't think so. She was part of a traveling circus that came to town one day—and he fell hard. But that's beside the point— the point being her insistence that Drake had a violent temper. It conflicted with the opinions of all the people who knew him, and it made me suspect she had an ax to grind. Only at first I thought it was another brand of ax—that she was protecting Drake and meant to put me off the track by pretending she had no use for him. Then I had a thought that was even more haywire. It was hard to believe Drake could stage a complete disappearing act unaided, so I began to divert more of my attention to his lawyer. I was less than half sold on the theory that Seager would abet a client who was the supposed murderer of his fiancée—but when I went to his office, one of those apparently meaningless little incidents cropped up to weaken my sales resistance. There was an empty picture frame jamming the bottom drawer of his desk. It seemed to me that he had only just shoved it out of sight, because he was struggling with the drawer as I entered. In any case, I knew it couldn't have been there very long.

An inconvenience like that would have irritated a less methodical man than Seager. He'd have had it attended to at once. So I wondered why a man so patently in the throes of grief should be so quick to rid himself of his loved one's picture. And my wondering led me quite naturally to the picture on Drake's bureau. I'd noticed it wasn't a publicity shot, and if Toni had warded off Drake's advances as stated, she'd hardly present him with an expensive studio portrait. Later I put temptation in the way of the reporter who stole it, hoping its publication might give rise to something."

"It gave rise to something all right." He tried to stop thinking of Ginette. "Why didn't you ask for an explanation then and there?"

"Because I'm not as impulsive as you. As Sammy says, there are more ways of killing a pig than slitting its throat. I had a few words with the receptionist on the way out, and I had Seager's financial affairs investigated."

"Well?"

"Shaky but not shady. He was struggling to pay the overhead, but there were no signs of crookedness. Nonetheless, I had him tailed long before the Jill episode."

"If you'd told me everything I might not have copped the world's champion fool record."

Nelson smiled bleakly. "You had no official standing—aside from which I couldn't have you wading in before I'd collected real evidence." His smile warmed. "And you didn't want to hear everything. You got pretty impatient whenever I mentioned my visits to Chilton. It was the day after the main event that I came upon big Mrs. Foster hanging up small undergarments outside the garage. It should have meant something to me, but I suppose I was too busy trying to sum her up. And I suppose I'd forgotten that old saw about choosing the most obvious place when you wanted to hide something. I didn't think of the garage again until I saw Sammy folding Kyrie's pants. Kyrie's built along the same lines as Toni. The similarity ends there—"

"You mean that's the reason we dashed off to Chilton with Seager?" He saw Ginette in Seager's living room. Ginette. But when there had been real cause to doubt her, when she was right there in that dog's apartment, he had not doubted. At least he had that.

"No—things were fairly clear to me by that time. Not that I wouldn't have dashed off anywhere for far less—but I had far more. You've forgotten the body washed up by the sea."

"But it wasn't—" Seeing Toni alive had made him forget. He gave Nelson his full attention.

"No, it wasn't. It was the body of Bobby Drake."

"What?"

"I know it's hard to digest. We had everything backward from the beginning—as intended."

Pierce tried to digest it. "Did you know it was Drake before you and Seager went in?"

"Yes, I was told on the phone. Drake had a riding accident years ago. He'd been patched up with a tin plate in his elbow. Dr. Traub's brother, a surgeon at Spruce Harbor, had performed the operation. The body was badly battered, the skull had been crushed beforehand, and everything possible done to make the features unidentifiable. Additionally, marine life had innings—the tin plate showed without benefit of X ray, and Dr. Traub recognized it as his brother's work."

Bitter saliva collected in Pierce's mouth. He swallowed. "And you thought if you confronted Seager with—with it he'd break down."

"Yes. I underestimated him—or over. As often happens, Seager's worst moments were the ones he spent waiting to see if he'd got away with it—that period when we mistook his nervousness for grief. In the final test he found his second wind."

"And when I met him I thought he was a man Dale Carnegie would be proud of." Then Pierce said, "But suppose a jury discounts Toni's story. She won't be considered reliable—and Seager's foxy-smart. How can you prove he murdered Drake? Did you really find Drake's hat and coat—or was that bluff?"

"There are a number of castoff coats and hats in that storeroom over the garage. I wouldn't be surprised if the ones we want are among them. Maddox is going to search in the morning. The suitcase might be there too. Foster must have taken it from the penthouse on the day he ordered the jewelry—just to make it look like a planned getaway." He lit a cigarette. "Seager didn't dare come near Chilton to tie up the loose ends after the event, and the Fosters have had their hands too full to dispose of anything. But even without the hat and coat and suitcase there's enough evidence to convict him now that we've got our corpse. Remember, Toni's offering her own head along with Seager's—and that will take a lot of discounting by any judge or jury. Then there's the car. You noticed it in the garage—the black one without license plates. A recent paint job—undoubtedly gray underneath, with stains on the upholstery that couldn't be washed away in spite of the Fosters' industry. I'm willing to bet it belongs to Seager. I'd checked to see if he had a car, and got the description but no record of sale. I'd even searched his own garage to see if it was there. Are you listening?"

"Yes." Pierce tore his mind from Ginette.

"Seager must have had a lot of blood smeared on him by the time he returned from rowing Drake out and dumping him. I guess he detoured on the way back to plant Drake's car and then got into his own without thinking to drive Toni to his house. Some of the blood was transferred, and after that the car was no good to him. He had to make the best arrangement at hand to put it under wraps until there was time to get rid of it entirely."

"What exactly was at stake? Drake must have made a will, so I don't see how Seager could have hoped to— Oh—of course."

"Of course. The cash Drake took from his bank. We haven't found that yet—but we will."

"How do you think Seager got him to play into his hands like that?"

"According to all accounts, Drake was easy-come-easy-go nothing of a businessman. He seems to have been prey to a number of wildcat schemes. It's my guess that Seager invented some tempting double-your-money proposition that demanded cash on the line—and that Drake bit."

A little later Pierce said, "Want me to drive the rest of the way? You must be all in."

"I'll manage. We're on the last lap." Then he said, "You never offered to drive before. I wouldn't have known you could if I—"

"Hadn't checked? Tell me—did you really suspect me? You made a dirty crack about my inheritance."

"I'm paid to make dirty cracks from time to time—and I work hard at suspecting everybody until tag day."

"Thank God it's tag day."

"Amen." Nelson yawned. "Almost time to start the day's work."

"You'll get some sleep first, won't you?"

"Too much to do. But I'll make up for it."

"You'd better," Pierce said awkwardly. "Guys like you should take care of themselves. I don't suppose I'll be seeing you again, so—I want to—"

"Moving out of town?"

"No."

"Good. When Kyrie comes home how about dinner? Bring Ginette Arthur."

"Thanks."

Nelson glanced at him. "I've had invitations accepted with more enthusiasm."

"I—I don't know if Ginette wants to have any more to do with me."

"Your I.Q.'s way down again," Nelson said firmly. "Of course she does."

"You generally know what you're talking about," Pierce said. He could feel her in his arms.

THE END

DEAD YESTERDAY

RUTH FENISONG

CHAPTER ONE

The maid tiptoed to the door of the large living room. The decorous expression settled upon her young impertinent face as soon as she crossed the threshold. The excuse lay ready to her lips. "Ma'am," she said tentatively. "Ma'am—?"

The countess answered with a snore. Chins pressed into her neck, she slept, her chair drawn close to the heat of the open fire.

The maid inhaled with caution. The air in the room was very stale, and the luxury of furnishings was dulled everywhere by layers of New York dust. Some faint stirring of conscience impelled her to move about, making small futile stabs at creating order. A sin and a shame, she thought, that such a beautiful apartment had got so out of hand. But it was not her fault. There was too much work for one person.

When she had taken the job there had been a cook, and a daily woman supplied by the house. But the attentions of the daily woman had been discouraged because they annoyed the countess. And then the cook had left. And what with seeing to meals and everything, it was impossible to do much cleaning. Not that the old bag complained or even noticed. She was easy to work for. Generous too. The maid gave her that. And she seemed content so long as she had enough to eat and drink. Mainly enough to drink. The maid had never caught her at it, but from the way she reeked of alcohol each morning, every night was binge night.

A funny sort of life for a real countess with plenty of money and stuff. No hobbies, no visitors, or at least none but that little gentleman, that Mr. Spencer, who came about once a month. The maid had become skilled at dismissing the few others who still tried. Mr. Spencer, however, was persistent and would not be turned away, although what pleasure he took in the visits was hard to imagine. Just a loyal friend who must have known her before she became such a mess, the maid guessed.

At first the maid had doubted her employer's right to the title, had regarded it as some sort of joke. But her boyfriend had put her wise. "Say, baby, don't you ever read the papers? Everybody's heard of *her*. Sure she's the goods. Married an Eyetalian count who died about two-three years ago and left her a fortune. Stick around. Maybe she'll take a shine to you and remember you in her will. Wouldn't mind having an introduction to her myself."

She had laughed. "Not your type, Dave."

She had a date with him now. It was his afternoon off, and he said if she could wangle it she was to meet him outside the Roxy. She had meant to tell the countess that a toothache was driving her crazy and that she had to see a dentist right away. But there was no sense in awaking her. There was no sense in writing a note either. Chances were it would never be read. Take for instance the mail littering that fancy desk in the corner. It had been piling up for months and none of it ever opened. Most of the time she was not even permitted to answer the telephone. "Let it ring," the countess said in her deep voice that somehow called out goose pimples. She was a funny old egg. Well, not so old, according to Dave. But how could you tell, the way she had let herself spread all over the place. Yet Dave couldn't be talking through his hat because there wasn't a gray hair in her head. Her hair was a red tumble, thick as anything in spite of the fact that she never brushed it. Natural too. No dye on the market could produce that color. The maid was hard to fool about such matters. She touched a hand to her own sparrow-brown locks and envied that hair as a freakish waste of nature.

Well, she had better be on her way or Dave would see the picture alone. Worse, he might pick up another girl. She was going to marry Dave, but he did not know it yet. She had to stick as close to him as possible. She had to look out for herself. But she would make sure that she was back in time to get dinner. She did not want to lose her job until she had saved enough for a wedding. Besides, she had nothing against her mistress. Sometimes she even felt sorry for her. Crazy, her feeling sorry for a rich slob who did not know which side was up.

She left the apartment hurriedly, not using the service exit because the other was quicker. If the elevator boy gave her any lip she'd tell him a thing or two. When she was downstairs she was troubled by misgivings. Had she or had she not heard the spring lock click behind her? Impatiently she cast her fears away and ran for a crosstown bus.

After a while the countess opened her eyes, once bright as her hair, and now like bits of scrap that had been allowed to rust and sink in the folds of her flesh. Her tongue was dry. She sent it questing for saliva. She swallowed painfully. She thought as she had thought since hell began that it was a mistake to sleep in the afternoon. It reimposed that gruesome task of facing life again. Once a day was enough for that. Yet what other way was there to shut out the mocking sun, to hasten the coming of dark? Only when dark came would she pander to her thirst. That much discipline she imposed upon herself. Except for a little wine at such meals as would have caused Dino's nose to wrinkle in disgust, she waited until dark to slake her thirst. And then she did not drink in the apartment that was Dino's. She drank in shabby bars that held no danger of encounters with people she had known in Dino's time. She had come to be accepted in these bars. None of the regulars gave her more than a casual glance. That was what she wanted, the illusion of drinking in company without the effort of sociability. It seemed important, because long ago she had despised solitary drinkers. But long ago sociability had been no effort at all. Her talk had flowed. She had called forth laughter, admiration, jealousy, love. She had called forth love with no more than a smile or a whisper. Long ago.

She heaved herself out of the chair. Her legs bore their heavy burden through her bedroom to the adjoining bath. She took great gulps of tap water, not swallowing, sluicing out the parched cavern of her mouth. Then she splashed her face and dried it, and began to comb her hair. Began only, putting the comb aside because it balked at a tangle, and pain reduced the importance of neatness. Not once during this sketchy toilet did she look in the mirror. When it was over she shivered, all heat being concentrated in her mouth and throat, and turned, and retraced her steps to the living room fire.

The fire was almost dead. With difficulty she bent over the wood basket and grasped a few sticks and flung them into the failing blaze. Straightening, her blank gaze settled upon a painting above the mantel. Without recognition she met the eyes of that slim lovely girl. A stranger from another world. She sank back into her chair.

In the next room, which had been Dino's study, the phone rang. She gave no sign of hearing, and presently it stopped. Vaguely she supposed that the maid was in the kitchen. She thought of calling for a glass of wine but resisted the temptation. This was the only game she played, this holding off until the hour came. It was the only game left her out of all the others she had played so zestfully.

Her lids dropped again. When she raised them twilight was in the room, twilight and a human presence. She thought, I must be dreaming. It is not time for him. Time does not pass so quickly as all that.

"Thea—are you here? Is anyone at home?"

Time had not passed. It had gone backward. This was not the hateful expected voice. This was a voice not heard in years. Yet she recognized it immediately. It seemed to come from somewhere behind the high back of her chair. If she sat very still perhaps its owner would leave. She did not want to see him. Above all, she did not want him to see her. It was the first touch of vanity she had experienced since the world's end. She had no need to study her appearance in a mirror. She could feel it in the misery of every move she made, in the meeting of hand with roughened hair, with cheek, with overlap of flesh that had been clean and smooth and taut.

He switched on a lamp and rounded the chair. He stared, and then he muttered, "No—Thea—my God—Thea! What have you done to yourself?"

She sighed. She said in that thrilling voice that was so completely divorced from her neglected person, "Grant Barstow—I thought you were away—on the other side of the globe."

"I came back yesterday—I—" He could not talk for staring. She said, mustering what will she had, to gentle words, "I'm seeing no one these days—no one, Grant."

He might not have heard. He found another lamp and lit it. With deliberation he turned a chair so that it faced hers. He sat down. He was going to be difficult. She remembered well the mulish expression that clamped down on his mouth. What had he done to the maid to make her forget instructions?

"Grant—it's no use—please go."

"Go?" His eyes swept the room, returned to dwell with unbelief upon the shapeless figure, the soiled and wrinkled dress, the raddled face. "Of course I won't go—not until we've talked. There's something very wrong—"

"There's something very wrong," she repeated tiredly, "something beyond the offers of help that you intend to make. Please—I told the maid—"

"What maid?" His voice was stiffened by a frame of anger. Remove the frame and it would collapse. "I've been phoning since yesterday. Naturally you were the first—one of the first friends I wanted to see. You never bothered to reply to my letters, but surely they explained my—well—never mind that now—"

"Never mind that now," she said. There might have been irony in the simple repetition.

He ignored it. "When I couldn't reach you by phone I decided to drop in. I rang and rang. If you have a maid she's—"

"She may have gone out to shop. How did you get in?"

"The door was open. I thought I'd write a note—"

She said a vast uncaring "Oh," knowing that she would have to speak to the maid, dreading it as a project quite beyond her will or scope.

"Why are you living like this—alone and—?"

"Dino is dead," she said.

"I learned of Dino's death from a man I met in Florence. It doesn't answer my question. I want to know why—?"

She moved her tongue over her dry lips. "What time is it?"

He said mechanically, "A little after five." The question echoed in his ears, completely irrelevant to the contents of his heart and mind. "We'll not talk about the time or the weather. Thea—you've got to— you're going to explain all this." He waited. Then he said doggedly, "Lots of women have lost their husbands and managed to go on more or less as before. There must be something other than that—" He battered against her silence. "You're sick. You should be under a doctor's care. Are you? If it's something to do with glands, Dr. Selig—"

Her shoulders heaved. Incredibly she laughed. The sound of it was heartbreaking, a bright souvenir stumbled upon among castoffs once cherished and now grotesque because of time and change. "It's nothing to do with glands," she said through laughter.

He sensed the danger, doubted the ability of the gasping flesh to stop now that it had started. He shouted brutally, "Then it's a psychiatrist you need—unless you're too far—"

The laughter ended. She cowered as from a blow. He forced himself to go on. "I've been out of the country five years. When I left you were—how old—thirty-seven—thirty-eight? And you looked younger. You looked as young as you were when that picture was painted." He took his shocked eyes away from her and raised them to the portrait over the mantel. For a moment it was as though the nightmare had been dispelled.

But he had to go back to it. "Thea—you were always so realistic— so sane. You can't be—you can't have chosen this strange way to mourn for Dino."

"I loved Dino."

"I know." It was wrenched from him even though the clean image he had carried for so long was gone, buried past hope of resurrection beneath an ugly tomb. "But you loved him only for a little while. Then you discovered that Dino wasn't—"

"Dino wasn't worth loving? Dino was an unlikely receptacle for love that endured beyond the transitory flare and sputter of his own emotions. Is that what you want to say?"

He could have sworn there was mockery in the voice, that the dulled eyes had cleared, that through them shone that Thea of the portrait. But when he leaned forward eagerly, the lids had dropped again and he was confronted by a great blank waste.

Dino was dead and forget him. Dino living had been a rotten stinker, worth at most a glance, a quickened heartbeat if it was a woman who glanced, but never a lingering thought, a sustained passion. That was what he wanted to say without benefit of euphemism. Personable? Yes. Nothing in his makeup of the sleek Latin gigolo. Dino had been endowed with the fair coloring of northern Italy, the charm and poise of an ancient culture. He himself had been fooled by it. He winced. It was a reflex unfailingly induced by memory of Dino. He looked to see if Dino's widow had noticed, but she was a static bulk in her chair, seeing nothing, hearing nothing, responding to nothing outward. Again he raised his eyes to the portrait. The real Thea.

He and Dino had met her at the same time. He had been introduced to Dino in the office of Seth Oswald, president of a large advertising agency. And damn Seth Oswald. Damn the man for all time.

He, Grant, had stopped in to discuss the handling of an account, had stayed after the campaign had been outlined, for a drink and a chat.

"Don't worry, Grant. The money couldn't be put to better use than advertising. We'll clear a place for you on the map—the place you've earned."

The young Grant was not at all sure that he had earned or even wanted the place that would be cleared. But he was sure that he needed more money than his father had left him in order to pursue his real career. He was a research chemist, and quite by accident he had stumbled upon a formula for removing hair from women's legs and arms.

"Yep, it's a gold mine," Oswald said. "Revolutionary. You're in from here on out. Hold everything. I've kept the best for the last. Take a gander at these." He pushed a folder of glossy prints toward Grant.

"Who is she?" Grant asked. His tone was casual. But he was normal. And no normal man could have resisted the impact of those pictures. He flipped them over, his eyes lingering on each pose. Studies of grace that was unstudied. Arrested motion of arms outflung, of legs at point of leaping.

"When you've time look at the face," Oswald said, grinning, "it's not bad either. Well—she's your baby. She's the 'Smoothy Girl.' Pretty soon she'll be looking at you from every slick magazine in the country, and unless I miss my guess she could sell boats on a desert. Excuse me a minute." He turned to answer one of the phones on his desk. "Who? ... Oh, he is? ... No, don't keep him waiting. Send him in."

Grant had risen. "So long, Oswald. I'll be—"

"What's your hurry? Friend of mind I'd like you to meet. Count Mazzini." He said the name unctuously. "You've heard of him. Not only one of the oldest titles extant but loaded—and shrewd enough to have tied the load in good U.S. investments. Besides, you're English, aren't you?"

"Half—my mother was an American."

"Well, he likes Englishmen," Oswald said, as though that settled it.

Grant had roomed with Seth Oswald's younger brother at Yale. He thought that snobbery must be a family trait. While he stood hesitant, the count made his entrance.

"Hello. I interrupt something? Splendid. You Americans work much too hard." He himself showed no signs of working ever. He propped his walking stick against a chair. He drew off his gloves and flung them on the desk. His hands were long and thin and innocent of wear and tear. His clothes had creases only where creases should be, and he smelled faintly of lotion and leather and fine linen. "Nonetheless, I adopt you. I adopt the whole country. This day I have applied for my first citizen papers. So we celebrate."

Oswald presented Grant as the coming white hope of womanhood and went into a detailed explanation. The count seemed much amused and spoke at ribald length about the pros and cons of Grant's discovery. He had a certain type of wit, and Grant could not help laughing. Grant was not a drinking man. Up to that time he had been too engrossed in his chosen field to be a playing man either, but after several rounds of Oswald's scotch he began to find Count Mazzini very entertaining and to feel that perhaps he had missed something. So he accepted his invitation, seconded by Oswald, to do the town.

"But we must have ladies also," Mazzini said, "and that, my friend Seth, is for you to arrange since I have quite literally gone through my own list. What have we here?" He seized upon the open folder. His face took on a rapt, bemused expression. "I change my mind. We must have lady—this lady."

"Well—I don't know about that," Oswald said.

And something had moved Grant to remark that you couldn't always tell about pictures. She might be a dreadful disappointment. She might talk through her nose.

"Who *talks* with a lady like this?" the count demanded.

So Oswald had arranged it, using as pretext the fact that it would be advisable for her to meet the man responsible for the product she was to make famous.

She did not talk through her nose. She had a voice that made every word she uttered seem like a jewel laid upon black velvet. And if the words, removed from their background and examined, proved to have no great depth or sparkle, it did not matter. She was a lovely girl. She was warm and gay and outgoing. She was at ease, relaxed in any company. And her red hair was something to fall in love with just by itself. And both Dino Mazzini and Grant Barstow fell in love with all of her.

Before the first lap of the race was over it became plain that Grant had no chance. She cheered Dino on, and he must have wanted her badly to take that hurdle of marriage without breaking stride. But he took it, and someone else became the "Smoothy Girl" because such an honor was not suitable to Dino's wife.

Dino's span of interest was hardly more than infantile. No one was surprised when his attention began to stray. The real surprise was that his constancy lasted for better than a year.

Yet even after she caught him out, even through his most flagrant infidelities, she allowed the marriage to stand. In the set in which she moved, people thought that she was being quite reasonable. They thought that the benefits received, the title and the wealth, compensated for her husband's peccadilloes. She had, after all, been a smalltown girl, a model, a nobody raised suddenly to a position of social prominence. And they assured each other that she had lost little time in following Dino's example. Gossip bedded her down with every man she met.

Grant alone suffered for her. And even he was forced to admit that she stood the strain, if strain it was, with marked aplomb. Certainly she managed to keep her beauty and her gaiety intact.

He returned to the sick bewilderment of the present. For fifteen years she had walked unimpaired through circumstances inimical to any woman. Why, then, this belated metamorphosis? Dino was dead. And even allowing for the sentimental investiture of the "dear departed" with qualities never vouchsafed him in life, why had she not, after a decent period of mourning, emerged into the sun again? He could have accepted the change in someone who had shown strong symptoms of neurosis. But not in Thea.

"Thea," he said, "open your eyes—look at me—listen to me. I've always loved you. Wherever I went—whatever I did—you were there—the real you—not—not—"

She opened her eyes. "This is the real me, Grant." Now the mockery was patent. "Will you have me? Will you marry me? Will you say to your friends, 'Congratulate me—meet the bloated hag I have singled out above all other women'?" She took answer from his involuntary recoil. "I thought not. No man would. That much I've learned from experience. I've learned exactly what attracts a man—what it is he seeks when—"

"Thea—stop—I won't have it—I'll help you—"

"Go away and don't come back."

"I won't go—or if I do it will be only for a while. I'll come back again and again until I've found out what it is that's made this happen and how I can put an end to it—because, by all that's sane, it can't be Dino. You lost Dino long before he died—and no matter what you had felt for him, his death was a deliverance—a finish to nothing but humiliation."

He spent more words. He spent all the words he had, and they were wasted. They bought him no admittance to her dark. He begged her to see a doctor, to give him the name of some relative who might stay with her, minister to her physical needs the while she convalesced from this—this unnamable disease. But she was like a deaf-mute. The only response she made reached him as a silent force that pushed him from the room.

Exhausted finally, he went, promising to return, all but threatening to return, since a promise implied hope or pleasurable expectation, and she had put such things aside. He missed the hurrying maid by a matter of moments.

The maid was relieved to find that she had closed the door after all, and annoyed because the thought of it had tormented her throughout the showing of the feature picture. But as soon as she reentered the apartment the strange sounds reached her. Cautiously her high heels carried her to the living room.

"Ma'am," she said, small-voiced, timid. "Ma'am—what is it—what's the matter?"

The Countess Mazzini did not hear. The countess was weeping, and it was as though the snows of the world's winter had melted and joined in one relentless flood.

CHAPTER TWO

"She's antisocial," Ranse said.

Mrs. Upjohn cuffed him playfully. "Don't torment your sister."

He ducked, repeating, "Antisocial antisocial anti—"

Gale clapped her hands to her ears. "Stop it."

"Aw come on, Gale, it's technicolor tonight." His last few words rang out falsetto. Unlike most boys of his age, he appeared to take huge delight in his changing voice. He was always experimenting with it. "Why won't you come?" And then in a deep bass, "Why?"

Gale was not amused. "If it comes to that, why are you going? Just so you can say it stinks?"

"'It appears no other thing to me,'" Ranse quoted, "'than a foul and pestilent congregation of vapours.'"

Mr. Upjohn said absently, "Shakespeare was referring to the world when he wrote that. Well, Gale, do you want to change your mind?"

"He was referring to the world," Ranse said, "because he didn't have movies to refer to—only the world. Poor Shakespeare. Gale—what's the matter with you lately?"

"Let me alone—just let me alone."

The three of them stood ranged against her, three giants crowding the walls of the ridiculous apartment like clowns stuffing a circus automobile. Ranse with his deceptively angelic face. Mother large and scrubbed and bursting with intelligence and good humor, but entirely lacking in understanding. And Father, a bull of a man. A kindly, studious bull, yet—

"Let's go, boys," said Mrs. Upjohn. "If there's anything I dislike, it's arriving in the middle of a picture. If previous experience hadn't taught me better, I'd swear that the audience was missing something from the way it grunts and groans when its vision is blocked for a minute or so. Why they build such narrow aisles in the first place is past understanding. Gale, you didn't eat enough at dinner. If you should get hungry take anything but the cold lamb. I want to use it in a new recipe I've been working on—"

"Stomachache for four coming up," Ranse said.

"You're being obnoxious, Son," Mr. Upjohn boomed.

Mrs. Upjohn went on imperviously, "If it turns out well, I'll pass it along to the woman across the hall. Her husband looks frightfully undernourished."

"Mother!" Gale said, and did not continue because it was useless.

Ranse tweaked her hair in passing. She slapped at his hand and he gave a realistic cry of pain. He had a deep affection for his sister and was constantly thinking up new ways to hide it. All the way to the door he yelled, "Antisocial—antisocial—"

"Father," she said, "Mother—Father—make him stop—he'll have everybody complaining again." She bounced in her chair as the door slammed sharply.

Gale Upjohn loved her parents and Ranse dearly, yet she could not help admitting to herself that at times they were hard to take. But this did not prevent her from despising a consonant attitude on the part of the New York neighbors who were quickly learning to use every means at their command to ward off Upjohn onslaughts.

Gale was an ordinary seventeen-year-old girl with more than an ordinary share of physical assets. She had red hair and an arresting white face which she usually managed to keep innocent of all expression as safeguard against portraying the embarrassment induced by her family.

Both of her parents had been graduated from their respective colleges with honors, and this they mentioned as often as they took breath from their self-appointed task of telling everybody how to do everything. But in spite of their high IQ's, she often felt that they were almost moronically insensitive to the climate of their relationships. Young Ranse, cut of the same cloth, also walked in darkness. Nor did it seem to trouble him that he had hardly been in New York a week before regaining the nickname of "Rancid."

Gale thought drearily that the widely proclaimed anonymity of the big city was a fraud and that life for her was going to be the same as it had been in Starwell, Connecticut. In fact, it looked as though it would be worse.

In Starwell the Upjohns had been tagged matter-of-factly as "Know-it-alls." And sometimes the inhabitants of Starwell hid behind curtains and refused to answer bells rather than subject themselves to lengthy advices on how to run their households, shop, cook, and bring up their children, the while their furniture suffered the wear and tear of Ranse's insatiable curiosity, Father's scattered pipe ash, and Mother's absent-minded habit of applying her shoes to clean upholstery. But the Upjohns and their parents and their parents' parents had been born and bred in Starwell, and if they were treated as a minor menace, the treatment held nothing of malice. Their value as a conversation piece could send any social gathering off to a gay start. And everyone recognized that Mrs. Upjohn's idiosyncrasies did not prevent her from emptying her purse when contributions were needed, or that Mr. Upjohn was always ready, if officiously, to lend his brawn and brains to a neighbor in distress.

Moreover, in Starwell it was conceded that Gale was different and not to be lumped with her tribe. But here in New York, after a few bouts with Mother and Father, no one bothered to distinguish one Upjohn from another.

Gale, moving restlessly through the series of little boxes that made up the New York apartment, could think with longing of the roomy old house in Starwell, of spacious green stretches, and of air that was not stiff with impurities. And she could wonder why she had been so elated when Father called a family meeting to announce his big opportunity.

"No more of wasting my genius in a backward town. I've received an appointment with the largest industrial engineering firm in the country." He broke in upon the fluent surprise of his wife and son. "I waited to tell you until I was sure of a place to live. You may or may not be aware that housing's rather tight in New York—due to bad planning and management." His tone indicated that he would soon put that to rights. "I don't mind admitting that it took quite a bit of doing to secure an apartment, but of course I managed. Oddly enough, enough, we'll be living practically next door to my sister Thea."

Here Ranse put in a few words. "Who cares about that stuck-up thing?" He was only echoing his parent's constantly expressed belief that people should say what they thought when they thought it. He looked surprised at the rebuke that followed.

"You don't even know your aunt. A boy of your age should be aware that valid judgment can be based only upon firsthand knowledge. In any case, 'stuck-up' is a ridiculous term."

"Tell us about the apartment, dear," said Mrs. Upjohn. "Is it—?"

"That will keep." Gale could understand now why he had not been eager to talk about it. "I'm sure my sister Thea will be delighted to resume family ties. Much as I dislike clichés, she'll have learned by this time that blood is thicker than water." Something in Gale's listening face had captured his attention. She was awarded a pat on the shoulder and a burst of his untempered frankness. "You're very like your aunt, child. Her mentality is no great shakes either. She became, of all things, a model. But at least she had sense enough to make a good marriage. An Italian count *and* money is a pretty rare combination. Yes—everything's turned out very well for Thea. The count is dead and she's left alone with the money." He had laughed his earsplitting laugh. "Not a bad achievement for a dumb beauty. Let's hope that you'll receive similar rewards."

Gale could not echo the hope. Her beauty had brought her no

rewards to date. And how was she to meet a rich man and keep him in sight long enough for the question of marriage to arise, when Mr. and Mrs. Upjohn and Ranse succeeded in discouraging the lowliest of aspirants to her hand? What hope she had she forthwith glued to Aunt Thea, viewed only once or twice from the cradle, and glimpsed thereafter through random words dropped over the years.

That Aunt Thea had dusted herself thoroughly of the Upjohns was no black mark against her in Gale's book. It simply showed that what brains she had were in the right department. And it seemed to follow quite logically that in her niece she would recognize a kindred spirit, and rescue her, and permit her to bask in a normal atmosphere at one with a normal intelligence quotient.

Even now, in the face of the evidence, Gale refused to admit that the glue was not holding. For if Aunt Thea was delighted to have the Upjohns near her she gave no sign. She neither answered her mail nor her telephone. So inaccessible was she that she might have been living in a castle with a moat around it instead of in an apartment house just a few blocks away from the Upjohns' shoddy quarters.

Gale had walked past that house many times, cursing herself for cowardice, and yet not daring to brave the hauteur of the doorman, the imagined splendor of the lobby. Mother and Father, engaged in the business of settling in, had not got around to visiting their fabulous connection, but when they did, Gale thought unhappily, all would be lost. Because once Aunt Thea refreshed her memory of the Upjohns en masse, she would want no part of them. She would not bother to accord her niece any special attention. So the important thing was to get there first and alone, to present the case before it was too late.

Bemoaning her lack of courage, Gale went to one of the room's narrow windows. She looked down at the gloomy street which seemed deserted even though it was only a little after eight. In Starwell she had often gone out at a much later hour. The trouble was that she had not yet reached such terms of familiarity with the city as to make its night attire seem anything but frightening.

She turned from the window. She said, "Hell," and glanced toward a massive chair that bore the impress of her father's frame. It was almost as though she expected it to play back a record of his views on profanity. "A lazy vent for emotional stress indicating the paucity of the average vocabulary. My dear Gale, it requires a modicum of searching to find words suited to every known tribulation." But the chair was empty, so she said, "Hell," again, and yet again.

She had refused to go to the movies because she loved them and her family did not. They went, it seemed, merely to criticize, to jeer at the "mawkish sentimentality," to laugh uproariously at the "fulsome tragedy," and to decry the fact that a constant diet of such fare was slowly undermining the nation. It would have been all right with Gale if they kept their reactions to themselves, but they shared them generously with everyone within earshot, and no one was ever grateful.

She chewed at her sweet full lips and bit down hard as the doorbell rang. It was not the downstairs bell. It was the one right outside the apartment. The clock sitting on Father's homemade bookshelves had dragged its hands to nine while she brooded. Her first thought was that the family had been thrown out of the movies, but before she had gone halfway down the long narrow hall she dismissed it. Even young Ranse was equipped with his own key, which he delighted in using, independence being part of the Upjohn creed.

Undecided, a little afraid, Gale stood midway between the door and the doubtful haven of the coffin-shaped living room. She had been warned that things unknown to Starwell happened often in New York. Then a second thought struck her. Aunt Thea—it could be Aunt Thea. Maybe the last note I sent— She raced to the door and flung it wide.

The unshaded bulb in the outer hall did not improve the complexion of the mustard-colored walls. The boy who stood there would have been attractive in any light. He was tall and fairish, with a well-shaped head and wide shoulders.

The expectancy drained out of Gale as she recognized him. Her "What do you want now?" was frigid.

He said, "I guess that means you remember me—Jack—Jack Channing."

She nodded. He lived in the apartment beneath. A few days ago his mother had sent him up to complain about Ranse, who was teaching himself to tap-dance. Ranse, at fifteen, was overgrown in all directions, and when he danced he came down heavily on nearly six feet. But the justice of the complaint had not made it palatable.

The boy was staring at her. There was nothing bold or wolfish about the stare. It stated honestly that he had found someone he liked to look at.

Embarrassment made her voice gruff. "My mother and father are out. If there's anything you want to see them about you'll have to—"

"I didn't come to see them. I'm sorry about the other day. My mother—well—you know—older people get nervous sometimes ..."

"She was right," Gale said uncompromisingly. "You don't have to apologize. If you'll excuse me—" She started to shut the door.

"I'm not here to apologize exactly. When I saw you the other day I—well—we live in the same house and all—so I thought we should get acquainted. We could go have a soda or something."

"Oh," said Gale. Then she said, "Come in."

She asked him to sit down, and he sat in Father's big chair. In her present mood it was a relief to see him there instead of Father. He did not dribble ashes all over the place, nor did he look as though he had to be pestered into visiting a barber. His hair was cut very short and tracked by a wet comb. And although his white sports shirt was open at the neck, he had topped it with what she instinctively knew to be his best jacket. He was nice. She would not have minded showing him off to her friends in Starwell.

"So the family's out," he said without sorrow.

"Yes—they've gone to the movies."

"We could go sometime if they wouldn't mind."

"They wouldn't mind. I'll be eighteen on my next birthday." She did not see fit to mention that her next birthday was seven months away.

"I'll be twenty-one." She made no comment, and he tried again. "You've got a lot of furniture."

"We moved here from a house."

"That must have been tough. Lose your money or something?"

She knew it for sympathy rather than prying. "No—we never had much money to lose. Everyone in a small town lives in a house. We had to come to New York because of my father's work."

"He's got some build—hasn't he?—like a heavyweight." Her silence constrained him to add, "Of course he doesn't act like a prize fighter." And then, "Your kid brother's big too—"

Firmly she ruled Ranse out of the conversation. "My father's an industrial engineer." Because he seemed impressed, she went on. "He's worked out the machinery needed for some important new chemical process—so they were glad to get him in New York. This apartment is only temporary until we find a decent—" She stopped. She was talking just like the rest of the family, belittling everything. Perhaps Jack Charming lived here from choice or, worse, from necessity.

He was not offended. "It must be kind of cramped at that—after a whole house. My mother and I are used to it though. I was born in New York and we've lived here ever since I can remember. Mother says it wasn't so rundown until they began to take in everybody." He moved uncomfortably, and although she was not very perceptive, she understood why. By everybody his mother had included people like the Upjohns. It was as plain as his slightly snub nose.

He changed the subject. "Say—I don't want to be forward—but it just doesn't seem natural to call you Miss Upjohn—that's why I haven't been calling you anything. You see—I get hunches about people—and I've got a hunch we're going to be friends—so I wish you'd tell me your first name."

"Althea Gale." Her tone was not encouraging.

"That's kind of a mouthful, isn't it?"

"I'm called Gale." She looked somber, thinking of what Ranse was called.

"I don't mean Althea isn't pretty," he said, misinterpreting her expression. "I just—"

"I was named for an aunt. My aunt Thea." She stiffened as an idea took hard shape within her.

"Well—I like Gale better. If you don't mind, I'll call you Gale. Where do you go, Gale?"

"What?"

"School, I mean."

"Oh. I don't—not now anyway. Later I might take a business course or be a model or something. I haven't decided yet. I was graduated from Starwell High last June and my parents wanted me to go to college, but—" She shrugged to signify that she had other more important plans.

"That's funny. I'd have sworn you were a college girl."

She was not flattered. "That's probably because I wear these clothes, but I haven't had a chance to shop yet." She took a brief contemptuous survey of her low-heeled loafers, her woolen skirt, her green sweater, and thought despairingly of the styleless winter coat in the hall closet. It had been the result of one of Mother's sewing bouts, and perhaps it was the chief cause of her failure to visit Aunt Thea. Mother's theories about sewing, like most of her theories, bore sour fruit, and how could a girl in such a coat pass muster in a place that swarmed with sleek and elegant New Yorkers?

"Did I say something to offend you?"

"No—of course not."

"That's good—because offending you would be the last thing I'd want to do. After all, college isn't everything—and whatever you do, I guess you won't have to worry much about *your* future. Anyway— I've always thought that women, unless they've got some really big ambition, are foolish to go in for a career—especially"—he brought it out shyly—"beautiful women. With a man it's different. I go to Columbia. I've never wanted to be anything but a doctor—"

"That's nice," she said absently.

But he was taking her interest for granted, elaborating upon his dedication to medicine with no awareness of her inattention.

He's heaven-sent, she thought, not sharing her parents' aversion to clichés.

"—my grandfather on my mother's side was a doctor. Mother kept some of his books and maybe they started me off. I used to read them the way other kids read comics—"

With him to companion her she could storm Aunt Thea's gates. Escorted, she could walk past the uniformed doorman with his cold, scornful face. She could enter an elevator as though she were an expected guest and demand to be taken to Aunt Thea. Nothing ventured, nothing gained, she thought.

"I hope I haven't been talking your ear off, Gale."

"Oh no." The smile she gave him was new to her lips but old in the annals of women.

He said shakily, "Well—if we're going to get that soda—" As though to match that smile, he became a tired man of the world. "Or you might prefer something stronger. I have to go easy myself because hangovers and concentration don't team up, but—"

"Would you mind if we didn't—um—indulge tonight? You see— your coming made me forget about it—but I'd been planning to walk over to my aunt's. She lives near here—"

His face fell. "Must you? I wouldn't want to interfere with your plans—but we're just getting to know each other and—"

She said graciously, "If you like, you may come along."

"To your aunt's? But she mightn't—"

"Of course if you've something better to do—"

"It isn't that—it's—I wouldn't want to horn in."

"I'm sure my aunt will be delighted," Gale said. To herself she sounded just like her father. "Wait a moment. I'll get my coat."

She brought the despised garment back to the living room. As he helped her into it she bolstered her morale by saying proudly, "My aunt's a countess." Then she caught a glimpse of his face and could not help giggling.

The pleasant little sound seemed to bring him relief. He stopped gaping. "You had me going for a minute. I thought you were serious."

"I am—she is. Come on—it's getting late." She tugged at his arm. "Will you be warm enough in that jacket?"

"I guess so. I didn't think we were going very far—I mean—sure— it's warm for February—anyway, I never catch cold."

Out in the street he began to laugh. "We can stop for a soda after all," he said, "because if she's a countess she'll be used to late callers. She probably holds a reception every night until all hours—with champagne and caviar and butlers and footmen—"

It sounded funny to Gale. Suddenly she was laughing with him, having a good time. Suddenly Aunt Thea seemed less important and New York less aloof. "Okay, Jack, if you think sodas will mix with butlers and champagne."

It was nearing ten before they reached the fashionable apartment house. Meanwhile they had become very important to each other, achieving by direct route the rapport that so often takes adults months or years to attain.

The doorman did not give them a glance as they entered the building. But Gale sobered somewhat in the subdued lights of the lobby. "Jack—I'm not sure of the apartment number. We'd better ask."

He said doubtfully, "But you're sure this is the right address? All right—there's a switchboard in that alcove. The fellow behind it will know."

The fellow behind it was old. He gave her a paternal smile. "Yes, miss?"

"Would you tell me the number of the Countess Mazzini's apartment?"

He said mechanically, "Twelve A." Then he took another look at her and shook his head as though to clear it. He said, "Why, you're—excuse me—I mean are you expected?"

"Naturally." She was off, pulling Jack Channing with her.

Now that's a funny one, thought the man at the switchboard. His hand went out to one of the keys. Nope—there's been no talk of a daughter—so it must be the eyesight's out of whack. He withdrew his hand from the key. Ever since the count's death it had been no use trying to announce visitors to the countess. The house could burn down before she'd pick up the receiver. She was probably out, anyway. He had sat at that board for twelve years and during that time he had seen many changes. The change in the countess was the worst of them. He sighed sentimentally.

Before they reached the elevators Jack Channing balked. "You weren't joking. She is a countess."

"I told you."

"Well—look—I haven't a hat—and this shirt and no tie—"

She said grandly, "Don't be silly. What difference does it make?"

But his mother had imposed upon him a strict code of manners, and although it did not cover dealings with a countess, he knew what was expected of him. "You go on up, Gale. I'll wait here for you."

"No—I want you to come."

"Please, Gale, it isn't that I wouldn't like to meet her, but she'd be bound to think it strange—seeing me for the first time without a hat or tie."

Gale said, "I didn't think you'd turn out to be such a drip." And right there in the lobby they had their first quarrel. She did not want to go up without him. She realized now that she did not want to go at all, but if at all, she wanted his support. He would prove to Aunt Thea that she was a personage in her own right, one who could attract nice handsome men. She tried to coax. "Please—she's only Father's sister—she's just like anybody else—she wasn't born a countess." But she could not move him. Then she thought that people were staring and listening, so she muttered passionately, "All right—don't bother to wait. It's been an experience to know you," and left him, and darted into an elevator.

Deserted, he stood forlornly looking after her. Maybe he was a drip.

But right was right, and how could he call upon a countess, so informally clad? He squared his shoulders. Never mind. Someday he would live in a house like this. He and his wife?

He decided not to take Gale's anger seriously. He had brought her and he would wait for her. He walked away from the elevators to the lobby proper, which was furnished with chairs and smoking stands. He sat down. He hoped that Gale would not be long. Countess or no countess, Gale was his girl from now on.

CHAPTER THREE

"Ma'am," said the maid for the third or fourth time, "you'll make yourself sick. Could I get you something, ma'am? Can you hear me?" But she was no competition for that dreadful sobbing. Helplessly she retreated to the kitchen and smoked a cigarette to soothe her nerves. People in their senses don't carry on like that, she thought worriedly. It's not drink either. I didn't smell a thing. I wonder if I brought her a cup of tea could I get her to take it?

At intervals she slipped into the foyer to listen, and at last to her relief there was a silence. She returned to the kitchen and dried and put away the lunch dishes as initial preparation for the evening meal. After that storm the apartment seemed so quiet that she jumped to hear the summoning bell.

"Yes, ma'am, I'm here," she said from the living room doorway. Embarrassed, she looked everywhere but at that streaked, salt-bitten face.

The Countess Mazzini was seated at her desk. She had pushed the pile of unopened mail aside. She was writing, and bits of torn paper littered the floor at her feet. To find her engaged in anything more strenuous than just plain sitting was a fresh shock. I ought to quit while I'm ahead, the maid thought nervously. She really is bats.

Her opinion was implemented as the sunken eyes turned toward her. Tears had washed away their film. They seemed shamefully overexposed. "Mildred, get one of the elevator boys in here—no, two."

"Huh?"

"I want two of the boys in here at once."

The maid scurried out. "No, I don't know what she wants you for," she said to the boy who answered her call, "but you don't have to be scared. She said, 'Two,' so find somebody else and make it snappy." In a few minutes she ushered them across the foyer and was dismissed by the countess. But whatever had been required of the boys did not take long. As soon as she heard them leave, chuckling and muttering to each other, she showed herself at the living room door again.

"Mildred, I want you to clean this apartment." The voice was waterlogged but firm.

"Yes, ma'am—I will—the first thing tomorrow—" She did not at all like the expression in those eyes.

"Not tomorrow. Now. You may start in here."

"Clean now? The whole place? But it's late—and I'm just about to fix your dinner—"

"Don't bother with dinner." It was as though she read what was passing through the girl's mind. "I'm not insane. I want a thorough cleaning done. If it keeps you later than usual you'll be compensated."

"It isn't that—it's just a funny time to—"

"There's a vacuum cleaner in the apartment, isn't there? I seem to remember hearing one—although not for quite a while."

"I do the best I can—if you don't like my work I'll—" Under that gaze the show of indignation sputtered out.

"I don't—but perhaps that's as much my fault as it is yours. After tonight you'll be free to look for other employment. I'll pay you a month's salary in addition to the remainder of this month—provided you do a satisfactory job."

On the verge of further protest, the maid held back. Humor her, she thought out of a storage of cinema-gleaned rules. Play along or she might get violent. "Yes, ma'am," she said, and fled the room. In the kitchen she took time out to consider the situation. Fired—me! Some nerve. And on top of that I'm to start housecleaning at half-past six. Who does she think she is? I'll walk out this minute and serve her right. I'll get my hat and—say—am I nuts too?

For common sense had come to the rescue. Two weeks to go in this month—that means six weeks' pay. Not bad. Better than okay. I can take my time looking around for a decent job. What if I do stay late tonight? I can sleep late tomorrow. Boy!

Revitalized by such clear thinking, she went to the closet where the cleaning implements were kept, and from the untidy welter routed out a pail, cloths, the vacuum cleaner, and the box that held its attachments.

On the way back to the living room she almost dropped her cumbersome load. If that isn't water running in her bathtub, I'll drink it. This sure is another kind of binge she's on. What's got into her? When I left this afternoon she was the same as always.

She had cause for astonishment because the Countess Mazzini's bathtub too rarely showed evidence of use.

In the living room she worked fast and with an efficiency she had not displayed since her first realization that she was to receive no more than token supervision. She dusted the furniture. She removed grime and soot from window sills and woodwork. She vacuumed the drapes, the upholstery, and the rugs, swept the surfaces between, and grumbling because the countess had not seen fit to use the wastebasket, held the uncapped tube over the litter of torn papers near the desk until every last scrap had been inhaled. That done, she wondered belatedly what the countess had been so busy writing. But her curiosity was blunted by anticipation of the near future. Of course the countess would supply her with a reference, and so armed, she could afford to pick and choose her next employment. Meanwhile she could also afford to splurge a little. A new hat. A new dress. Why not a whole new outfit?

She surveyed the results of her industry, and as an added touch built up the fire again because the heap of dead ashes spoiled the general effect. Satisfied, she went on to the next room, a small study that had obviously been the count's. She was familiar with it, having from time to time given it perfunctory swipes with a duster and more painstaking swipes with her eyes. Books, as befit a study, although books such as these? Guns, riding crops. A regular sportsman, she thought with vicarious pride, not knowing that the late count had taken as much joy in shooting a song sparrow as in larger game. What a handsome man. Often she lingered over the picture of him which dominated the desk. A real heartbreaker. Her smile of approval became pitying. And a real dumb cluck when you thought of the countess. There were other pictures in the study, too, but she had never allowed her eyes to dwell upon them for long, even though no one watched. Nor had she mentioned them to Dave. Might give him ideas. Not that he didn't have plenty. Wait until he saw her new outfit.

Next she went to the countess's bedroom. The countess was not in it. Neither was she in the bathroom, which had been left in a disgraceful state. The maid sighed. Oh well. Do it and it's done. Between fastidious thumb and forefinger she began to pick up underwear, washcloths, and towels, thrusting them into the hamper.

It was nine o'clock before she had worked her way back to the kitchen. She was tired and hungry. Dave had wanted to stop for a snack after the movies, but she had been in too much of a hurry. Really, it didn't pay to be conscientious. Now she'd have to drop everything while she ate a bite to keep her from keeling over. But she certainly did not intend to get dinner for the countess. Her hands were full enough with the kitchen still to do, not to mention the room off it. Was she glad that in the beginning the countess had stipulated that she was to sleep out. At least she wouldn't have to pack her things or struggle with a suitcase.

She gaped when she saw the countess standing at the kitchen sink. She was eating salt crackers and washing them down with claret. Judging by what was left in the bottle, the crackers had needed a lot of washing down. That was not remarkable. But the change was. The countess's hair had been washed and brushed to shining beauty. And she was wearing that coveted blue velvet house gown so long imprisoned in a plastic bag in the closet. So help me, if you worked at it you could almost see what a knockout she must have been and why a handsome count had married her. Yes, you could see a real resemblance to the painting in the living room, even if the velvet gown, designed to flow loosely, was all but bursting at the seams.

For once the maid's respectful tone came without labor. "I'm almost done, ma'am." She set the vacuum cleaner down behind the door. "If you want to see how everything looks—"

"I'll be out of here in a moment. You'd better eat something too." She had rouged her lips, but the maid credited wine for the bright high flush on her cheeks.

"Yes, ma'am." The expression in the countess's eyes still made her uneasy, but the depleted wine bottle was somehow reassuring. It proved that she was still dealing with a known factor. "Ma'am"—the words were produced without conscious intention—"now that I've got onto the way you want things done I'd just as soon not leave if—"

"I won't need you. I'm planning to go away."

"Oh—well—I'm sure I wish you the best of luck—"

"Thank you, Mildred." She walked from the kitchen. There were tattered remnants of grace in the way she moved her heavy body.

Watching her, the maid felt her brittle young heart contract. The spasm was too brief to be analyzable, even if she had been adept at analysis. Phew—what came over me? Suppose she'd said yes when I asked to stay? The sooner I get out of here, the better.

She drank a cup of instant coffee and ate some bread and cheese. On the way to the sink with her dishes she thought absently, I mustn't forget to turn in my key or she might get the notion I'm coming back to steal the crown jewels.

A moment later she stuck her head into the foyer. Association had brought the key to mind, the unmistakable sound of a tumbler falling in a lock. She ducked back just in time to avoid being seen.

So that's the reason behind all this dolling up. What do you know? And the other times he came he rang the bell as respectable as you please. Now whoever would have believed it? And me fooled all the while into thinking he was only a friend of the family.

While she did the remaining chores she amused herself by spinning out a tale for Dave. Honest, Dave, you could have knocked me over with a feather. The funny part of it is that, except for being kind of short, Mr. Spencer isn't bad. He dresses like a million and he has swell manners. I think he must be English because he sounds like that fellow in the movies who plays butlers. So wouldn't you swear he could do better than her? I guess it's the money, even if he doesn't look as if he's that hard up. Some romance. I wish you could have seen her. For all the world like a blue velvet sausage—could scarcely make both ends meet. For in retrospect she wondered how she had been able to contain her laughter at the sight of that tight gown. Every once in a while she stopped communing with Dave to speculate upon the modes and manners of the so-called upper classes. With the countess expecting him and all, it was pretty barefaced to ask me to stay, knowing I'd get onto the fact that he had his own key. Probably figured it wouldn't matter with me out of the picture as of tonight. Still—it doesn't explain that sudden soap-and-water routine—unless maybe he laid down the law—said he'd leave her flat if she didn't spruce up—him being so clean himself. It must be something like that.

But it was nothing like that.

The Countess Mazzini had not at once returned to her chair in the living room. She walked the apartment like an unwieldy robot whose mechanism had rusted from disuse. She forced herself to take in the results of the maid's labor, finding all as it should be, as now it must be since pride had trickled back into the dry wells of her being.

Grant had summoned pride. Poor Grant. Her own dull misery she could endure, but that its poison might infect another had not occurred to her. She had refused to think of Grant until he appeared like a knight on a charger, assuming in his white innocence that such weapons as he bore would effect a rescue. Yet the pain of his defeat rather than the battle he had waged had been the instrument designed for her release.

She wandered into Dino's study. She handled one of a pair of pistols and slowly returned it to its case. She touched the elaborate frame of Dino's photograph. Dino's cardboard face looked up at her in the remembered way, calling a sadness from her heart because the death of grief is also to be mourned. Here in this room, she thought, is all of Dino blatantly displayed. And the thought was powerful enough to make her quit the room in superstitious fear that the glittering facets of his personality, the well-stocked liquor cabinet, the nudes, the riding crops, might actually reassemble to confound her.

Sweating, she sat down at the desk in the living room. She took a fountain pen and a sheet of paper from the drawer. She wrote laboriously, grasping the pen in her thickened fingers. Her handwriting had never been too legible, and when she was finished she went over the whole, striving to clarify some of the wavering words. The pen, which she had filled that afternoon, seemed to go dry, and she shook it impatiently, getting ink on her fingers and on the desk's surface. She hardly noticed. She addressed an envelope, folded the sheet into it, and suddenly, with a sweep of her arm, thrust it and the accumulation of unopened mail on the desk into the wastebasket beneath. The movement seemed compulsive, as did her desertion of the desk for the chair near the fire.

Spencer had crossed the room's threshold. He had eyes the color of coffee beans set in a round, bland face. As he took in the room and its occupant he looked like a knowing baby pursing its formless mouth to a whistle. "Strike me pink," he said.

"What are you doing here?" she said quietly.

"Now that's not much of a welcome, is it?" His cockney voice sounded hurt. With finicking care he placed his hat and coat and walking stick upon a tufted sofa.

"You've had your welcome this month."

"And who's to say we must keep it as cut and dried as all that? I should think you'd be pleased to have a bit of company. It almost looks as though you might have been expecting some. What *is* the spring cleaning in aid of—if I may ask? It couldn't be your anniversary? No—of course not. Your birthday, then? Say the word and I'll pawn my watch to buy you a present."

"You can save your breath, Spencer."

"What with the high cost of living—not to mention a bit of a financial setback—breath is about all I *can* save. It's a good job I've a pal like you to lend an helping hand—"

She looked puzzled. "I didn't hear the bell ring."

"That's right—you didn't." His rubbery mouth stretched. The smile was gummy, as though the short white teeth had yet to complete their growth. "My old key happened to be in my pocket."

She moved her tongue over her lips. It might have been anger that she tasted, but she downed it with no more comment than the lift of her shoulders.

He seemed, if anything, disappointed at his failure to arouse her. A wariness entered his eyes. "I must say you're taking it like a perfect lady—even if only a lady by marriage. Nearly look the part too. What *are* you celebrating? I don't mind admitting you gave me a bit of a turn—sitting there wide awake and queening it. Almost like old times—" He gestured toward the painting over the mantel. "Almost."

Automatically she followed the gesture.

He laughed. "Oh well," he said, "we none of us get younger—those of us as aren't cut off in our prime—and who's to say that your dear departed wasn't one of the lucky ones—not living to see the change in his lovely bride—"

She said harshly, "That's enough. You may go."

Conditioned to such commands, he had turned to obey before he remembered the way things were. To cover his lapse into servility he said, "Back in two shakes," and continued on out of the room.

Her eyes did not mark his exit. She was staring at the painting, seeing it, tracing with love and sorrow the shape of its vivid beauty.

I am a murderer, she thought. I have tortured you beyond recognition. I am at once a murderer and a suicide. No crime is left me to perform—nothing but anticlimax.

Spencer had returned with a tray that held a pinch bottle, a siphon, and two glasses. He placed it on a low table and sat down next to it. "A very proper sentiment, I'm sure—leaving the count's study as it was—but perhaps under the circumstances you're carrying things too far. It does seem a shocking waste for you ever to seek elsewhere with all that beautiful liquor in stock. Say when." He held the bottle poised over a glass. She shook her head. He poured scotch, added soda, and drank, making a sound of appreciation deep in his throat. "That's a bit of all right. Lucky I'm not a sensitive chap or I might fancy you balked at drinking with me, when the reverse would be more—"

The deep voice of Thea Mazzini said aloofly, "It doesn't matter what you do or say. It never has mattered."

"Come now—you can't expect me to believe that—not when your interests and mine lie close as peas in a pod."

"No—I can't expect you to believe that."

He looked at her uncertainly. "I wouldn't be here tonight if I didn't have your welfare at heart. The straight of it is, I popped into your favorite pub first and waited there for as long as my nose could take the stink of it. You being regular as clockwork in your nightly rounds, you can't blame me for getting the wind up when you didn't appear. You might have been taken queer and no one wiser, what with you turning a thick ear to bells and the little maid not sleeping in—so if you're put out about the key you can see that I had no choice but to—"

She had arisen from her chair. She was walking toward the desk. She took a wallet from one of the cubbyholes and started to count out bills.

He watched her. "Now that's a bit more like it." Then he said, "Come again, old girl. I can't use chicken feed."

She placed the bills beneath a paperweight. She hoped that the maid would finish her work soon and come to claim them. Then she could get on with what must be accomplished. "The money is not for you," she said, and her eyes reduced him to insect size.

Some of the confidence he had brought with him turned tail. With something like horror he heard the old familiar whine in his voice. "I don't mind taking less than I had in mind if you're strapped," he said. "I never was one to press my advantage." Because he had managed to banish the whine he gathered momentum. "But there's no hurry. I'm enjoying myself." He refilled his glass. He went on reflectively, "Even those stinking pubs of yours are better than some places I could mention—"

"Damn you," she said. She half-filled the other glass with whiskey. She drained it.

He whistled. "That's putting it where it belongs. Now then—now that we're all cozy and sensible again, how about—?" He broke off, this time completely unnerved by her eyes. They held a kind of suppressed violence that made his flesh creep. She's balmy, he thought. I must watch my step.

To his relief she looked away. The "Damn you" had not been aimed at him but at herself. She had not meant to drink. She had hoped that the wine would see her through. She did not want them to come and find—

His tone was propitiating. "I'm not an unreasonable man," he said. "If it isn't convenient " He had got up and was edging toward the desk.

"You're not anything, Spencer. You've never frightened me for a moment."

"Frightened you?" He parodied injury. "Course not—Coley Spencer wouldn't harm a hair of your head. He's your friend—your true-blue friend—"

"I made you a part of my punishment," she said. "It wasn't your threats—"

"Have it your way. Have it your own ruddy way." He saw that she was staring straight ahead. He was at the desk now, busily pocketing the money and the wallet, stooping to root in the wastebasket. He found the envelope he was seeking in a matter of moments. She was paying no attention to him, so he drew out the contents and read rapidly. He was empty-handed as he made his way back to his chair. "So long as your way works out to my advantage," he said, his eyes thoughtful. He was a very small man. His only moments of power had been experienced in this room. He could not forego them without struggle. "Glad to see you've got over your scruples about drinking the count's liquor—but no sense in—" Again he stopped.

She was refilling her glass. Hardly more than the reflection of a smile touched her mouth. Yet its slight upward curve seemed to him to be heavy with evil. "I could have crushed your life out at any time," she said. "I'm wondering now how I resisted the temptation."

"Here—" He shot up straight in his chair. "What kind of talk is that?" He had a dreadful feeling that unless he had an immediate brain wave the end of a long and prosperous holiday was drawing near. He said weakly, "You wouldn't want to let anybody else hear you go on like that—might give the wrong impression—when all's said and done, you haven't so much to grumble—" The doorbell put a period to his dithering. "Who might that be?"

"It might be Grant," she said quite pleasantly. The whisky had taken effect. There was something she had to do, but whatever it was, it seemed less urgent than before. "He said he would come back, but I didn't think it would be so soon." Her deep voice became imperious. "Let Grant in," she said. "I'll give him a better memory of me. He deserves it." She did not quite know what she meant, but she knew it was a part of that something that had to be done.

"What are you talking about?"

Neither of them heard the maid as she went to answer the door. The maid was ready to leave. She had her coat on and all she had to do was tie her scarf about her head. She welcomed the ring because it would provide her with an excuse to intrude upon those unlikely lovebirds in the living room. She did not intend to let anyone else in, even if this was her last night on the job. But she would announce the visitor's name, and the countess, seeing her dressed for the street, would get the idea and pay her.

She opened the door. She said, "Yes?" impatiently.

I want—I'm calling on—is the Countess Mazzini at home?"

The maid stared, trying to recall where she had seen the girl before. Young—younger than me—couldn't be a movie star—not in that getup—though I've heard they run around Hollywood wearing any old— Before she could prevent it, Gale Upjohn had stepped into the foyer.

The maid held out a restraining arm. "Sorry, miss. The countess don't—isn't seeing anyone."

"She'll see me," Gale said, so firmly that no one could have told how far from firm she felt. "I'm her niece."

"Her niece?" No wonder she looks familiar, the maid thought. She's the spitting image of that picture—could even be closer than— She shrugged. Such thoughts were neither here nor there except as added tidbits for Dave. "Look, miss, whoever you are, you better come back some other time because—"

"I can't," Gale said. All things considered, it seemed a true statement of fact to her. "She's at home," she said, "I hear her." And permitting herself no further thought, she slipped past the maid and strode toward the sound of voices.

When she entered the living room she saw the two people sitting there talking quietly. She knew a moment of disappointment because that huge woman was so unlike the Aunt Thea of her imagination. But otherwise the scene was normal enough. Then the two pairs of eyes turned her way and there was a moment of silence. Her young lips parted to frame the set speech of introduction which time and again she had rehearsed. "Aunt Thea—I'm your niece, Gale. I guess you must have been away because we wrote—" But the words she uttered were drowned in indistinguishable gutturals. Screaming, the woman had sprung from her chair.

She was advancing upon Gale, ruthless as an act of nature, a flood, a tornado, a tidal wave. The little man, trying to stop her, went down in her path and came up again, mouthing phrases that were meant to be soothing but failed to soothe. He disappeared from view, but she came on, the heat of her mad eyes enough to shrivel flesh off bone.

Someone else came into the room. It was full of people and sound. Gale only sensed this. She cried out in terror, "Aunt Thea—why? I'm your—Don't—don't—" Then she fought blindly for her life.

CHAPTER FOUR

Until the little glass dot under Number 12A turned yellow, things had been rather dull at the switchboard. Before the operator answered the signal he glanced diagonally across the lobby and made a bet with himself. He bet that the young man sitting there so patiently was about to receive a message from the redhead who had gone to the Mazzini apartment. He even went so far as to predict that the message would either ask the young man to come up or tell him not to wait, and that it would be delivered by the girl herself, since the maid must have left long ago, and the countess never used the phone.

"Hello," he said, grinning.

Into his ear a voice cried in high desperation, "Help—murder— police—" Then quite gently the receiver was returned to its hook.

He stared stupidly at the place on the board where the light had been. He drew out the plug and immediately inserted it again to reestablish the connection. No one answered. The high voice still ringing in his ear might have been a dream voice, and there was nothing to tell him he had not dreamed. He scratched his bald head. He tugged at a flabby ear lobe. Help—murder—police. I heard it plain as anything. What the—? She drinks—she could be drunk— only that was never her voice. Got to use my head. Mr. Voss always says— He exhaled breath gustily. Oh sure—Mr. Voss.

He rang Apartment 2C. Almost at once the manager's wife answered. "It's Adrian," he said without finesse. "Put Mr. Voss on … I can't help it, ma'am … That's right … Yes, important … Okay, I'll hang on.… Mr. Voss? … Sorry to disturb … A call from Mazzini's." He rimmed his lips with the mouthpiece to prevent leakage. "Sounded like trouble—someone yelling murder … Yeah, I tried to call back— couldn't raise anybody … No—I don't think it was her voice … Yeah— but the phone clicks off before I get a chance … Okay."

In a very short time Mr. Voss appeared in the lobby. He nodded his distinguished head graciously to tenants passing in and out of the building. With no trace of urgency he made his way to the switchboard, one of the elevator boys keeping pace with him.

"Fred will relieve you for a while, Adrian," he said. "There's something I want you to do for me."

Adrian got up, trying to achieve a matching degree of nonchalance. He admired Mr. Voss. He felt that he really deserved his exalted position. He had seen managers come and go, and some of them had looked at him doubtfully and made tactless remarks about his age, but Mr. Voss was not like that. With the assurance that everything was now in good hands, he dogged him to the elevator that Fred had left unmanned.

"Best not to let any of the others in on this unless we have to," Mr. Voss said.

"Sure—that's right." Adrian took the elevator to the twelfth floor and made an expert landing. "She had a visitor," he said, "a young girl who—"

"We'll soon see," said Mr. Voss as they walked to Apartment 12A. He pressed his finger to the bell. He repeated the action three times at carefully spaced intervals. Then his habitual calm began to strain at the leash. "There seems to be no one at home, Adrian. You're sure about that call? With a busy switchboard, perhaps you might have confused the number—"

Adrian said reproachfully, "It wasn't a busy switchboard, Mr. Voss"—his voice sounded loud in the silent hall—"and even if it was, I know my job too well to—"

"Shhh—I didn't intend to cast doubt upon your ability." He tried the bell again.

"There's got to be somebody there," Adrian insisted. He elaborated upon his mention of the young girl who had inquired for the Countess Mazzini. "So you can see why I'd be extra-interested in her—the way she looked just like —"

"The countess never had a daughter," Mr. Voss said flatly. "You mustn't let your imagination run away with you."

"No, but from my place at the board I've a pretty good view of the lobby and I was sort of watching for her to come down and she didn't."

"You might have missed her," Mr. Voss said.

"Uh-uh." He kept his voice down, but at the same time managed to inject it with triumph. "The boy she was with is still sitting in the lobby waiting for her."

"Oh," said Mr. Voss. Then he said, "I don't like this," and produced a key ring from his pocket. Before he selected and inserted the right key he said, "Everything seems quite orderly and quiet inside."

Adrian took it for a rebuke. In spite of himself he could not help sharing the manager's unstated opinion that he was at fault for even daring to hint that all was not well in that well-run building. "But I heard it," he said weakly. "'Help—murder—police'—and it didn't sound like no gag—"

"Very well—we'll investigate. We shall have to make an excuse, of course. We shall say that there appears to be a seepage of moisture on the ceiling below which might possibly stem from the countess's pipes." Cautiously he swung the door inward, closing it as soon as he and Adrian had stepped into the foyer. "There are lights on," he said unnecessarily, and then called out in rounded tones, "It's Mr. Voss, the manager. Is anyone at home?"

There was no answer. Adrian ended the overlong silence. "They must've heard you—"

"Follow me," Mr. Voss said.

They looked into the kitchen. It was tidy and empty. "She's only got one in help," Adrian said, "a maid who don't sleep in—"

"I know," said Mr. Voss, his voice omniscient.

Adrian went on babbling nervously, "It's cockeyed—screeching helpmurderpolice in a guy's ear and then not a peep." Somehow the fact that everything seemed to be in order added to his discomfort. It was as though he had told a skeptical doctor he was deathly sick, yet could produce no convincing symptoms. "I can't make heads nor tales of it," he said.

Methodically, starting with the little room off the kitchen, Mr. Voss toured the apartment. Adrian, close at his heels, was impelled by his unquiet nerves to a running commentary. "Clean as a whistle," he said, "which just goes to show you. Last time I was on day shift that fresh kid, Cass, came down from helping the maid in with some bundles and said it looked like a pigsty. Not that I want to make trouble for him if he *is* a liar, but—"

"I hope you watch your language at the switchboard," Mr. Voss said absently. He glanced into the study and saw nothing there to provide a legitimate cause for staying. He proceeded to the living room. It was tenanted, or had been recently. There was a smell of liquor in the room, and under it the flat metallic smell of warm blood.

"Holy hat!" said Adrian. Here at last was his vindication, yet he took no joy of it. He reached out to clutch the arm of Mr. Voss. Unexpectedly that pillar of strength felt strangely soft. "Hey," Adrian cried, giving rather than receiving succor. "Hey—Mr. Voss—you're not going to pass out on me!"

"Don't be absurd," said Mr. Voss in a sick voice. There was a glass and a bottle within reach. He poured a drink, and when he had swallowed it he was able to set down the glass with a steady hand. "Anybody would be shocked," he said defiantly. "Anybody."

"Sure—sure." Adrian looked at the bottle and decided against it, fearing disaster to his protesting stomach. "Do you—are they dead?" He had to turn away. When he could look again, Mr. Voss was kneeling beside the body of the girl, gingerly touching the region of her heart, gingerly raising the limp hand by its wrist.

"I guess I should've called the police right away," Adrian said miserably. "I guess I shouldn't have waited—"

"No—you did the right thing." Mr. Voss dropped the hand and looked surprised when it hit the floor with a small thud. "It's better that I have some grasp of the situation before they—before—" He took out a handkerchief, returned it to his pocket without using it. "There's a test they make with a mirror, but—"

Adrian swallowed. "Side by side," he said, "like they was laid out—"

Mr. Voss arose, adjusting without heart his well-creased trousers. All business, he went to the second body. It lay head toward the fireplace, the loosened hair flaming around it like fire, or like blood. He stopped short, the business stance deserting him. "Countess," he said softly, "Countess Mazzini—can you—?" He might have been a horse confronted with a jump beyond his courage. He raised his voice, pronouncing each word with extreme care. "She's breathing. Perhaps the less we move or touch— Obviously the thing to do first is to get medical advice. I'll see if Dr. Aldington is in his apartment. Where's the telephone? I don't want to use the house phone. Fred might— Wait here— I believe the count had an extension put in the study."

Adrian waited. He thought that the inevitable had been put off long enough and that it was sure as hell a case for the police. Any fool could see the signs. The heavy stand that held the fire irons was overturned and there was blood at the poor girl's nose and under her head. You could not tell what was under the head of the countess on account of her hair. But Mr. Voss said she was breathing. He could hear her breathing. He had heard it the moment he entered the room, but he had not identified the sound which was like some far-off erratic tide. He averted his eyes. There was something shameful about that mammoth helplessness. He turned again to the girl. Poor soul. She looked finished for sure. He tried to imagine what had taken place. He was unequal to it. A little sheepishly he produced a mirror from his breast pocket. He polished it on his sleeve, squatted, and held it to her lips and nose. Then he eyed it sadly. He thought he heard a noise and dropped the mirror. He picked it up, thanking God piously that it had not broken. Mr. Voss was taking a long time to telephone. He did not really blame him for being reluctant to call the police. The house had a good name. Not since the death of Count Mazzini had there ever been so much as a noisy party. Full of life the count had been. Full of life. Adrian shivered and hugged his old bones for warmth. He did not want to look, and yet his eyes performed of their own accord. Funny, the change in her after the count's death. Mr. Voss had been too well mannered to mention it, but the smell of alcohol was enough to— The bell of the apartment rang and he went gladly to welcome whoever it might be.

It was Dr. Aldington, a large, reassuring man. He said, "So we're having a bit of trouble, Adrian," and Adrian would have liked to bask for a while in his aura of vitality, but Mr. Voss appeared and took over.

"You may go, Adrian. I'll feel more comfortable with you at the board. I needn't tell you to say nothing of this?"

"No, sir." Adrian went, heavy with dissatisfaction. It was as though he had been shown one scene in the middle of a play and would never know its beginning or its end.

He had to ring for an elevator because one of the boys had taken Fred's car down. "What goes, Adie?" the operator asked, and Adrian mumbled something about a leak and no plumber at this time of night and himself a jack-of-all-trades. Mr. Voss, he thought resentfully, had no need to caution him not to talk. All the same, he had to clamp down hard to keep from speaking to that young fellow who was still waiting in the lobby.

It was only when he tried to settle at the board that the strangeness of the whole affair came into full focus. There seemed to be a large screen behind his eyes upon which was intermittently projected the picture of those two lying on the floor upstairs. It made no sense. That young visitor to the countess was surely not responsible for whatever had occurred. But—? The light of 12A flashed on and he answered it with almost hysterical eagerness. "Yes, Mr. Voss. Yes?"

"Are there many people in the lobby?"

"No, sir—a couple of men going out—Wait a minute—old Mr. Lindemann just walked in with a lady. He's heading for the elevators—and that fellow is still around—the one I told you—"

"If he starts to leave, stop him. It may be important. I'm putting you in charge down there until the police come. They'll be in plain clothes, I hope—but in any case, get them into Fred's elevator at once and put Fred back on the board. Try to keep it as inconspicuous as possible. If anyone notices and asks questions, say that one of the tenants slipped in the bathtub and is severely injured. That will account for the ambulance."

"Ambulance? Does that mean she's still—?"

Mr. Voss had hung up. Adrian began to feel quite warm with excitement. If he was to act as usher for the police he would soon know everything. He peered across the lobby. The young fellow was growing fidgety, changing his position every minute. Suppose he should take a notion to get up and leave? It was all very well for Mr. Voss to say, "Stop him," but how? And come to think of it, why? Speculation got him nowhere. He concentrated upon the coming of the police. He was confident that he would spot them immediately, with or without uniforms. He hoped that the tall gentleman heading toward his little alcove would not cut off his view. He greeted him without cordiality. Under other circumstances he would have given him high marks as the sort of caller who added tone to the house.

Instead of making one of the usual inquiries, the gentleman produced a leather folder and held it for Adrian's inspection. At Adrian's dumfounded expression he smiled and said, "I could have knocked you down with a feather, couldn't I? Let's go."

Later, in relating the incident to his cronies, Adrian said, "And damned if he didn't take the words right out of my mouth." But that was later. Now he left the switchboard and led Acting Captain Gridley Nelson of Homicide to the elevator, comforting himself with the thought that if he had been fooled into taking a policeman for a gentleman so would everybody else in the house. Only when he had sent Fred back to the board and started the cage on its ascent did he attempt to justify his mistake.

"You see, officer, we expected more than one man."

"I'm the vanguard."

"What's that? Oh. Where's the ambulance?"

"On its way." He had a friendly voice. His eyes were friendly, too, but they would know Adrian next time they encountered him.

"On its way?" Adrian felt urged to speak with defensive toughness. "A person could die—"

"I understand that the call wasn't put in until quite a while after the accident occurred."

"Accident?"

Nelson said something softly. It sounded like, "I can dream, can't I?"

Walking down the hall behind the strong, long-legged figure, noting the way the good coat lay wrinkleless across the wide shoulders, Adrian thought that they didn't have policemen like that in his day, and wondered how old the man might be with his shock of thick white hair and his young olive-skinned face.

Mr. Voss opened the door. He was breathing fast. He peered around them to see who else might be there. "Come in—You're—?"

Nelson introduced himself.

"One man? They've sent only one man?"

"I happened to be in a squad car nearby when the call from headquarters went out. So I came on ahead. The others will be here soon."

Mr. Voss said distractedly, "But I don't know whether I should be here or downstairs to see that they get in without causing undue—"

"Stay here for the time being," Nelson said, and said no more until they reached the living room. He stood in the doorway for a moment or two. Then he moved aside to allow Mr. Voss and Adrian to pass him. When they were well within the room he said, "Is this the way you found them?"

Adrian, who had studiously avoided the area near the fireplace, turned stiffly and saw that the girl lay as before but that the older woman had been covered by several blankets.

Mr. Voss cleared his throat. "We—that is—Dr. Aldington covered the countess. He's in the bathroom—"

Nelson drew back the blankets a little way. He seemed to be concentrating his attention upon her right hand. He straightened and said, "Was she conscious at all?"

"No—but she groaned a bit. The doctor believes she's suffering from a severe concussion—and heat seems to be essential to the treatment of—"

"She drinks a great deal?"

"Well—she— you mean because of that bottle on the table?"

"I mean I can smell it. Is she an alcoholic?"

"I don't know—she was never troublesome. She would not have been allowed to remain if—"

Nelson had moved to the body of the girl. He was staring down, his pointed, sensitive face bleak. "Her position's been shifted," he said.

Mr. Voss shook his head. "No—she—I touched her to see if I could find a pulse—that's all."

"Who is she?"

"Why—I believe she's the maid." He looked at Adrian for confirmation.

Adrian spoke up. "Sure she is—was, I mean—by the name of Mildred Ketchell—"

"Did she live here?"

"No—and it ain't usual, her staying as late as this—right after supper she'd be on her way. I know because when I'm on night duty she's often leaving just as I come on. And that ain't the only thing that's—"

Mr. Voss broke in anxiously: "Please excuse me, Captain, but I've a great responsibility on my shoulders. About your men coming—and the ambulance. The tenants might grow panicky—and with that boy at the switchboard so inept—"

Nelson cut him off with a nod. He came back into the normal area of the room and said, not without sympathy, "I've a man stationed outside in my car who'll take charge. You've a service elevator, haven't you?"

Mr. Voss breathed deeply. "Of course—obvious—they'll use the service elevator. It's larger—better able to accommodate the stretcher. Thank you, Captain, for appreciating my position. I've been under such stress, I'm afraid I wasn't thinking too clearly—but it was all a bolt from the—"

"I'd like to take a look at the rest of the apartment—and to telephone."

"Certainly—I'll show you where the phone is. You'll find that whatever cooperation you ask will be cheerfully—"

Dr. Aldington came out of the bathroom to find Adrian alone. "Have they come?" he asked.

"Just one so far." Adrian turned his back while the doctor went to take a look at the dormant countess. He heard him mutter, "Pulse the same." Then he heard a long-drawn groan that made him want to plug his ears.

"Will she—is she going to die too?"

The doctor left her side. "I wish," he said, "that doctors were as clairvoyant as some laymen believe them to be."

Adrian did not attempt to unravel that statement. His eyes were on the painting above the mantel. He slapped his forehead. "My gosh—I—What time is it, Doc?"

"Eleven-fifteen."

"An hour—almost an hour he's been sitting there. I clean forgot—"

"Who's been sitting where?" Nelson said from the doorway.

"The fellow who came with the girl who was up here visiting the countess when—"

From behind Nelson, Mr. Voss murmured reproachfully, "I gave you instructions, Adrian—I—Captain, wouldn't it be wise for me to go down and bring him up? Even if he has only a remote connection—"

"All right," said Nelson.

Mr. Voss hesitated. "If I should need any help with—"

Nelson said patiently, "I doubt it. If he's been sitting out in the open for almost an hour I expect he'll come peaceably—if he's still there." He left the doorway as Mr. Voss went through it.

Dr. Aldington came forward. "There isn't anything else I can do here, officer. The Countess Mazzini doesn't happen to be a patient of mine. I've given her an injection to stimulate the circulation. She's received a bad blow on the back of the skull—probably impairing one of the vital centers—and that's as far as I can go without X ray—"

"I'd be grateful if you'd stay, Doctor. The medical examiner will want to talk to you."

"Very well." Dr. Aldington adjusted a lamp that had been shining on the face of the countess.

Nelson said none too gently, "Please don't touch anything else. The lab squad will have a difficult time as it is."

The doctor's large face reddened. "It was I who put in the call only a few moments after I'd been summoned." He sat down near the desk. "And if I may say so, officer, your lab squad and your medical examiner are slow to get here. As for the ambulance—it's a disgrace—"

"These are busy times for my department," Nelson said. Then he smiled. "Sorry I barked, Doctor. I don't like murder."

The doctor's good humor was restored. He eyed him with benevolent curiosity. "You don't look like a man who would make a career of it."

"The career is a logical follow-up to the dislike. Can you give an opinion as to the cause of the girl's death?"

"The skull fracture inducing bleeding at the nose and mouth would be enough to cause it. I made no more than a superficial examination after I was certain that she was dead. It seemed more important to do what I could for the countess."

"Yes—of course." Then he said, "The girl did not die in this room. She was carried in after death. There are blood stains in the hall near the service phone."

"That so? Well—" The doctor shrugged.

"Do you happen to know the name of the countess's physician?"

"A Dr. Selig. At least he was her physician. A sound man—on the staff of the Parkside Hospital. I ran across him once in the lobby of this house—but that was some time ago—more than a year, I believe."

Adrian had been listening closely to the conversation. He said, "So it must've been the maid who phoned me."

Nelson turned to him. "Suppose you tell me about it." He thrust a chair toward Adrian and perched on the arm of a facing one. "You might as well sit down to it."

"Well—thanks." Adrian sat down. Against his always tired back the chair's upholstery felt like a great soft hand. He looked up at the gentlemanly officer. He said, "I'm at the board and I get a buzz from 12A—and when I answer it a party says, 'Help—murder—police,' in my ear and hangs up before I can get a word in. I try to call back, but there's no answer—which is nuts because a little while before it happens this young girl comes in with her young man and asks for the Countess Mazzini's apartment—and what's further, she heads for the elevators, leaving her fellow—the one I told you about— waiting in the lobby. And I don't see her come down again either— nor does the fellow, or he wouldn't be waiting all that time—would he?" He paused to allow the logic of this to sink in. "Anyway, I think the best thing to do is call Mr. Voss—he comes down to the lobby right away and I run him up here—both of us making like nothing's going on so as not to start any fireworks. Well—to cut it short, we find them on the floor. They both look dead—because I guess we're so upset we don't notice right away that there's a kind of low jerky rumble which turns out to be *her* breathing." He glanced at the whisky bottle and the glass on the table and decided not to mention that Mr. Voss had taken a drink to steady himself. "Mr. Voss feels for the girl's pulse and knows she's gone. But when he gets onto the countess being alive he calls Dr. Aldington while I wait here. I let Dr.

Aldington in and myself out. Then Mr. Voss rings me at the board and tells me you're coming. That's about it."

"Did you touch anything while Mr. Voss was telephoning?"

"No, sir. I—well, I just thought I'd make sure so I had a mirror in my pocket and I held it to the poor girl's mouth and nose. I didn't do anything else."

"You'd make a good witness. Could you describe the girl who asked for the countess's apartment?"

"Yes—I could. I could describe her to a T because she's the image of that picture there." He pointed.

Dr. Aldington said, "That's a painting of the countess, Adrian."

"Sure, sure—I know. That's why I'm so surprised when she walks up to me. It hits me like a bullet, is she—well—a relative that's been kept dark?"

Nelson said, "If this is the much-publicized Countess Mazzini, her doings were very well lighted until a few years ago."

Dr. Aldington nodded. "You can say that again, officer. And you may find it hard to believe—but up until a few years ago that painting was a good likeness." He smiled at Adrian. "The truth is that all redheaded women look alike to most men."

Nelson, his eyes going from the painting to the blanketed form on the floor, made no comment. "Did the girl give you her name?" he asked Adrian.

Apologetically Adrian shook his head. "Generally I'm particular about announcing visitors—but even when people called the countess on the house phone—her private number not being listed—I could ring my guts out and there'd be no answer."

"I see. Did you find out which of the operators brought the girl to this apartment?"

"I didn't ask. When Mr. Voss sent me back to the board he told me not to say beans to a soul. But she came up all right, even if we didn't find hide nor hair of her. Must be she left by the service stairs."

"Or the service elevator?"

"Nope. Because if she didn't come down the regular way—and she didn't—she was up to no good—and she'd have known that the man on the service elevator would guess there was something fishy about her using it."

"He might have mistaken her for a maid."

Adrian thought it over. "As far as her clothes went, he might. For a fact, most of the maids in the house dress better—but no—she didn't look like a maid—more like a high school kid—sixteen or seventeen, maybe. Besides, Alvin, who's on the service elevator, is acquainted with most of the help in the house. He'd be suspicious all right—or if he wasn't he'd think she got mixed up and lost her way and he'd direct her back to the other cars."

"We'll check," Nelson said.

Something in his expression made Adrian really want to help him. "I guess she's long gone from here," he said sadly. "I guess I should have called the police when I heard that voice, but—"

"We'll find her," Nelson said. "Try to recall as much as you can about her clothes."

"Sure. For one thing, the coat. Green—a kind of heavy goods— didn't fit too good—"

Nelson was listening attentively. "Go on."

Adrian's face fell. "I didn't notice anything else—except I guess she had low heels—she walked kind of free." He brightened. "The young fellow will— Say!"

"Something else you've remembered?"

"No, sir." He had been about to exclaim that Mr. Voss was taking a long time on his errand, but it was not his place to call attention to that.

Nelson glanced at his watch. He sighed inwardly. His day's labor was beginning where it should have ended. There was so much to be done and so little that could be done until the others arrived. A girl had been murdered, a woman injured, and there were any number of potentially lethal objects in the room. There were also probably more than enough fingerprints scattered over them to confuse the lab squad, and he saw no need to add his own until the tests had been made. He got up off the arm of the chair and did a little jig step to flex his long legs. His voluntary ride in the squad car had climaxed a tedious and difficult case. He thought longingly that a few hours of sleep would have been a helpful bridge to this new claim upon him. He thought additionally that he hated upperworld murders more than those of the underworld, where stool pigeons could almost invariably be counted upon to provide clarification. He went to the desk and stared without apparent interest at a blot on its bare gleaming surface. Ink stains on the fingers of the countess. On the desk. He looked down at the full wastebasket.

With all the patience he could muster he plowed on. "Is it your opinion, Doctor, that the blows could have been administered by a woman?"

"It would depend on the woman—and on the weapon," Dr. Aldington said cheerfully.

"You saw nothing on the floor that might have been employed?" He included Adrian in the question.

"No, sir," Adrian answered. "Unless one of them fire irons—or sticks of wood."

Dr. Aldington said, "There's a possibility that the young visitor had nothing to do with it. She might have found things as we found them and made herself scarce as a perfectly natural reaction. I'll go

further and suggest that in a drunken rage—and please don't tell
Mr. Voss I used that expression—the Countess Mazzini struck and
killed her maid and then tripped and knocked herself unconscious."

"If there had been no call for help—if the maid had been killed in
this room—and if the countess is given to drunken rages," Nelson
said, "I might bid on it."

"But there was—and she ain't," Adrian said warmly.

Dr. Aldington fought for his hypothesis. "The girl could have put in
the phone call before she ran away."

"She couldn't—her voice was deep—more like the way the countess
spoke—it was the maid all right—" Adrian broke off. "There's
somebody at the door—"

He understated. There was a safari at the door. It trekked into the
living room, headed by Mr. Voss. Directly behind him was a bewildered
hatless youth in sports attire. Then came the medical examiner, two
white-coated stretcher-bearers, and a straggle of men with cameras
and cases.

CHAPTER FIVE

"I'm hungry," said Ranse.

"That picture didn't pander to any of the appetites," Mr. Upjohn
said.

"I was deprived of most of it," Mrs. Upjohn said happily.

"Perhaps you should hire that woman with the hat to sit in front of
you at every movie. The expression on her face when she turned to
glare was worth the price of admission."

"The pie in the window of that restaurant looks almost edible,"
Ranse said.

Mrs. Upjohn's voice was firm. "It's nearly eleven o'clock. Gale's been
alone long enough. We'll have our feast at the kitchen table."

But they feasted without Gale. At first no one expressed worry
about her absence. After a survey of the refrigerator, Mrs. Upjohn
decided to postpone testing the new recipe for lamb and made a
round of sandwiches. She chewed hers with less enthusiasm than
she usually displayed at table. "Gale didn't eat a thing," she said.
"She's been picky since we moved to the city."

"She's a sad sack," Ranse said with his mouth full. "I think she's
having a change of life."

"Ranse!" Mrs. Upjohn, who seldom used restraint of any kind, was
trying hard to bridle her features.

"Son," Mr. Upjohn said, "I've told you before that unless you have a
good grasp of your subject matter it's wise to be silent."

"Well—I only meant she's been acting droopy—and I thought—"

For once his father did not want to know what he thought. "Perhaps Gale needs a tonic, Elsie. I believe I'll make inquiries about a good doctor."

Ranse was never willing to be excluded from the conversation for long. "That guy downstairs is studying medicine."

"What 'guy'?"

"The one who complained about my tap-dancing. But he forgot what he came for when he saw Gale."

"I've always felt rather sorry for parents who had ugly children," Mrs. Upjohn said complacently.

"He was far from ugly." Mr. Upjohn thrust the remains of his sandwich from him.

"I was referring to Gale's good looks," Mrs. Upjohn said. She got up and stretched her opulent, unfettered body. She began to clear the table.

"We take after Father's side of the family," Ranse said.

"Finish your milk and go to bed," Mrs. Upjohn said shortly.

"I'm not sleepy. Where *is* Gale, anyway? It isn't as though she's made any friends to visit."

"You looked into her bedroom, Elsie?"

"Yes—of course."

"You'd know she wasn't home without looking," Ranse pointed out. "The walls are so thin you can hear people's eyes close. Some joint."

"I can't say New York has done much for your vocabulary," Mr. Upjohn said. There was an unusual note in his booming voice. He sighed heavily. "Sometimes I find myself questioning the wisdom of the move."

"I miss Starwell too," Ranse said.

"There's nothing wrong at the plant—is there, Lawrence?"

"Nothing I can't remedy. It's merely that I'm beginning to be of the opinion that Starwell is a healthier place to bring up children."

Ranse laughed falsely. "We're brought up already. The damage is done." Neither his father nor mother responded. Pauses were a rarity in the Upjohn ménage. He swished the milk around in its glass. "Want me to go out and look for her?" His voice, ending in a squeak, was as casual as a changing voice can be.

"Where do you propose to start looking in a city of this size?"

"I wouldn't worry, boys," Mrs. Upjohn said in a worrying tone. Then her blunt face brightened. "I know. As soon as we left, Gale changed her mind and decided to go to a movie herself."

"It's well after eleven, Elsie. I don't like her being out alone."

"Now, Lawrence—we've always taught our children self-reliance."

"It can be carried too far in a place like New York." He looked at his watch again. He seemed to be answering some protesting voice within himself. "Gale *wanted* to come to New York. I remember how pleased she was—"

"It's this joint gets her down," Ranse offered. "Now take me—I'm adaptable. I tell myself I'm camping out—"

Mr. Upjohn surveyed the kitchen gloomily. It was long and narrow. The stove faced the refrigerator, leaving very little working space between, so that his wife was in constant danger of freezing her generous hindquarters or burning them if her activities were reversed. Mr. Upjohn boomed in sudden anger, "Designed for pygmies by a sadistic architect. But I had no choice—"

"The apartment has nothing to do with it." Mrs. Upjohn turned from the sink, banging her unwary head on a jutting wall cabinet. "The apartment's fine," she said gallantly. "Very—um—step-saving. And home—in the last analysis—is anywhere that contains a happy family. The picture will change for Gale as soon as she meets some young people. Not attending school, it's difficult for her to make contacts—but Thea should be able to help—"

"Have you by any chance heard from Thea?"

"No—but I suppose a woman in her position has so many social obligations that—"

"Are you saying that social obligations take precedence over her own flesh and blood?"

"Well—no matter. The moment she sees Gale she'll be only too proud to—" A plate dropped from her hand to the linoleum. She wheeled to face the living room.

"I'll answer it," Ranse said, but his father spun him out of his path. At that he gained the telephone only by a nose.

"Yes?" they heard him say. "Who? … I beg your pardon, madam?" And then in an outraged roar, "But I must ask you to control yourself—My good woman, that's absurd … I know nothing of your son's announced intention to call upon my daughter … No—she is not at home … Madam, I neither doubt nor accept your word. Since we are unacquainted, there has been no opportunity for me to form an opinion as to your veracity … Just permit me to point out that it is I who have the greater lien upon anger, and certainly the tone you are using does not lead me to believe that any son of yours is a fit companion for my— There is nothing to be gained by continuing this conversation. In a word, if your son has not delivered my daughter into my keeping within the next—"

He came away from the telephone, nursing his ear. "Hysterical," he bellowed. "Hysterical woman. Hung up on me. Why people should be so undisciplined as to lose their tempers—"

"Lawrence—"

"The woman underneath us—and how symbolical. A Mrs. Channing. I pity her husband—"

"She's a widow," Ranse said.

"Then I don't pity her husband."

"Lawrence—what did she say?"

He screwed his large face into his conception of Mrs. Channing's face. He mimicked her voice. "My poor misguided son, out of the kindness of his heart, and much against my better judgment, decided to pay your daughter a neighborly visit. He left me at eight-thirty this evening. If you had any consideration at all you'd have sent him home long ago—or perhaps you are not aware that he has early morning classes and that I refuse to allow *anyone* to lead him astray."

Ranse guffawed. "I told you he was drooling for Gale. The signs were unmistakable."

Mrs. Upjohn dropped into a chair. "Then that's all right," she said comfortably. "They're out together. I'm so relieved. It's exactly what Gale needs—and he seems unusually decent for a city-bred boy."

"I'm not so sure it's all right. I see nothing decent about keeping a young girl out until—" He consulted his watch again and added an incredulous "Midnight! We know nothing whatever about him—"

"I trust my own judgment, Lawrence. I've never found that my first impression wasn't substantially correct—"

"Why, Mother," Ranse said, "let's not exaggerate. Time and again you've changed your mind about people—"

She said, "Tomorrow's a school day. How do you expect to concentrate upon your studies if you don't get enough sleep?"

"My studies are a pushover. I'll bet that Channing guy needs more sleep than I do. He looks like the type who learns the hard way." A thought struck him. "We could have stopped for that pie after all. Somehow I'm still—"

"Nonsense. You didn't even eat your sandwich. Heavens! I haven't finished the dishes. While I'm at it I think I'll whip up some pancake batter for breakfast. Sit down, Lawrence. Read—or listen to the radio."

"The neighbors take a dim view of nocturnal music," Ranse said.

"Well—you can play it softer than usual." She went to the kitchen. She finished the dishes. She set the table for breakfast. She mixed pancake batter. She made herself very busy, but she was not engrossed in the tasks she set for herself. When she returned to the living room her husband was pacing the floor and Ranse was carrying on a monologue that sounded like a dirge.

"Now there's no use in that," she said. Then she clapped her hand to her bosom.

"Yippee!" Ranse shouted.

"Go press the buzzer."

He pressed it and came back into the room. "I guess that poor square's mother doesn't trust him enough to give him his own key. But Gale has one—"

"I shall have a talk with Gale," Mr. Upjohn said.

"I shall have a talk with Monsieur Channing." Ranse thrust out his chin. "Maybe I'll pop him one in the kisser. I think I could."

"I sincerely hope that physical violence will not be demanded," Mr. Upjohn said pessimistically. But he had stopped pacing.

"Lawrence, you're not going to play the heavy father at this late date. Gale has done nothing wrong. I always say, if you can't trust your own children, who can you trust?"

"I trust her. But I do not trust the city at night." He strode down the narrow hall to the door. He pulled it open with such force that the insecure knob came away. He stared down at it expressively. "Everything in this miserable cave comes apart sooner or later," he said. "It *is* a joint." Then he raised his head and took a backward step. "Sir? I thought you were my daughter."

A smile touched Gridley Nelson's mouth. It was gone in a moment. He said gravely, "Mr. Upjohn?"

"Yes. Are you another good neighbor? Come in—come in—although why you should choose this hour—"

Nelson crossed the threshold and waited for his host to lead the way. Mr. Upjohn closed the door, wondering aloud about the location of a screw driver. In the living room he said, "My wife—my son," and made indicatory gestures with the doorknob.

Disappointment and curiosity fought it out on Mrs. Upjohn's face. She left her chair. "It wasn't Gale?" Then she said, "Lawrence, if this is a relative of that young man's, I want you to explain that we're the ones with the real grievance—"

"In italics," Ranse said. He moved protectively to his mother's side. "My name is Nelson—"

"It doesn't mean a thing to us," Ranse said.

Nelson looked at him. "Sit down," he said firmly. He turned to Mrs. Upjohn. "I think you'd better sit down too."

They sat. Mr. Upjohn said, "I resent your—" and found himself swallowing the rest of it.

Nelson took the leather folder from his pocket and opened it. "You'll want to see my credentials," he said.

Mr. Upjohn had snatched the folder from his hand. His wife and son were on their feet again, crowding him. For once only their faces spoke.

Nelson took the folder from Mr. Upjohn's flaccid hand and returned it to his pocket. He said, "Please sit down—all of you. So far as we know, nothing has happened to Gale."

"That had better be true," Ranse said hardily. But his young face had paled.

Mrs. Upjohn's hand was clutching her thick firm throat. Mr. Upjohn's mouth was opening and closing, but not so much as a syllable came through.

Nelson said, "I was hoping she'd come home." His deep-set brown eyes went from one to the other.

Mr. Upjohn managed to produce a fraction of his normal volume. "We went to the movies. Gale refused to join us. While we were away the young man downstairs called, and it seems that he took her out." Even the muted version of his voice was not quite steady. "Has there been an accident?"

"Not what you mean by accident," Nelson said. "Do you know the Countess Mazzini?"

"Of course. She's my sister."

Nelson said, "Your daughter and the Channing boy went to visit her—but when they got there the boy decided to wait in the lobby. It seems he did not consider himself suitably dressed for the occasion. He waited for a long time, but your daughter did not come down. At least she did not use the front exit."

"Then she's there—with Thea," Mrs. Upjohn said. "Gale's impulsive. She's always taken an interest in her famous aunt—although why—"

After a glance at Nelson, Mr. Upjohn silenced her. "Well?" he said.

Nelson shook his white head. He spoke rapidly. "She's not there. A short while after she arrived a murder was committed in the Countess Mazzini's apartment. The maid was killed—the countess injured. But there was no sign of your daughter. Yet the elevator boy who took her up remembers her perfectly. He even led her as far as the door."

It was too much for them to digest. All three swallowed at the same time. They might have been rehearsing for it. Mr. Upjohn said, "Thea injured? My sister Thea—seriously—fatally?"

"We don't know yet. Are you on friendly terms with her?"

"Certainly—but we haven't seen her for years. She drifted out of our orbit even before she married Count Mazzini."

Mrs. Upjohn was paying no attention to the exchange. She said, almost making a plea of it, "Gale will be home soon. She wouldn't stay out so late with a strange boy unless there was some good rea— I guess you were right, Lawrence. We should have warned her that the mores of Starwell cannot be applied to New York—"

"Haven't you been listening, Elsie? She's not with the boy."

"Why not? He must be a fool—waiting—and not going up to find out what was keeping her—"

"It didn't occur to him," Nelson said. "He's at home now. I brought him back with me. But he can give no explanation of your daughter's disappearance."

"Then surely Thea—what does Thea say? Didn't she—?"

"We couldn't question her. She hasn't regained consciousness."

Suddenly Mrs. Upjohn wailed, sounding like any ordinary mother whose brood was threatened, "I want my little girl." The tears were streaming down her face.

"Mother!" Ranse had never seen her cry. His Adam's apple performed a series of frantic maneuvers. "Mother—she'll be found— the Missing Persons Bureau handles at least ten thousand cases a year and solves ninety-nine per cent of them—I read it—"

"Ninety-nine per cent," Mr. Upjohn repeated dully.

Nelson said, "Have you a photograph—?"

"Plenty," Ranse squeaked. He was glad to leave the room. He came back with an album of snapshots and a small photograph. "In her high school graduation dress," he said, looking everywhere but at his mother. "She hasn't aged much. It was last June—"

Nelson studied the photograph for a moment before he pocketed it. He leafed through the album of snapshots and returned it to Ranse. "I won't need this."

Mrs. Upjohn's need tears had stopped flowing. She was on her feet. "You won't need anything," she said vigorously. "I'm not going to have Gale's picture bandied about. It might spoil her chances." She thrust out her large arms, and automatically Ranse and his father moved within their sweep. The three stood together, united against Nelson. "I make it a rule to worry about nothing, Mr.—er—Policeman. You are free to go about your business. We'll manage ours. Good night."

Nelson, eying that stalwart lineup, wished that he could accept the dismissal. Briefly he entertained the notion that if Gale Upjohn was to be found they would find her without his offices. Briefly he yearned for his wife, for home, for hot water, food, bed. Patiently he said, "I'm afraid that for the time being at least you'll have to consider me as a partner in your business. There's been a murder. You'll need my help—and I yours."

"There are always murders in this city," Mrs. Upjohn said. "It's— it's criminal. But what has my little Gale to do with—?"

"We shall have to question her. She was on the scene during or immediately after the maid met her death. It's possible that she can provide some clue." He controlled a sigh of pity, thinking of the one black clue she might provide. "You don't want to obstruct justice, Mrs. Upjohn." It was half question, half statement. "You must try to tell me—"

"But we should be out looking for her. Before you came her father was saying —"

"Where would you look? Has she friends—or relatives other than the Countess Mazzini—to whom she would be likely to turn?"

Mrs. Upjohn said, "We've been in New York a mere few weeks." Her accents made it manifest that she considered him an idiot not to know this. "How would Gale have had time to make friends? As for relatives—with the exception of Thea, both my family and my husband's had sense enough to remain in Starwell. Our roots are in Starwell. We—"

"She was graduated from high school." His eyes were on the laden bookshelves. "What about college? Hasn't she any fellow students who might give her shelter if—if for one reason or another she preferred not to come home?"

"She doesn't attend college. Gale's a darling—but not as intellectual as the rest of us. She—" Then she said angrily, "Why, may I ask, should she prefer not to come home? Do you suppose for one moment that she's done anything to be frightened or ashamed of—or that she has the sort of parents who would not give her sympathy and understanding no matter what she—?" She broke off. It was as though her own words had bitten her. She gripped her husband's arm. "Lawrence, we're wasting time. Get your coat and hat—I'll get mine. We'll—"

Mr. Upjohn had been standing like a statue, or like a man in deep shock. Now he jerked his wrist out of his cuff and stared at his watch. He performed the same motion twice, both times unseeing.

Nelson said, "Mr. Upjohn," his voice low but reaching. "Please tell your wife that the police have every necessary facility for conducting a search of this nature—and that for you to try it alone will be futile—unless you have some lead that you're withholding."

Like a large agonized dog, Mr. Upjohn shook himself. He said hoarsely, "Elsie—use your intelligence. If there's anything you can tell this man, do so. I, God help me, can offer no light on the matter. I am away—occupied most of the day. I have no time to maintain the vigilance so patently required in this—this rotten metropolis. Ranse— Son—what about you?" Nelson gave him points for trying to lighten his voice so that the burden of his fears might not descend upon the boy. "You always seem to have your ear to the ground. I'm sure you know far more concerning your sister's activities than we do."

"She doesn't confide in me. She thinks I'm a kid. I follow her around some, but it isn't very interesting. Since we moved here she hasn't talked to a soul except maybe good morning or good evening if anybody says it first. If it wasn't for having to open her mouth when she goes to the store or the library she'd probably get lockjaw. I keep tabs on her only to see that she isn't molested by wise guys, but it makes her so angry you'd think I was her worst enemy. Hell!" He blinked his blue eyes. "Excuse it, Father."

"How angry does she get?" Nelson felt like a monster.

"You know—redheaded mad—and then it's over." He made a sputtering sound that came to an abrupt stop. "She never actually admits she's sorry—but I can tell she is."

"Go to bed, Ranse," Mrs. Upjohn said. "At once."

"Why? How can I go to bed when—?"

She was beside herself. "Do you hear me?—leave the room." She turned on Nelson. "He's tired. He's only fifteen—he doesn't know what he's talking about. Gale has no temper. She's a sweet charming child. All of the Upjohns are noted for their even dispositions—you can ask any—"

Nelson raised a hand to stem the flow. The telephone was more successful. Mr. Upjohn choked it on its first shrill ring. "Hello … Yes, child, yes. You've had us—"

"There," said Mrs. Upjohn. "There."

"Be still," Nelson said effectively.

"What? … Gale—baby … But where? … Please—I beg— Don't— You're being stubborn and foolish … No—no—you must tell … Wherever you are, I'll come to take you home … Listen to your father … Sweetheart, you don't know what you're—Gale—Gale—Gale?" He was jiggling the hook with the frenzy of a thirsty man at a dry pump. "Operator—operator—"

Nelson forced the instrument from his hands. He, too, jiggled the hook. After a moment of it he dialed a number. He spoke, and above his tense low words Ranse and Mrs. Upjohn made clamor.

"Father—tell us—"

"Lawrence—where is she—why doesn't she come home—what's happened—is she all right?"

"She—she—"

Nelson set down the phone. He faced them, waiting.

"She wouldn't say where she was. I couldn't—the connection was broken. She says we're not to worry—she's safe—but she's not coming home because it's better that way—better for all of us—that's what she says." He tore at his collar. "Not coming home—and that—that's all—"

Nelson said, "Did you hear any sounds in the background to indicate the sort of place she might be in?"

"Nothing—only her voice—Don't stand there—"

"It *was* her voice?"

"My own daughter—you're asking me if I recognize my own daughter's voice?" He clenched his fist. "Do something—"

"I'm trying to have the call traced," Nelson said. Then, hating to quench their sudden radiance of hope, he added, "It can be done provided she didn't call from a pay phone."

CHAPTER SIX

Slowly Gale left the telephone booth. The heaviness of her heart seemed physical, so that to carry it was a straining effort. An alarm clock behind the counter of the all-night restaurant said that the hour of two was near. She did not believe it. She did not fully believe in anything that had happened or was about to happen. Even Father's voice had sounded strange, containing an unfamiliar blend of anguish and kindness that warred with her memory of him. For he was a memory now, as were Mother and Ranse. And Jack, with whom she had giggled and chatted so recently, was also a figure of an irrecoverable past. A dead past. Death. Father had said, "Wherever you are, I'll come to take you home." But of course he did not know about the death. She must not think of it. Fiercely she shook her head, accepting as part of the strangeness the missing caress of loose-flowing hair against neck and cheek. "Hide it—it's a dead giveaway," the man had said. Dead. And he himself had made a tight turban of her scarf. The man! He might be angry if she was not there waiting when he came out of the drugstore across the street. She had wanted to go in with him, had tried to explain the need to phone her parents. But he had said firmly that it was not advisable, and because she could not summon the strength to oppose him, she had made for the restaurant the moment his back was turned.

There had been no telephone in the place to which he had led her after the nightmare exit down flights and flights of stairs. "I'm taking you to my digs," he had said, and she had allowed him to take her, numbly grateful for his supporting arm when they reached the street. He had seemed her only safety, someone to lean upon until she could make the climb back to reality. "My digs may not be so grand," he said, "not what you're accustomed to, I expect, but I'm a busy bloke— and since I'm seldom home, a place to hang my hat is all I want. Make yourself comfortable. Have a bit of a wash and put some iodine on those scratches. You'll find some in the medicine cabinet. Brew a cup of tea if you like. You wouldn't care for anything stronger? No— thought not. Well—ta—I'm off to make some necessary arrangements. You won't take offense if I lock you in? Just a precaution. There's a Nosy Parker lives opposite, and he might do a bit of spying. So don't answer any knock and I'll be back in two ticks."

He did not come back in two ticks. He gave her ample time to think with desperate longing of the wholesome clutter in the Upjohn apartment, to sit in one of the grease-stained armchairs and dream in feverish sequences of an animal lunging for her throat, of hatless dematerializing boys, of Ranse grimacing and uttering frightful screams, of an animal with the curving fingers of a woman—

When the man returned he looked pleased with himself. He looked different. Inimical. "Upsa-daisy," he said. "We're going for a nice ride into the country."

Again there were stairs, and this time a waiting car, and later a suburb that made her for one choked moment remember Starwell's main street. He had pulled up at the drugstore, bidding her to sit quiet and wait. Only she had seen the restaurant, and the urge to touch home even at this distance had been stronger than apathy of limb and spirit.

She quickened her lagging step. A hard-eyed woman seated at the counter turned to stare at her, saying with mock sympathy, "I'd get rid of that bad old cat, honey, if I was you," and someone's laughter followed her out to the pavement.

She crossed the street and got into the car. She sat there, a huddle of cold misery. The man slid behind the wheel, unnoticed. His voice startled her.

"Was I long?" he said. He tossed a package into her lap. "I think you'll find your wants for the night in there. A proper department store, that was."

"Thank you," she said mechanically.

"And welcome." He started the car. "It's not the first time I've shopped for the fair sex. What did you say you're called?"

"Gale." She pronounced it without conviction. She was no one she had ever known. She was a stranger riding with a strange through an endless night.

He removed a hand from the wheel and shoved it into his overcoat. He might have been reassuring himself that some prized possession was safe. "But your true name's Althea," he said with satisfaction, "for *her*."

She shuddered.

"Oh well—what's the odds? I'd as soon call you Gale as anything. And you're to call me Coley. So long as we're to be in each other's pockets for a while we don't want to stand on ceremony. Don't smoke, do you?"

"No—"

He produced a flat gold monogrammed case, handling it stealthily, watching out of the corner of his eye to see if she observed it. "Not what you might call sophisticated, are you?—for this day and age." He puffed away. He said, "Do you know—I'd be the last man to boast, but hunting out the doings for you in that shop was the least of my activities since we met. I've had the old brain spinning like a top and I flatter myself I've got everything settled to a fare-thee-well."

"Settled," she said dully.

"Chin up—there's a good girl. What's done is done—and you're in luck I happened to be on the spot when you did it."

She tugged at the door's handle. "I want to—"

"Here!" He reached out and gripped her arm. He snarled, "Less of it. Are you planning to do yourself in? I'd ought to—" His voice emerged from the snarl, persuasive and smooth. "If anyone was to ask me, I'd have taken my oath you were as sensible as they come. You're not going to let me down, are you? Not after all the trouble I've been to."

She said laboriously, "It isn't that I don't appreciate what you're doing for me. Only it just isn't fair to bring you into it. I'd rather—I think I'd rather be alone—"

"Poor little girl—you've had it. I'd be the last to deny that. But you'd be surprised at how different you'll feel in broad daylight. Leave it to Coley Spencer. He'll tuck you in safe as houses. He'll be as tender as a mother to you and no thanks asked—"

"I can't," she said. "I must have been crazy to think I could. Please—stop the car and let me out. I'll go to the police—I'll tell them—"

"Do I trust my own ears? Could your heart be so stony that you'd bring disgrace upon your poor dad and mum—that same dad you wanted to ring up because you couldn't bear to cause him a moment's worry? Now listen to me. I don't mind saying I took a fancy to you on sight. And when Coley Spencer takes a fancy to someone there's nothing he won't or can't do to help them out. Make no mistake about that. I told you I've thought this thing through—and I have. I'm a man with connections—see? You might have been wondering where I got this car—even though it isn't exactly out of the top drawer. Well, I don't own a car of my own—taxis being more my speed. But did that stop me? No. I borrowed it from a pal I met at the race—a pal of mine. That's the sort of reputation I have—pals who'll lend me their false teeth for the asking. And what's more to the point—I've borrowed a house—a farmhouse, you might call it—" In his zealous bid for her attention he was dropping and retrieving aitches with sleight-of-hand dexterity. "This house has nothing near it for miles around—" He paused. "How old did you say you are?"

"Seventeen." The age, too, belonged to another. She, this stranger in this rattling car with this talkative man, was ancient or unborn. She was ninety. She was nothing. She was moldering away—

"Well," he said, "it's not as though I'm driving you across the state line—nor is it as though I've anything nasty in mind. Of that you can rest assured. Not that I don't relish a spot of fun as well as the next—"

Her brow wrinkled. She was commanding herself to listen, to comprehend, but could do neither.

He laughed. "I'll lay odds you wouldn't be averse to it, yourself. Not with your coloring and that mouth and those— But we can't have everything, can we? And it's business first with Coley Spencer. Ever hear of amnesia?"

She had caught and isolated one phrase. "We can't have everything." She prayed silently. I'll never want anything again—never ask for anything—never be dissatisfied—if only—if only— She set her lips against a welling sob. It was too much to expect of God. He would not cancel out that which had happened. He would not waste His miracles upon such an undeserving girl.

"I say—you haven't gone to bye-byes? S'truth—you're like your old auntie in more than looks. Miss—Gale—pull your socks up. I promise you there'll be time and to spare for sleeping where we're bound. What I'm asking is if you know anything about amnesia."

She said, "Amnesia." And with schoolgirl obedience recited the dictionary definition. "Loss of memory due to brain injury, fever, repression. Also a gap in one's memory."

"Good. Now we're getting somewhere. I knew you were a clever girl. Trust Coley Spencer to place his dibs on the right horse. Of course I would have worded it different, myself, but the main thing is you've got the idea. You might not think it, but I do quite a bit of reading in my spare moments. Why, you can hardly name a magazine or newspaper I haven't looked into at one time or another. That's how I chanced upon this article about amnesia. Can't say I expected it to come in handy, but that just goes to show." His elbow jabbed at her ribs. "The way I look at it, amnesia's the answer to a maiden's prayer."

"Prayer," she said. "The answer to—"

"With bells on." Satisfied that he had gained her attention, he went on. "You lie doggo in this farmhouse for a week or so—and then I pack you into the car and drop you near some busy center. Naturally I let you out in a spot where there aren't likely to be any witnesses. And what do you do?"

She did not know. She signified as much. "What?"

He said triumphantly, "You start marching—that's what you do— keeping your eye peeled for a busy—for a copper. When you find him you tell him you've lost your memory and don't know what your name is or where you are or even the day of the month. He might be a bit suspicious at first. According to the article, it isn't customary for the young to get taken that way—but if you stick to your sad story there isn't a thing he can do but act on it—and there are two ways he can act. If he recognizes you by the description—"

"Description?"

"Look here—can't you do better than throw my words back at me like that? It puts me off."

She laid a palm against her feverish head. She aborted speech from her dry lips. "What description of me could he—?"

He said irritably, "You don't think your dad and mum are going to sit back and do nothing about you? Doubtless they screamed for the police the moment the clock struck twelve." He misinterpreted her gasp of despair. "You've no call to worry your head. Because the police aren't wizards—far from it—and where are they going to start looking? All you've got to remember is that you never went to see your auntie—and you've got to forget everything else. It's as simple as that. When you wanted to telephone home a while ago I you said your people hadn't the foggiest notion of what you'd been up to—"

"Jack knows," she said.

"Who?"

"Jack Channing—he went with me—"

"What are you giving us?" They were rolling down a country road. He pulled over to its side and braked sharply. "You never said a word about any Jack."

"I—he lives in my house. He came to call and I asked him to go to—to go there with me. But he wouldn't come up—he— Please—"

He removed his biting fingers from her arm. He spat out a word. It hung in the close stuffy atmosphere of the car like a tangible lump of ugliness. Then for a time there was silence except for the motor and the sound of the wheels churning gravel. When he spoke again it was thoughtfully.

"I may have to change my plans a bit. What sort is this Jack Channing? What's he do for a living?"

"He's—he goes to school. He's studying to be a doctor."

"Wasting your time with schoolboys. I should think you could do better than that. Was he intending to wait until you came down so's he could see you home like a proper gentleman?"

"No—we—I told him not to."

"Your people—how do they take to him?"

"They don't know him—at least, they only met him once."

"Then it isn't to be supposed he'd run straight to them with a report—there being no reason for him to get the wind up. More likely he'd carry on as usual—going to bed and rising at the crack of dawn for school—which means that the news of what was what would reach him later than sooner. So there's no use fretting about him—not for the time being, anyway."

She made a desolate little moan. He took it for agreement. "All right then—let's get back to amnesia and your copper. He's heard you out—and if he's slow-minded and doesn't put two and two together, he'll cart you off to a hospital. And if you're still not recognized—or even if you are—tests will be made to prove you're really off your chump. But you don't have to worry about that either— because those tests are all my eye and won't prove a thing—not after you've had a few lessons from Schoolmaster Coley Spencer.

With me to coach you, I promise you'll be ready to do a star turn in any state in the land. First on the list will be an electroencephalogram of your brain to see has the amnesia been caused by an injury or a tumor or some such. It won't hurt any more than parting your hair—and when it's done they'll be no wiser than they were before—because hysteria could cause the condition, and that's what they'll have to believe in your case. Not that they won't try to catch you out. A lot of fakers try it on for one reason or another—runaway kids to escape a hiding—husbands who've got themselves into a spin and haven't the guts to face their loving wives—or vice versa. Yet with all the scientific tricks going—including the truth drugs, which don't do more than relax you and make you talkative the way drink would—and the questions chucked at you by psychiatrists who are mostly all potty themselves, you can pull it off. Because why? Because by the time I get through with you you're going to be the best little liar alive—and there'll be nothing to connect you with Auntie at all. You see, I took the precaution of having a go at the fingerprints in the room—and aside from the question of this Jack—which we'll get around to presently—there's no reason why you shouldn't look forward to a very good life indeed—" He lit another cigarette. "Now you might be wondering," he said, "why I'm so—"

She was wondering about nothing. She had decided to escape from him as soon as possible and, so decided, had shut her eyes and ears against his voice.

He turned his head for a moment and saw her exhausted white face disturbingly outlined in the morning's first light. "I'll be damned," he grumbled.

But he let her sleep. She was a valuable piece of property. She was his insurance against a lean future, his meal ticket. The old one had expired, and with great presence of mind he had immediately replaced it. He spent the remainder of the journey in self-congratulation. Of course there were hurdles to be taken, but he would manage. How sharp of him to have spotted what Thea Mazzini was up to before he had even entered the room. How clever of him to have read and pocketed the telltale page before the hoo-ha started. Luck had entered into it, he admitted modestly. Yet the true test of intelligence was in knowing how to use luck.

Very carefully, as befits the owners of a valuable property, he drove on, muttering to himself the directions supplied by his generous racetrack pal. He found the place at last. It was well set back from a narrow dirt road and almost hidden by a tattered weaving of scrub-oak branches.

He saw, as soon as he had made the turn, that it possessed few other virtues. It lay rigidly and without conformation along a stretch of frozen earth, much as a man in workaday clothes might lie on the top of an unyielding bed. He snorted indignantly.

Then for a space of minutes he was quiet. His generous racetrack pal had neglected to inform him of the rooted stump that was almost in line with the uninviting front door. It fetched the car a blow that made glass crash. A splinter struck his cheek. But that was not the worst of it.

"Here," he said roughly, "come out of it. This is no ruddy time for play acting."

She did not hear him.

CHAPTER SEVEN

Captain Gridley Nelson had a wife. She was an ash blonde with violet eyes. She refilled his coffee cup and said, "Any self-respecting woman required to breakfast at cold dawn would proceed to file her first papers—and I don't mean citizenship."

"I'm sorry I woke you, Kyrie."

"I'm glad. To see you at any hour has become a rare pleasure. I didn't hear you come to bed. How much sleep have you had?"

"Enough." He looked at his watch. "It's almost eight o'clock—not exactly dawn."

"Don't even think of leaving until you've eaten those eggs—or I'll send Sammy to headquarters with a lunch pail."

He smiled. Sammy was their cook, by-product of a former case.

He said, "I wouldn't mind one of Sammy's lunches, but I don't expect to spend much time at headquarters today."

"You're lucky Sammy starts work at a reasonable hour. She wouldn't approve of those shadows under your eyes—and she wouldn't hesitate to tell you so." She buttered a piece of toast. "Grid, are you listening to me?"

"I'm giving you my full attention." He was. He was staring at her beautiful mouth.

"That's not what I mean." She sounded serious. "Look—aren't you overdoing it? You don't have to be a leg man now. With Inspector Furniss away, you're supposed to play the big executive—the desk sitter."

"And black is black and white is white. A nice dichotomy—only in my job it doesn't work out. It never worked for Furniss either." He did not go on with that. He did not want to remind her that if Furniss had been content to sit behind a desk he would not be in Florida recovering from a gunshot wound. He changed the subject by reaching across the table for her hand. She, too, was a by-product of a case, and so precious to him that even to touch her lightly was to start a chain reaction. He arose and pulled her into his arms.

She said against his mouth, "Don't think I don't know what you're doing, trying to divert me with your Princeton double talk."

"Not with my Princeton double talk." But he released her.

"Grid, I don't mean to nag—"

"You haven't even mastered the rudiments of nagging."

"Are you on a tough assignment?"

"It may not be so tough. I didn't get wind of it until late last night. But there's a youngster involved and—"

"A youngster?"

"Your girl of seventeen."

"You suffer too much, Grid. You identify too much with everybody concerned in those cases of yours."

"It would be pretty difficult—even for me—to identify with a seventeen-year-old girl and a fat old woman."

"Who are they?"

"The Countess Mazzini and her niece."

"The Countess Mazzini? I know her."

"You know her?"

"Well—not exactly know. About ten years ago—I must have been about fifteen or sixteen—I came to New York to visit Louise and Charles—and they took me to an opening night. The count and countess were sitting right beside me. She was beautiful. Do you mean she's been murdered? Where does the fat old woman come in?"

"Look—let me tell you about it tonight. I'll know more then."

"Will I see you tonight?"

"I don't give you much of a life, do I, Kyrie?" His intelligent face wore an unusually helpless expression.

She flung her arms around him. "Just try to get rid of me and find out how I prize these seconds we spend together. Think you can carry a small piece of news on your rounds? Me, I've been carrying it for more than a month."

"Kyrie—?"

She nodded. "I decided to have a little mobster of my own to hold Papa's attention."

"Why—?"

"Cause and effect," she said solemnly. "Did they leave that out of your education?"

"I learned about it somewhere along the way. What I was trying to say when you interrupted was why didn't you tell me sooner?"

"I wanted to be certain. I didn't want to raise your hopes and then have you disappointed." She added slowly, "You would have been disappointed. You're happy about it, aren't you? You're not going to start thinking that this isn't any world to bring children into?"

He said, "This is the same world it ever was—only more so." His expressive mouth curved. Rays of the smile lengthened his deep-set eyes.

She was satisfied. "In that case," she said, "we should celebrate."

"Kyrie—love—I've never had greater cause, but—"

"It could be a modest celebration," she said, "like basking in each other's company say for another ten or fifteen minutes while you finish your breakfast. Remember, you're eating for three now."

He laughed. He finished his breakfast and basked for a half-hour. He had everything, he thought, looking at Kyrie. Everything plus.

"Grid, do you want a girl or a boy?"

"Thanks be that's one decision I'm not required to make. Anyway— either is preferable." He meant it.

Kyrie beamed at him. "What a fortunate he or she it's going to be on the distaff side. What is the antonym for distaff?"

Suddenly the thought of the pedantic Upjohns obtruded. His face clouded.

"Don't worry," she said. "I'd hate you if you had all the answers. And don't get the idea your whole life is going to be revolutionized. We'll clear out a room next door for a nursery—and you'll be spared the mechanics of the business."

He pulled himself back to her. "I don't mind where you hang them," he said. "But won't these stairs be too much for you later on?"

"I doubt it. I'm strong as a horse."

"Anyone less horsy I never expect to see." He had lived in the walkup apartment on Lexington Avenue ever since coming to New York. He had married in the thick of the housing shortage and the best he could manage in the way of enlarging his quarters was to take the apartment next door as soon as it fell vacant. "Just you be careful," he said. "Doubly careful."

"And you be triply careful." She helped him into his coat. "It's only fair."

He conceded the justice of it. He sang in a low tuneful baritone as he walked the winter streets to the garage. Thoughts of Kyrie and the baby walked with him. They went along in the car as far as headquarters. But there he left them, as was fitting for a man whose work demanded full concentration.

He had come to his present position by way of a circuitous route, including such roads as Princeton, Little Theater, assistant in the laboratory of a criminologist, and sundry other occupations. He had been able to take his time, differing from an army of fellow job-seekers in that his mother had left him an adequate income which enabled him to exist whether or not he toiled. With the criminologist he had learned much, but his strong appetite for individuals made work on group theories tasteless fare, and only when he took up his duties as a raw rookie did he at last feel himself to be a round peg in a round hole. He was not particularly ambitious, nor could he play at politics. His steady advancement had been earned. He would have been content to remain a lieutenant working with his immediate superior, Inspector Waldo Furniss, who was also his friend. But like it or not, in the old man's absence he had been called upon to take the reins as acting captain. And that was that.

He entered the building on West Twentieth Street, wondering how Furniss would have dealt with the Mazzini case. He believed that he would not have to wonder long and that in no time after the newspapers carried the story he would receive a letter or a phone call with detailed advice and instructions. Meanwhile he would do the best he could, which, even according to his chief's high standards, was not bad.

A small cluster of reporters caught up with him before he reached his desk. He told them most of what he knew and said truthfully that soon he hoped to know more. He did not mention Jack Channing's vigil in the lobby, being of the opinion that it would serve only as material for a sob story. He also tried to minimize Althea Gale Upjohn's share in the proceedings and asked them not to jump to conclusions about her. Two plainclothesmen were sitting in the anteroom of his office, nondescript citizens, provided with a perpetual disguise of anonymity. Both of them smiled as he entered, and one of them said, "Hi, Captain. Your picture's in the paper. Aren't you getting too big to ride in squad cars? You might have been shot. One down in this department is about all we can spare with business so good."

Nelson looked blank for a moment. He had shelved the squad car episode almost at the door of the Mazzini apartment. He hoped that Kyrie would not see his picture in the paper or read the accompanying story. The role he had played could not be catalogued as careful in anybody's book.

"Congratulations, Captain," the other detective said. "Some wind-up. That's one set of murdering drug peddlers bankrupt. Coffee?" He offered a paper cup. "We sure as hell thought you'd be sleeping on your laurels this morning."

"They've withered. I've got to go after fresh ones. No, thanks—no coffee, Judd. I've had some. Were you or Lathrop here last night when the Mazzini call came in?"

Lathrop answered, "Nope, off duty. But Berman, who was on the desk when we arrived, treated us to a run through. Sounds like a poem in my kid's picture book—about a gingham dog and a calico cat. Seems these two characters ate each other up. It figures, don't it? The maid sassed her mistress, who was drunk and didn't like it— and the brannigan was on."

"On the strength of that, maybe you can get the day off," Judd said.

Nelson took Gale's graduation picture from his pocket. "Judd, take this to Bessemer of Missing Persons for the regular channels. He has all the dope he needs. Lathrop, you see if any of the lab reports are ready on Mazzini."

"We being assigned to this case, Captain?"

"No—I wish you were—but you've got your hands full with that Bronx stabbing."

Lathrop grinned. "I thought maybe I could rest my dogs by keeping an eye out in the countess's apartment."

"Sorry—I've got a man stationed there." He went into his office and called the Parkside Hospital. He spoke to the policeman on guard duty and learned that the Countess Mazzini was still in a coma and that the doctor in charge was not optimistic. Even if she regained consciousness, any hope of questioning her would have to be indefinitely postponed.

Nelson took it philosophically. Clarification from that end would have made everything too easy. Seeing in memory that inert form, smelling again the fumes of alcohol, he took his emotional pulse and decided that here was one case where his sympathies need not be involved. It was plain enough, he told himself, that whatever had happened to the woman was surely by invitation, and that for once he could proceed unobstructed by the compassion that usually attended him. But the young maid was something else again. And so was Althea Gale Upjohn. He sighed.

While he waited for the reports, he delegated Judd to visit the morgue of the city's leading tabloid and unearth every scrap of newsprint available on the Countess Mazzini's past, she who had been born an Upjohn of Starwell, Connecticut, and rebaptized by a cover girl agency as Thea Gerard. He chose the tabloid because it would be certain to afford more particularized data than a conservative paper.

He sent a man to question the day staff of the Park Avenue apartment house. He outlined briefly the nature of the information required: the habits and haunts of the countess, her visitors within the last few months, descriptions of them, conversations overheard, a line on the maid's general character, her visitors if any, her boyfriend or friends.

Watching the men depart to carry out orders, he felt very virtuous. He felt like Kyrie's big executive. But this did not prevent him from feeling restless, too, although the time spent at his desk was fully occupied. People came to consult him about departmental matters. His phone rang constantly.

The Upjohn family preempted a slice of the morning. Twice Mrs. Upjohn called to demand news of Gale, and once her husband called, delivering a lengthy stricken monologue postscripted by concern for Thea Mazzini's state of health. Nelson referred Mrs. Upjohn to

Missing Persons for all future inquiries. But first he permitted her to blow off a considerable amount of steam and promised to take note of her advice and comment on the shortcomings of the metropolitan police.

Mr. Upjohn he referred to the Parkside Hospital for word of his sister. He sincerely regretted that he could ease neither of the parents, whose suffering was valid even if unreasonably translated. His need to take action became as tormenting as a physical itch.

It was almost noon before the laboratory reports reached him. He devoured them. Then he got up, left word as to where he could be reached that afternoon, and went to lunch. He did not taste what he ate. He was too busy digesting the reports.

It was the lab's opinion, based on a series of smudges found on certain surfaces in the room, that someone had made an unsuccessful attempt to erase fingerprints. In spite of this they had brought out seven sets, including Adrian's, the manager's, the doctor's, the maid's, and Thea Mazzini's. The last two had been taken before removal of corpse and near corpse, in order to isolate them from the others. The remaining two sets were unidentified. One of them had been found on the wastebasket, the other on a chair back in the study.

The maid's death was attributed to multiple skull fractures. The reports confirmed Nelson's discovery that her body had been moved from the hall containing the service phone to the living room. This fact made it appear possible that the missing seventeen-year-old girl had fled in panic rather than in guilt. Unless, of course, she was more than ordinarily muscular and could manage to lift a weight heavier than her own. Remembering the slim, intensely feminine child in the graduation picture, Nelson discarded this possibility. She would have had to lift the body, since there was no evidence that it had been dragged. Nor was there evidence, apart from the unidentified fingerprints, of an accomplice. Adrian and the others on night duty had said that they knew of no one else who had called upon the countess that evening, Adrian adding positively that at least no one else had asked to be announced. But this was not conclusive. There were eight apartments on each floor. The elevator boys had taken numbers of people up to twelve, some of them familiar, some not, and had neither asked, nor been told, nor noticed their destinations.

The countess had fallen where she stood, victim of one blow. It could not be determined if the same blunt instrument used on the maid had inflicted that blow. The countess had suffered no wound or abrasion. She might have struck her head upon the hearth. The swelling was indistinguishable from any other swelling. But there were scratches on her hands, as though she had gripped someone who had struggled and clawed to break free. Scrapings from her fingernails, containing minute shreds of flesh, supported this theory. Yet scrapings from the nails of the dead maid were innocent of flesh, which seemed to dispose of the gingham-dog-and-calico-cat premise advanced by Lathrop. Whoever had fought with the countess had lived to fight another day.

The overturned fire irons provided no clue. Neither their handles nor their business ends showed traces of hair or blood. The wood in the basket was clean of foreign matter. And by the nature of the wounds, hair or blood must have adhered to the murder weapon. Moreover, the fire irons bore the prints of both countess and maid. Theirs and no others. No attempt had been made to obliterate them. As for the other manipulatable and therefore suspect articles in the room, no hair, no blood, no telltale clues.

Nelson added "Murder Weapon Unknown" to his mental notes and conceded that it seemed to raise the score in Gale's favor. According to all indications, the murder weapon was sizable, which made it unlikely that she would hamper her flight with it. Or had she taken it without realizing what she was doing and dropped it en route? If Adrian's powers of observation were to be trusted, she had brought nothing with her, and certainly, no matter what her exit, her entrance had been open enough to signify lack of premeditation.

Trying to trace her exit, he and his men had investigated both sets of service stairs. Nothing relevant had been found. Even as high up as the twelfth floor the stairs were used constantly; by maids carrying garbage to the incinerators placed on every landing, by tradesmen who had deliveries to make on several floors and were too impatient to wait for elevators, and even by tenants calling upon friends who lived above or below them. To search for any particular fingerprints among the embarrassment of riches that decorated the walls would have been wasted effort. Footprints were nonexistent. The stairs had been treated with deck paint. Only on a wet night would they have recorded the steps of those who trod them.

Nelson went back to the fingerprints on the wastebasket, and the possibility occurred to him that someone had searched through its contents. He shrugged his wide shoulders. All of the discarded mail had been ripped open by one of the lab men in the hope that some of the prints within might match those that were unidentified. None had. Nor was it of any help to believe that the wastebasket had held something of significance for the murderer. Not without knowledge of what that something was.

Nelson came up for air, paid his check, and left the restaurant. On the way to his car he saw white lilacs in a florist's window and stopped to send a box of them to Kyrie. The transaction seemed to take place below the level of his conscious mind, which continued to plow away at the ifs and buts and maybes of the Mazzini case.

He drove to the house on Park Avenue. Apparently it had weathered the tragedy without quickening or slackening of its normal pulse. He did not see his man in the lobby. Unchallenged, he took an elevator to the twelfth floor and rang the bell of the Mazzini apartment.

A young man in plain clothes answered the door. He said pompously, "Captain Nelson? May I congratulate you on—"

"Thanks. Any visitors?"

"One. An overgrown kid. He wouldn't give his name at first. Then he claimed to be the missing girl's brother."

"What did he look like?"

"Big build—bigger than lots of men, fair complexion, reddish hair, blue eyes—and a butter-won't-melt-in-my-mouth expression. But it would all right." The detective looked at Nelson smugly.

Nelson nodded. "Did he say what he wanted?"

The detective took a deep breath. "He said it was his inalienable right as a citizen to aid and abet the slow-witted processes of the law." It was evident that the encounter with Ranse had not amused him. "If I hadn't sent him about his business he'd have been into everything."

"You used sound judgment," Nelson said, and added pleasantly, "I don't remember your name." What with a recent political probe which had exposed many an unsavory mess, he found it no easy matter to keep track of replacements.

"I'm Lester Weems, Captain."

"All right, Weems, go back to whatever comfortable chair you've selected. I'll have a look around."

But Weems was either ambitious, curious, or uneasy about sitting idle in the presence of a working superior officer. He stuck close. "Anything special you're after, Captain?"

"Yes—but I can't name it." Nelson was standing at the kneehole desk in the living room. He stared at the ink stain on its surface. Then he bent to retrieve a scrap of paper that lay near the wastebasket.

"Something the lab overlooked?" Weems asked eagerly. "I guess they figured it was too small to take a print."

"It may have come from one of the envelopes when they tore open the mail."

"They opened her mail?" Weems's humorless face was shocked. "Is that allowed?"

"It had been thrown away." Nelson gestured toward the stuffed wastebasket. He opened the top right-hand drawer of the desk. It was fairly tidy. Right in the front were two packets of white monogrammed paper. One of them was intact. On the other, the wide band that held the sheets in place had been torn. Nelson matched the scrap to the top sheet. After a moment's thought he closed the drawer. He sat down. He drew the wastebasket toward him and sorted out its contents. Bills and advertisements he set aside. He made another pile of appeals for funds from various organizations, wondering in passing just what the countess had ever done to justify her existence. He slit open three telegrams which the lab men had left sealed, and scanned their messages. All three were from people who wanted to know why the countess did not answer her mail or telephone, and the most recent one was more than six months old. He subdivided the personal mail that was left. With one exception, the friends of the countess had not been very persistent. Out of the lot, only four had written more than once. But that one exception had written fourteen times. Nelson studied the sender's name and sampled portions of the letters. He reached into the wastebasket and drew out a handful of envelopes. He examined postmarks. Throughout all of his activities he was conscious of Weems breathing down his neck.

Annoyed, he looked at him. "You could have saved me trouble if you'd gone over this stuff."

Weems said stiffly, "I didn't know I had the right to read personal mail."

"In a murder investigation it's often necessary to violate personal scruples. Besides, as I pointed out, the mail had been thrown away." He knew he was being unjust.

"The countess was not murdered," Weems said, disposing of the rebuke. "She's still alive." Then he said brightly, "Excuse me, Captain, but about all those letters that came from Italy—the last was postmarked eight days ago—and perhaps you've overlooked the fact that the sender could have returned to this country to do the countess injury. Travel these days—"

"I'll check that," Nelson said. "Right now."

"There's an extension phone in the study."

"Thanks. You seem to have done some exploring."

"I was looking for something to read." He not only sounded defensive, he actually blushed.

Nelson, on his way to the study, put correct interpretation upon the blush, having marked last night the count's taste in literature and art. He smiled to himself, feeling a bit kinder toward Weems.

He called headquarters and submitted the name of Grant Barstow. As a starting point, recent passenger lists of incoming liners were to be checked to determine if and when he had entered the country.

He hung up, speculating not about Barstow but about the countess. What had she, that worst of correspondents, been writing on the eve of her accident? For she had been writing. The ink stain on the desk, the ink stains on her fingers, and the torn scrap of paper testified to that, as did the slightly lowered block of stationery in the drawer.

Was it her essay for which the busy murderer had searched in the wastebasket? And had it been carted off along with the murder weapon?

Another hunt through the apartment seemed indicated, a patient leisurely hunt into nooks and crannies that in the initial excitement had gone unexplored. He preferred to conduct it without benefit of such a witness as that disapproving Weems.

He returned to the living room. Immediately Weems bounced out of the huge comfortable chair near the fireplace to stand at attention.

Nelson said, "I'm going to be here for a while and you could use a change of scene. Report back in an hour."

"If you're sure you don't need me? Someone might come—"

"I'll manage."

"I didn't mean that, Captain. Everyone knows your reputation—"

"Relax," Nelson said.

"Yes, Captain. I'll be back in one hour sharp."

"Right." Nelson tried to sound as though it mattered.

His search began at the desk. He worked methodically, taking drawer by drawer, first making certain that there were no secret compartments, and then returning with almost mathematical precision each article to its original place. He did not find what he was seeking, the sheet or sheets of paper upon which the countess had spent a portion of her last conscious hours. But he did find that his sympathy for her was somewhat less dormant than he had imagined.

She was or had been sentimental. Witness the box of souvenirs in the bottom drawer. He set it upon the desk's surface. Its contents amounted to a sketchy diary. There was a florist's pin stuck through a card on which had been written, "I hate pressed flowers. I hate anything dead, so I'm saving this instead of the orchids—my first from Dino." There was a menu from the Waldorf, and scrawled upon it, "Our first meal alone. I couldn't eat. I wanted Dino to switch his empty plate for my full one so that the waiter wouldn't think I didn't know which fork to use. Dino laughed and everyone turned to look."

There was a racetrack card which said, "Dino didn't even see the horses. He says he stares at other girls because he likes to compare them with me. He didn't mean to hurt my arm."

There was a yellowed snapshot, uncaptioned, of a man and a girl. It had been taken on what appeared to be the terrace of a restaurant. The girl was anybody's conception of radiant youth. She resembled Gale in her graduation picture. The man was fair and seemed well made. His hands rested on the knob of a walking stick. Even in the faded snapshot it was possible to glimpse the arrogance with which he faced his world. Nelson had seen his face before, prominently placed in the study, and long before that gazing out over his obituary in a newspaper. He did not like any version of it. He tried to recall how Count Mazzini had met his end. He made an involuntary turn toward the painting above the mantel. He shook his head. How difficult it was to connect beauty with that Countess Mazzini he had seen last night.

He examined the rest of the souvenirs and found among them three that seemed out of keeping. The emerald ring had more than sentimental value. It should have been worn proudly or consigned to a jewel box or to a locked safe. And what sweet memories could be evoked from that wispy blood-clotted handkerchief, or from the leather address book stamped with Dino Mazzini's initials and crowded with names, not one of which was masculine?

He was closing the drawer upon the box when the doorbell rang. He felt that his work had barely started and hoped that Weems had not returned early to prove what a good conscientious boy he was.

"Yes?" he said, opening the door wide.

The man standing there did not speak for a moment. Instead his puzzled eyes went to the metal number over the bell. "This *is* 12A?"

"Come in," Nelson said.

The man came in and halted a few steps from the threshold. "Who are you?" he said bluntly. Then he seemed to take reassurance from Nelson's appearance. "Excuse me. I don't mean to be rude, but I understood that Thea—the countess was seeing no one."

Nelson shut the door behind him. "You're right about that, Mr." — he played the hunch before he realized he had it—"Mr. Barstow."

"You know my name? I don't remember meeting you—"

Nelson said, "Suppose we sit down to the explanations."

CHAPTER EIGHT

Grant Barstow wrinkled his brow to which a receding hairline contributed unnecessary height. Incredulously he looked around the living room.

Nelson saw a lean tall man who, in spite of tweed coat and horn-rimmed glasses, resembled a medieval scholar. "Sit down, Mr. Barstow."

"This room," Barstow said, "yesterday it was— I don't understand. Where's Thea?"

"You were here yesterday?"

"Yes—I don't know—I'm beginning to think it was some sort of aberration. For heaven's sake, who are you—and what are you doing in—?"

Nelson pushed a chair toward him. It faced the fireplace, half the width of the room away. "That's better," he said gently. "I'm not trying to add to your apparent confusion. I'm Captain Nelson, Homicide."

"Homicide?"

"Will you please explain your aberration of yesterday?"

"No!" It was not a refusal to answer the question. It was a refusal to accept what the presence of a Homicide officer might imply in Thea Mazzini's apartment.

Nelson said quickly, "The countess is alive."

"Thank God."

"Would you like a drink?"

Barstow shook his head. The color was returning to his face. Nelson sat opposite him. "Don't you read the newspapers? I'm sure the story's out by this time."

Barstow cleared his throat. "I've only been back in America for a few days and I'm not—I'm out of touch with American newspapers." He paused, obviously trying to frame his thoughts. "I'm sorry—I'm usually fairly quick—but I find it hard to take any of this in. You say you're from Homicide and you say that Thea's alive. Did someone make an attempt upon her life—or did she—?"

"Did she what?"

"Suicide. Was that it?"

"Have you reason to believe she might try to, commit suicide?"

"I don't know—she was unhappy—I tried—"

"Yes?"

"It wouldn't interest you." The eyes behind the horn-rimmed glasses welled misery. "It's purely personal."

"But it does interest me. When you came in you spoke of the room. You said that yesterday it was something-or-other. What did you mean?"

"It was—it hadn't been cleaned. There was a close smell—dust everywhere—an accumulation as though the neglect was not just a matter of a day or even a week—and Thea sat in the half-dark in that big chair near the fire." He lit a cigarette with stiffened fingers, as though if he relaxed his hand might tremble. "It was very— disturbing. I think she must have been sleeping. I think I woke her."

The point, thought Nelson, is did you put her to sleep again? He said, "What time did you come in?"

"About five."

"Who let you in?"

"No one. The door was open."

"Was it customary for the countess to leave the door open for you?"

"No—no—How could it be? She was not expecting me. I hadn't seen her for years."

"And yet you walked in unannounced?"

"I telephoned several times, but no one answered—so I decided to come. I'd found out from mutual friends that she still lived here and that she had been something of a recluse since Dino's death." Dino's name sat sourly upon his mouth. "But I never dreamed it had gone so far." His voice went lame. "Well—I came. I rang the bell and I suppose that automatically I tried the door. It opened and I walked in. I intended to leave a note."

"It must have been a matter of extreme importance that made you write to her so many times and then call as soon as you returned to America."

"Important? God!" The stark sound of his own voice seemed to fill him with horror. He made a successful attempt to pull himself together. He said with dignity, "I see nothing to be gained on either side by this conversation."

"An attempt was made upon the life of the countess. That's reason enough to continue it."

"What?" Then he said, "Who—?" And then, "Please—is she in hospital? If you'll tell me where—"

"I'll go further than that. I'll answer any questions you may care to ask, after you've answered mine. You say the place was dirty when you arrived yesterday—and that the maid wasn't here?"

"I don't—I didn't believe there was a maid. I thought that some remnant of pride made Thea say there was."

Nelson appraised the ring of sincerity in his voice and judged it to be pure gold. But he admitted to himself that he might be mistaken, that his judgment might easily be affected by the man's looks and general bearing. He based his next words on the premise that if Barstow had committed murder no one knew it better than Barstow. "There *was* a maid, and someone, for some reason, killed her. That's why I'm here and that's why I must have whatever information you can give me—personal or otherwise. Any recent visitor to this apartment is on the suspect list. So please describe what happened yesterday."

"But if Thea—she *is* alive? You're not breaking it gently? No—of course not. You couldn't possibly know how I feel about— But if the murderer hurt her, too, she must have seen him—identified him."

Nelson decided that there was a limit to frankness. "She's had a severe shock and the doctor won't allow her to be questioned." He glanced at his watch. In twenty minutes a refreshed Weems would report for duty. He said, "You arrived at about five. Go on from there."

Barstow went on from there. Once under way, he wasted no words, omitting nothing in the reconstruction of yesterday's visit but some of the things he had said and all of the thoughts that had passed through his mind. "It was about six when I left. There was still no sign of a maid." Then he said, "I told Thea I would return. I wish I hadn't waited until today. Perhaps I could have prevented whatever it was that happened."

Nelson did not commit himself. "Where were you sitting?"

"Near Thea—in that chair opposite the large one."

"Do you remember touching anything?"

"The chair arms, I suppose. I see. You're after prints?"

"Were you in the study?"

"No."

"Would you mind providing a set of your prints now? It will at least help to eliminate the deadwood."

"At least," Barstow said. His voice held a hint of humor. He set his prints on a square of metal that Nelson took from his pocket.

"Thanks." Nelson returned the metal to its chamois case. "What did you do after you left here?"

"I walked downtown—quite far—almost as far as the Battery."

"It was a cold night for walking. Do you live down that way?"

"No—a few blocks from here—at the Clovelly House." He went on almost apologetically, "I'm planning to settle in New York. A hotel will do until I can find a suitable vacancy."

Nelson looked at him speculatively. People who stayed at the Clovelly House did not apologize for it. It was an exceedingly expensive address. "What sort of work do you do?"

"I'm a research chemist. I've been working for the government—in England. The project ended several weeks ago and I decided to travel around a bit before I came back to the States."

"I see." His tone was deliberately skeptical.

"You mean you don't see. Very well. After I got out of college—I was born in England, by the way, but this is my mother's country and she wanted me to study here—I stumbled upon a formula for a depilatory which is marketed as 'Smoothy.' It continues to add to my income." He seemed to brace himself against comment. Into the silence he said, "You want me to supply an alibi for last night? I can't. I walked because I wanted exercise. I met no one I knew. I stopped nowhere. I returned to Clovelly House around midnight. I had coffee and a sandwich sent up from the grill and went to bed."

Abruptly Nelson changed the subject. "What's your opinion of Gale Upjohn?"

"Who?"

"Gale Upjohn—the countess's niece."

"I didn't know there was any family." Barstow frowned. "Thea never mentioned any. Why?"

"Considering your long-term friendship, it seemed a logical question."

"Look here—I don't know exactly what you're after, but I do know you're wasting your time."

Because the complaint was usually, "You're wasting my time," Nelson warmed to him. "In a way I almost hope I am."

Barstow continued earnestly, "I wouldn't hurt Thea—and what motive could I have for killing a maid I've never met?"

"You might have met her. She might have been employed by the countess before you went abroad."

"I doubt it." Barstow's voice was dry. "Dino, whatever his faults. was clean in regard to his person and his surroundings. And he had a general factotum who was supposed to keep things up to scratch in addition to his other duties. A woman slovenly enough to allow the place to look as it did yesterday would not have lasted a moment unless—" He shrugged.

"Unless her physical attractiveness compensated for other shortcomings?"

"You knew Dino?" He seemed to be seeing Nelson for the first time. His slightly myopic gaze traveled the custom-tailored suit to the good shoes, and rose again to meet the sensitive, well-cut features. He said, "You say you're a police officer?"

With a gesture perfected by endless repetition Nelson brought the leather folder out opened. "Credentials on demand."

"Yes—well—Captain Nelson, I repeat, you're wasting your time."

"What happened to the general factotum?"

"Coley Spencer? He wasn't that exactly. He was a valet—but he managed to thrust his nose into everything. I don't know what happened to him—care less—although I must say he had a peculiar loyalty to his employer, who treated him like a dog or a prince, according to his mood."

"How long have you been out of the country?"

"Five years."

"Then the Count Mazzini was alive when you left."

"He was. Am I to be suspected of his murder too? At that, it would make more sense."

"Was he murdered?"

"No—he died of pneumonia." His voice became mildly ironic. "Don't *you* read the papers? I'm sure the event was given considerable play."

"How did you learn of his death?"

"Through an acquaintance I met in Florence."

"Is that what decided you to cut your travels short?"

"Yes, damn you, that's what decided me." His voice could not sustain the anger. It broke. "I've loved Thea for a long time."

It was not news to Nelson. Yet he still found it hard, in spite of the snapshot and the painting, to accept the fact that the woman he had seen last night could ever have inspired love. He looked away, not wanting to witness the discipline that was being imposed upon Barstow's suffering mouth. He said briskly, "When you came in yesterday, did you ask to be announced?"

"No." Barstow had recovered enough to speak firmly. "But I did ask the boy who took me up if the countess was at home, and he said he hadn't seen her go out. As a matter of fact, the same boy took me down. He might possibly remember the time of my entrance and exit."

"All of the boys are being questioned," Nelson said.

"They are? Well—have you considered that a burglar might have entered the apartment?"

"Nothing appears to have been ransacked, but of course there might be things missing. I'm checking with her lawyers and the insurance company for a listing of valuables kept in the apartment. What, by the way, was she wearing when you saw her?"

Barstow said unhappily, "Something shapeless and not very—black, I think."

Nelson gave a moment's thought to the tight clean blue velvet. "Any jewelry?"

"No—I didn't notice any." As though unable to stop himself, he said, "Jewelry would have been out of keeping with—with her mood."

"Was she a possessive woman when you knew her—materially, I mean?" Barstow moved restlessly. "I realize this is painful for you. It's not idle curiosity."

"She didn't marry Dino for his money—if that's what you're thinking."

"That's part of it. Would you say then that she was careless of wealth and of the things wealth could buy—her personal belongings, for example?"

"No—she has—when I knew her she had good taste—she liked good things—but the possessions that held the most significance for her were those to which she could attach sentimental as well as intrinsic worth." Then he said, "Careless? Dino wouldn't have permitted carelessness of that sort." A bleak smile crossed his face. "He treated the symbols of his wealth with great respect. He dictated what Thea wore and kept all jewelry not consigned to a vault in his wall safe. It's in the study behind one of his charming pictures."

Nelson nodded. "We discovered it last night when we were looking for clues." The safe had not been tampered with. One of the lab men had opened it easily to find it quite empty. "Do you know the combination?" he asked.

The bleak smile came again. "Obviously you did *not* know Dino."

Nelson left his chair and went to the desk. He stooped over the bottom drawer and came up with the emerald ring extended on his palm. "Any enterprising burglar would have found this."

Barstow got up and went to him. He looked at the jewel.

"You've seen it before?"

"It's Thea's engagement ring. It's priceless. Dino chose the stone and had the setting designed by an artist friend of his. Thea was like a child—so proud—she hated to take it off her finger for a moment."

Nelson replaced the ring among its strange bedfellows. "She took it off—and kept it with some souvenirs that by any objective viewpoint are singularly worthless."

"She couldn't have—not while Dino was alive. He kept track of everything. If she took it off after his death that means—that surely means that her love for him is dead too. I wonder—" Barstow retired into himself. The act was all but visible.

Nelson called him back. "You wonder?"

"Nothing," he spoke slowly, absently. Then sensing Nelson's eyes upon him, he made an effort to give some sort of answer. "Unless the maid realized the state of Thea's mind and managed to salt the ring away for future reference. Perhaps she was making a test to see if it would be missed before she committed herself to actual theft. Or perhaps she planned to make an even bigger haul." Clearly the words were shaved from the top of his mind, but suddenly he seemed to believe at least a part of them. His voice crisped. "Hasn't it occurred to you that the maid could have been responsible for her own death by calling in an accomplice who had no intention of sharing with her?"

Nelson had been listening attentively. He said, "The maid's background is being investigated. That angle will be worked too. One more question, Mr. Barstow. Had the countess been writing—or did she write at any time during your visit?"

"Write? She could hardly bring herself to speak."

"Thank you. And now, for your information, she's at the Parkside Hospital. But I doubt if she'll be permitted visitors for a while."

"Is her condition serious?"

"She's had a bad blow on the head. She's receiving all possible care."

"Thank you, Captain Nelson. I'm sorry we met under such unpleasant circumstances. I gather I'm not under arrest?"

"No."

"Well—goodbye."

To Nelson's surprise he found himself contemplating Barstow's proffered hand. He shook it, steeling himself against being unduly impressed by its warm vigor. Experience had taught him that limp, fishy clasps were not limited to scoundrels and that it took more than a forthright grip to make an honest man. He saw Barstow to the door.

As soon as he was alone he rang up Clovelly House. Barstow was registered there. No, he was not in his suite. Nelson said chattily, "I'm wondering if he's my Mr. Grant Barstow," and described him. The telephone operator could not say, but she transferred the call to a desk clerk who could. Nelson went through the routine again, elaborating upon it. "If he's the Grant Barstow I knew, we attended University together and I'd like to renew the acquaintance—but naturally I don't want to annoy a stranger. My name, by the way, is Mortimer VanSlandt." He made it sound like anything but by the way. He made it sound like half a page in the social register, and the desk clerk assured him respectfully that his description fitted Mr. Grant Barstow to a T.

Grinning, Nelson hung up. The impression left with him by Barstow made him almost certain that he was taking unwarranted precautions. But only *almost* certain. So he called the Parkside Hospital and gave orders that the Countess Mazzini was not to be left unguarded for a moment. That done, he glanced at his watch and credited Weems with being less of an eager beaver than he seemed. He had overstayed his leave by twenty minutes. If he had returned on time he could have been assigned to tail Barstow, insuring his absence indefinitely and providing him with good experience. Then Nelson thought seriously that there would be no harm in arranging a suitable tail for Barstow, someone less obvious than Weems to melt into the decor of Clovelly House. He rang up headquarters and voted in his candidate for the job.

He sat on the edge of the count's desk, impervious to the count's taste in pictures and reading matter, and pondered his interview with Grant Barstow. At first glance it seemed to consist wholly of chaff. Yet there were a few puzzling elements that might be wheat. For one, why should an apartment containing vintage dirt be cleaned after the hour of 6 P.M.? For another, why should a fat woman in soiled, shapeless black respond suddenly to the lure of blue velvet? The Upjohns had insisted that Gale's was an impulse visit. He believed this because a woman immune to letters, telegrams, and telephone calls could be expecting neither Gale nor anyone else. And if she was not preparing for a human visitation, for what was she preparing? Death? Was it a suicide note she had been writing? He knew that not infrequently women dressed to meet death by suicide. But what of subsequent events? What of the maid?

He swung himself off the desk. He strode across the foyer and turned at the angle that led to the kitchen. The garbage pail was his first stop. It needed scouring. It held scraps of bread and meat and the detritus of other foodstuffs. It held no scraps of paper.

He searched further. He saw the vacuum cleaner behind the door. It was still assembled. He knelt and opened the tank. The metal cover and the hose came away in one piece, and he reached in to extract the bag. It was tight-packed with that massed black dirt peculiar to vacuum cleaners. He found some newspapers in an unappetizing cabinet beneath the sink and spread them on the linoleum to catch what seemed like the hoard of months. He took off his coat, rolled up his shirt sleeves, and rooted.

He brought to light hairpins, orange pits, cotton wool, a pencil stub, an earring, several corks, and many scraps of paper. Some were large and some were small. Some were blank, but some had words inked upon them. All of them he extracted carefully, and carefully set aside. Then he salvaged the earring, decided that the pencil was not worth saving, rolled the newspaper into a bundle, and deposited it in the garbage pail. He gave himself a good scrub at the kitchen sink, contemplated his nails sadly, wriggled into his coat, and went to the living room.

He was piecing the scraps together at the kneehole desk when the bell rang. He let in Weems and the operative he had assigned to questioning the staff. To Weems he said severely, "You're very late," having no idea how late it was.

Weems said stuffily, "I understood that detectives were required to use their own judgment, so I joined forces with Sergeant Emmett in order to facilitate his work."

Behind him, Emmett, the old-timer, grimaced at Nelson. "That's right, Captain. He's a great facilitator."

Nelson led them to the living room. "Well?"

At his nod Emmett sat down wearily. He took a notebook from his pocket. "Want the works?"

"Later. Girst give me what you think is important."

"Well—I got very little under haunts and habits. She didn't go out worth a damn in the daytime—and most of her evenings were spent in a bar on Third Avenue. The handy man lives over that way and he spotted her there at least four times. She didn't know him from a hole in the wall and was anyway too far gone to know her best friend. Will I be checking with the bartender later to see has he got any ideas?"

"You will."

"Well—a couple of funny twists. Two elevator boys came in here yesterday at six-twenty, fetched by the maid. Seems the countess needed them to witness something. But whatever it was, she had it folded so they could see only the place where they put their monikers. Then she slipped it into an envelope, sealed it, stamped it, and gave it to one of them to mail, along with five bucks apiece and a thank you. So far not so funny, but—"

"Did they read the address?"

"The fellow who dropped it into the mail chute did, but it went in one eye and out the other—or most of it. He remembered it was three names and some number on Broad Street."

Nelson went to the desk. He found what he wanted, a letterhead engraved with the name of Barnes, Desmond, and Maxon. The letter itself was merely a notification of stock dividends paid to the Mazzini account.

"Her lawyers are on Broad Street," Nelson said.

"Glad it adds up for you, Captain. Now—"

Weems spoke importantly: "I told the sergeant it would have helped if they'd noticed whether or not it was written on legal-size paper."

Emmet said in disgust, "Legal or toilet paper—it was all the same to them. They could have been wearing blinkers—except they *did* notice—"

Weems cut him short: "My line of reasoning is that the countess might have had a premonition—might have made her will." He looked at Nelson, prepared to take a bow. But the applause was not forthcoming.

Unable to resist, Nelson said kindly, "Don't strain, officer. Legal paper isn't a requisite. The law doesn't require a will to follow any particular form so long as it states plainly the intention of the testatrix." His eyes went toward the scraps of paper on the desk. "In all probability the document mailed by the elevator boy was a will. A holograph written on her own stationery." He added solemnly, "I didn't have to violate my principles to discover that—unless opening a vacuum cleaner could be termed a violation." He turned to Emmett. "You were saying they noticed the condition of the apartment."

Emmett chuckled. "Did I get that far? Hope you won't dock me or my wasted day, Captain. Mirrors?"

Nelson laughed with him. "Not exactly. I had a visitor while you were working."

"Yeah?" His voice quickened. "A dapper little pudgy guy—maybe English?"

"No—a tall thin man—maybe English."

Emmett was consulting his notebook. "Classy tweed overcoat—glasses—a professor-type guy?"

"That's the one."

Emmett read, "Came yesterday, five minutes to five. Same boy took him down at six—or nearly. Boy's been working here a year—one of the pair who signed the document. Says he never saw this guy before and wondered on account of she has no visitors to speak of." Emmett glanced about the orderly room, his bland face puzzled. "Says he was surprised the guy stayed so long in such a pigsty."

"When had the boy been here before?"

"About three weeks ago was the last time—to help the maid with some bundles—and once before that to raise a stuck window because the handyman wasn't handy. The maid was a nice chick, he said, but she'd kind of let the place get out of hand. Don't look like it to me— or has the force gone into the housecleaning racket?"

Nelson said, "Your professor type was an old friend. It might have been his visit that opened the countess's eyes to the state of her surroundings. According to the night switchboard operator, the maid usually left after dinner. It looks as though she was ordered to stay late last night to tackle a long-delayed cleaning job."

"Seems if it waited that long it could have waited until morning. And what's with making a will all of a sudden—unless Sonny Boy"— he glanced at Weems—"has got something with his premonitions."

Nelson said, "She could have been tidying up for a suicide."

"Say—that makes sense. From all reports she was mixed up to start with, so she cashed in the maid's chips instead of her own."

"Not according to the lab's version." He saw that Weems was edging toward the kneehole desk where the scraps of paper lay. He said, "Don't bother with that. It's only a portion of the will—no more than a rough start before the countess got down to the final draft. Call Barnes, Desmond, and Maxon. Identify yourself. Find out if they've received a communication from the countess. Then ask if they'd prefer to give you the gist of it now or discuss it with you in person."

"Yes, sir." Weems made for the study.

"Fat chance of lawyers giving out the gist of anything over the phone," Emmett said. "Sharp as a pretzel, isn't he?"

"He'll learn. Now we come to your 'dapper little pudgy guy.'"

Emmett turned the pages of his notebook. "About five foot six— visits once a month or so. Don't stay long. Natty dresser—no bill collector, unless bill collectors carry canes. Maybe in the forties— light hair—pink complexion—barber chair smell."

"Announced?"

Emmett shook his head. "Just comes up. Nobody knows his handle. Elevator boy got curious once and peeked. Heard him call the maid by name when she opened up, but didn't hear what she called him."

"Perhaps he was visiting the maid."

"Don't think so. I'll get to that. The doorman who's been here longer than the rest of the help says his face is familiar, only he can't place him. Thinks he dates back to when the count was around."

"Anything else?"

"About him? No. A few miscellaneous dames from time to time. But not lately—so nobody remembers what they looked like except they looked rich. Seems a safe bet they're out of the picture."

"What other angle on the maid?"

"No pushover. An independent soul—poor thing—faithful to her very own boyfriend. Used to sneak off to the movies with him sometimes of an afternoon. Name of Dave Rapp. Works at Collins Garage and secondhand car emporium on West Forty-sixth. Service elevator man gave me that. Knew because he told Mildred he was thinking of investing in a jalopy and she tried to drum up trade for this Dave. Service man went there. He didn't buy, but they had a drink together. Seems Dave's a nice fellow but without honorable intentions toward any dame."

Weems strode into the room looking peevish. "I spoke to a Mr. Desmond who is in charge of the Countess Mazzini's affairs. He said he had received no recent communication from her."

"Blame it on the U.S. Mails, sonny," Emmet said. "What used to take a day takes three or four or never—"

"Mr. Desmond was most uncooperative," Weems said. "He wouldn't give me any other information either."

"Other information?" Nelson said.

"Sonny's been using his own judgment again," Emmett explained, grinning. "Yes, sir! The post office ain't what it was—and come to that, neither is the police force."

Weems ignored him. "Do you want me to run down there and—?"

"No, you sit tight here until further notice."

About five minutes later Nelson left the Mazzini apartment. He descended and walked toward the side street where his car was parked. Deeply preoccupied, he had turned the corner before he realized that he was being followed.

CHAPTER NINE

Experimentally he broke into a run. At once the footsteps behind him accelerated. Obviously the follower was unskilled. Choosing his moment, Nelson slowed, came to an abrupt halt, and pivoted, thrusting out his elbow.

Ranse Upjohn said, "Oof."

Nelson eyed him dispassionately. "If you're going in for this you'd better take a few lessons. First of all, it's wise to keep a good distance away from your suspect."

Ranse had recovered his breath. "Suspect is right." He spoke out of the side of his mouth, but panting spoiled the effect. So did the smudges under his angelic blue eyes and the bang that the wind had laid across his broad forehead.

"I hope I didn't hurt you," Nelson said.

"That will be the day, bud."

Nelson started walking. Ranse caught up with him and kept stride. His sockless feet had been thrust into moccasins. Gray flannel slacks and a green sweater flaunting a large yellow C completed his attire.

"I can give you a lift home if you like," Nelson said. "You're not dressed for the great outdoors. You're not dressed for tailing, either. That outfit's too distinctive. What's the C stand for?"

"Carter High," Ranse said automatically. "It's in Starwell." Then he squeaked, "I'll file your advice in the nearest trash can," and went on in a creditable bass, "And that's enough horsing around. I don't want anything from you but my sister. Where are you keeping her? I won't even ask you to explain what you were doing so long in my aunt's apartment. I'm not interested in minor police corruption—"

"Hold it," Nelson said. He got into his '51 car. He did not close the door.

"No, you don't," Ranse said, and slid in beside him. His teeth were chattering. "You take me to Gale."

Nelson reached across him to slam the door. He started the car and turned on the heater. He said conversationally, "What sort of police corruption *are* you interested in?"

"I've read all about the methods used. When you're trying to frame someone for a murder you keep shifting him—her—from one jail to another without booking her and without giving her a chance to call a lawyer. You do that until she breaks down and confesses. Well— my sister Gale is lucky she's got me to see that you don't get away with it." He stuck out his rounded jaw. "The New York City police is the worst of all. It doesn't even bother to keep records of half the crimes that are committed because it thinks that what people don't know won't bother them—and with the unsolved cases not written down it can keep right on boasting about how much less crime there is here than anywhere else."

Nelson sighed. He had read that article too. And he hated it because it was founded upon fact. Ever since the "Big October Shakeup" newspapers and magazines had taken lethal shots at the metropolitan police, potting it sitting or standing, and remaining supremely indifferent to the men of integrity who numbered among its ranks. "Have you finished quoting?" he said.

"I'm not quoting. You wouldn't be interested in Gale either if a countess wasn't involved. You're not going to make me believe a dead servant girl is anything to send your blood pressure up. If that was all there was to it you'd be sitting back on your butt until it was time to go out and collect some more graft. Yes, I mean you. Don't tell me this is a police car or that you bought it on your salary. It hasn't even got a siren." Just for a moment he sounded wistful, as though he regretted the missing siren.

That childish note of wistfulness restored Nelson's balance. He replaced the hand which had involuntarily sprung from the wheel. He had been torn between two strong compulsions, one to clout the boys on the ear, the other to go into a defensive exposition about his chosen career.

Ranse said loudly, "If it wasn't true you'd take a poke at me."

"In your present state that would be as futile as trying to convince you that I'm an honest man."

"Ha."

"Try listening to me for a moment. Try to keep any secondhand thoughts from clogging your hearing. I don't know where your sister is."

"Sez you!"

The urge to clout him almost won out. "But I hope that wherever she is she's safe."

"Safe so that you can frame—"

"A great deal of the evidence so far points to her innocence."

"What? Do you mean that? But if she's innocent why doesn't she come home?"

"You haven't much faith in her, have you?"

"I have too." He was close to tears. "Anyway, I don't care—she's my sister—"

"Blow your nose. Not on your sleeve—here." Resignedly he handed over a handkerchief, noting that it was a monogrammed present from Kyrie. He had lost several dozen in the course of his work. He must remember to tell Kyrie that the recipient of this one was male. "Here's your street," he said.

Ranse blew, and crammed the handkerchief into the pocket of his slacks. "I'm not getting out. If you really don't know where Gale is I'll help you to find her."

"I think we'll get more accomplished if we work separately."

"I don't trust you. I'll admit you're plausible, but how do I know—?"

"Out." He stopped the car. Ranse did not move. Nelson laid a deceptively gentle hand on his arm.

"Hey—quit. All right—I'm getting out." On the sidewalk he shook his fist. "I know judo, too, but you had me at a disadvantage. If you want to try again I'll take you on and—"

Nelson drove off, not at all heartened by the encounter. He felt that he should have been able to influence Ranse by other means. That thought led to another. He hoped fervently that he would be able to do better when his own child came along. He hoped that he and Kyrie would produce nothing like Ranse. Then he smiled at his own idiocy and trusted that they would produce no worse. Too bad he could not have taken time to establish a better relationship with the youngster. Time—good lord. The clock on the dashboard ticked smugly. Five-thirty, it said, like it or not. He drove across town, expertly weaving his way through the car-clotted streets, but it was six before he covered the distance he could have walked in fifteen minutes.

He rolled his car into the parking space near the entrance of the Parkside Hospital and climbed the broad steps of the building.

The Countess Mazzini's room was in the luxury pavilion designed for patients with bursting pocketbooks. Outside her door sat a middle-aged man with a hook on his knee.

Nelson smiled at him. "You'll do, Lowry. You look exactly like a visitor who's been sent out while Nurse tidies her patient."

"That's what I'm trying to look like, Captain. The hardest part is remembering that this is a hospital. If it wasn't for the uniforms, I'd swear I was in a hotel lobby." His eyes roamed the spacious hall. "My wife could sure use a couple of those easy chairs and a few feet of the carpet."

A young intern strolled by and stopped at a desk in the center of the floor. The white cap in charge gave him a ravishing smile.

"He's got it soft," Lowry muttered. His eyes followed another white cap carrying an armload of flowers. "Our bird got flowers too. Came just a little while ago. I saw the card. It said, 'With love from Grant.' No last name."

"Barstow," Nelson said. "I've met him. Has there been any change?"

"She's giving out with words now instead of just groaning. The nurse says they don't make sense though. Not that she'd tell me if they did. She's got a lot of professional etiquette. I ought to be sitting in the room to do any good, but the doctor won't hear of it. They sure protect their customers here. Where my wife had her first, it was like Madison Square Garden, only not so fancy. The doctor's in there now. Name of Selig."

"What time is your relief due?"

"Seven. I was spelled out for an hour at lunch time."

"Want to stretch your legs?"

"Among other things. I'll be quick about it." He arose, took his bearings, and walked away, a tidy self-respecting man in a well-pressed blue suit.

Nelson saw the lights above the doors flash on and off, saw nurses hurrying to obey the summons, saw trays wheeled by that looked far more appetizing than the general run of hospital food. He wondered if Kyrie would choose to have her baby here and was grateful that she could if she so chose. He seldom thought about finances, and realized humbly that this was because he had no need to think of them. He wished that nobody's wife need go to overcrowded wards to be delivered. He thought that he would phone Kyrie as soon as—
He woke up sharply and said, "Good evening, Dr. Selig."

The doctor stepped out of the room. Behind him the door swung silently into place. He was a short slight man of about fifty. He had a thin, deeply lined face. His smile made it charming. "Good evening. You are someone I should know but—"

"I'm Captain Nelson, Homicide."

"Oh—I see." He extended his hand. "I am glad we meet, Captain Nelson—yet I am afraid I have no good news for you." His face became grave. "I am shocked with the change in the countess. So beautiful she was you would never believe."

That was true enough. No matter how often it was confirmed,

Nelson could not accept it. "Will she live?"

"I do not know. If it were just a matter of the blow she received—then yes."

"Are you referring to her drinking?"

"I am referring to what has caused her to drink."

"How long have you known her?"

"Let me see. She was recommended to me soon after I arrived in this country—perhaps fourteen years ago. I attended her for a while, but—" He bit his lip. "Her husband and I were not in step together. Then, too, I went back to Europe to make some studies in endocrinology and returned here after the outbreak of the war. So except for one meeting three years ago I did not see her."

Lowry came up behind Nelson, whose back hid the little doctor. "Very tempting gents' room, Captain. Oh, beg pardon, Doctor, I didn't mean to interrupt."

The doctor said, "But there is unfortunately so little to interrupt." He looked at his watch.

Nelson said, "Could we go somewhere to talk for a few minutes? I'll keep it as brief as possible."

"Very well." The doctor led him across the hall and down a corridor to a small sitting room. "I doubt we will be disturbed here," he said. "It is for the relaxation of the staff physicians, but seldom do they have time to relax. Please." He gestured toward a deep leather chair and took the one beside it. "I think I cannot tell you very much," he said. "You understand my position, naturally."

"I am trying to solve a murder," Nelson said. "What you tell me will be held in confidence."

"Surely you cannot believe that my patient has murdered her maid."

"Not unless she's been extremely clever about confusing the evidence. But I do believe that the murder was not committed by a stranger to her. That's why it's necessary for me to question as many people as possible who know or have known her—on the chance that one of them might unwittingly hold the missing key."

"Key? Oh—you speak figuratively." The doctor nodded. "Perhaps your work and mine are not dissimilar. You wish to know what factors lead to murder as I wish to know what factors lead to disease. Good. I will answer what I can without violating my profession."

"You say you saw the countess three years ago. Was she drinking then?"

"No. She came to my office on impulse. She was much as she had been—not so gay—so ebullient—but all in all she had made a good recovery—" He did not go on.

"Recovery from what?"

"This cannot be relevant. However, it is no secret. About a year after her marriage she was pregnant—and as the result of a fall she miscarried. She wanted a child very much—but she had courage and she made a gallant adjustment to misfortune." He spoke to himself. "That is why I do not understand her present state."

Nelson found the subject too close for comfort. Kyrie— He frowned, endeavoring to detach himself.

The doctor was watching him. "May I say you are a sympathetic man, Captain Nelson? Regrettably my opinion of the police was formed abroad. You encourage me to revise it."

Nelson could not very well reject the compliment by confessing that he had been thinking of his wife. He made a project of lighting a cigarette. "Perhaps two tragedies in a row were too much for the countess. You realize, of course, that her husband died since your last meeting with her."

"This was no tragedy," the doctor said bluntly.

"She loved him."

"She loved him once. It was over when she lost her child." He raised his hands helplessly. "I do not handle well your questioning. Perhaps you are more dangerous than you seem. Would it not, under the circumstances, he more logical to approach those who have known the poor maid?"

"That's being done too. But murder is often a far cry from logic. You've as much as said that the count was responsible for the miscarriage."

"I did not mean to say it. I did not learn it from a creditable source. She would have bitten her tongue rather than tell me—and naturally her husband was not one to admit guilt."

"Who did tell you?"

"His man."

"Spencer?"

"Yes—how do you know of him? She cannot have kept him on? No—I thought not. I treated him at the same time for a split lip. He was unspeakably frightened and resentful—not at the injury to the countess, but at the injury to himself. He told me in that while everything of discredit to his master."

"The count was a lovable character."

"Please? Ah! You are wondering why my English is no better for having been so long in America? But I lost much of it on that return visit to my homeland."

"Your English is excellent," Nelson said patiently.

"Thank you." He added simply, "The Count Mazzini was swine."

"Pneumonia caused his death?"

"I believe so. I was not called to his bedside."

"Do you know who was?"

"I know the name of his physician—Dr. diSilvio. It was probably he who wrote out the certificate." He stared at Nelson. "I begin to follow your mind, but I cannot concur. This little man—this Spencer—you think he has murdered the count for revenge and now comes back for further revenge?" He shook his head. "It is not likely. A physician, to be worthy of his salt, must know something of psychology. To my judgment this little Spencer is not a moral man—he is given to petty breakings of the law, perhaps—but not to murder. Or if he murders it is on a desert with a mute standing by to whom he can lay the blame. You understand?"

"Yes. Can you recall what Spencer looked like? Enough to give me some sort of description?"

"Of my height—but fleshier." The doctor made a grimace of distaste. "Women might say he had not yet lost his baby fat. Nor yet his baby pink. A certain elegance in his attire. I think he aped the count in every detail. For with his hatred was mixed a cringing respect for power wherever it might lodge—and correspondingly a contempt for weaknesses that were not his own." He shrugged apologetically. "But this is not what you want."

Nelson said, "We could find a place for you in the department, Dr. Selig." He steered back to the countess. "You say that the concussion is not necessarily serious?"

"That is true. Rather I believe it is a matter of glands. Some deep emotional disturbance has unbalanced them. To this directly—more than to the amount of alcohol she has consumed—do I attribute the abnormal gain in weight. If I were able to do a basal metabolism I would know how to proceed—to correct with whatever injections are needed. But there are other symptoms present and readable—the way her eyes react to a moving object, for one—the amount of white revealed because the lids remain stationary as the eyeballs shift— Excuse me—I ride my hobbyhorse."

"Her eyes are open?"

"She opened them while I was in the room." He added defensively. "Yet this cannot be termed consciousness. She gave no sign of recognizing me. The nurse says it has happened at intervals during the day."

"The nurse also said that she speaks occasionally."

"This is also not to be called consciousness. Aside from coramine to stimulate the circulation, she has been given drugs to relieve tension—not so much for the concussion as for the glandular condition. It is not surprising, therefore, that her mind wanders."

Nelson decided upon the direct course. "Would you permit me to see her?"

"I do not think it would gain you anything."

"Perhaps not. Perhaps I merely want to reassure myself that I've neglected nothing."

"I respect your conscientiousness, but—"

"Doctor, you spoke of a deep emotional disturbance as accounting for the physical change. Yet it could not have been the loss of her baby because you saw her after that and remarked upon the recovery she had made. Nor could it have been the loss of her husband, since you are certain she no longer loved him. My own findings bear you out." Nelson told him about the box of souvenirs.

The doctor listened sadly. "It is the whole story, no? Plain to read as a graph. First the corsage and the little dinner—then the doubt of his faithfulness in that he looks at other women—then the poor stained handkerchief which she sends to join the happier souvenirs— perhaps so that if she feels herself softening again toward this swine she has always tangible reminder of his true nature—and finally the lowest point of the graph—the prized ring—the period to everything." He added sheepishly, "You will be asking yourself what kind of scientist is this who so romanticizes." He got up and looked meaningly at the door.

Nelson arose. He said, "Thank you for your patience. I've a feeling you've helped me more than I had any right to expect."

"So? I do not—"

"And now—if you'll allow me to follow through and see the countess I'll be very grateful indeed."

"Well—" He hesitated. "I find it difficult to refuse you. Come then— but I must be firm in that you make your visit brief." He smiled. "And I must exact that at some time you explain to me how I have helped."

"I will—when I've fitted the pieces together."

Lowry's hands met in silent applause as Nelson and the doctor passed him to enter the room of the countess. The young nurse saw Nelson first. She was seated in a chair a few feet away from the bed, and she jumped from it, obviously to do battle.

The doctor said, "It's all right, Nurse."

"Dr. Selig—I didn't know you were coming back—"

"This is Nurse Rissiger, Captain. Nurse, this is Captain Nelson."

She returned Nelson's greeting with a frank stare of appraisal. She said, "How do you do," in an interested voice.

"Will you leave us for a little?" the doctor said.

"Of course, Doctor." It sounded reluctant. She glanced again at Nelson before the door closed slowly and silently behind her.

The room was large and airy. Except for the hospital bed, it looked like part of a suite in one of the better hotels. Two great windows were veiled against the evening. Several lamps glowed pleasantly.

The doctor walked over to the bed. Nelson followed him. The supine figure seemed to hear or sense their approach. The lips parted. "Grant?"

The doctor leaned forward. With tenderness he touched the hair, violent beneath the white bandage. "Hush," he said softly. "Hush."

She said clearly, "Grant—I recognized your voice—"

"You're going to be well again soon," the doctor said. "Hush now."

Nelson could have shot him for the silence that followed. Deliberately he coughed.

"Grant—I'm glad you've come again. I've dressed for you. Now I can say goodbye properly. You needn't remember this afternoon—"

The doctor opened his mouth. Nelson raised a peremptory hand. He stepped closer to the bed.

"Grant?"

"Yes," Nelson said. "Yes."

"Don't let him—please don't let him—I won't look at her—"

It was a muted, disembodied sound. He had to strain to hear. He said, "I won't let anyone hurt you," and meant it. He had a lump in his throat. The quality of the voice had placed it there, a voice untouched by the abuses which had undone the flesh. If he closed his eyes he could see the girl who had been loved by Grant and by this gentle doctor. The girl who had been taken in marriage by Dino.

The doctor thrust him back from the bed. The unexpectedness of the attack made him stumble. He righted himself, fleetingly surprised that the small physique could contain so much strength. He saw that Thea Mazzini's head was raised, that she was staring straight ahead.

"Will it never be done?" she cried. And the music of her voice was dissonant with fear. "You are really evil. I will not—I will not be faced with that dead self—I am punished enough—I will put an end—"

The doctor's knowing hands spread against her shoulders. He was sweating. "Dear lady—please—rest now rest—" He turned his head toward Nelson. His voice was low and bitter. "You have done damage enough. Ring for the nurse—and then leave."

She was struggling. Nelson moved toward the bell and stood directly within her line of vision. He saw, as surely as though it were actual substance, the cloud lift from her wide-open eyes. "You—" she said. "Who are you?"

"Your friend."

Her eyes closed. She succumbed to the pressure of the doctor's hands.

CHAPTER TEN

Dragging his big feet, Ranse entered the shabby vestibule. Preoccupied, he bumped without awareness into a small well-padded man. "Watch it," the man said, but Ranse did not even hear. She'll be home, he told himself. Why shouldn't she be? Captain White-top said she didn't do it, didn't he? He ought to know. I'll act as if I didn't miss her at all. I'll— He stopped before the row of mailboxes, not because he was interested in whatever letters might be there, but rather as a delaying action. For if Gale was not safe upstairs, he was in no hurry to refresh his memory of his mother's anguished face. As for father— "Be upstairs, Gale," he muttered.

His eye happened to light upon the Channing mailbox. The jerk, he thought, taking a girl out and not bringing her back safe and sound. If he'd gone up to Aunt Thea's with her it couldn't have— nothing could have happened. Resentfully he placed a finger on the Channing bell and held it there. That will give *them* something to shout about, he thought. Then he realized that he had an audience. He removed his finger as though the bell were hot. With wonderful innocence he whistled a few bars of "The Afternoon of a Faun," no mean achievement because his mouth was dry. The angry rattle of the buzzer was lost to him.

The man he had bumped was still in the vestibule. He was standing with his back pressed to the street door. He was no longer watching the bell. He seemed fascinated by the big C on Ranse's sweater.

Ranse said, "Are you looking for someone?"

Coley Spencer winked. He whispered conspiratorially, "Not any more. I take it you're Jack Channing."

Ranse drew himself up tall. "People get hurt jumping to conclusions."

"Oatsy chap, aren't you?"

"Oatsy?"

"Full of the old what it takes. Well—nothing like it for a bloke just starting out to make his mark. Look here, Jack—"

Ranse said grandly, "Jack Channing is dead. They've removed his carcass to address unknown. And good evening to you, sir."

"Come off it. I've got a message for you."

"You have?" He was even in less of a hurry than before. Added to his larger problem was the Channing door, which there was no way of sidestepping. Undoubtedly Mrs. Channing would be lurking behind it to intercept the ringer of the bell. "You wouldn't be the bearer of bad news to the late Jack Channing?" he said hopefully.

"I told you to come off it, didn't I? My message is private-like, and I don't intend to chance its being overheard. As to bad news—that's all in the way you look at it." He beckoned to Ranse. He stood on tiptoe to reach his ear. "Gale sent me."

The boy's heart began to thud. "Gale—?"

"Shut up, you ruddy fool." Alarmed, he looked about him. "You come along with me."

Like an obedient dog, Ranse followed him out of the house. They walked for two and a half blocks. Ranse made several attempts to ask questions, but his companion would not answer. He did not speak at all until he stopped short before a dirty black car with a shattered windshield. "Here," he said, "in with you." He pointed to a stack of newspapers next to the driver's seat. "Heave those into the back—or toss them on the sidewalk. I've done with them anyway, and I don't want her— Never mind—least said, soonest mended."

Ranse, as he tossed the papers into the back, was mindful of his recent ride in another car. For some reason he found himself wishing he was with Captain Nelson now instead of with this butterball who spoke like one of the minor characters in an English film.

"All set? Here we go."

The way he drove, it was no wonder the jalopy had so battered an appearance. "Hey—look out!" Ranse shouted. "You shaved the enamel of that truck."

"Nervous, my lad? That won't do—not for a promising young grave-filler."

Ranse said robustly, "Are you taking me to Gale?"

"Righty-oh—and you've cause to be flattered. She asked for you first crack out of the box."

"She asked for *me?*" The words were colored by incredulity.

"S'truth. 'Jack will know what to do,' she said."

"Oh." He was completely deflated. He opened his mouth to explain but thought better of it. Gale was the important one. If he could find her and bring her back to Mother and Father! He said, "Where is she?"

"A long way from home, but we won't have to stop on the way. I've had the tank filled—and bought splints and tape. I'd have let you fetch your own kit except that someone might think to ask why you wanted it."

Ranse looked stupid.

"But perhaps, you being only a student, you haven't got your own kit. Anyway, we'll make do."

"Is my—is Gale hurt?" His heart was thudding again.

"She hit her knee a whack against the dashboard. Shouldn't be surprised if something's broken—not that she'd let me get near enough to find out—and I can't have her crippled at this stage of the game. That's where you come in."

Ranse cried hotly, "Why didn't you get a doctor for her? Why didn't you let my—her mother and father know? They're worried sick. You must have read about it in the papers—and you were right there in the house—"

"Take it easy, nipper. You don't act like much more than a nipper at that—regardless of your size. They must be hard pressed for doctors these days to let you into the sacred portals." He added darkly, "I read the papers all right and found more than I bargained for—but even if they did find her fingerprints, how are they to prove she didn't leave them there another night?" His voice took on a small load of satisfaction. "Not without you stepping forward they can't prove it, and they haven't got around to you yet or it would have been mentioned. So at least that worked out according to schedule."

A broken leg, thought Ranse. Golly, that must hurt—

"If you really want to help your girl you'll have to take me on trust. And believe me, I've my reasons for doing and not doing."

Ranse stuttered, "W-when did she—how did she break—?"

"What's the odds when or how so long as you're far enough along in your studies to set a bone or two?"

"I—" He was a Boy Scout. He had learned first aid. But you could maim someone for life if you let bones knit the wrong way. His eyes started to water. He took Nelson's handkerchief from his pocket and blew his nose. He would have liked to hang one on this butterball, but he seemed too old and too soft to hit. And besides, Father said that physical violence was the trademark of those too stupid to think their way out of a situation. Could he think his way out of this one? He had to. He cleared his constricted throat. He said nonchalantly, "Please stop the car at the next drugstore."

"What for? I've got the doings."

"It isn't that. I—I want to break a date." He remembered that he had spent his last dime for newspapers and added, "I'm—I'm temporarily embarrassed. Would you lend me a—?"

"You're a cough drop, you are, keeping your mind on dates while your own true love is waiting. Who do you think you're leading up the garden path? Shouldn't be surprised if it was me. No, my lad, we don't stop—not for dates or anything else."

"Where do you come into this?" He was striving hard for maturity. "How did you meet Gale?"

"I met her. That's what counts. And she was a lady in distress if ever I saw one—and I'm the gentleman as came to the rescue."

Rance wished he would talk sense. Or was he talking sense? For the first time in his short extrovert life he wondered if he was quite as smart as his mother believed him to be. If the man in the driver's had been the oily-haired gangster type of movie fame, the whole business would have seemed more comprehensible to him. But—

The car had stopped for a traffic light. Experimentally his hand played with the door release. No, that wouldn't do. By the time he had borrowed a dime and telephoned, Butterball would be off in a cloud of dust without him. And he had no idea of his destination, which meant that he had no information to give either to the police or to his stricken parents. So there was no choice but to sit tight until they got to wherever it was that they were going. As soon as they did he would act, even if it meant taking Butterball apart.

"I don't believe I know your name." He tried to be casual.

"Pudding Tame will do until I decide whether or not you're to be trusted."

"It suits you," Ranse yelped.

Spencer stepped viciously on the gas. The resulting jolt bounced his passenger almost to the roof. When he had resettled himself he said aloofly, "I can drive pretty well if you're tired."

"Meaning you can manage this rattletrap better than I can? Have another pipe dream, Mr. Particular. And where would you drive, may I ask?"

"Wherever you say."

"I'm not saying. I'm trying to think. So put a sock in it."

Ranse saw that he really was trying to think and that his thoughts seemed unrewarding. He kept quiet, not because he understood the injunction put upon him, but because he did not know what to say. They had left the city behind. The cold twilight, the bared shivering branches of trees brought home the iciness of his own feet. He wriggled his toes. Suddenly he did not believe that he was being taken to Gale. What would she be doing way out here? It was crazy. It was a rib of some kind, or else the man thought that the Channings had come into a fortune and was kidnaping him for ransom. He said, "Look, if you think I've got money or something, you're mistaken. We're—"

Spencer took his eyes from the road for a moment. "Money—you!" He gave a wet-sounding chuckle. "Sure. You can't fool me. You're an eccentric millionaire in disguise—and what a disguise —and I'm intending to hold you in durance vile until your nearest and dearest cough up the nuggets." His voice became mournful. "So you don't believe I'm giving you a chance to play the hero, eh? You don't believe I'm leading you straight to the arms of your chosen bride. And me just about deciding to take you to my bosom and tell you the whole sad story."

Ranse said with intent to pacify, "You can't blame a guy for wondering how Gale got way out here? It does seem kind of strange—" He clutched his throat.

Spencer said suspiciously, "How old might you be, anyway? Your voice hasn't even settled. What are you—a child prodigy?"

"I'm—I'm twenty," Ranse said, giving the most impressive age that came to his mind. He went on improvising. "My voice trouble springs from a rare impediment called vocalemia. The professors in school use me as an example when they lecture—"

"Vocalemia? Well—we learn something every day. Look here, old chap, to get back to common ground, what do you know that they haven't printed in the papers?" The car bumped over a depression in the road. Spencer hawked up a series of brief harsh words.

Diverted, Ranse catalogued them for future use. He was rudely dragged back to the present.

"Can't you answer a simple question? Living in the same house, you must have heard talk—something the girl's family let drop to the neighbors—"

Ranse thought of Captain Nelson again. "I heard that the police think Gale's innocent."

Spencer showed his gummy teeth. "They do, eh? Well—so far, so good, unless I'm compelled to alter my plans. But you can take it from one who knows—they've got another think coming—and that's just between the two of us."

"You were there—in the apartment when—?"

"Now wherever would you get hold of a notion like that?"

"But you—"

"Never mind, I'm asking the questions—and once you've had a few words with Gale, you'll discover that my whereabouts are irrelevant and immaterial." He added, "Barring me being called as a witness, which won't happen if you use your loaf and influence Gale to use hers."

He was juggling his aitches with a speed that made Ranse dizzy. "Hirrelevant? I mean—" He bit his knuckles. "The police won't think so, because you're as good as admitting you were there and saw Gale do—do something bad. Not that I believe it—she couldn't. Ask my mother. My mother says she's a sweet gentle—"

Spencer broke in sarcastically, "So your mother's given her blessing to love's young dream? Very nice, I'm sure, but it will need a lot more than that to cheat the hangman—so let's get back to ways and means. Mind you, I've admitted nothing—"

Ranse shouted, "You've admitted being an accessory—that's all you've admitted—because the police are trying to find Gale—and if you really know where she is and haven't told, it amounts—"

"It does, does it? Well, you wouldn't give us away—not after you've heard the ins and outs of the matter you wouldn't. And to come right down to it, you're holding back information from the police yourself. They'd be glad to know of your existence. They'd be all ears when you told them you took Gale to see her auntie on the crucial night and that she was up there so long you couldn't be bothered to wait. I expect it would even make them change their minds about her innocence. Oh yes—I know all about it. I've been talking to Gale for half the night. She told me you'd quarreled and that she sent you packing but that you promised to wait for her anyway. Perhaps you didn't wait because you didn't like the look of things. Perhaps she let slip that she didn't get along with her auntie. Do you know—it wouldn't surprise me if that's the way the police would view it."

Ranse was silent.

Spencer said, "You never thought of it like that, did you? Well, you listen to me. Your girl did two people in—sent them to kingdom come—"

"Two? My—the—the countess isn't dead."

"Worse luck," Spencer grumbled. "But she will be unless they're keeping something back." His pink face darkened.

Captain Nelson had said that the evidence pointed to Gale's innocence. Ranse was clinging desperately to his calm statement. He said, "You're nothing but a barefaced liar."

"No offense taken. I was young once myself. Perhaps you'll change your tune when you hear the facts from her own ruby lips. You might even feel called upon to make me a handsome apology. But that will keep. What we must hope for now is that the countess doesn't regain consciousness. Not that she's been conscious for donkeys' years." He seemed to feel the demand for an explanation. "Because she could give the show away—see? And if the worst comes to the worst— which it won't—Gale's no worse off with two murders than with one. Do you have a fag?"

Ranse had not. That ended the talk. He looked out of the window, but dark had descended. He could see nothing. And in any case there was nothing he might have seen to ease his troubled heart or his physical discomfort. He was chilled and hungry. He had left the house immediately after breakfast that morning, skipped school, and eaten a chocolate bar for lunch. The man, the moocher, the butterball, had decided not only to smoke his own "fags" but to share them. And refusal seemed out of the question. It was not the first time Ranse had smoked, but his stomach, which had been audibly protesting its emptiness, now threatened to reject what little it contained. The remainder of the ride was spent in a feverish and successful attempt to quell it. At least it took his mind off Gale.

"I should think she'd get the hump for fair—lying alone in the dark," Spencer said.

"Huh?"

"Are you going to sit there all night?"

Ranse realized that the car had stopped. He saw without belief the dingy house picked out by the headlights. "Gale—here?" he said. And in his sudden hurry he almost fell out into the cold, reviving air. He barked his shin against a thick tree stump and felt no pain, only sharp urgency.

"Wait a moment," Spencer shouted to him. "You can't get in without me." He came scuttling after, a key ring jingling in his hand. "Now where's that ruddy lock? Ah—got it."

The door creaked inward. Spencer muttered, "Queer she hasn't lit a lamp. I placed one where she could reach it." The flashlight in his hand clicked on. "This way—I've put her in the parlor." He prodded Ranse into a small square room at the right of the entrance. He swept it with his light.

It held a chill and rusted stove, a horsehair sofa. It held a smudged oil lamp on a rickety table which also contained a coffee pot, a cup, and a plate of bread and butter. It held a few straight chairs and a number of unframed pictures tacked to the torn discolored wallpaper. It did not hold Gale.

The flashlight hovered over the empty sofa. "Now that's a rum go," Spencer said. Then he cleared his throat. "She'll be back." He pointed to the open window. "The poor girl must have somehow managed to hoist herself out that way—but her being sensitive. like, I couldn't suggest any other arrangement for—" He went to the table and lit the oil lamp. "That will help her to find her way back, though how she can drag her leg—"

With a mighty effort Ranse lifted his voice. "Gale," he bawled, "Gale—where are you?"

"Here—where's your natural delicacy? Do you want to embarrass her?"

Ranse shoved him aside and made for the door, still bawling her name. Half formed in his mind was the thought that he must see her alone first, warn her that he was supposed to be Jack Channing and not Ranse. But more than that, he wanted to reassure her, tell her that he had come to her aid, that no longer need she bear whatever it was alone.

Out in the moonless night he stumbled about like a great animal. From the doorway the yellow eye of the flashlight followed him, and he heard the voice behind it tisk-tisking with a horrible joviality about the shocking manners of the younger generation. He evaded the light's focus and moved blindly until he found the outhouse. He beat against its flimsiness and the door sprung open. He stepped away and said her name again. There was no answer. He knew that, broken leg or no, his sister would have screamed in outrage against such intrusion.

By this time Spencer had joined him, flashing his light around the empty interior. "Shamming, was she?" Spencer said. He swore prolifically. "Well, she can't have got very far—not without a lift— and you can count on one hand the number of cars that pass here in a week. Since we saw no sign of her driving out, I expect she's lost her bearings and gone the other way. Silly little fool. She'll find nothing but a dead end there. For a starter I move we comb the road on foot. You wait here—there's an hurricane lamp inside that will serve us better than this."

Ranse took him by surprise. He snatched the flashlight from his hand and raced toward the road. He wheeled and kept going toward far-off town. He knew that Gale had a good sense of direction. If her goal was New York City she would not have taken the opposite way. Yet it seemed unlikely that she could have managed to attain the distance to the main highway without a lift. So she must have bogged down, he reasoned, and sneaked into the uncleared land at the right or the left to rest.

Pebbles skidded under his crashing feet. "Gale!" he bellowed. "Answer me—Gale! Please—if you're anywhere around, say so—it's me, Gale—it's me "

He lost track of time. He forgot the past, and there was no future. He was a lost child, and there never had been and there never would be anything but this dreadful, endless wandering. "Gale— answer me—you gotta—"

Once he fancied that his mother was at his shoulder egging him on, and he turned and saw far off the bobbing light of the hurricane lantern. But the real and the unreal had become so indistinguishable to him that even when he heard at last the voice he needed to hear it, too, seemed part of the nightmare.

"Ranse—"

It was so weak it hardly grazed his ears. He stood stock-still until it came again. Then he cried hoarsely, "Coming," and dived into the tangled brush at the right of the road. "I'm coming, Gale—keep talking so's I'll find you." Twigs snapped. Branches reached out to scratch his face and neck. His haste tripped him. He crashed to his knees and the flashlight rolled from his hand.

"Ranse—have you gone? Don't go—"

"I won't." The flashlight shone dully from a pile of dry leaves. He recovered it, righted himself, and went on, seeking his will-o'-the-wisp.

"Here—by this tree."

"What tree?" he called hopelessly, and a moment later the light of the dwindling battery outlined her small white face.

She was lying against the tree trunk, her hair wild about her shoulders. He knelt and put his arms around her, his own cold body warm against her chill. "Gale—you dope," he said, "you dumb dope."

"It's you—it's really you—"

He muttered crossly, "Sure it's me. How long have you been out here? Are you trying to catch pneumonia?"

"I've been here hours, I guess. It got dark, but I wasn't afraid. I was saying poems to myself. My coat kept me warm—it's so roomy. See—it almost wraps around me twice. Ranse, do you remember how I cried when Mother made it?"

"Look—what about this leg business? I've got to get you indoors."

"There is no indoors—only that awful place. I can't go back there. I must tell the police—"

"They know," he said.

"They know?"

"Sure—so that's all right—but you're not—you're freezing. Come on." He tried to raise her.

"I can't walk. The car crashed into something. I bumped my head—and my knee must have banged against something. He thinks I broke it and I let him think so because I wanted him to leave—and I knew he wouldn't if he thought I could get away. Today as soon as he was gone I started out, and it wasn't so bad at first—but then it got worse and I couldn't put my foot down anymore. So I've been hiding in here, thinking it would get better any moment, only it doesn't— No don't touch!"

"I won't hurt you—I only want to see. Don't be a sissy." He felt her knee, himself wincing as he heard her indrawn breath of pain. The knee was swollen all right. It felt hot and puffy to the touch. "I guess I'll have to carry you," he said.

"Home?"

"No—that's too far, dopey."

She sighed. "I know—I just wanted to say it. It sounds so easy—but of course I know I can't go home—ever. Oh, Ranse, what shall I do?"

"You can't stay out here all night. That's for sure."

"I don't want to go back to that dreadful house. He tried to give me some capsules this morning before he left. He said they'd stop the pain, but I think he just wanted me to sleep so that I wouldn't try to escape. I pretended to take them, but I didn't. At first he seemed all right to me, Ranse—but now I don't like him—he—"

"I hate him myself," Ranse said, "but don't worry. Just let him try something."

She slumped against him. She said in a small empty voice, "I wish I was dead."

He babbled nervously, "Gale—Sis—no, I mustn't call you that—he thinks I'm Jack Channing. You'll remember—won't you?—I'm Jack Channing." He gave a bloodless laugh. "Isn't that something, Gale—hey?"

"Yes," she said, "that's something. I'll remember. Ranse, how did you know where to look for me? It's all so crazy—I can't think. What about Mother and Father?"

"I'll tell you on the way back." There were questions he wanted to ask her, too, but he could not think either, not beyond the moment's necessity, which was to get her back to warmth, to feed her something hot as his mother would have done, and to try to strap her knee. Immobilize it. That was the word. "Immobilize," he said loudly. It made him feel more competent. He turned so that his back was toward her. "Gale, if you put your arms around my neck I'll give you a piggyback ride. I'll try not to bounce much."

"I'm too heavy for you. You'll get a rupture. Ranse, do they really know I killed Aunt Thea?"

"She's not dead."

"But he said she was—"

"He stinks. She's in the hospital."

"You're making it up?"

"I'm not. For Pete's sake, I'm sick of squatting. Will you grab me around the neck?"

She did. He could feel the sob that shook her as he managed to stand upright. "Try not to mind. I'll fix it as soon as we get back. Cold compresses ought to help—and keeping off it. Hold tight."

"Wait—I took his cane to help me walk. We've got to find it—it's around here somewhere."

"I'll come back for it—I can't bend down now to get it. Look—I'll tie my handkerchief to the tree to mark the place."

Once he got out to the road, the going was easier. It would have been a cinch, he thought, without the heavy coat she was wearing. Good thing she had it, though. He picked his way carefully, trying not to jog the injured knee. She had a bump on her forehead, probably the result of the car crash, but he wondered unhappily if the bushes were responsible for those scratches on her face. He wondered.

Her breath touched his neck. "Ranse, I've been so nasty to you lately. I'm sorry."

"You can't help it if you've got a rotten disposition."

"Yes, I can help it. If only Aunt Thea doesn't die—if only I'm not a murderer—you'll see—" She gasped. "Oh, Ranse—"

"Stop talking. It tickles." He thought that she was remembering the maid. He became a very busy boy, trying not to stumble, trying to wield the flashlight, trying to hold her bad leg firm against his side, trying not to release the questions that beat against his lips. But the warm wet drops that trickled down his neck were not the sweat of his labors. "All right, talk," he said. "I'd rather be tickled than soaked. Stop crying. Tell me anything you want to and get it over with. So you took a notion to see Aunt Thea and—?"

"It wasn't a notion. I'd wanted to see her for a long time, only I didn't have the nerve to go alone—and then Jack Channing came and I got him to take me—but he wouldn't come up—so we had a fight and I went up without him—and a maid let me in—and Aunt

Thea was sitting there with a man—*the* man. She wasn't the way I pictured her at all—"

"I know—fat. Go on."

"She looked at me—"

He felt the quake along his back. "So—?"

"Ranse, she looked at me and it was terrible—and she got up and threw herself at me—she hit—scratched—"

"Why? What had you done?"

"Nothing—I hadn't done a thing. I'd only just come into the room, and then it seemed to—I don't know—there was yelling and screaming and I was fighting too—trying to keep her away from me—and then—then I guess I must have knocked her down because she was lying there—"

He said scornfully, "Were you wearing your knuckle dusters?" For some reason not analyzed, the heaviness in his chest lifted a little. "The papers said she's enormous, and you don't weigh much over a hundred." He made it sound as though she were boasting. Then he remembered the missing weapon and the heaviness descended again. "What *did* you use, anyway?"

"I don't know—I don't know. The next thing I was running down the stairs with him—and he took me to where he lives. He said he wanted to help me. He left me there and came back with a car and we drove out here, but I don't think he wants to help me—I—"

Ranse said judicially, "Personally I think he's a—a cough drop. Still, he let you phone last night."

"He didn't. I sneaked out of the car when he was buying things. I didn't want Mother or Father to worry."

He groaned. "You poor nitwit—then why didn't you tell them where you were? They'd have—"

"I couldn't—I couldn't—I was mixed up—I—"

"You're still mixed up. What's that butterball's name?"

"Spencer—Coley Spencer. Ranse, you shouldn't have come. Now you're in it too—and he's got some scheme—"

Ranse wished he had a scheme himself. He wished he was not so hungry. He wished he could do something about the blisters that had formed on his sockless heels. "I'll scheme him," he said.

"He's going to be angry when he finds out you're not Jack. He wanted to stop Jack from talking to the police because Jack was the only one who knew I was there. Then when he thought I had a broken leg he said he couldn't very well get a real doctor so he'd kill two birds with one stone."

"He isn't going to kill anything. Jack has talked to the police, but don't tell him that. Not that he had anything to say—the drip."

"Oh, Ranse, what must he think of me?"

"Who?"

"Nobody—it doesn't matter. I wish you'd go home. It's bad enough for Mother and Father with me gone—"

"I'll get word to them somehow." The words were brave, but he had no feasible way to implement them. A house without plumbing and electricity could not be expected to have a telephone. And he would have to know a great deal more about everything before leaving her alone with that—that— He thrust the problem aside. "I still don't get it about the maid," he said baldly.

"Is she—is she really dead?"

"Yes."

She said drearily, "Then he must be telling the truth—I killed her."

"Don't you know?"

"I don't—honestly I don't. He said she came in and tried to pull me away from Aunt Thea, and he said my redheaded temper was up and I went for her—but it's—when I try to remember my mind's a blank."

He had memorized almost word for word the newspaper stories which described in gory detail the condition of the maid's head. He asked again, "What did you use to hit with? You've got to remember— or if you can't, he must have told you—"

"He didn't—and I didn't ask him. I guess I just picked up something."

"On your honor?"

She sobbed, "I'm telling you everything I can think of—but, Ranse, I haven't got that kind of a temper—I don't hit people, I say mean things the way I did to Jack, but I never— Ranse, I don't understand. It makes me afraid—not just of him—of me if that's the kind of person I am. Must we go back in there? He can get awfully angry—"

He could not think of anything else to do. "It will be only for tonight." As an afterthought he added toughly, "Listen, I'm with you—and you can take it from me, he's chicken. I'll show him who's boss around here."

Chicken or not, Coley Spencer had evidently given up the search. The hurricane lantern was nowhere in sight as they turned down the path. But he heard their approach, and the door of the house was flung open before Ranse had a chance to kick it.

"Strike me pink," said Spencer. "Come in—come in." Relief and not anger shaded his voice. "So your heart led you to her straight as an arrow. Here—set her down on the couch." He shook a playful finger at Gale, but the effect was spoiled because his voice was shaking too. "Silly little thing—you gave me a turn, you did."

Ranse, freed of Gale's weight, had grabbed a piece of the limp bread and butter and was stuffing it into his mouth. He swallowed and said loudly, "If there's anything hot to eat in this trap, get it and get some cold water too—I suppose ice would be too much to expect in this dump. After that you can make yourself scarce because I've got to do some doctoring."

CHAPTER ELEVEN

Nelson called the Collins Garage from a booth in the hospital lobby and asked to speak to Mr. Dave Rapp. Mr. Rapp's boss regretted that this could not be arranged. "Dave quit early," he said. "He felt kind of puny due to one of his tomatoes dying on him. You could maybe catch him at home. His landlady has a phone. Hang on—I got the number written down someplace."

Nelson hung on, recorded the number, and fished for another dime.

Dave Rapp's landlady grumbled about needing at least another pair of feet, but she obliged, and presently an aggressively male voice said, "Yeah? This is Dave."

Nelson explained himself briefly.

"Oh—well—sure—I'd be glad to help, but I'm strictly ignorant about the whole business. When I seen Milly's name in the paper I pretty near shed my skin. I was out with her yesterday afternoon and she was just as alive as you or me. It don't seem right. A great kid—Milly. Wouldn't even so much as let you lay a hand on—"

Nelson managed to interject a question.

"Sure—sure—she did a lot of gassing about her job, but most of it went in one ear and out the other. I guess I'm a guy with a one-track mind, if you get me. What she said mostly was stuff like the countess being a lush—and nothing much exciting happening—no visitors, for instance, except some old friend who looked in once a month or so—"

"Did she mention his name?"

"Yeah—Spencer—like in Spencer Tracy. Poor Milly sure loved the movies. Honest, I hope you find the louse who killed her. I wouldn't mind giving him a workout myself. Something I *can* tell you. I read in one paper that Milly and Mazzini had a fight, and that's a lot of malarky. They got along fine. She trusted Milly so much she sent her to the bank every month to draw out two thousand dollars without her being bonded nor nothing." He paused for a moment. "What was left from the rent and food and Milly's salary must have gone for liquor, because Milly said she never spent a cent on clothes. I'd kid with Milly about how far she could get with two grand in her fist—" He remembered that he was talking to the law. He said hastily, "Just kidding, you understand—good clean fun. Milly was too honest for her own good. I mean—well—"

Nelson asked if he had ever seen the countess.

"Nah. I was curious on account of she'd been such a looker, but

Milly said she wasn't anymore—and besides, she might get mad if I came around, and it was such a good job there was no sense taking risks."

"Had Milly any relatives or other friends that you know about?"

"Not a soul in the world. She was always singing the same song about wanting to get married and raise a family of her own." Then he said defiantly, "Maybe I would've married her at that—"

Nelson told him to stand by and said he might be summoned to headquarters for more extensive questioning.

"Sure—any time—just call Collins Garage. The boss will let me off whenever I want. He better."

Nelson went out into the air, breathed of it deeply to rid his nostrils of odors that no hospital, however deluxe, could exorcise, stepped into his car, and drove to headquarters. No information had come in on Althea Gale Upjohn, not even as yet the usual stream of false clues that cranks and crackpots could always he counted upon to provide. Going through the messages on his desk, he came across several from Mr. and Mrs. Upjohn, who wanted to know, among other things, his opinion about inserting a personal in the papers begging Gale to come home. His opinion was that it could do no harm, and he gave instructions that this be relayed the next time the question was put. While he was at his desk he called the Motor Vehicle Bureau and learned that one Coley Spencer had renewed his driver's license. He took down the facts that the code card contained.

Then he looked at his watch, battled with himself, won out over his intense desire to go home, and drove to Coley Spencer's address. He found it to be a remodeled tenement house on Fifty- fifth Street between Second and First avenues. The sign outside said, "Furnished One-Room Apartments, Light Housekeeping," and attached to it was a "No Vacancies" board.

He climbed the tall stoop and rang Spencer's bell. There was no answer. He rang the bell next to it and the door clicked open. He went up three steep flights of stairs and knocked, pretending not to notice the bony head sticking out of the door opposite.

"You ring my bell?" the head demanded.

"Sorry—I meant to ring Mr. Spencer's."

"He ain't in."

"Thanks. Do you know what time he'll be back?"

"What do you take me for—his secretary? You a friend of his?"

Nelson weighed the tone of voice and found it politic to say, "No."

The man came out into the dirty yellow light, setting the latch behind him. He was thin and stooped. He needed a shave and a bath. He needed a complete reupholstering job from top to bottom. He moved close to Nelson, his myopic eyes busy. After a detailed inspection he chuckled cynically. "If you're a bill collector you've got your work cut out for you. He owes me plenty—a buck here and a buck there till I learned my lesson. All he gets from me now—" He belched.

"Doesn't he work?"

"Him? He don't know what work is except to figure the horses. But a shortage of money's got nothing to do with his chiseling. I've seen him with a wad as big as a pillow. Got a cigarette? I'm clean out."

Nelson gave him a cigarette and lit it for him. He would have given him the pack, but he did not want to seem too eager. "Was he at home last night?"

"Now why would you want to know?" He drew in smoke greedily. "I guessed wrong the first time, huh? You're a private eye." Again he peered at Nelson's clothes. "Business must be good. Her husband sic you onto him?"

Nelson said, "Is she here often?"

"Listen—I don't miss a trick. Last night was the first time she came, and I couldn't hardly believe it. He's always bragging about knocking 'em over, but his kind is plain wind with no trimmings—so I didn't take any notice—"

"Last night," Nelson prompted.

"Yeah—last night. It must've been after eleven—dunno for certain because my clock's broke—I hear him unlock his door and I hear him talking and it wasn't to himself. I hear her voice just as sure as I'm standing here. And then what does he do but go out again and leave her in there by her lonesome. First I thought he went for some beer—but who buys beer for an hour?" He grinned and no teeth showed. "Get a load of me. Wouldn't you think I was being paid for this? What about it?"

Nelson put his hand in his pocket for the identification folder, change his mind after another look at the man's general air of decay, and weakly produced a five-dollar bill.

"That all?"

"That's all from me. If you want it there's got to be more from you."

"Sold." He snatched and pocketed the bill before he said, "But I ain't got much more to give. When he came back the second time it was only for a couple of minutes. Then he left with the skirt, and that was that—except I'll be glad to oblige if you want me to swear they was in there together long enough to—"

"That won't be necessary," Nelson said. "Did you see the woman?"

"Only the back of her. When I heard them going down the stairs I ran out for a gander because it don't do no harm to keep your eyes open and it could do some good—like now. She had a loose coat on, so I couldn't make out her shape—and she was wearing one of them turbans on her head."

"A turban?"

"Well—not a big one like them Indian fellows wear—but wound around so's it hid every bit of her hair."

"Did you notice the color of her coat?"

He shook his head. "The light ain't so good, and they was halfway down the stairs."

"Have you seen Spencer since?"

"He ain't back. I ought to know. I'm not working right now—and I ain't stirred from the house for two days."

"Is it usual for Spencer to stay out all night?"

"Nope, he keeps pretty regular hours—got to say that for him. Listen, mister, I'd like to run down to the corner grocer before it closes. I ain't trying to welsh or nothing—"

"Go ahead—and thanks." Nelson dared not speculate upon how much or how little thanks were due.

Coley Spencer's neighbor drew his thin stooped body erect. "A pleasure. Anybody don't push me around I'm always glad to oblige." He went into his apartment and closed the door. A few moments later he came out wearing an overcoat that matched for shabbiness the rest of his attire. "You still here, mister?"

"I think I'll wait around for Spencer."

"Suit yourself. If he comes before I get back, hold up the fireworks. I wouldn't want to miss nothing."

Nelson waited until he had gone down the stairs. Then he listened at the other doors on the floor to make sure that there was no threat of an immediate exodus.

Spencer's lock responded to the cellophane trick. Nelson stepped over the threshold and bolted himself in. It did not take long to search the place. While he was at it he received a distinct flash of Weems's humorless, shocked face. But he was not deterred. He felt justified. He felt that what he was doing, if not in the book of regulations, needed to be done.

The "light housekeeping" advertised on the sign meant a two-burner gas stove, a sink, and a small refrigerator standing unscreened at one end of the combination dining room, living room, and bedroom. The cabinet above the sink was empty of dishes. The sink was full of them, to the enrichment of several cockroaches. The door to the tiny bathroom broke the same wall at a distance of only a few feet away. The apartment's movable furnishings consisted of a day bed, two grimy upholstered chairs, a straight chair, two iron floor lamps with fringed rose shades, a gate-legged table, a varnished chest of drawers, a spindly desk, and a pile of magazines on the mustard-colored cotton rug. A venetian blind with its slats closed against a narrow dark court covered the room's one window.

Coley Spencer, Nelson thought, was either a man without taste, a man without means, or a man who could manage to rise above his surroundings. He opened the door of the closet and immediately discarded the "without means" hypothesis. A considerable outlay was represented in the carefully hung suits, the treed row of hand-sewn shoes, the heavy maroon silk robe, the tie rack filled with Sulka and Bronzini models, and the two obviously unused pieces of luggage bearing a Mark Cross imprint. The chest of drawers presented similar evidence of a man who lavished affection upon himself. The spindly desk showed nothing but old racing forms, a cheap writing tablet, and a folded envelope which had evidently served as an address book. It bore penciled memoranda of two names and addresses. Nelson looked around for a phone book in order to check the names. There was none. Neither was there a telephone. He pocketed the envelope.

He went into the bathroom. It was clean. There was nothing out of place except a small bottle of iodine and a box of absorbent cotton on the washstand. The iodine bottle had been opened, but the inroads made upon its contents were hardly perceptible. A piece of drugstore wrapping paper had been thrown into the wastebasket. There was nothing else in the basket but a few small wads of cotton. He knelt to examine them and saw that they were flecked with blood. Rising, he opened the medicine cabinet and nodded thoughtfully as his eyes picked out a styptic cylinder. He rescued the wrapping paper and packaged the bottle of iodine and the discarded cotton. He took it for possible future reference.

After one last look to make certain that nothing in the apartment could have served as a portable weapon, he let himself out, grateful that Coley Spencer's neighbor was not spending his five dollars with profligate haste. He was sorry that he had not given him more. It was beginning to seem as though he deserved more.

He made still another trip to headquarters to place his findings in the proper hands. Then he drove home. He was suddenly very tired too tired to use his key. Sammy opened the door to him. Her heavy-lidded eyes blinked in surprise, and her handsome coffee-cream face broke into a smile of welcome.

"I can't believe it either," he said.

"You come right in, Mr. Grid-dely. I going to run a nice hot bath for you and you going to soak yourself before dinner."

"I'll take a shower."

"This once you take a bath. It going to rest you."

He followed her down the hall. She was as tall as he. She moved strongly and with grace.

"You mean you haven't had dinner yet?" he asked.

"No, sir," she said in her rich dark voice. "We hoping you get home. We ain't expecting—we hoping. Miss Kyrie, she right pleasured with your flowers."

He wondered briefly what explanation, if any, anthropologists gave for the fact that most colored voices were easier on the ear than white voices. Of course there were exceptions. Thea Mazzini—Kyrie— He shook his head. He really was tired. He said, "How is Miss Kyrie?"

"She fine," Sammy said knowingly. "You don't have to worry none about Miss Kyrie. She next door dressing. I going to tell her you here soon as I fix your bath. What you been doing to get so messed up?"

"Vacuum cleaning."

"Then must be you got promoted," she said solemnly.

He smiled. Sammy had never thoroughly approved of policemen. She had simply been elastic enough to make an exception in his case.

He shaved while the water was running in the tub, and then he bathed, trying to slough off the day's work along with the day's dirt, and not quite succeeding. He had just finished dressing when Kyrie came into the room.

"You smell soapy clean," she said, her arms around him. "Thank you for my flowers."

"Thank you for making me want to send you flowers. New housecoat?"

"Cocktail coat. Yes—do you like it, Grid?"

He nodded. "I think that particular soft shade of green is my favorite color for you."

"You say that no matter what color I wear. You're strikingly satisfactory." She whirled, the circular skirt billowing about her.

"Is it all right for you to do that?"

"Buy new clothes? No, I suppose it's extravagance—considering that they won't fit for very long."

"You know that isn't what I meant. I meant the *pas de seul*."

"Grid, if you should ever start being a fusspot, I couldn't stand it. Come on—Sammy's mixing martinis."

Arms around each other, they went into the warm colorful living room. There were vivid drapes on the windows, sturdy armchairs, overflowing bookcases, and white lilacs in squat satisfying vases. Kyrie surveyed the long ash table set for two.

"Sammy has the Carole Stupell touch," she said. "Maybe we could do without her, but I wouldn't like to try."

Sammy came through the archway bearing a tray with two frosted glasses and a pitcher of martinis. She placed it on a coffee table and moved majestically back to her chosen realm.

They sat down and enjoyed their drinks and each other. For the first time that day the tight spring in Nelson's chest began to unwind. Other ways of life receded because his own way seemed so absolutely perfect.

Dinner was a thick broiled steak, a froth of mashed potatoes in a garlic-rubbed bowl, broccoli, watercress with a special dressing, crisp hot bread, and for dessert a steamed rum pudding for which there was no room but which nonetheless went down with miraculous ease.

They took their good black coffee back to the comfortable chairs, and Kyrie gave a sigh of pure pleasure. Nelson echoed it, and they both laughed.

"Aren't we the smug pair," Kyrie said demurely. She lowered her eyelids. The long lashes, slightly darker than her hair, curled back upon themselves.

"Smug isn't the word. Want some music?"

"Not enough to have either of us walk as far as the gramophone."

"What was your day like?"

"Unexciting. I had lunch with Stella, and I put in my Wednesday stint at the Red Cross. Stella's little girl is going into the Parkside for a tonsillectomy." She stared at him. "Grid, did I say something?"

His smile was quick but not spontaneous. "If you didn't, I'll never trust my ears again. Weren't you telling me about Stella's little girl?"

"Stella's little girl didn't conjure up that ghost in your face."

"It was your mention of the Parkside," he said. "I visited the Countess Mazzini there this afternoon."

"Oh, damn. I would have to bring your work into the room just when you were looking so relaxed."

"You've only prepared me gently for the fact that sooner or later the telephone's going to intrude on this euphoria—"

"Would you be preparing me gently for the fact that you'll have to go out? Poor Grid." She did not say, "Poor me," but he heard it just the same. "At least," she said, "it was nice of the phone not to spoil our dinner."

"Let's sit on the couch."

They sat close on the couch. Sammy came in to clear the table. She looked at them with benign approval.

"Grid, if you'd like to talk about the case it might help to clarify your thoughts," Kyrie said.

Nelson talked. He told her what came to his mind, withholding the doctor's tale of Thea Mazzini's miscarriage, which was paramount in his mind. He thought he felt Kyrie shiver. He said in self-reproach, "You should be looking at beautiful pictures or reading edifying literature instead or listening to—"

She kissed his chin. "Nobody believes in that stuff anymore. Grid, why didn't the poor woman get rid of those pathetic souvenirs? Wouldn't you think—especially with that devoted research chemist standing by—that she'd have pulled herself together and started again? But going to pot like that—I can't understand it. If the position had been reversed—if she had been the one to ruin the marriage—then I'd say she was punishing herself out of guilt—" She broke off to listen. "I'm beginning to regard the telephone as I would some shrill-voiced hussy who was trying to break us up. Grid, do you think for once it could be some nice normal social call?"

She would not let him move until Sammy announced severely that a man wanted to speak to Mr. Grid-dely. Then she released him.

The call was a long one. When he returned she studied his face. "I give up," she said.

His set mouth curved. His voice was as casual as he could make it, but the excitement seeped through. "New developments."

"Don't be any more exasperating than necessary. Will you or won't you have to go out?"

He sounded shocked. "To do leg work? I'm the big executive." He sat down beside her again. He said seriously, "I don't think I'll have to go out—not for the time being, anyway."

She smiled beatifically. Then she said, "Grid—you're not neglecting your work because you think I need to be humored? I can invite people in—or go to bed with a piece of edifying literature—" She shook her head. "No, I'm flattering myself. If it felt the urge, our conscience would have dragged you away from me by your beautiful hair."

"I've given my conscience battle on several occasions. This isn't one of them."

"That's good." She sighed. "I expect I'll change plenty within the near future, but I won't have you changed. What are the new developments? Is the countess any better—or—?"

"They have to do with Spencer," he said. "We're looking for him in earnest now. I've set all the wheels in motion. For the moment there's nothing I can do singlehanded."

"Tell me about it. Pretend I'm Inspector Furniss." She added a little awkwardly, "You know, Grid, that nothing will be repeated—"

"I know." He touched her with his eyes. It was difficult for him to believe that this slim, beautifully made ash blonde who looked as though a breeze might sway her had a dark strength that could, when she summoned it, be counted upon to keep her on her feet.

She might have been reading his thoughts. "Do you ever remember, Grid, that I worked for the FBI?"

"Not when I can help it." He turned his eyes front. "About Spencer—they found fingerprints on the iodine bottle that match one of the unidentified sets in the Mazzini apartment."

"Then he's it. Because if the apartment was cleaned and polished at six he must have been there later—"

"We've reason to believe that the iodine prints aren't his."

"Am I being stupid?"

"No—you see, after the bottle was checked a detective went to Spencer's address and lifted a raft of prints off cups in the sink, walls, and about every other surface in the room. A few matched those on the bottle, but the majority didn't—although they did match another of the unidentified Mazzini sets—"

"Wait a minute—let me sort it out. One of the sets belonged to the seventeen-year-old—to Gale—"

He nodded. "Yes, it's been checked against those found in his own bedroom as well as with the one on the bottle."

"Grid, he took her to his apartment first—and then he took her to heaven knows where."

"That's the way it adds."

"What made you hit on the iodine bottle—or was that just lucky break?"

"There were bits of flecked cotton in the wastebasket. My first thought was that Spencer had cut himself shaving. But there wasn't much blood, and a man wouldn't normally put iodine on minor shaving nicks—not if there was a styptic stick handy—which there was. And since the countess had shreds of skin under her nails to prove she'd scratched someone—"

Kyrie looked puzzled. She said, "But if Spencer did the killing he'd be the one the countess scratched—he'd be the one who needed the iodine. So why were Gale's prints on the bottle?"

"You tell me."

"Could he have made her play nurse?"

"He could—or she could have been the one who got scratched."

"But wouldn't that mean she was the—?"

"Not necessarily." Unexpectedly his mind played back a portion of the scene at the Parkside Hospital. Thea Mazzini had cried, *"You are really evil. I will not—I will not be faced with that dead self ... I will put an end—"*

"Grid?"

He said slowly, "The Countess Mazzini had been drinking—and when she saw Gale—"

"Well?"

"I don't know—I haven't much to go on—only a few words that the countess said this afternoon—but there is—or was—a marked resemblance between them. Couldn't she in her drunken state have thought that Gale was the ghost of her old self come back to torment her—something like that?"

"And attacked Gale?"

He nodded.

Kyrie said doubtfully, "I'd rather believe it than believe that the poor child committed murder. But if Spencer did the killing and took her away with him because she was a witness, I don't like that either—it looks bad—"

"It looks bad, but it doesn't look logical. Assuming that Gale was a witness and that the maid was a witness, why should he kill one and not the other? Unless—?"

"Sex? Oh, no, I can't bear it—a little beast of a man and a young—"

He took her hand. He said firmly, "We're not going on with this. It was a mistake to begin with. Anyway, I think you can rule out that angle. I mentioned, didn't I, that I'd spoken to his neighbor? Well—among other things, I received the distinct impression that Spencer is not a ladies' man and that petty conniving's his main interest in life."

"Murder isn't petty conniving."

"And we're far from sure he's a murderer. Grant Barstow hasn't been cleared of suspicion even if the fingerprints he gave me so willingly don't match any of the others. Remember that someone made a definite attempt to remove fingerprints." He was only trying to divert her.

"You leave Grant Barstow out of this. He's a darling."

"Anything to oblige. Speaking of petty conniving, Spencer visited the countess regularly—and he hardly seems the type she'd have welcomed to the exclusion of all others. Doesn't that point to something?"

"Blackmail?"

"Yes—especially since the maid drew out two thousand dollars each month and remarked to her boyfriend that the countess spent nothing on clothes. Even allowing for a high rental, food, lights, liquor, and the maid's salary, there must have been quite a bit leftover—and there was no money at all on the premises."

"Spencer could have stolen it."

"He could have. I think I'll know more about the financial end of it after I've seen her lawyers. They'll have received a copy of her will by morning." He got up and stretched. "Now let's have one or two records and then—"

"There goes that hussy again. You might as well answer it, Grid. It's sure to be for you."

This time she did not have to study his face when he came back to the room. "No good?"

"Missing Persons. Something they thought I'd want to know. They've just had word that Ranse Upjohn didn't come home for dinner—an unheard-of thing according to his parents because he's always hungry." He told her of how Ranse had tailed him, an incident left out of his earlier telling. "So I drove him home," he ended, "but it seems I should have carted him upstairs. Under the circumstances I don't blame the Upjohns for being worried, but I have a feeling he can take care of himself."

"You mean you aren't doing anything about it?"

"I'm Homicide, Kyrie. This is Missing Persons' pigeon—and probably a clay one at that. I've asked them to keep me informed."

He put a record on the gramophone. It was Debussy's *Reflets dans l'eau,* a favorite with both of them. But neither of them really heard it.

CHAPTER TWELVE

Ranse fought a losing war with the single cotton blanket, growled, sneezed, and awoke. He had gone to sleep as close to the stove as he could get. He got up from the floor and gingerly fixed his cramped limbs.

A weak morning light strained through the bleared windows. He shot a quick look at the horsehair sofa and saw Gale's outline blunted by the covers. She had refused to let him carry her upstairs, and after investigating the conditions there, even his own habitual indifference to surroundings had deserted him.

Coley Spencer had elected to sleep on a cot in the kitchen. "I wouldn't feel right leaving you two alone down here," he explained. "No telling what rash notions you might take." Ranse could hear him snoring. He muttered, "Oil it, buster, oil it," and made a monstrous grimace toward the source of the rasping sounds.

Gale moaned. He went to her and whispered, "Are you awake?"

"Go away—Ranse!" She sat up. "I was dreaming —I— Oh!"

"Yeah—oh," he said, and gave her time to get her bearings.

"Is it morning?"

"Just about. How's your knee?"

"I don't know—it kept me awake most of the night, but—" She felt for it. "It still hurts." They were both whispering.

"Do you think you'll be able to walk?"

"I'll try."

She was wearing her slip. He took her coat which had been used to eke out the blankets and helped her into it. She hung her legs over the sofa and tried to stand. She gave a little scream.

"Quiet—you'll get him up. Nope—you can't walk, so that's out. I'll have to go alone."

"Ranse—please—don't leave me here. I'm afraid."

"Afraid of him? I still can't figure out what he wants with you, but if he meant to hurt you he had plenty of chances before I came."

"If I had that walking stick I could—"

"Not very far you couldn't—and we'd have to make the main highway before we could expect a lift. Anyway, by the time I found the stick and came back he'd be awake and it would be too late—

unless I knocked him out or—"

She shuddered. "No."

"Sis, you've got to be reasonable. Think of how Mother feels not knowing where we are."

"I'll be reasonable. Only when he finds you gone he'll—"

"Where's that stuff he wanted you to take to make you sleep?"

"Why?"

"Never mind why."

"Under the sofa. I hid it there so he wouldn't think of it again."

Ranse tried to crawl under the sofa. It was too low to accommodate his bulk. He swept the dark area beneath with his arm. He withdrew it dirty to the elbow, but his fingers grasped a small bottle.

"This it?"

"Yes—I won't—"

"Who's asking you to? How many did he try to give you?"

"Two—"

"Okay." The label read "Sedafin." The light was not yet sufficient for him to make out the smaller print even by holding it close to his eyes. He slipped the bottle into his pocket. "Do you have to go outside or anything?"

"Yes, but—"

He had gone to the window to look out. "Gosh—my watch says half-past six. It shouldn't be that dark out. I'll bet it's going to rain." He came back to her. "Here are your shoes. I'll go first. Then I'll come back and taxi you to the mansion house door. You can hop the rest of the way, I guess."

"Ranse, I feel awful. If I had some hot water to wash with—"

"Girls! Well—I'll see what I can do about it."

About a half-hour later Spencer opened sticky eyes to the clatter that Ranse was making at the iron range. Ranse never had to exert himself much to produce noise. When he really worked at it the effect was noteworthy. Spencer shot up from the cot. "Here—what's the row!"

Ranse said meekly, "I'm not used to a wood stove. You'd let the fire go out and it was kind of hard to get it going again. I had to take some hot water to Gale. I'll just see if she's finished with it, then I'll make the coffee."

"Coffee? That's different." He thrust back the lion's share of blankets and emerged in the unquiet splendor of scarlet silk pajamas. Rinse blinked.

Spencer had arranged his clothes neatly on a kitchen chair. He padded over to it. "Save some of that hot water for me."

"Sure." Ranse left the kitchen.

When he returned, carrying a basin and a towel, Spencer was tucking his shirt into his pants. "How's her ladyship?"

Ranse opened the door and dumped the basin outside. A gust of cold air blew in. He slammed the door quickly. "Her knee's pretty bad," he said.

Spencer showed his gummy teeth. "Shouldn't wonder if it wouldn't keep her out of mischief." Grunting, he bent to the task of putting on his socks and shoes. Then he took out a comb and ran it through his sparse upended hair. "Can you cook? There's no eggs, worse luck, but you'll find a can of bacon and some pancake mixture in the cupboard."

"Pancakes and bacon coming up," Ranse said.

"Well, get on with it." He wrapped himself in his overcoat and opened the kitchen door. He uttered a sound of protest against the cold and plunged.

Ranse gave the door a savage kick. He hurried with his preparations. As soon as he heard Spenser's returning footsteps he poured a cup of coffee for him. "Thought you might like this to start with," he said. "The pancakes aren't ready yet."

"I say! Nothing like a bit of service. Creamed and sugared too." Spencer seized the cup and took a few gulps. "Hot all right—if not to the king's taste in other respects." He poured in more condensed milk from the opened can and drank the rest of the cup. "Think I'll have the next cup black with a spot of brandy in it." He took a flask from his overcoat pocket. "First I'll take some in to her ladyship."

"No—I will. I've toast for her and bacon. She won't want pancakes. You watch to see they don't burn."

"Perhaps I'd better—if that coffee's a sample of your cooking."

Ranse set a battered tin tray for Gale. The toast was black in spots and pale in others. He covered it with the bacon and wished ruefully that he had something with which to cover the bacon.

He looked at Gale's drawn, scratched face and said, "Maybe there's something to washing, after all. You'll pass in a crowd. Now eat everything and get the coffee down while it's hot." He watched her sip for a moment. "How's it taste?"

"Delicious."

He grinned. "I was the best coffee maker in my scout troop—but Butterball would never believe it."

Her eyes widened. "Ranse, how can you be so cheerful? You've got something up your sleeve—what is it?"

"Tell you later. If I don't eat soon, I won't even have arms up my sleeves." He went back to the kitchen.

Spencer was seated at the table eating pancakes and bacon without enthusiasm. Ranse did not wait for an invitation to join him. He sat down, filling his plate and his mouth without a noticeable break in the continuity of motion.

Spencer observed him gloomily. "Cor—to be young," he said. He loosed his hold on knife and fork. "Seem a bit off my food—and small wonder, what with the night I had. Hardly closed my eyes."

"Why don't you take a nap now?" Ranse said helpfully.

Spencer yawned. "And you up to who knows what? Not half. My stake is too big to risk, thank you."

"Just what is your stake?" Ranse said through pancakes.

"Close your pecker when you chew, there's a good chap." He sounded pained. "Let me tell you, it's no picnic being shut up here with you—and coming on to rain. All I hope is the blasted roof don't leak. That would be the last straw."

"Oh, I don't know," Ranse said. "It's not so bad."

"You're a cool customer, you are. Fact is, I can't decide what to do about you at all—and I don't mind admitting it's giving me a bit of an headache. Mind you, I've nothing against you personally, but in this world, as you're bound to learn sooner or later, it's every man for himself, and I'm hanged if I can see any place for you in my plans." His eyes were fixed on Ranse's face and they were suddenly colder than it was outside.

Ranse, in the act of helping himself to more bacon, saw with surprise his hand wavering above the dish. He withdrew it foolishly and tried to smile. But something had happened to his stomach. He was no longer hungry. He said, "I guess I've had enough. I don't want to put on weight—football and stuff—"

"You're an husky chap at that," Spencer said, still eyeing him in that cold appraising way. After a pause he said, "What sort of a yarn do you intend to spin when your family asks where you've been?"

"My father's dead." Ranse had his fingers crossed under the table. "And yesterday my mother went to California to visit my uncle. She'll be away for a month, so I won't have to think up any yarn." He added angelically, "It's a good thing, because in school they kid me about not being able to lie—they've nicknamed me George—for George Washington—"

The climate of the eyes had changed somewhat. Spencer spoke almost benevolently, "Lying's a mug's game all right. So you're free as a bird—are you—and no one to answer to? But what about your schoolmates and professors?"

"I'm on my midterm vacation," Ranse said glibly, "but it wouldn't matter anyway." He hoped that Spencer knew nothing about the school system. "They're used to students dropping out in college—they never bother about it."

"Well—well! We don't have to decide anything straight off, do we? Suppose you start clearing up. I'd give you an hand except that what with one thing and another I'm fagged." He staggered as he made for the cot, and muttered something about brandy not being such a good idea in the morning.

Anxiously Ranse watched him stretch out.

"Here, you—before you start would you mind legging it upstairs? I left some magazines in the room next to the landing—and you might fetch my razor, too, while you're about it. My motto's always been, 'Improve your mind and keep up appearansh—appearances, redardlesh of where you find yourshelf—"

Ranse went upstairs. The small expensive bag was incongruous in the filthy bedroom. He opened it, extracted a *True Crime* magazine and a digest, and rooted about angrily among the clean shirts and underwear for the shaving kit. His anger was for himself because of the wave of sheer fright that had overtaken him at table. He stood disarranging the contents of the bag after he had found the razor, dawdling purposely, giving his still thudding heart time to quiet down. He came upon a leather manicure set, extracted the scissors, and with great satisfaction snipped the toes from a pair of Argyle socks. These he struggled into defiantly, almost hoping that Butterball would notice and bring the fight out into the open. Then he removed the socks and put them into his pocket, remembering that this was no time for open warfare, that he, too, had embarked upon a round of the sneak's own game. Miserably he speculated about the possible outcome of that game. But the sneak had only himself to blame, hadn't he? Trying to give Gale capsules that might—that might—?

Ranse descended the stairs slowly, muttering, "Every man for himself."

He brought the magazines and the razor kit to Spencer, and Spencer said, "Ta," without moving. "Put 'em on shair—might take forty winksh while you wash up—if you're quiet about it."

Ranse was quiet about it, so quiet that his mother or his father or anyone closely associated with him would have immediately felt for his pulse. Deep down within himself he sang as he worked, not permitting one note of the lullaby to escape his lips. Yet his effort to impart the lullaby's message telepathically was so great that sweat broke out upon his intent face. And presently all the noise there was came from the cot.

Spencer lay on his back. His puffy little mouth was open, the corners wetted by runnels of saliva. His snores had the quality of an engine that nothing could silence except a thrown switch.

Ranse leaned over him, touched him experimentally, shook him without effecting a marked change in the rhythm. "Man," he breathed in awe. "Man!" He ran outside and picked up the coil of rusty clothesline he had discovered and cached behind the outhouse on one of his trips. Returning, his eyes lit upon the car standing unkempt in its unkempt surroundings, looking as though it had grown there or as though some artist of the realistic school had brought it there to balance his composition. Why not? thought Ranse. Sure—what a dope I am. Why not? He stuck his head in to investigate. The key was not in the ignition, but he found that the gas situation was fair. He went back to the house.

He cut the clothesline into several lengths with a kitchen knife. He extracted a key ring from Spencer's pocket, rolled him over, and bound his hands behind his back. He turned him face upward again so that he would not smother, and bound his ankles, connecting both sets of bonds with another length of line. During the process he used his repertory of Boy Scout knots, throwing in a few of his own invention for good measure. And all the while he labored, the snores continued.

His final "That will hold you" was no figure of speech. He bolted the kitchen door, lowered the cracked window shades, and clumped into the living room.

Gale, too, was sleeping, but her sleep seemed natural and peaceful. She looked, for the first time since he had come, warm and comfortable and secure. That's my sister, he thought, staring down at her lovely, innocent face. I've got to take care of her. And I will. Yes, sir, I will. The resolution swelled his chest. He hated to awaken her, but it was better than having her wake alone to the feeling that she had been deserted.

"Gale," he said. "Hey—for Pete's sake—"

She opened her eyes and smiled lazily. Then the smile faded. "What is it?"

"Keep your shirt on. Everything's under control. He's tied up in the kitchen and I'll be back in no time at all."

"Tied up?"

"You bet—with reef knots and—"

"How did you—? No, I don't want to know—I'm going with you."

"No, I'm taking the car, but I may have to walk back because there isn't much gas—and where would that leave you? It's going to rain, and with the shape you're in, a soaking's all you need."

"I don't care—"

"Look—all I expect to do is flag somebody on the main road—if I get that far—and give them a message—"

"Can't you buy some gas?"

"With what—not to mention where? Have you got any dough?"

"No—I—no—not a penny—but he—"

Ranse shook his head, confused by his own scruples. "Look—I tied him up and I—never mind—but stealing money—well, that's plain stealing. Besides, I don't know where he keeps it and I'm not going to untie him again to find out. Honest—I won't be long—and another ride in that rattletrap isn't going to do you a bit of good—especially if it rains." He avoided her face, knowing that the forlornness and the fear had repossessed it. "I'll put some more wood in the stove so that you can keep warm and I'll get you a couple of magazines from inside. You won't even miss me."

"Don't pay any attention to me," she said. "I have no character, I know you've got to go—only don't be too long."

He took another look at Spencer, wished he had thought of a way to tie him up without the aid of Sedafin, brought Gale the magazines, attended to the stove, said a falsely hearty "Goodbye," and left.

He had absorbed the theory of driving when he was about eight or nine and had started to practice secretly not much later. That part of it was easy. Figuring out a message to give to a passing motorist was harder, provided he was lucky enough to stop one. A note would have been the best thing, but in all that forsaken house he had not come upon even the stub of a pencil, and Gale had forgotten or mislaid that versatile tool, her lipstick.

He stopped the car near the place where he had found Gale on the previous night. The clouds were massing with definite purpose, and told himself that he might as well pick up that walking stick since it might be impossible to locate it in a downpour. Gale could certainly use it, he thought as he waded into the bushes. He scouted about and after very little trial and error came upon the tree he had marked with his handkerchief. Captain Nelson's handkerchief. He rescued it and returned it to his pocket. The stick was not very far away. He found it half sunk in a mound of leaf mold. He picked it up, examined its heavy gold handle for a moment, and went back to the car. The crook, he thought. I knew he was a crook. Walking sticks with other people's initials. D. M.—doesn't stand for Coley Spencer, that's a cinch. I wonder who he crooked it from. Weighs a ton—like real gold. But he was not really wondering. He was only trying to justify the course of action he had taken.

Not passing a single dwelling, he bumped along the rutted road and at last turned triumphantly onto the main highway. Then for a brief while he considered taking a chance and continuing as far as he could toward the city. Now he regretted that he had left Gale behind. According to the gasometer, they might have traveled as far as a gas station and told their story and begged for either gas or leave to use the telephone. While he was trying to remember the location of the last gas station passed on the trip out, two things happened almost simultaneously. The clouds ripped open and his right rear tire went flat. The car slithered to the side of the road, and his first dazed thought before he braked was that the clap of thunder had been perilously close. Then he yelled, "Oh, you dope—you prize dope. Thunder in February. Yah!"

He got out and was drenched to the skin before he reached the rear of the car. The wheel sat hard on its rim. There was, of course, no spare tire.

He shrugged, somehow vindicated, because it was a good thing

Gale had not come with him after all. As it was, she would be having fits worrying about him. The thing to do was to get back to her as soon as possible. But first he had to stop a car headed for New York, tell the driver as much as seemed necessary, outline the position of the house, and ask him to get in touch with Captain Nelson of the Homicide Squad. That was all. Nothing to it.

There was a steady but not heavy stream of traffic flowing from both directions. He planted himself near the flat tire and signaled vigorously. No car stopped. Several drivers slowed down and veered to escape hitting him but were on their way cursing before he could launch his plea. He must have looked an ominous outline standing there in the pelting rain, but by the time he stopped signaling he contained a frustrated weeping child who wanted home and mother.

He gave up at last and crawled dripping into the car. The jerks, he sobbed, the mean jerks. A guy could die of pneumonia. He mopped himself with Nelson's handkerchief and then looked around for something drier to use. He pulled open the dashboard compartment and was rewarded only with an empty carton that had once contained tissues, one greasy glove, a tailoring establishment's circular addressed to some unknown character, and a pencil. A pencil! He forgot his abject discomfort. He began to generate heat. When he abandoned the car about ten minutes later his confidence in Ranse Upjohn was restored. The rain won't last forever, he thought. Someone's bound to notice and stop for a better look. You were cooking with infrared that time, fellow. Really cooking.

He started the trek back fairly light of heart in spite of sodden clothes and sodden blistered feet. But he had not sloshed very far before another problem began to ride him. He called it, "What to do with Coley Spencer until the doctor comes," and no matter how he turned it over in his mind, he could arrive at no feasible treatment. In the light of what he had seen in those cold eyes, to untie Coley Spencer seemed to be asking for it. To leave him tied? He did not know what Sedafin contained, but he supposed that it contained a drug. Probably morphine. And when someone had an overdose of morphine, wasn't the cure to walk him back and forth and feed him black coffee until the effects wore off? He could not envision himself walking Spencer back and forth. But if he didn't Spencer might— Might? Maybe he was!

No, he could not envision himself untying Spencer and walking him back and forth and later being humped for his pains the minute he slept or turned his back. But he could envision Ranse Upjohn being visited by grief-stricken parents in a dank cell, Ranse Upjohn taking that last mile, cut off in the prime of his manhood, unable to walk without stumbling, not because of a burden of fear—he would go smiling—but because of the leaden conscience he had been doomed to carry to the chair.

He stumbled on. He did not notice that the rain had stopped or that the sun was trying to come out. He did not notice it even though he had thrown his head back to gaze directly at the sky.

CHAPTER THIRTEEN

When Nelson awoke, Kyrie's arms were wound around him and it took a lot of discipline to free himself. Kyrie murmured in sleepy protest, "Is it that hour already?" And he said, "Shhh," and kissed her, and got out of bed with her drowsy "Take care" following him.

It was not that hour already. Morning had barely opened its wet eyes. He put in his appearance at headquarters, damp with the drizzle that promised to work itself up into a serious rain, and found the night shift still working under the dreary unshaded electric bulbs.

This time he accepted the container of lukewarm coffee which someone thrust at him and which was no auspicious beginning to any man's day. Nor was he otherwise warmed and nourished. Althea Gale Upjohn and her brother Ranse were still missing. The Countess Mazzini was "resting comfortably," that elastic hospital phrase which covered so much and so little, and the senior Upjohns were doing the reverse and loudly admitting it.

The stakeout at Coley Spencer's house had nothing to report. Visits by a detective to the two names found by Nelson on Coley Spencer's desk were not revelatory. One of the names, Francis Mallory, had turned out to be a solid businessman. Mallory had met Spencer in a bar, had exchanged addresses with him under the love-the-world spell cast by alcohol, and had forgotten the incident until the detective refreshed his memory. It was the detective's opinion that Mallory was telling the whole truth.

Al Ferris, the second name, was not at home. The superintendent of his apartment house had to be reminded sternly of his duty as a citizen before he would talk at all, and even then he cast few pearls. He said that Mr. Ferris was a good tenant, paid his rent on the dot, often spent nights out, sometimes even a week of nights, but where, he could not say. He, the superintendent, minded his own business. He had heard that Mr. Ferris was keeping a little chick uptown, and if you were to take him out and shoot him he could not supply the address or her name because he did not know either. And no, he could not even guess what Mr. Ferris did for a living. He placed no stock in the rumors, unfounded, mind you, that Mr. Ferris was a bookie.

Nelson took the detective off the assignment, put on another who looked like the village idiot and who was actually one of the best operatives on the squad, and gave him free rein.

At nine o'clock he went out into the drizzle again. He drove downtown, parked on Broad Street, entered an ugly old building, and took an elevator to the law firm of Barnes, Desmond, and Maxon. He showed his credentials, stated his business, was asked to wait, refused politely, and was directed to the office of Mr. Desmond.

Mr. Desmond was not busy. He was drinking coffee that smelled as though it had been freshly made. He was drinking it out of a thin cup, and Nelson's intrusion annoyed him. "You say you're from Homicide?"

"I *am* from Homicide. Have you opened your mail this morning?"

Mr. Desmond, a clean-shaven elderly man whose most prominent feature was a bright hand-painted necktie, seemed genuinely shocked. "My secretary opens my mail."

"Then please ask her if she received a communication from the Countess Mazzini."

Mr. Desmond relinquished his cup. He said with slow deliberation, "Even if there has been a communication—which I doubt—you could not expect me to confide its nature."

"I do expect it," Nelson said pleasantly, and added in what he hoped was a convincing tone. "In fact, I demand it and have full authority to enforce the demand."

"Surely," said Mr. Desmond, "you cannot imagine that my client is involved in the murder of her maid."

"I am not an imaginative man," Nelson said untruthfully. He did not say, "I might very well become a violent man if you persist in drawing this out." It was hard not to say it. His day was slipping away and there was so much he needed to accomplish. "What makes you doubt there's been a communication?"

"I have entire charge of the Mazzini affairs—investments—charities—and so on. The countess trusts me so implicitly that she seldom sees fit to send me instructions. I have not heard from her in over a year." He touched his lips tenderly with a fine linen handkerchief and picked up the coffee cup again.

Nelson said, "Nevertheless, she sent you her will the day before yesterday."

"Her will? Good. I advised her to have a will drawn after her husband passed away, but she kept deferring it. In fact, my first thought when I read of her more recent trouble was that it would be a great pity for her to die intestate. But I telephoned to the hospital and was told that she was resting comfortably, so it may not be too late—"

"It's not too late—"

Mr. Desmond listened to no one when he could listen to himself.

"Strange how women shy away from wills—"

"Will you please ask your secretary to bring the mail?" Nelson's tone was disciplined. Nevertheless, Mr. Desmond looked up at him and further responded by pressing a button on his desk and muttering into the intercommunications system.

The secretary brought the mail. She was pretty. Mr. Desmond seemed entranced by the undulations of her rear as she left the office. Nelson took advantage of this. He leaned across the wide desk and swept the mail toward him. He scrutinized it rapidly, envelope by envelope.

Desmond awoke, shouting, "Stop that at once."

"You're a busy man," Nelson said, "I hated to disturb you." He brandished the thick square envelope. "This is it. Will you open it or shall I?"

Desmond took the envelope from his hand. He searched for a paper cutter. He said, "You are very highhanded. In all my experience as a lawyer I have never come across such—" He took an eyeglass case from his breast pocket. He extracted a pair of glasses, did a really professional polishing job, set them upon his nose, and carefully adjusted the earpieces before he slit the envelope.

Exactly three quarters of an hour later Nelson left Mr. Desmond alive and well, a feat which had required almost superhuman effort. He stopped on the way uptown for breakfast, and some of the needless energy he had expended upon restraint flowed back, permitting his brain to circulate again.

The Countess Mazzini had left her fortune to her niece and namesake, Althea Gale. This seemed on the surface to establish a clear motive for the attempt upon her life and to brand clearly Althea Gale as the assailant. But Nelson had never been one to accept what appeared on the surface. And in this case, which involved the future of a seventeen-year-old girl, he was more than ever impelled to roil the surface in an effort to determine what lay beneath.

If, as he suspected, a man named Coley Spencer had been blackmailing the countess and had been present at the time of the murder and of the near murder, it was logical to assume that Coley Spencer was connected with Althea Gales's disappearance. It even made sense to go further and assume that he had abducted her.

Several possible reasons for the abduction reared their heads. One, Althea Gale was evidently an unusually pretty girl.

But would a blackmailer, intent upon the pursuit of his career, permit himself to be sidetracked by a pretty girl? Nelson doubted it. He thought that monetary and not amatory considerations would continue to dominate the impulses of such as Spencer.

And so, on to the next possible reason. Suppose Coley Spencer had attacked a countess grown restive of his hold upon her. And suppose that Althea Gale and Mildred, the maid, had witnessed the attack. And suppose Mildred had died for it and Althea Gale had been spirited away for it.

He shook his head. Why would Coley Spencer murder one and abduct the other? With two victims and a setting for his fell deeds conveniently at hand, and with the penalties for murder and kidnaping made equal under the law, why would he draw the line? Obvious answer, he would not unless he was actuated by something much stronger than his conscience. And almost anything was stronger than a blackmailer's uncertain conscience. And money was stronger than anything.

Nelson buttered a piece of toast, set it neatly on the edge of his plate, and contemplated it. But that would mean— He could not finish the thought without going entirely into reverse, and this he grimly forced himself to do. Coley Spencer, deprived of the original goose that laid his golden eggs, would of necessity seek another source of supply. He would transfer his attentions to Althea Gale. But he could not do so unless he contained within his dirty self the magic formula which would command her to produce for him. And what formula could exert more magic than the knowledge that she had committed a crime? And since until that night Althea Gale had led a sheltered existence, and since until that night Coley Spencer had not set eyes upon her, what could the crime be but that night's crime? So it was turnabout. It was everybody change places. It was Coley Spencer who had witnessed Althea Gale's attack upon the countess. And the unfortunate maid's ringside seat for the spectacle had been none of her own choosing, and she had been struck down in the passion of Althea Gale's rage when she attempted to intervene. And Coley Spencer had said to Althea Gale, "Just you come along with me. I'll see that you get off scot-free, and you can reward me for my kindness later." He had discovered, of course, that Althea Gale was the countess's sole heir.

Nelson drove uptown, giving no more thought to the mechanics of driving than he gave to his legs when he walked. This time, he told himself as he slid into a parking space near headquarters, this time I'd rather be wrong than President.

A few minutes later he was surprised to find himself at his desk, his mind retaining no record of the bridge between it and a lawyer's desk on Broad Street. He examined the fresh stack of messages and pressed a buzzer. A uniformed policeman answered the summons. Nelson held up one of the messages. "What's this about a truck driver waiting to see me? I didn't notice him as I came in."

The policeman smiled. "Captain, you didn't notice me neither, and I was standing right beside him." He gestured with his thumb toward the anteroom. "Out there."

"What does he want?"

"He wants to talk to you. I couldn't get him to say more than that, but I don't think he's a crackpot even if he is carrying his umbrella wrapped up in brown paper. Captain—if you'll excuse me—you don't look so good."

"A trick of light," Nelson said bleakly. He was consulting another of the messages. "I've got to make a phone call. I'll see the truck driver in five minutes."

"Right." The policeman went back to the anteroom.

Nelson picked up the receiver. "Get me Dr. Selig of the Parkside Hospital," he said.

The fact that the doctor had called did not contribute to his well-being. The doctor had pulled no punches yesterday. He had expressed contemptuously his opinion of Nelson's callous behavior in upsetting a sick and perhaps dying woman. He had looked as though he would have enjoyed thrashing Nelson, and Nelson, with no pride in his own performance, would not have blamed him for trying.

"Dr. Selig?" he said. "This is Gridley Nelson, Homicide." Then he relaxed because the doctor's voice was unexpectedly cordial.

"Captain Nelson, you must permit me to apologize for my rudeness to you—"

Nelson produced a lame "But—?" let it hang, and said quickly, "How is the countess?"

"That is why I called. She has had a good night. This morning she has even eaten a little—"

"She's regained consciousness?"

"I think so—yes. I was not with her when she awakened, but the nurse tells me she glanced about her as if puzzled by her surroundings but yet did not make the effort to ask where she was. The nurse quite naturally said some words of reassurance which were accepted, because soon afterward she closed her eyes again and now sleeps peacefully." He paused. Nelson could visualize his shrug. "It is far from conclusive," Selig went on, "but it is hopeful—no? There seems so very much that we of the medical profession do not understand about the wedding of the human body and the human mind. However, I wish to tell you that your visit did no harm—that you may even have exercised some healing effect upon my patient."

"Thank you, Doctor. Then when she wakes again—and if you think her condition warrants it—may I—?"

"I will not prevent—I will inform you the very moment it is possible for your questions to be answered."

Nelson thanked him again and hung up, feeling somewhat cheered. He hoped fervently that the moment for questioning the countess was not far away.

He had been more stirred than he cared to admit by Thea Mazzini.

He wanted her not only to live but to be restored to a better life than had been hers since her marriage to the Italian count But aside from that, he had his job to do. And if he could talk to her, the stubborn case would be broken and he would learn exactly what had happened, and why. And he would be free to devote himself to those tough, unlovable characters who provided policemen with the major portion of their activities, and among whose numbers seventeen-year-old girls were, thank God, a rarity.

He heard a cough. A squat barrel of a man stood in the doorway clutching a soggy cap and a long thin object covered with blistered brown paper.

"Come in," Nelson said, and gestured toward a chair near his desk.

The truck driver stepped over the threshold, his eye roving to take in the somewhat battered furnishings of the office. He inspected Nelson briefly, sat down, placed the long thin package on the desk, and began to peel off the brown paper. He gave a running commentary as he worked. "Maybe I'm a rummy to waste my time on this—maybe it's some kind of a joke—but you never know—and I wouldn't have felt easy if I didn't do something about it. I went to Centre Street first and they told me where to find you. It's got your name on it—see?"

Nelson leaned forward. "Where did you get it?"

"On the road—a couple of miles from Paltzville. It's about ten o'clock and I'm rolling along and I'm soaked on account of it's only just stopped raining cats and dogs and I've got a busted window which lets everything in due to an accident I had and didn't reach no place to stop for repairs. I'm thinking about a cup of hot java and damned if I don't nearly bump into this jalopy which some goon's left almost in the middle of the lane. I give with the language and then I get out wanting to slug somebody it being too much of a rotten shake what with everything else that's happened on the trip and me never having an accident before in my life so help me. Well—there's nobody in the jalopy which ain't surprising because it has the kind of a flat tire which spells curtains—and no spare—but there's this thing"—he pointed—"stuck out of the window like a flagpole and wedged between the glass and the frame. I give a look—and like I say I don't know if it's some kid's joke or what—but I figure it's a pretty expensive joke—so maybe it ain't." He gazed at Nelson, his heavy weathered face expectant.

"Maybe it ain't," Nelson said absently. He, too, gave a look. His fingers were busily untying the piece of crumpled linen and the elongated woolen sock which were knotted together over the stick's gold knob. When spread upon the desk, the sock proved to be toeless, the linen an indescribably dirty handkerchief. He shirred his brow, gazing without belief at the small G. N. in the corner. Not a handkerchief. His own handkerchief.

"I didn't touch them things," the truck driver said. "I figured they was just put there to attract attention. But I read what's on that paper—only I couldn't make heads or tails of it except your name." He added proudly, "I put it back like it was—thinking it could be evidence or something."

Nelson unrolled the tailor's printed circular that twined the lower end of the stick. It sprung back as he tried to spread it out.

"The other side's where the writing is," the truck driver offered. But Nelson had already turned it over, weighted it down, and was studying the printed message.

Across the top and underlined several times was, "For Captain Gridley Nelson, New York Homicide Department." Underneath it a map had been drawn, its points of interest clearly lettered. There was a straight line representing the main highway, with an arrow pointing to New York City. The highway branched into a winding road marked "Dirt," its windings stating whether left or right, and ending in a simple economical drawing of a house.

Below the map there was a fuzzy scrawl. It said, "I can't give details. My pencil point's wearing out. Whoever finds this should have sense enough to tell you where—and you follow the map from there. Hurry. We've got our hands full." And it was signed, "Ranse Upjohn."

The truck driver said heavily, "So I brought it—so I'll be on my way to the wife and kids. Jeez if it ain't almost one o'clock." But he hesitated. "I'd sure like to know if I done the smart thing?"

Nelson looked at him. He took the shirring out of his brow. He stretched his expressive mouth to a wide warm smile. "You did the smart thing. Leave your name and address and I'll let you know how it turns out."

"Well—I don't want to get mixed up in nothing." He supplied his name and address.

"Before you go can you give me as nearly as possible the location of the abandoned car?"

"Hell—I can give it exact. You cross the George Washington Bridge—" He went on to describe routes and landmarks.

Nelson took it all down. Then he sacrificed his hand to a vigorous pumping. "Thank you, Mr. Grogan. Tell your wife for me that you're a top-flight citizen."

"Well—sure—that's okay. I kept thinking maybe I was a rummy to waste—" He was embarrassed by Nelson's approval. He would have repeated the entire story if Nelson had not eased him from the office.

At least, Nelson thought as he returned to his desk, young Ranse is safe. At least his family will have some consolation. His face darkened. He picked up the cane by its middle. The overbalancing weight of the gold knob pulled at his wrist. It was monogrammed. It was monogrammed D. M. He dropped it to the desk. He read the note through again. "We've got our hands full," it said. "We." A kid's joke? His hand was not quite steady as he reached for the telephone. "Crime lab," he said tersely. When he was connected he gave a terse order. Then he summoned the policeman. "Take this to the lab. No— not by the handle. They know what I want—have them stop everything else and do this report in less time than they've ever done one."

"Got it, Captain. Anything else?"

"Yes—notify the Paltzville sheriff that a car's been abandoned here—I've written down the location." He handed him a slip of paper. "Have him bring it in."

Nelson was talking on the telephone to a Dr. deSilvio when a vacant-faced man in baggy clothes entered the office.

The man saluted and said, "Detective Sergeant Clevis reporting, Captain, re, Al Ferris—"

Nelson hung up the receiver. "Not now, Clevis." He left the desk and started to put on his overcoat. "I've got to leave as soon as or even before I get a report from the lab."

The deceptively slack jaw hung open. Clevis firmed it and found his voice. "Remember me, Captain? You sent me after Al Ferris and I got something important to tell you. Don't you want it anymore?"

"All right—it it's important. Shoot."

"I'll jet-propel," Clevis said, and proceeded to make a record for rapid speech. "I made like a cleaner's boy, hung some clothes over my arm, and got into the Ferris guy's apartment. I told the super I had orders to take Ferris's blue suit out to be pressed because he wanted it uptown in a hurry. It worked like a charm. The first thing I saw in the bedroom was a dame's picture signed with love and kisses to Papa Al from his little baby, Winnie. I figured she was it because she had star billing over a lot of other pictures. The super was on me like a hawk, so I said to him, 'Mr. Ferris told me to help myself to a beer from the refrig,' and the super said, 'I'll bet,' but he tracked for the kitchen like he had a sudden thirst—so I got a sure-enough blue suit from the closet and I got a rent bill of an apartment leased to a Mrs. Winifred Morris before the super came back from the kitchen saying there was no beer. I streaked up to Mrs. Winnie's on Eighty-sixth Street, and sure enough, Al Ferris was there. I talked to him like a brother and he responded real sensible. He admitted Coley Spencer was a friend of his, but not dear enough to stick his neck out for. Near twelve o'clock on the night of the murder—this being the first he'd heard of a murder, and it grieved him like anything—he'd lent Spencer an old car and an old farmhouse he wasn't using—and he didn't ask questions because Spencer knows Winnie's husband, who, believe it or not, is a traveling salesman—"

Only then did Clevis pause for breath. "The house—"

"Just outside of Paltzville?"

"Yeah—a fast two-hour drive. Holy cow—you knew it all the time!" His skinny frame wilted beneath the baggy clothes.

"Not all the time—not until a short while ago—and you've added to my information. Want to take a ride?"

"There?"

"Yes—right away. We won't wait for the lab report."

The policeman steamed triumphantly into the office, waving a sheet of paper. "I didn't wait for it to be typed up, Captain. Doc says you're a good at making out his hieroglyphics. He also says it ain't complete—"

"You going to study that now?" Clevis said.

"No—I'll read it on the way."

"Then let's go. Ferris was a lousy giver of directions, but we'll find it."

"We'll find it," Nelson said, slipping the report and Ranse's map into his pocket.

CHAPTER FOURTEEN

Ranse tried his best to hurry back to Gale, but several times the state of his feet forced him to rest by the roadside. It was long after one when he reached the farmhouse. He opened the door to a deadly quiet.

Gale was crouched at the end of the horsehair sofa, white-faced and jittering. She muttered disconnected phrases to herself, half-formed thoughts that seemed to be bursting out of her inner turmoil. "And when I went up she was—and she saw me and—"

"Gail—hey, Sis—I'm back."

Her shadowed eyes cleared. She said normally, "I thought you weren't coming—I wouldn't have blamed you."

"That's a dumb thing to think." He dropped into a chair. "I took so long because I was unavoidably detained by blisters. Why were you talking to yourself?"

"Was I? I've been trying to remember everything that happened that night."

"And do you?"

"No—only what I've told you."

"Oh."

"Ranse—I hopped inside and I saw him. You shouldn't have tied—"

"I had to, so there's no use talking about it." He removed his shoes. His feet looked raw. He flexed them, wincing.

"Your poor feet—and you're drenched—"

"You should have seen me before I started to dry."

"Did you hit him? His eyes are closed and he's breathing funny. If—well—" She leaned toward him. "You must promise me something—you must promise to say I did it—because in a way I did—"

"You're nuts. Sure his eyes are closed. Since when do people sleep with their eyes open? He's sleeping—that's all."

"But he looks so—"

"He couldn't look a bit worse than he ever looked. I'm going in there in a minute—just let me take a little rest will you."

"You gave him some of those capsules—that's it—isn't it?"

He groaned. "They were his capsules in the first place. He's entitled to them."

"But—"

"Are you hungry?"

She shook her head. She said hopelessly, "I know you did it for my sake—so if—if anything happens you've got to say I did it. It won't matter anyway because—"

"Quit. Do you have to be such a pain in the neck? Why don't you change the subject? Why don't you ask if my mission's accomplished?"

"Is it?" she asked dutifully. She seemed past caring.

"Sure. Bet you we don't have to stay in this dung heap much longer.

"Ranse, you ought to take off those wet clothes—you'll be sick "

"Who—me?" He pulled himself out of the chair and padded in his bare feet toward the door. He said nonchalantly, "Maybe I'll get us both something to eat. I think I'm hungry." He was certainly empty, but it was unlike any hunger he had ever experienced.

"You'll untie him—won't you, Ranse? I'm not afraid with you here— truly. I'd almost like to see him try to—to hurt us. It would—"

"Anything you say. Anything for a little peace." He closed the door behind him. All I need, he thought, is to get splinters in my blisters. He began to whistle a shrill martial tune, but his steps lagged in spite of it. It was all he could do to cover the distance between the kitchen door and the cot.

Somehow Coley Spencer, in his deep sleep, had managed to turn himself over. His face was buried in the pillow. He lay still, apparently untroubled by his bonds. It seemed to Ranse that he was producing no sounds at all, neither the sounds of snoring nor of breathing.

"No," Ranse whispered. "Please, no." He rolled him upon his back. He shuddered as he saw the suffused skin. "But I didn't mean it," he said. "Honest, I didn't mean it. What else could I do?"

He worked at the knots, his hands cold and slippery with sweat. He was afraid to use a knife, afraid that it might slip. He grew hopeful as he saw the color receding from the purple face, but when it dwindled to a mottled white, hope dwindled. Whatever else had happened to Spencer since morning, he had developed an unmistakable rash. It stood out patchily against the now pasty skin. Without success Ranse tried to recall what he had read in medical books. Nothing he had read explained the rash.

Struggling with the knots, he did not hear Gale's thumping progress toward the kitchen. He became aware of her when, like an injured bird, she hopped across the floor boards. He turned and said roughly, "Why didn't you stay put?"

"You forgot to bring the walking stick," she said, making a statement rather than a complaint. "Is he—?" Then she was near enough to see.

She swayed on her one leg. Ranse caught her. He set her in a chair and used the only possible vent for his aching fullness. "Hell and damnation! Must a guy have a sister like you—must you bother me now!"

She leaned back. She said meekly, "I just want to help."

"Then help by letting me alone. I'm busy. I haven't even finished untying him." He turned his back on her. He hated his clammy fingers that earlier had been so remarkably adept. He hated Ranse Upjohn, lock, stock, and barrel. Ranse to the rescue. Ranse putting his foot in it, making it twice as bad. I'll hide the clothesline, he thought. When they come I'll pretend I don't know how he—how it happened. I'll say he was all right when I took the car. No—they'd realize that was a lie. If he'd been all right he wouldn't have let me take the car. Worse—they might think what Gale wants them to think—that she did it. As if I'd let her— Zooks—if I could only get an idea—something that wouldn't make Mother and Father feel any worse than they do now.

His large hands hovered uncertainly over his victim. He noted with surprise that he had all of the tangible knots untied.

"Ranse—" She stood behind him, holding to the back of the chair. She was pushing it along the floor, using it as a support. "He's breathing. I saw his chest move."

Ranse held his own breath as he looked. It was true. But it did not seem to him that it would continue to be true. "Of course," he said. "I know it. Naturally if he was dead he'd be stiff by this time, and he's as limp as an old potato." It sounded plausible, although he had no idea of how long it took for rigor to set in. He wondered if he should try to rub some warmth into those limp cold limbs. He said aloud, "Nope—it might create a thingamabob—an embolism. I read that somewhere."

"A what?"

"I've got to get him on his feet." He felt sick to his stomach. He wished that he did not have to touch Coley Spencer again for any reason, or see him again if it came right down to it. But there was no point in wishing. Or if he wished, why not go the whole hog and wish that the Upjohn clan had never left Starwell? He got a grip on Spencer's shoulders and pulled him to a sitting position. Spencer's head lolled.

"Ranse—you should support his back."

"You're thinking of babies," he said crossly. The tug of the inert form loosed his grip. Spencer fell to the pillow. "He sure is limp all right. I guess that's a good sign. But how am I going to walk him?"

"If there was poison in those capsules maybe an emetic would help. Mustard and hot water—"

"I tell you, they couldn't be poison—not if he wanted to give them to you. Use your head. Why would he take the trouble to bring you way out here if he only meant to poison you?"

"How many did you give him?"

"I opened six in his coffee. Coffee—yep—that's what he needs."

"S-six?"

"Sure. He told you to take two, didn't he? And he's a man, so it stands to reason he must be at least three times as strong as a girl—and they belonged to him, so it's likely he's taken them before and built up a tolerance for them. That means—"

For the first time she was annoyed. "I know what a tolerance means. I'm not exactly a moron."

"Not exactly." But he was somehow cheered to find that she could still be angry with him. It made him feel as though he were back on a patch of familiar ground. "Look—I'm going to try my best to walk him. Could you get over to the stove and make some strong coffee? That is, if the fire hasn't gone out completely. If it has I'll have to light it for you."

She was edging her way toward the stove, alternately hopping and resting on the chair back. "I can manage the stove. Do you remember Mrs. Rathbun in Starwell? She had one and— The fire's not quite out. All it needs is poking and more wood." Her relief at doing something was apparent.

"All right. Don't burn yourself." He filled the coffeepot with water, got a can of coffee and a spoon, and brought them to her. He stubbed his big toe on the return trip to Spencer but made neither vocal nor mental comment. It was all part of the general picture. He put one strong young arm behind Spencer's back, another under his knees. The little man weighed more than his stature indicated. It was not easy for Ranse to lift him. It was harder to stand him on his feet and keep him there. It was impossible.

"If only I could take his other side," Gale said.

"If only—if only." It came in a frustrated wail. "Well—you can't, so that's—" An idea struck him. "Bring me that chair. I know what I'll do. I'll have him straddle it like a kiddy car and I'll tie him to the back of it and I'll keep moving his legs one at a time. It will have the same effect as walking—it will start the circulation—"

She giggled nervously. "It—it sounds like a Rube Goldberg invention—" The poker she was holding dropped with a clang. "Ranse!"

Unnoticed, the hapless Spencer collapsed in a heap on the floor. Ranse ran to the window and raised the grimy blind. "Him," he said, "his car—and there's another man with him." Pride entered his voice. "See—I told you my mission was accomplished. Gosh—he must have driven like sixty. What time is it, anyway?"

"Half-past three," Gale said. The flat dull quality of her tone reminded him that he had little cause for rejoicing.

He wheeled. "Listen," he said fiercely, "You've got to forget that stuff about you being responsible for this. They'll know you're lying anyway. Policemen aren't as dopey as you suppose. So you keep still and I'll take care of everything. I'll let them in—"

But there was no need for him to go to the door. Acting Captain Gridley Nelson and Detective Sergeant Clevis had entered the house. Drawn by his voice, they came straight to the kitchen.

Ranse stood tall. He met Nelson's eyes and said squeakily, "So you got my message?"

Nelson took in his bedraggled appearance. He took in the heap on the floor and the pale redheaded child who hugged the back of a chair as though it were her only friend in life. He said, "Yes—your message reached me—and you weren't exaggerating a bit. You have got your hands full."

Clevis, after a sharp look at Gale, had walked across the room to Spencer. "Brother!" he said. He squatted for a closer inspection. Three pairs of eyes watched. Clevis arose, dusting his hands. "Smells to me like this one's celebrating Mickey Finn's day." Efficiently he hoisted Spencer to his feet and dropped him on the cot.

Ranse swallowed. "Mickey Finn's day?" He gawked at Clevis, whose baggy suit seemed to contain nothing at all. Then he felt of himself as though he might be reappraising his own brawn.

Nelson was at Gale's side. Gently he unfastened her tensed arms from the chair back. "Sit down," he said. "We're going to help you as much as we can."

She looked up into his face. She nodded submissively. He said, "You're Gale Upjohn, of course."

"Of course," Ranse said. "Would I be here if she wasn't?"

Nelson did not comment. He said, "Clevis?"

Clevis turned from contemplation of Spencer. "I'm no medico, Captain, but it's my guess we can't do much for him. I think it's too late for the salt-and-hot-water routine."

Ranse scrapped all claim to bravado. "I thought—coffee—if we could get him to drink coffee—"

"How would you go about making him swallow, son?"

"We'll all have some coffee if it's ready," Nelson said calmly. He lifted Gale, chair and all, and set her down at the table. "Pull up the other chairs, Ranse, and get the cups."

"Yes, sir."

He got the cups and filled them. He got canned milk and sugar from the cupboard. His own will played no part in what he did. His will said, Run. Gale will be safe now, but you'll never be safe again, Run. He could hardly bear the smell of the coffee. It brought back the enormity of what he had done. He looked down at his bare feet. Run? He slumped into a chair next to Gale.

Nelson was stirring sugar and milk into her coffee. He was all but spooning it into her mouth. He looked like a friend. The hypocrite! And the man drinking so unconcernedly at his side looked like that harmless Gussy Briggs who wandered the Starwell countryside communing with nature. Harmless! Hiding his muscles under a sloppy-joe outfit.

Nelson raised his eyes from Ranse's untouched cup. "You put something in his coffee?"

Ranse nodded. Wordless, he stuck his hand into his pocket, took out the small bottle, and set it on the table.

Nelson picked it up, examined it, and passed it to Clevis.

"Yeah," Clevis said, squinting at the small print. "I thought so from the rash. I was on a case where they used it once." He scratched his head. "Whenever Consumers Research makes a stink it's taken off the market and put out under another name. And there are always suckers who'll take chances for the sake of a little sleep. Chock-full of chloral. Only I always thought it needed alcohol to make it that much effective." He gestured toward the cot.

Ranse said miserably, "He told me the coffee was rotten, so he put some brandy in to make it taste better—"

Clevis nodded. "The mixture will do it every time."

Nelson got up. He beckoned to Clevis, and the two of them walked over to the cot. There they conferred in low tones.

When Nelson returned to the table Ranse said defiantly, "He wanted Gale to take the capsules, so I thought they were only to make you sleep—and I had to put him to sleep before I could get away to—" He clenched his hands. "I guess I gave him too much—I—I guess I should have knocked him out instead—but—"

Gale spoke suddenly. "It wasn't Ranse's fault—I—"

He glared at her. "It was too—"

"Suppose you tell it from the beginning," Nelson said. "It must have started about the time I drove you home yesterday. Your parents said you didn't go upstairs—"

"Mother—does Mother know where we are?"

"She's been notified that you're safe. Of course I wasn't sure that Gale was with you— Hold it a minute." He addressed Clevis. "Want any help?"

"Not unless you've got a stomach pump on you." He had slung Spencer over his shoulders. Again Ranse gawked at him as with seeming ease he carried his sacklike burden toward the door. He said cryptically, "A feather might do the trick. Nothing like fresh air and a feather—or a reasonable facsimile."

Nelson got up to open the door for him. Cold air blew in. Then the door slammed shut and he was alone with the two unhappy Upjohns.

Ranse wet his lips. "What's he going to do?"

"He's not going to bury him, if that's what worries you. Let's have it."

He listened without interrupting while Ranse gave a recital that began with Coley Spencer's error in believing him to be Jack Channing. Ranse became more relaxed as the telling went forward. He even stopped at intervals to bring his cup to his lips, as though in talking he had purged himself of the coffee's unpleasant association. He took Nelson along on the drive with Spencer. He took him along on his search for Gale, after the discovery that she had left the farmhouse. He led him into the wood to the very tree where he had come upon her.

He was carrying Gale pickaback down the dark road when she herself brought him back to the present. "Ranse was wonderful," she said huskily. "He put cold compresses on my knee and got food for me and—and everything. A twenty-year-old man couldn't have done any better."

Nelson tactfully ignored Ranse's blush. "How did you hurt your knee? No—never mind that for the moment. How did you manage to get so far from the house with it?"

"I took Coley Spencer's cane and used it as a crutch. Oh, Ranse, it's valuable. I think the knob is gold—and we've left it there in the wood—"

Nelson looked at Ranse inquiringly. "Perhaps you'd better finish your side of it first. Then we'll let Gale talk."

"Gale has nothing to say. She doesn't remember anything. You ought to take her home. Her knee's very swollen. She needs my mother—"

"We'll be leaving soon," Nelson said. He waited.

Ranse finished the story. He became so engrossed in it that he did not notice the reappearance of Detective Sergeant Clevis.

The expression on the sergeant's face was at once disgusted and smug. He winked at Nelson and sat down at the table.

Ranse concluded defiantly, "So you see—after he gave me that dirty look at breakfast I wasn't sorry I put the capsules in his coffee. If I hadn't done that I'd have had to tie him up some other way. I couldn't leave him around loose with my sister while I hiked to the main highway—I just couldn't—even if I was to hang for it."

"We don't hang people in New York," Nelson said. He studied Ranse's face. "I'm not going to lecture you about what you should or should not have done. On the whole, you managed quite intelligently and I'm sure that never again will you administer drugs without full knowledge of their properties." He added dryly, "Sergeant Clevis seems to think that the patient will live."

Ranse became aware of Clevis. "Where—?"

"Parked in the other room," Clevis said cheerfully. "Believe it or not, I found a feather, got his jaws apart, and tickled his throat. He don't feel good—but he'll live to feel worse."

Rance had his purely selfish moment of happiness. His face worked as if it were trying to roll itself into a tight ball. The moment fled as Nelson turned his attention to Gale.

She did not need to be prodded. She spilled it all out. It was neither more nor less than she had told Ranse. But it sounded worse to him with repetition. And Nelson made her repeat it more than once.

"You say you have no recollection of striking either the maid or your aunt?"

"I didn't strike Aunt Thea—I couldn't—I was trying to catch her hands to keep her from striking me—"

"And yet you ran away because you thought you'd killed her?"

"He said I did—he said so—"

"All right. Let's get back to the maid."

"She opened the door to me. After that—I don't know—she must have screamed because I heard a scream—"

"When did you hear her scream?"

"It was after Aunt Thea was lying on the floor—and I must have wanted to go to her to see if she was badly hurt—and Spencer came between—and I ran out of the room. I didn't know why—I didn't know where I was going—but the maid was at the living room door when I went through—"

Ranse cried, "You never told me that."

"You never asked me." She stared at Nelson. "I'm remembering—you're making me remember—but how could I have killed the maid? I didn't go back in there."

"What did you do?"

"I saw a door—I was mixed up—I thought it was the way out—but it wasn't—it was another room. There were books in it—books and pictures. Spencer found me there and I went with him."

"Yet according to Spencer, the maid tried to interfere when you struggled with your aunt, and you killed her." Nelson's voice was neither believing nor unbelieving. "What did he say you used for a weapon?"

"He didn't say. I didn't even ask him—it doesn't matter—"

"It matters very much. Didn't he say you struck them both with the heavy knob of the cane?"

"No, he didn't—how could he? I didn't have the cane. It was his. I would have had to take it away from him, and why would he let me take it to hit—to hit people with?"

"He had it in his hand?"

"I don't know—"

"Think."

"I'm trying," she said, her hands pressed to her head. She was like a little girl told by the teacher to put on her thinking cap.

"You must have seen the cane." Nelson's voice was infected by her obvious strain. He wished he could let her rest. "When you were hunting for a crutch didn't you remember it and look to see where he had put it?"

"Yes—yes—that's true—I did remember. He had it under his arm when we were running down the service stairs. He prodded me with it once to make me go faster, and I turned my head to look. Yes—he had it when we left his apartment too. He was carrying it in one hand and his suitcase in the other. I don't think I noticed it in the car—but he tossed some things on the back seat so—"

"And where did you find it when you wanted the crutch?"

"Well—I'd looked everywhere without finding it—except upstairs because I couldn't get upstairs—then I gave it up and thought that maybe there might be a broom handle or something long enough for me to lean on in the kitchen—and I found the cane behind some stuff in that closet over there—"

Ranse said, "For Pete's sake, can't you see how tired she is?"

Nelson ignored him. "Gale, tell me again what explanation Spencer gave for bringing you here."

"He said he'd taken a fancy to me and didn't want me to suffer for having made one mistake. Something like that. He said he could help me to live it down." She bit her lip hard. "I know it must sound crazy, but I wanted to believe him—he seemed so kind at first—and I needed—I needed someone—" Her eyes filled.

Ranse saw Nelson put his arm around her. He did not know what to think. Nelson said, "Was that his only explanation?"

She stayed within the circle of his arm. She shook her head. Then she said, "No—later he said he had some scheme—something about amnesia. I was to get amnesia and forget I'd been to Aunt Thea's. He got me so confused that I almost did forget everything until you came and started asking questions. You see—Jack Channing was the only one who knew where I'd been." She told him fragmentarily of Spencer's plan. "Afterward he said he might have to change or—or modify it. But that would depend, he said. I didn't ask him what it would depend on because by then I knew I had to get away from him and give myself up to the police."

She moved away from Nelson, as though the word "police" had brought his official status home to her. She sat straight and stiff, her hands clasped on the table top.

Ranse said to Nelson, "What's the matter with you, anyway? You told me yourself that everything pointed to her innocence. Was that a lot of hot air—or are you one of those people who keep changing their minds all the time?"

"I changed my mind about Gale once," Nelson said gravely, "and now I'm trying to change it back again. Be patient with me."

Clevis was emptying his pockets of miscellaneous objects, setting them in front of Nelson. There was a wallet, an envelope, a corkscrew, a racing form, and a gold cigarette case. "If you're through, Captain," Clevis said, "get a load of this. I took the liberty of rolling our host before I went to work on him. I figured it would save arguments later. Read what's in that envelope—then take a squint at the monogram on the cigarette case."

Nelson extracted the sheet of folded note paper. When he was finished reading he returned it almost tenderly to the envelope and put it in his pocket. He glanced at the cigarette case and got up. He said to Gale and to Ranse, "I think that in a few weeks both of you will find it hard to believe that any of this really happened. We're going to start for home very soon—as soon as Sergeant Clevis and I have attended to something."

"Home?" Gale asked carefully. "You mean the police station."

"I mean home. Your home. Wait here."

He left them staring at each other. Clevis scooped up the objects on the table and followed him.

Spencer sat on the horsehair sofa, his hands supporting his head. He did not look dapper. He looked soiled and sour. He could have walked along Skid Row unnoticed.

Nelson said, "It didn't work this time, did it, Spencer?"

He raised his red puffy eyes. "Who the hell are you?"

Clevis said, "He's Captain Gridley Nelson of the Manhattan Homicide Squad—and he always gets his man—meaning you. On your feet."

Spencer showed no interest. He groaned, "I feel rotten. Don't know what hit me—damn near lost my ruddy guts."

"We'll get you a doctor," Clevis said. "We've got some real fashionable ones in the prison hospital."

That seemed to alert him. "What are you driving at—prisons and homicide squads?" The fog was lifting almost perceptibly. "Comes to that, what are you doing here on private property?" He pointed a shaking finger at Clevis. "I'm minding my own business—sleeping peacerful-like—and I wake up to find you mucking me about—sticking something down my throat. I haven't done anything—"

"You haven't done anything but two murders and a kidnaping," Clevis said.

"Two! Come off it. I expect you're here because of the girl. Well she came of her own free will. She'll be the first to bear me out."

Nelson sat down opposite him with an air of permanence. Clevis stood at ready. "The captain's going to ask some questions and you're going to answer them truthfully and respectfully unless you want to be busted right in that sore head of yours."

Nelson said, "I don't think there'll be any need for violence. I think that when Mr. Coley Spencer realizes the strength of the case against him he'll be glad to save himself additional trouble by cooperating. First of all, Mr. Spencer, I'll read you the letter that the Countess Mazzini left in her apartment. You've read it, of course, but that's not quite the same thing as hearing it read."

Spencer was patting his sides with both shaking hands, thrusting them into pockets, bringing them out empty. His puffy blotched face was the face of fear.

Nelson read:

For Grant,
   Tonight I intend to take my life. I send this explanation that it may be produced if, as sometimes happens in a case of suicide, there is suspicion of foul play. I also send it because of my debt to you.
   The foul play occurred long ago. The guilt for it is mine.
   The death of my husband was ascribed to pneumonia. The doctor who made out the certificate did so in good faith. But I killed my husband.
   He was sick in body. He had always been sick in mind, and his excesses had left him with nothing to resist physical disease. He had come home to me after being away on one of his weekend absences. But that is not why I killed him. I put him to bed and tended him, aided by a trained nurse, and by Coley Spencer, his valet—his man in every sense of the term.
   It happened when the nurse went for her afternoon walk. I was alone with Dino. Spencer was in another room. Dino awakened. He looked at me. He seemed better—or rather he seemed himself. He began to speak of his recent adventure. He said that pneumonia was not too high a price to pay for its enjoyments, which he went on to describe in detail. His words did not affect me. Almost at the outset of our marriage he had

inoculated me against his particular brand of cruelty, but he would never accept the fact that I was immune. Then suddenly he tried to humiliate me with more than words. And that I was no longer able to bear. We struggled. At last he gave up. He lay back white as the sheet, smiling his cruel smile. And Spencer, who had been standing unnoticed in the doorway, came forward.

I stumbled from the room. A short while later Spencer came to me and told me I had killed my husband. He said he would be silent if I paid for his silence. I agreed to pay—and I have been paying.

It would have been no punishment then to pay the law's penalty for my crime. I would have been glad to die in any way by any means. But knowing that swift sharp death would be no penance, I imposed a greater penance upon myself. I destroyed Thea Mazzini. Little by little, hour by hour, day by day, I killed her. Now it is enough—I have suffered enough. And it is wrong, Grant, that my suffering should spread to you.

My house is in order and I have made my will, leaving my earthly goods to my niece and namesake, Althea Gale Upjohn. I remember her as a small lovely child, such a child as I might have borne. To you, dear Grant, I leave release. Your coming today was a kind of deliverance.

Thea

Spencer said hoarsely, "She never paid me a cent. My word's as good as hers. She hated me—"

"We don't intend to prosecute you for blackmail," Nelson said. "The charge is murder—two murders."

"Are you telling me she's dead? Well, then—I've nothing to worry about. Who's going to pay any attention to the scrawl of an old witch when all and sundry know she was raving mad?"

"The countess is not dead," Nelson said. "I was referring to the maid and to—"

"You're mad too." He gestured frantically toward the kitchen. "I don't like to give that girl away, but if it's a matter of protecting myself—"

"You're past protecting. You don't want to give that girl away and you didn't want to give the countess away—for identical reasons. You battened on the countess, and when you expected her to die you shifted your operations to her niece. In both cases we have sufficient evidence to arrest and convict you as an accessory to murder. But we prefer to prove that you and you alone are guilty. I've read the accounts of Dino Mazzini's death and I've spoken to his physician,

Dr. diSilvio, who is willing and ready to testify that he found Dino Mazzini dead on arrival, that the cyanotic condition of his face indicated smothering, and that when questioned you stated he'd had a violent fit of coughing which strangled him."

"I may have said that. You're not going to hound me for trying to shield a lady. Mazzini treated her something chronic—"

"He treated you something chronic too. You hated him. You saw your opportunity and smothered him to death, didn't you?"

"She did—she choked him with her bare hands—"

"Notice her statement that his face was white when she left him—notice that the doctor's report made no mention of marks on his throat, which would have been present if choking was the cause of death. Perhaps you used a pillow for a weapon that first time—but on your second go around you used quite another weapon. After Mazzini was gone you helped yourself to some of his possessions—among them the cigarette case and the loaded walking stick he always carried—the one he used so frequently on you. That stick is in the crime lab now. There are traces of blood around the ferrule and in the carvings of the knob—blood doesn't come off easily, no matter how hard you try to remove it—"

Spencer shrieked. "No, you don't—you've torn it. That walking stick is never anywhere but behind the—"

CHAPTER FIFTEEN

Clevis produced a pair of handcuffs and managed to lock them on Spencer's wrists. It was no easy job. Spencer kept contorting himself like a fat and frenzied eel equipped with tongue. Even handcuffed, he had to be carried out to the car, twisting and writhing and shrieking obscenities every step of the way. Clevis plumped him on the back seat. He got in beside him and clamped a hard hand over his mouth.

"I can hold this pose all the way to New York," Clevis said, "or do a real job of gagging if I get bored with it. So you shut up." When he removed his hand experimentally, Spencer was quiet except for his eyes.

Nelson went back to the house for Gale and Ranse. They sat in the front with him. Neither of them turned around once to look. There was very little conversation on the long ride home. Ranse made a few limping attempts. He said that he sure would be glad to get to his bureau drawer and put some socks on his feet. He complimented Nelson on his driving. He said laboriously that he guessed Nelson was a pretty good detective. Then he subsided.

Nelson made no attempt to keep the ball rolling. He suspected that Gale was nearly at the end of her rope and that even the effort of listening would tax her. His thoughts were largely occupied with the ugly little man in the back seat and with the unpredictable minds of juries. He concluded that to make the case absolutely jury-proof further testimony was needed from Thea Mazzini. He hoped she would supply it.

It was a quarter past seven when he stopped the car. Gale gave a little sigh. "You meant it," she said. "You've brought us home."

"You haven't been sitting there all this time doubting me?"

"Not doubting you—just being afraid to believe you."

"Slide over behind the wheel. I'm going to carry you upstairs."

"I can manage her," Ranse said.

"I don't doubt it—but this time I'll make sure you're both safe inside the door."

Ranse grinned.

Nelson got out and took Gale in his arms. She hid her face on his shoulder while he said a few words to Clevis. Clevis assured him that everything was under control.

A young man was coming out of the vestibule as Nelson climbed a stoop with Gale. He stood holding the door. The vestibule light shone on his face.

Gale said, "Jack!"

"Gale!"

Ranse, tagging close behind, growled, "Later, buster," and elbowed him aside. Jack Channing looked after the procession open-mouthed, too stunned to move.

"I'll see you later, Jack," Gale called huskily. And Nelson smiled and thought that she was not nearly at the end of her rope. He stopped smiling and hoped with little faith that she could somehow be spared the ordeal of testifying in court.

On the way up the stairs she said, "Ranse Upjohn, you had no right to talk to Jack that way—"

"We're home all right," Ranse said.

Nelson knocked at the Upjohn door. Then he rang the bell. Then Ranse produced his key and turned it in the lock and ran through the hall, roaring, "Mother—Father—we're back—"

But there was no one there to answer.

Ranse said disconsolately, "Now I guess I've got to go out and hunt for *them*."

Nelson shook his head. "You're to stay here—understand? You're not to leave the apartment until your parents get back. I want your promise."

"Okay, Captain. Okay—but I bet you never would have found Gale if I hadn't—"

"Never in a hundred years," Nelson lied. He deposited Gale in Mr.

Upjohn's great armchair. Impulsively she caught his hand and brought it to her cheek. She said, "Thank you," but her eyes were more eloquent than the words.

"Do you have a family doctor?"

Ranse answered, "Not since we came to New York." He looked around the room. "Say—this old dump isn't so bad after all—is it, Sis?"

"It's wonderful," she said.

"Sit tight, both of you," Nelson said. "I'll send a doctor to treat that knee—and, Ranse, it might be a good idea for you to soak some of the grime off your feet while you're waiting—so that the doctor can see if those blisters need attention." He might as well start practicing to be a parent, he thought. "Even a full-sized bath wouldn't be a bad idea."

"Sure—whatever you say. Think I'll raid the icebox first, though."

Gale, a wan hostess, said that he should offer the captain some refreshment, and Nelson confessed gravely to being pressed for time.

Ranse said, "Take a rain check on it. Mother isn't a bad cook—mostly."

"I will." On that note he left.

Jack Channing was standing on the stoop, talking to a neat elderly woman. He looked as though he would like to intercept Nelson but as though he did not dare. Nelson smiled at him encouragingly but did not stop. Jack Channing would have to begin solving his own problems sometime.

He drove to headquarters with Clevis and Coley Spencer. He left Clevis to deal with the mechanics of the arrest and with two on-the-spot reporters.

He closeted himself in his office. He phoned Kyrie, apologized for not having reached her sooner, and said that she was to save something to eat for him. She answered that she had gathered he would not be home and added politely that she hoped the something she saved would not decay before he returned. She asked no questions. She said that she was well, and seemed satisfied when he told her that things were picking up. He had all he could do not to send a kiss through the receiver like any lovesick swain.

He arranged for a doctor to visit the Upjohn apartment. Then he drove to the Parkside Hospital, where visiting hours in the private rooms were from 9 A.M. to 9 P.M., and where in most instances passes were not required.

Neither Lowry nor his relief was stationed outside the countess's room. Nelson frowned. Then he knocked on the door. Then he walked in.

Thea Mazzini lay staring at the ceiling. Her eyes were lucid and very unhappy.

Mrs. Upjohn stood near the bed, flanked by her husband and by a red-faced man whom Nelson recognized as Lowry's relief. He was tugging at one of her arms, her husband at the other. But so monumental was she in her anger that they might have been a pair of stingless gnats. Backed into a corner, helplessly wringing her hands, stood the night nurse.

"Thea!" Mrs. Upjohn's plain scrubbed face had become the face of a lioness. "You were the last one to see Gale—tell me what happened to her—"

"Elsie," boomed Mr. Upjohn, "you must stop—this is a hospital—Thea's sick—you're only making matters worse—"

"Sick? She's a selfish, pampered, overfed woman—all she needs is to go on a diet. Thea, I won't leave this room until you answer me—Can't you understand?—they're saying Gale committed murder—and the poor child's afraid to come home. I know you never cared a snap for your family, but—"

Nelson stepped forward. The nurse cried ineffectually, "Who are you? The countess is not supposed to have visitors. I had to let this woman in—she was creating a disturbance in the corridor—and I can't go for help because my orders are not to leave the room under any—"

"Thea—if you don't know where my children are, then at least tell me what happened—at least let me publish it in the papers so that Gale won't be afraid to come home—"

"Elsie—Elsie." The big man was completely at a loss.

"Quiet," Nelson said. It was either the commanding note in his voice that did it or the element of surprise. A lull took place.

The detective released Mrs. Upjohn's arm. He said, "Chief!" and mopped his face with his hand.

Nelson walked over to Mrs. Upjohn. "Gale and Ranse are home worrying about you. You ought to be ashamed—letting them come back to a deserted apartment."

She stared at him. She was blessedly mute.

Mr. Upjohn said fearfully, "Is—is it true?"

"Of course it's true."

"Elsie—do you hear—?"

Nelson was unprepared for her swoop. She hugged him to her bosom. Then she pushed him from her and grabbed her husband. "Hurry—" The floor shook with their passage from the room.

"Holy smoke!" said Lowry's relief. "Chief, I couldn't deal with it. She was causing such a commotion outside—and everybody sick—and not a nurse or an orderly in sight—and she like to have knocked me down and stepped over me if I didn't let her pass. I couldn't very well shoot—"

"Go outside. I'll see you later."

"Yes, sir." He went.

The trembling nurse was trying to regain composure. "Thank you," she whispered. "But you'll have to go too."

Nelson hesitated. He looked toward the bed. The patient's eyes were closed.

"See how flushed her cheeks are," the nurse said. "I'll have to take her temperature again—and I had her all settled for the night."

Nelson sighed. He had hoped to give Thea Mazzini news that would buy her a really good night's sleep, but the Upjohns had blasted that hope. She was probably in no condition to digest news of any nature.

"Very well," he said, "I'll go—but I think the doctor should know of the disturbance. He might want to assure himself that she's all right."

Reluctantly he left. Outside, he was not too hard upon the perspiring detective. A similar situation was unlikely to arise, and if it did he, himself, could present no blueprint for coping with it. He guessed he was tired. Tired and hungry and disappointed. He went home to Kyrie, who took care of everything but the disappointment. Perhaps tomorrow would do that, he thought as he lay beside her. Perhaps—

Then it was the next morning and he had overslept. Kyrie, fully dressed, kissed him awake. "I hate to do this," she said.

"Since when?" he murmured dreamily.

"I mean wake you—not kiss you—as if you didn't know. But it's late and you'll be angry with all of us if I let you sleep any longer."

He did not reach his office until eleven. Grant Barstow had phoned. So had Dr. Selig. Nelson called Dr. Selig back, and after a series of misses tracked him down at a children's clinic.

"I think she has suffered no ill effects from last night's visitation," the doctor said, but his voice was not cheerful. "She seems beyond outward disturbance—and that is a bad sign. However, since her physical condition is fair and since—short of a miracle—I can predict no change for the better in her mental state, I see no reason to delay your visit."

Nelson told him in brief of the developments in the case.

The doctor was jubilant. "This is it—this is the miracle—I am sure of it. I am grateful to you also and I hope you will recall enough to supply you with the testimony you need. You will be gentle—yes? For it is not only bad news which can greatly shock.... Good—I will leave word for you to be admitted at any time you call."

Nelson thought that there was no time like the present. He started to put on his coat.

Clevis came into the office. He was unshaven and almost cross-eyed with fatigue. Nelson felt a pang of guilt for his own resentful night.

"Got a copy of his confession for you," Clevis said. "Of course he denied it the moment it was spilled—and of course he'll plead duress—but I swear I didn't even hit him with my pinky. Let's hope the countess will provide the clincher."

Nelson ran his eyes down the typed sheets. "You're going to be recommended for a promotion, Clevis."

"Thanks. You ought to promote that Upjohn kid too. It was the hangover from the Mickey that weakened Spencer's resistance."

"Go home and go to bed."

"That's the kind of music I got an ear for. See you, Captain."

Nelson's progress across the hospital lobby was intercepted. He met the harassed eyes of Grant Barstow.

"Captain Nelson—I telephoned, but you weren't in your office. How is Thea? I went upstairs, but they wouldn't allow me to see her. The nurse came out and said that she was resting comfortably, but— Please, Captain, I think I have the right to—"

"Wait here," Nelson said, "I'll have more to tell you when I come down."

"I'll wait."

Lowry was at his stand outside the Mazzini door. "Hear there were big doings last night, Captain. The nurse and I just turned away an anxious soul named Barstow. Want to bet five you don't get in either?"

"I'm tempted to take you up on it just to teach you there's no such thing as a sure gamble." Nelson knocked lightly upon the door. The day nurse opened it. He said, "Good morning, Miss Rissiger," and she said cordially, "Come right in." He wasted a moment before he crossed the threshold in wishing that he could see Lowry's expression.

The nurse said, "A friend is here to see you, Countess Mazzini. I'm going to leave you alone with him so that you can enjoy a nice little private chat." She went out, closing the door behind her.

Thea Mazzini looked freshly bathed and combed. Nelson wondered who had been thoughtful enough to purchase the new silk jacket she wore over her nightgown. She no longer lay flat. Her bed had been wound to the angle of convalescence.

He drew a chair within her line of vision and sat down. Her sad eyes searched his face. She seemed puzzled.

"You're trying to place me, aren't you?" he said quietly. "I've been here twice before."

"Twice?"

"Yes—once the day after you'd been injured—and again last night. Other than that, we haven't met—but I know a great deal about you."

"About me?"

"If you'd rather I'd go now and come back when you're stronger, I will. I want you to get well."

She said poignantly, "I'll never be well again."

"The things I know will make you well."

She smiled faintly. The smile was sadder than her eyes. "You say that with conviction. But you would have to be God to cure me. Who are you?"

"My name is Nelson." He did not know how to proceed, or even if this was the time to proceed.

She seemed to sense his indecision. She said, "Don't go. It's been a long time since I've had visitors—pleasant ones."

He let instinct take over. "Grant Barstow visited you."

"Do you know Grant?"

"Yes—and I know he loves you."

"Poor Grant."

"He needn't be poor Grant."

"Did he send you here? Perhaps you even know about the note I left for him. It doesn't matter. I told him I meant to take my life. I told him why. Who are you—really?"

"A police officer." He waited tensely.

She said without alarm, "Then you've come to arrest me. I'm glad. That's the way it must be since I was prevented from taking my life."

"I've come for the opposite reason. I've come to set you free. I have proof that you did not kill your husband. Spencer killed him after you left the room. He—"

"Spencer? Oh no. Nothing so final as murder for Spencer. Little crimes—endless chains of little crimes—not murder—"

"Murder if he thought he could escape—burden someone else with the blame." He recalled Dr. Selig's metaphor, something about Spencer committing murder only on a desert where he could lay the blame to a mute. He saw that her hands were gripping the bed. clothes. He said, "Shall I call the nurse? Perhaps—?"

"Proof—you said you had proof. Please—"

He told her as much of the story as he saw fit. He omitted mention of the maid, since he doubted that she knew of the maid's death.

She was quiet for a while after he had finished. Her eyes were closed. He felt oddly let down until she opened them. They shone new and young in her ravished face. "I knew you were a friend," she said.

He was disconcerted by her eyes. No one owed anyone that much gratitude. He looked away. He said, hating the light cheap sound of it, "Then perhaps you'll help a friend."

"Anything."

"Will you tell me as much as you can remember about the night you were injured?"

"If you want me to. Where shall I start? Grant had come in the afternoon. I had given Grant nothing—ever—and that afternoon I robbed him of his last hope. I had been living squalidly—I, myself, was squalid. I took Grant's coming as a sign that I might put an end to it at last. I told the maid to give the apartment a thorough cleaning—and I bathed and groomed myself for death. I made my will and mailed it—and wrote the letter to Grant. Spencer arrived just as I had finished it. He used his key, which apparently he'd never relinquished. I had paid him the usual monthly sum. His coming startled me. I did not want him to see what I had written. I knew that since I was his livelihood he would do anything he could to prevent me from committing suicide. So I swept the letter into the wastebasket along with some other mail that was on the desk, and I went to the chair near the fireplace and sat down. He took the opposite chair. He commented upon the unusual cleanliness of the room. He asked what I was celebrating. He would not leave. He got some scotch and two glasses—"

"There was one glass," Nelson said involuntarily.

"Two. Perhaps he put one away later—to hide the fact that he'd been there—especially since Mildred—" She stopped. "You said nothing about Mildred. Did he confess to her death too?"

"Yes. I wasn't sure you knew she had been killed. I thought I'd wait until you were well."

"I heard my sister-in-law say it last night. Poor Mildred—" Her eyes were somber again. "If I hadn't kept her—"

"No," Nelson said. "That sort of reasoning has no future at all." He prompted her. "Spencer sat drinking scotch—"

"Yes—he was determined to stay until I gave him more money. I had no intention of drinking with him. I wanted a clear head—and I wanted—when they found me I wanted to be in a decent—"

"I know—but the scotch was there—"

"And his hateful face was there, and so I drank. I should have given him money and sent him on his way—but I—the more I drank—" She paused. "I don't think I'm really an alcoholic. I started to drink deliberately—after Dino's death. It was part of the business of punishing myself—part of the degradation—the slow destruction of my—well—I'd been a model. It was my physical being that had attracted Dino. But I haven't wanted a drink since I've regained consciousness. I don't think I'll ever want one again." She said wonderingly, "I don't know why I'm unburdening myself to you— you haven't come for that sort of confession, but—" She did not go on.

"But you've been bottled up for a long time and I happen to be handy. What happened when Gale came?"

I was thoroughly befuddled by then. Just before her entrance Spencer had gone over to the wastebasket and was examining its contents. He'd seen me writing, of course, and was curious. I didn't try to stop him. I had reached the state where nothing seemed important—"

Nelson said, "Good—that helps. It's a very necessary bit of evidence which he left out of his confession—the business of learning you'd left your money to Gale before and not after he went into his act."

"I don't understand."

"It gives him a clear motive for killing the maid and for attempting to kill you. If he had found the letter afterward it might plant a doubt in the minds of the jurors. They might reason that the murder had been done by someone else and that he was merely using it to suit his ends."

She said with a flash of humor, "Then I mustn't dwell too strongly on having been under the influence, must I? Or they'll refuse to accept my word for anything."

Nelson did not commit himself. "We won't worry about that now. You were up to the part where Gale had arrived."

"I didn't know she was Gale. I thought she was a kind of *Doppelgänger*—my old self come back to mock at me. And at the same time I knew that wasn't true. I thought that Spencer had found someone who resembled me as I had been—and that he was using her to try to drive me out of my mind. I struck out at her. *Doppelgänger* or trick, it was too much. I wanted to hurt her—to drive her from the room—and then—then something hit the back of my head and I fell. And there was nothing until I awoke here."

"Did Spencer carry a cane when he came in?"

"Yes—he always carried it. He made it a symbol of power. Dino's cane. Dino had used it on him more than once—and now it was his—he was the one who possessed it. He flaunted it whenever he came for his money, knowing I knew he had stolen it—knowing that Dino had once turned in a rage upon—"

Nelson said hurriedly, "And Gale had it at no time while she was in the room?"

"Of course not. She was unarmed and unprepared, poor baby. Is that why Elsie came last night? I'd been given a sedative. She seemed to be shouting at me, and yet I gathered little except that somehow the maid had been killed." Her voice was tired. "Little Gale—how shall I make it up to her?"

"Your difficulty won't be there." Nelson brought her a glass of water from the bedside carafe.

She sipped. She looked at him inquiringly. "You mean the trial will be difficult—that I'll be called upon to testify?"

"Yes—but with Grant standing by—"

"I'll testify gladly. I've nothing to be afraid of anymore. But I won't ask Grant to stand by. I've brought him only unhappiness."

He arose. He said, "You'll have a hard time convincing him of that. He's downstairs. Will you see him? Not now—but later, when you're rested."

She did not answer. She said instead, "Is Nelson your first name?"

"No—I'm called Grid."

"Grid—do you have a wife?"

"Yes." He was puzzled. His broad brow shirred.

"Is she beautiful?"

"Altogether beautiful."

"Grid—can a man love an ugly woman?"

His brow cleared. "Some men see further than meets the eye—but no woman with a voice like yours is ugly—and if you cooperate with Dr. Selig he'll make you altogether beautiful again."

She smiled at him. "Then give Grant my love," she said, "and ask him please if he would mind waiting a little longer."

THE END

More murder mysteries featuring Lt. Gridley Nelson from…

Ruth Fenisong

"Fenisong's prose style is layered yet immediately accessible, and feels as contemporary today as it must have over 60 years ago. She is fond of complex plots with multiple characters, and introduces these elements with precision and clarity."
—Alan Cranis, *Bookgasm*

"Her tales are not cosy, with the more painful aspects of life being carefully woven into the fabric of the text, but neither are they gory, nor overwhelmed by despair – even when the ending avoids fairy-tale-like closure."
—Kate Jackson, *crossexaminingcrime*

$19.95 each in trade paperback.

Murder Needs a Name / Murder Needs a Face

"Good writing here with some telling points on sweet charity."
—Dorothy B. Hughes

The Butler Died in Brooklyn / Murder Runs a Fever

"… a full-scale wartime mystery, dealing with the FBI and suspected Nazi spies; yet there is also a legitimate murder problem to be dealt with too. "
—Curtis Evans, *The Passing Tramp*

Dead Weight / Deadlock

"Lieut. Gridley Nelson is in himself enough to make any book, whatever the murder-plot—and the Fenisong plots are usually better than average. Never better, however, than in *Deadlock…*"
—Anthony Boucher, *New York Times*

Stark House Press, 1315 H Street, Eureka, CA 95501
greg@starkhousepress.com / www.StarkHousePress.com
Available from your local bookstore, or order direct via our website.

9 7 9 8 8 8 6 0 1 0 8 0 0